SERPENT'S BANE

Cover art by Beth Alvarez

Edited by Savannah Grace Perran

First Edition: August 2020

ISBN-13: 978-1-952145-08-7

SERPENT'S BANE

BOOK THREE OF THE SNAKESBLOOD SAGA

BETH ALVAREZ

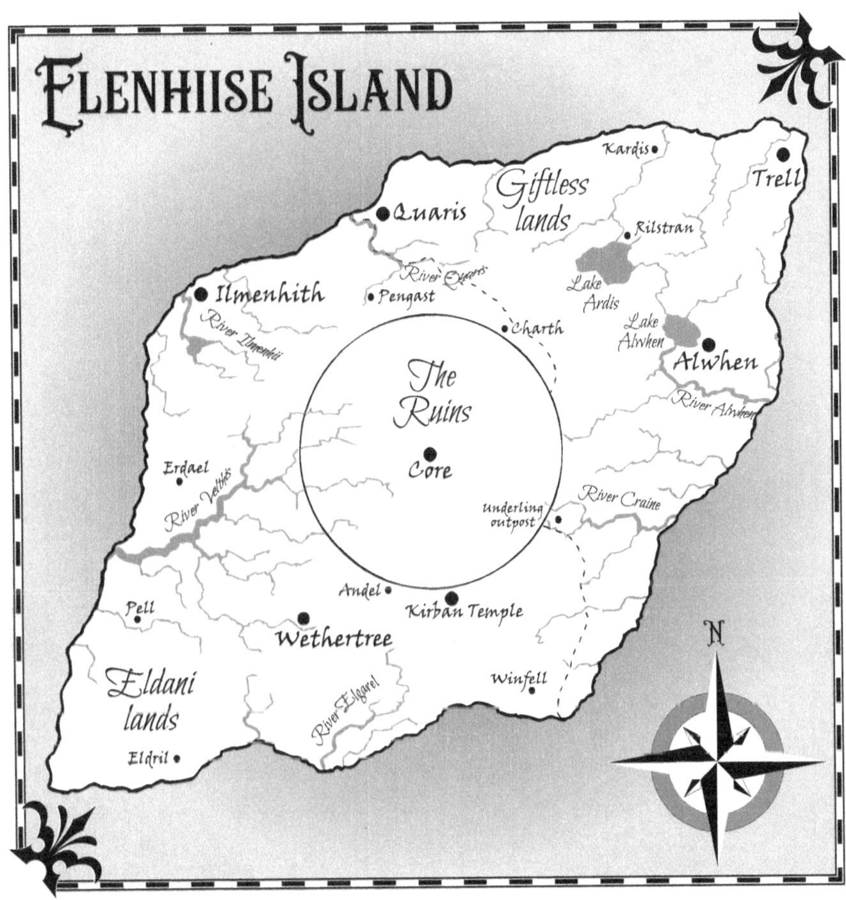

Elenhiise Island
Kardis
Trell
Giftless lands
Quaris
Rilstran
Lake Ardis
River Quaris
Ilmenhith
Pengast
Lake Alwhen
Charth
Alwhen
River Ilmenhii
The Ruins
River Alwhen
Erdael
Core
River Veltis
River Craine
Underling outpost
Pell
Andel
Kirban Temple
Wethertree
N
Eldani lands
River Elgarel
Winfell
Eldril

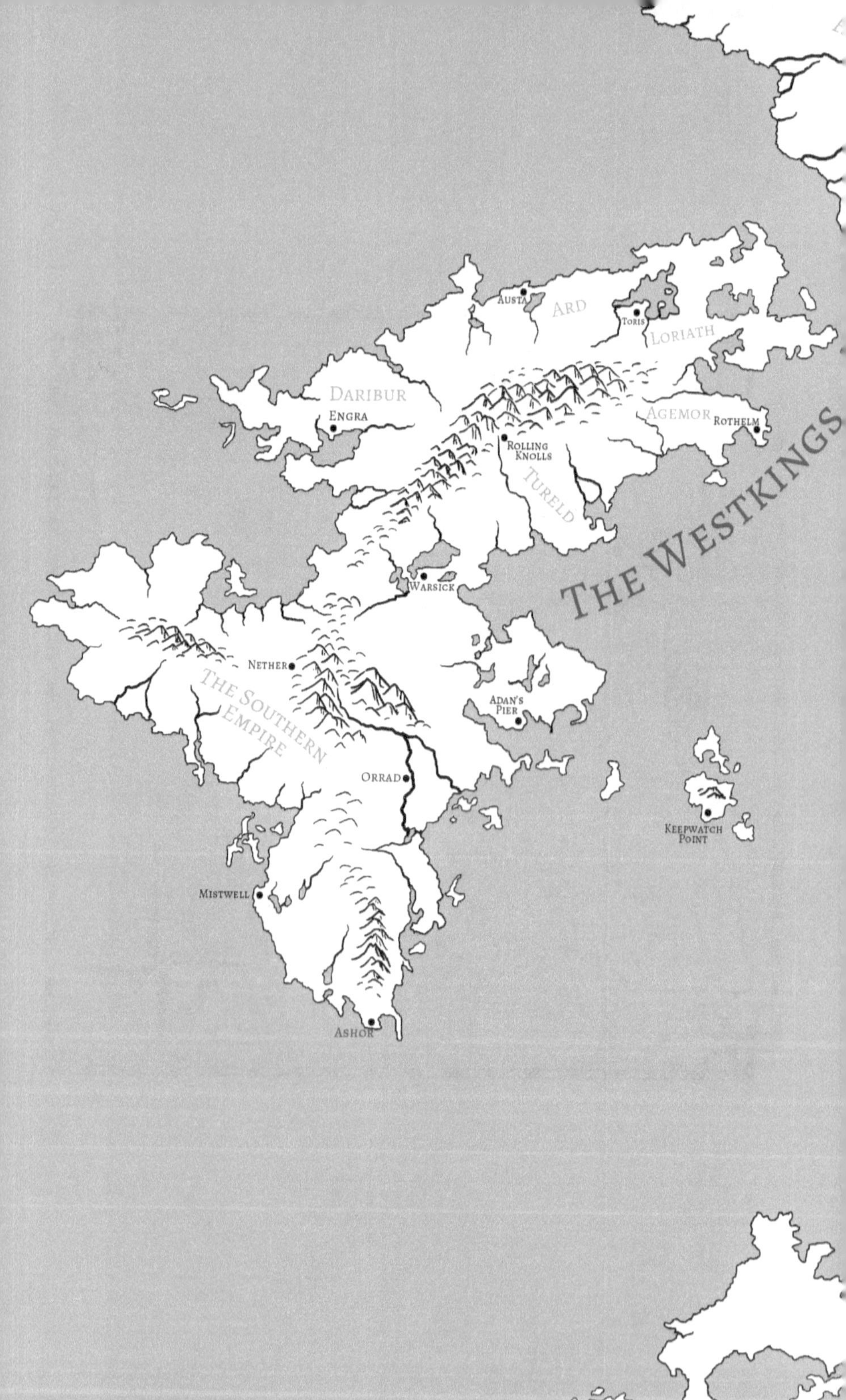

AUSTA
ARD
TORIS
LORIATH
DARIBUR
ENGRA
AGEMOR
ROTHELM
ROLLING
KNOLLS
TURELD
WARSICK
THE WESTKINGS
NETHER
ADAN'S
PIER
THE SOUTHERN EMPIRE
ORRAD
KEEPWATCH
POINT
MISTWELL
ASHOR

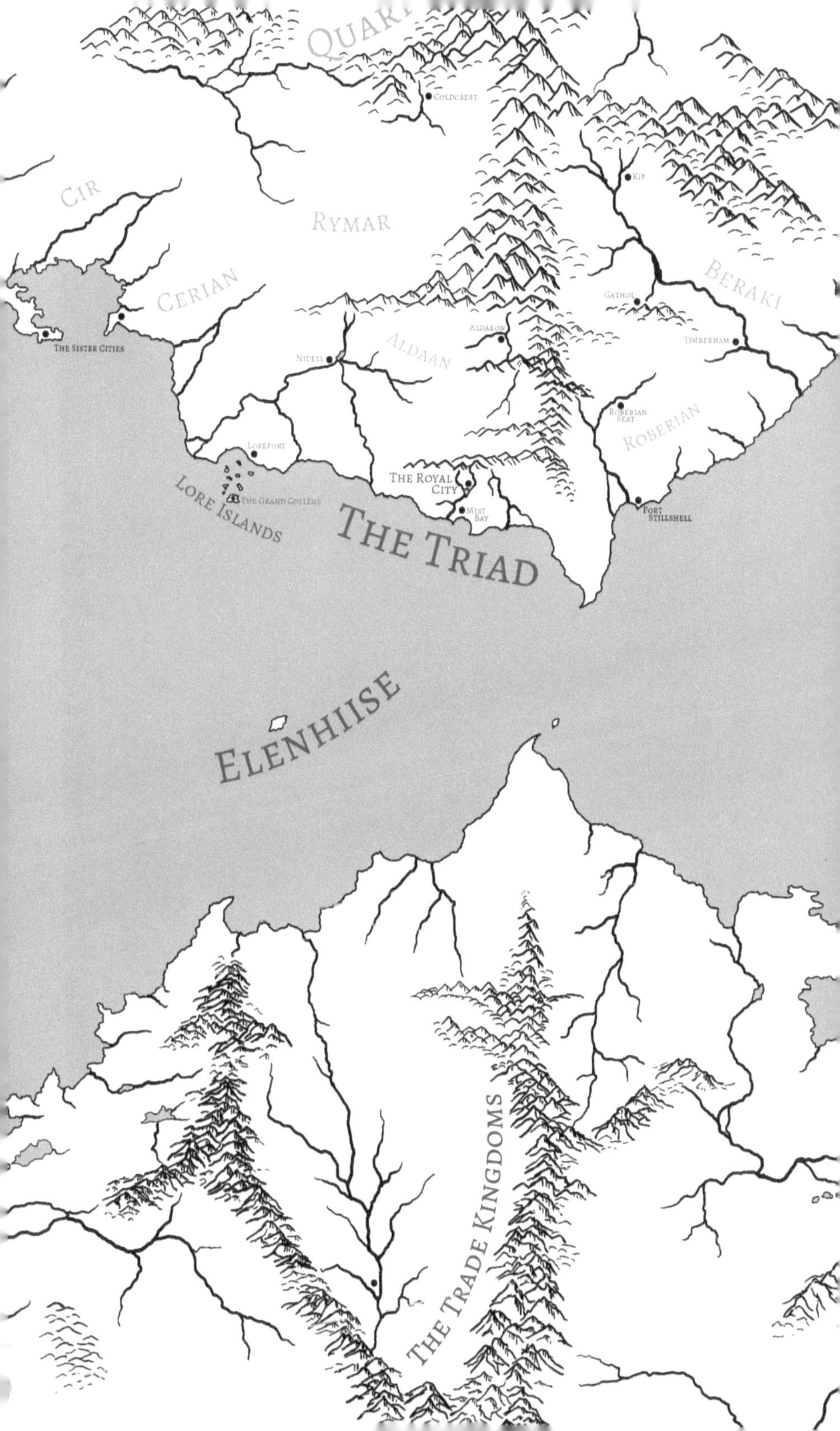

QUARI
CIR
RYMAR
BERAKI
CERIAN
COLDCREST
KIP
GATHOL
ALDAEON
TIMBERHAM
THE SISTER CITIES
NIDELL
ALDAAN
ROBERIAN
SEAT
ROBERIAN
LOREPORT
THE ROYAL
CITY
PORT
STILLSHELL
LORE ISLANDS
THE GRAND COLLEGE
MIST
BAY
THE TRIAD
ELÉNHIISE
THE TRADE KINGDOMS

CONTENTS

KINGSWORD

"What is it now?" Captain Garam Kaith was not a man one wanted to displease. From the moment his foot touched the bottom stair, it was obvious he was unhappy to have been summoned.

The guard at the table in the forefront of the prison stood up. "We have an unusual problem, sir. I thought you'd want to see it."

Garam glanced to the second guard by the mouth of the hallway. The man nudged his helmet and nodded in agreement. The cell keys in his hand rattled against his helmet's rim.

"Show me," Garam ordered. The last thing he wanted to do was look at prisoners, but it was his duty. One of many. The mile-long to-do list in his head already clawed at the back of his mind, but duty bound him, sure as chains.

Both guards led the way between rows of prison cells.

"We found it in the market, sir," the guard with the keys said. "Thieving from a merchant's shipments. Took three grown men to pin the thing down, not to mention getting it down here."

"It?" The question was sharp, but neither of the men winced at Garam's tone. They were used to it by now.

"That's just the thing, sir," the guard said. He licked his lips, betraying his nerves. "We aren't rightly sure what it is."

Garam eyed them as they stopped, then turned to peer into the cell beside them. A figure sat hunched in the back of the cell, dressed in clothing little better than rags. The captain jostled the iron bars. The figure's head lifted, its eyes glowing a baleful red in the dark.

"Lifetree's mercy," Garam breathed.

It pushed itself up and strode forward on feet like those of the dragons in old legends. Green scales glittered in the feeble light. Whatever the creature was, it had the form of a man, though his features reminded Garam of the unusually beautiful Eldani that sometimes came in from the forests. The angry glow in the creature's eyes pulsed as his feet carried him toward the cell door.

"Watch its hands," one of the guards warned. "It's got claws. Tore up the men that nabbed it pretty badly."

Garam took a step back. "He's as tall as I am," he muttered as he looked the prisoner up and down. The man—or monster—on the other side of the bars blinked at him, and he realized with a start that he was being studied as well. He frowned.

He was not a small man, over six feet in height and broad-shouldered enough to be imposing even without his gleaming plate armor. Garam fostered that appearance, choosing to keep his dark hair cropped close and his beard meticulously edged. Everything about him was stern. Serious. And the miserable creature in the cell in front of him matched his posture as if to declare himself an equal.

Clawed hands grasped the iron bars. The color in the prisoner's eyes flickered strangely as his gaze fell to the sword at Garam's side.

"Hey now." The captain rested a hand on his weapon and took a half step back.

The clawed creature's expression twisted with anger and spat words in a curious, lilting language.

The guards exchanged startled looks.

"It can speak?" Garam glowered at the men.

"We didn't know, Captain," the guard with the keys said in a rush. "The men said nothing of it, and it's done nothing but growl and glare at us since we locked it up."

"What language is that?" Garam asked.

"It sounds a bit like Aldaanan to me," the other guard suggested.

The captain glanced at him. "Send a message to the king's council, then. Request a scholar. If we put in a request now, we might have a translator before the day is out."

The guard bowed and hurried away.

"Sir?" the remaining guard asked. "Why does it matter what language he speaks?"

"Even if I was allowed to keep someone prisoner without explaining why, I wouldn't be in the business of doing it." Garam turned back toward the cell and gave the prisoner a thoughtful look. "And who knows. Maybe we can find out what you are, too."

"He had some things with him, sir. Would you care to see?" The guard jerked his head in the direction of the doorway and the shallow crates just beyond. They were often filled with belongings stripped from prisoners, but there hadn't been much crime of late. Garam supposed he should be grateful.

The captain gave the prisoner one more glance, then turned away. "Show me."

The guard led the way around the corner and reached for a bundle of cloth and a small leather purse. He moved it to the table for the captain to inspect.

Garam tugged open the purse and spilled part of its contents across the table. A few curious square coins looked to be copper, tarnished almost as brown as his skin. But they bore no mint or mark he recognized, which made them worth less than the metal they were made of. It was no wonder the creature was caught stealing. A narrow leather cord inside the purse caught his eye, and he pulled it free. A pair of gold rings were strung upon it, the right size to nest together, though an odd purple stone was set in the smaller of the two.

"It got awful angry when we took that," the guard said, glancing toward the cell.

"Enchanted?" Garam asked.

"Mundane, sir. As far as the seeker found."

The captain grimaced at mention of the artifact, a small ring that glowed when it touched anything imbued with magic. He recognized the tool's usefulness to his men; Garam simply didn't trust magic. "I'd prefer if you called an artificer from now on. Just to be sure." He turned the rings over in his hand and jingled them together.

"You requested my presence, Kaith?" The question came from the stairs.

The captain suppressed a groan. He should have been pleased to receive a response so quickly. But he recognized that voice, sniveling and arrogant. Of all the scholars they might have sent, it was that one. Naturally.

"Ran into him in the courtyard, as luck would have it," the guard on the stairs said, glancing between the scholar and the captain as if unsure it was lucky at all.

"Lord Survas." Garam struggled to keep his tone neutral as he turned to face the short-statured noble. "I called for you, yes."

Survas gave a lofty sniff and his pointed ears seemed to quiver. Garam wasn't surprised at the man's indignation. Few nobles ever visited the prison, and fewer by choice. Still, as Captain of the Royal City Guard, Garam ranked most men who walked in the palace as mere assistants to the king. A fact few of them seemed to remember.

"My men apprehended a... man..." he tested the word, ignoring the sneer Survas gave him, "who does not seem to speak our tongue. One of the guards believes it to be a form of Aldaanan. I trust you would be happy to translate for us."

"You're fortunate the king holds you in such high esteem,

Kaith." Survas snorted and looked down his nose. Despite his effort to look important, the difference between their heights meant he craned his head backwards until he looked ridiculous. "Otherwise, I doubt he would take kindly to you wasting our time."

The scholar held his chin high as he followed Garam to the cell. When he made eye contact with the creature, he gave a most unbecoming shriek.

The guards burst into laughter and earned a sharp look from the captain. The humor faded rather quickly.

"Ask him his name," Garam ordered.

"I did not come down here to converse with animals," Survas spat with a glare.

"No, you did not," Garam agreed. "Now ask the gentleman in the cell what his name is."

The scholar set his jaw, turned toward the cell, and cleared his throat. He rattled off the question in words Garam didn't understand. When no reply came, Survas tried a different tongue. When he found the right words, the creature in the cell started and moved back a step. His eyes narrowed, and he replied.

"Well?" Garam asked.

Survas grimaced. "He asked for his rings. Quite angry. He said rings first, then he'll speak to you."

The captain raised a brow. "Little bossy for a man behind bars."

Heavy silence fell over the group and Garam sighed. The leather cord was still in his hand. He slid his thumb over it, thoughtful. "We'll throw him a bone, then, and see if that makes him more cooperative." He crossed the floor in a few easy strides. The prisoner inched forward and waited, and when Garam held out the rings, clawed hands snatched them from his grasp with startling speed.

Eyeing the captain distrustfully, the creature pulled the cord over his head and settled the rings under his shirt. Then the reddened glow faded from his snakelike eyes, leaving a soft shade of violet.

"Strange things in the dungeon today," Garam muttered. "Survas, ask him his name now."

The small man made a face and brushed at his sleeves as if they'd gotten dusty. He relayed the question with a little more flourish than necessary.

The prisoner looked between the men on the other side of the barred door, uncertain. His gaze shifted down to his hands, resting on the iron bars. His eyes lingered on his left hand. "Rune."

Garam chuckled. "Now that I understood." He stepped closer. "Ask him if he knows why he's here."

Survas cleared his throat again, clearly displeased at having become a translator. But he did as he was told, growing even more displeased when the prisoner did not look at him again. The creature stared right at the captain as he answered. He never even blinked.

"He says he is here because you put him here. As punishment for his actions, which were stealing to feed himself and fighting off the men who tried to stop him." The rattle of Survas's voice made Garam frown.

"Do you feel no remorse for your crime?" the captain asked. The delay between his question and the translation made him tense.

"He says he feels no shame in surviving. He says he does what he must and would repay what was taken if he had the means."

Garam's expression shifted between amusement and consternation. "But you don't have the means. You seem to understand your position and why you are here, and you have no regrets. So what am I to do with you now?" The last came in little more than a murmur, a mere voicing of his thoughts. He didn't realize he'd spoken it until Survas translated and erupted into laughter.

"What's so funny?" the captain demanded.

"He says you could fetch his things and let him go!" Survas crowed and slapped his thigh as if it were a joke.

Garam raised his eyebrows. "Really?"

The noble coughed and stilled his laughter as he translated the single word.

This time, the prisoner's snakelike eyes dropped to Survas as he spoke, a furrow in his brow.

The small man grew solemn, then troubled. He gave Garam a sidewise look. "I do not think he is a common thief, Kaith."

Garam eyed him. "What makes you say that?"

"I dare not repeat it, Captain, but no peasant would speak in that manner. None would dare to." Survas shook his head. He did not translate what had been said and did not look at the cell again.

The captain stared at the two of them for a long time. Unsettled, he returned to the table and the bundle upon it. The cloth wrappings did little to disguise the sword held within. He tore them away.

Beneath the coarse burlap, the sword's twisted hilt gleamed a polished black, inlaid with blood-red stones. The cross guard curled inward, bent toward the flared blade like black horns. A three-pronged claw on the pommel grasped a ruby the size of an egg.

"Oh," one of the guards remarked. Despite the bland response, his eyes grew wide with wonder.

Garam hesitated. "That's certainly no peasant's sword."

"What's it made of?" The guard reached out before he thought better of it. His fingers stopped just shy of the blade. "Ain't no metal I've ever seen."

"A kingsword," Survas said, the words barely more than a breath.

"A what?" Garam gave him a hard look.

"Forged by magic for rulers alone." The scholar rubbed his hands together, though whether it was with nerves or scheming,

Garam couldn't say. "Stolen, no doubt, Captain Kaith. It should be confiscated immediately and presented before the king."

Garam's eyes darkened. His jaw clenched as he looked toward the cell. "Slop rations and prepare him for the arena."

"But Captain—" The guard cut off at Garam's raised hand.

"A thief as well as a monster. We'll let the champions take care of him." The captain rolled the sword back into its wrappings and tucked it under his arm.

"Ah, Captain..." Survas licked his lips and slid closer, eyeing the bundle. "Perhaps I should take that, being that I'm to speak with the king this afternoon, and—"

"Your work here was appreciated today, Lord Survas," Garam said. The sudden appearance of title and respect in the way the man spoke to him didn't go unnoticed, but it was too late for flattery to get him anywhere. "This is my city, and I shall see to the matter myself."

He did not wait for acknowledgment from Survas or the prison guards before he made his way up the stairs and back to the daylight that waited outside.

The sword was a curiosity, but at least weapons were something he understood. Man or monster, whatever that thing in the prison cell was, Garam had never seen anything like it. Like *him*, he reminded himself. Regardless of what the prisoner was, he was a person—a man with a name. Not that Rune was much of a name to go off of.

Still, a name was a name and it was a start, even if it didn't give him much of an idea of where their unusual guest might have come from. He'd never heard of any such mix of animal and man, not even in the deep, peculiar jungles that bordered his homeland.

Garam twitched his head and tried not to think of it any further. It was of no importance, not now. Thieves went to the arena and kingswords went to kings, even if he wasn't sure which king this one belonged to.

The streets of the Royal City felt empty in spite of the people around him, but the tall buildings that loomed on either side of the wide avenues still made him claustrophobic. It was his nature as a soldier, he supposed; any one of those buildings would make a perfect hiding place for archers. His dark eyes swept the windows before he caught himself. He pretended to study the carved stone reliefs that adorned the fronts of houses and businesses, instead.

Most of the city was constructed of pale gray stone, doubtlessly ferried in from elsewhere, given the ruddy color of the rock and earth in the fields beyond the city walls. Despite their ornate decoration, the buildings were sturdy, defensible, and he liked that. It almost excused the absurdity of the Spiral Palace.

The Royal City was the pinnacle of civilization in the north. The Spiral Palace stood at the juncture where the Triad's three provinces met. Each of the three regions—Lore, Aldaan, and Roberian—were relatively self-managing, though they were held under one rule. King Vicamros seemed a stable leader and Garam looked to him with deep respect. Still, every time he looked at the soaring white structure that towered over the capital city, Garam wondered at the wisdom in letting the three provinces carry on as they were instead of uniting them as one country under one name.

Garam tore his eyes away from the palace and shifted the wrapped sword tucked under his arm. The palace library would be the best place to find information about who the blade might belong to, but so soon after dealing with Survas in the prison, he was loath to seek the man's colleagues. Instead, he made his way toward home.

The guard barracks were housed within a building indistinguishable from any others, needlessly decorated with fluted columns and elaborate reliefs that all looked the same after a while. The Royal City often felt something like a grand maze. The notion made Garam wonder how long their newest prisoner had been thieving without being seen, and he didn't like the possibilities that came to mind. He'd have to remember to increase the number of patrols in days to come. No matter, though. There was time for that.

He tried to push thieves and prisoners out of mind, but as he carried the wrapped blade to his private quarters above the barracks, the captain couldn't help but think of the haunting glow of the prisoner's eyes.

"THAT'S A VERY old language you speak."

Rune's head jerked up and he squinted against the weak lantern light of the dungeon. Jolted from sleep as he was, even that seemed too bright.

He almost thought he'd imagined the words. The prison was quiet, save the occasional rattle of chains or weak coughs from prisoners in cells farther down the row. Then he caught the sound of the guard snoring at his station beside the stairs.

"No, not your imagination. I wouldn't speak to you if the guards were awake. I wouldn't want to risk making myself useful." The words were accompanied by a quiet chuckle, and Rune moved closer to the door of his cell.

He crouched beside the iron bars and peered across the hall. He'd noticed the old man in the cell opposite his, but hadn't paid him any mind. Of course, from the way the man spoke, perhaps he'd made himself unworthy of attention on purpose.

"You understand me?" Rune asked, keeping his voice low.

"Of course," the old man laughed. He never looked up, never made eye contact, behaving almost as if he didn't see anything at all. Rune might have thought him blind if he hadn't caught the way the man watched the wall. His eyes were sharp, trained too intently on the stone for his gaze to be anything other than deliberate. "Any scholar worth his salt would know the tongue. It's for that reason I'm surprised Survas was able to speak to you."

Rune snorted. "It wasn't much of a conversation."

"No, it wasn't," the man agreed. "He could have at least warned you what you're in for now." When Rune did not reply, the old man sighed. "They'll have you off to the arena in a day or so. Can't have too many folk sitting about in the dungeons like I am, after all."

"Arena?" Rune asked. The weight his fellow prisoner put on the word was enough to make him dislike the way it sounded.

"Of course. You're young enough, able-bodied from the look of you, and should put up a decent bit of entertainment for the nobles. They turn a whole gaggle of prisoners out into the arena each week, send lords and knights and nobles out with weapons to cut you down. Scares most people into behaving, and the betting puts a lot of coin into the pockets of the rich."

"Well, I hate to have to disappoint them." Rune wasn't chained, and having had time to rest and some semblance of a meal to replenish his strength, he saw no reason to stay put—especially if some sort of execution awaited. Shifting back from the bars, Rune closed his eyes and waited to sense the eb and flow of energy around him. He was a mage, after all. Not a skilled one, perhaps, but a strong one. If he could catch hold of the power in the air, there wasn't much chance that prison bars could stand in his way.

A delicate shift in the air gave him the direction he needed and he reached after it with his own energy. But the flow did something he didn't expect, bending around his reach as if it knew to avoid him. He opened his eyes, his brow furrowed. Despite his shaky grasp of magic, that had never happened before.

"If magic could get you out, don't you think I'd have tried that already?" The old man chortled, turning his head to peer across the walkway. The distinct, frigid blue of his eyes spoke volumes.

"You're a mage?" Rune regretted the words the moment they left his mouth. Of course the old man was a mage; no one had eyes that color naturally. It was one effect magic had on its wielders, the tax of bending energy to their whims. The raw power changed their eyes and scoured away the color of their hair, leaving them pale as ghosts. Rune focused on the man across the hall. The Gift of power prickled in his senses. He'd been too distracted to notice it before.

"Yes, unfortunately. You'd do well to mind your Gift if you make it out of your first arena visit alive. They don't take kindly to mages here."

The statement gave Rune pause. There were a lot of reasons a mage could fail to garner respect for themselves, either by actions or accident. But for mages as a whole to be ill thought of? That was unfathomable. The rank of Master mage carried weight and power on Elenhiise island. Masters were considered nobles in every way.

But he wasn't on Elenhiise anymore. Rune tucked the knowledge away and tried not to let his thoughts show. The information was surprising, but useful, given his own Gift. Useful knowledge wasn't often given away for free. "Who are you? Why would they put an old mage in prison?"

"Because old mages are the frightening ones. We're too tired of the world to care about keeping our tongues in check." Again the old man chuckled, though now he sounded tired. "I am Redoram Parthanus, highborn mage, scholar, and former member of the king's council. Of course, even that rank doesn't protect you if your opinions are unpopular." He grimaced and shook his head. "They've put wards here to prevent our kind from breaking free. I don't believe the same wards preside over the arena, but they wouldn't dare include me. My opinions are unpopular with nobles, but not with the masses. They won't risk aggravating the people. Instead, I suppose they'll just wait for me to rot."

More useful information. Rune considered it carefully. If he had access to his power in the arena, it bettered his chances of coming back alive. Coming back to what, though, he wasn't entirely sure. He supposed there were worse places to be than prison, though escaping one on Elenhiise only to land in another once he returned to dry land hadn't exactly been the plan.

And what was the plan? He'd never stopped to think about what he would do once he made it off that blasted ship. Too many regrets had clouded his mind. They rose into his head now, as if summoned. He tried to stifle the thoughts, fingering the rings on their cord around his neck.

"You lied to the jailers." Redoram's voice brought his focus back to the present, to the dank and musty prison in which they both sat.

"What makes you think that?" Troubled, Rune shifted to sit on the floor and lean back against the cool stone wall. He didn't know the man's game just yet, couldn't risk being seen in a moment of turmoil.

Redoram leaned against the bars and rubbed his bearded chin with a frown. "Your name. I once knew a man who spoke your tongue and bore the same accent. An esteemed mage from the college out in the isles of Lore. The language as he spoke it would never favor a name so simple." He paused and his mage-blue eyes narrowed. "I'm not sure what sort of training you've had for your Gift, but if it's of the sort that makes you think true names have any kind of power, you'd do well to learn otherwise."

He snorted. "It is my true name." He gave Redoram a look from the corner of one faintly glowing violet eye. "It just wasn't given to me until later in life."

For a time the old man said nothing, regarding him in thoughtful silence. Then he nodded. "I see." Redoram drew back from the bars and chuckled once more. The sound of the old man's laugh was beginning to grate on his nerves. "Well then, Rune, was it? Best of luck in the arena. It's been a pleasure speaking with you. Come back alive and I may do it more often. I'd be happy to teach you what you need to know to survive here, assuming you'll be keeping me company for a while."

Rune arched a brow. "If I come back alive, I don't think I'll need you to teach me to survive."

Redoram gave a hearty guffaw at that, letting the laugh fade into a cough when the prison guard stirred at his station.

Content to let silence fall, Rune stared at the far wall of his cell and played with the rings at his throat. If participating in some sort of arena combat was all it took to guarantee he'd make it back to the prison, he liked his odds. He'd be escorted to and from the event, he assumed, which would give him the opportunity to see where the prison was located within the city. He'd get to see the city itself, too, and having a clearer scope of its size would tell him how likely he was to find his father's sword. The rest of the plan could come later. Future conversations with Redoram could help him plan escape and choose a destination. The old man was one resource he planned to pick clean while it was at his fingertips.

As for the arena itself, simply staying alive until the event was over didn't sound difficult. It didn't come at the best time, with him weakened and out of practice after two months on a ship and a few more starving while ashore, but he would have to make do. There would be rations in the evening and likely more in the morning as well. For the moment, all he could do was rest.

Rune folded his arms over his chest and tried to make himself comfortable against the wall as he let his eyes drift closed. Preparation was the easy part. Survival might be a bit more of a challenge. Then again, he reminded himself as a half-healed scar on his back rubbed against the coarse stone, he had lived through worse.

THE COLLEGE OF LORE

Envesi gritted her teeth, rubbed her eyes, and tried to ignore her. If the girl didn't stop, she'd pay penance for it later. Envesi had half a mind to stripe the girl herself.

Penance was an ugly word, one she'd heard far too often since their arrival in the mainland college some eight months before. She was Archmage of Elenhiise, not someone to be switched and scolded like a misbehaved mageling. Or she had been Archmage of Elenhiise, before the three of them had been sent away.

"Oh do be quiet," Envesi snapped at last, giving Alira such a glare that the girl sniffled and quieted down. She shouldn't fault the girl, not really. Alira had barely worn the white robes of a Master mage before she'd been named Master of her House of affinity. But between her and Melora, the other Master exiled alongside them, Envesi had heard quite enough.

"Best mind the way you speak to her. We're all on equal footing now." Melora's voice was too calm, too even. The former Master of the House of wind had done an admirable job of pretending to accept their punishment, but Envesi knew her too well to think her acceptance was genuine.

Biting her tongue to keep it in check, the former Archmage turned back to the tub of suds before her. She snatched a white robe from the water and scrubbed it against the washboard with a renewed vigor.

It was not the first time Envesi had worked the laundry basins at the Grand College of Lore. It was here that she'd received her training and scaled to the rank of Master mage before she was forced to fulfill an arranged marriage. There was no consolation in the fact that none of the mages she'd trained under seemed to be a part of the college any longer, though perhaps there should have been. Doing their laundry for a second time in her life would have been even more humiliating.

"I've heard they plan to test us soon, raise us to the rank of gray." Melora spoke in a short, clipped tone. She did not look at the other two women as she pinned the wash to the many lines strung across the ceiling. If any of them had been allowed to use their Gift, the laundry would have been done hours ago. But that would have defeated the purpose of penance. "Imagine, a gray mageling at my age. My robes would match my hair."

Alira wiped her nose, then coughed. "I'll be glad of it, to be honest. At least it would get us out of the laundry."

Envesi couldn't help but agree, which she resented. Alira was young, her hair only just turned white from the continual shock of twisting raw energy into usable flows. Being set back to the lowest mageling rank was not quite so devastating to her as it was to Melora or herself, women who had worn Master white for longer than Alira had been alive. Still, it did provide a measure of relief. At least if they wore mageling robes, they'd be allowed to touch magic again. Envesi had sorely missed the sensation of power at her fingertips.

"I don't understand the need to test us. They know perfectly well that all three of us wore the white." Melora scowled and wrung water from a shirt until her knuckles turned as white as the cloth.

"It ought to be obvious. They want to see that we understand the mainland's practices for magecraft before they decide whether or not they'll grant us access to power. The political climate involving mages is different here." Envesi couldn't keep bitterness from her voice; admitting the energy lines were held beyond her reach was difficult to bear. At the same time, she scolded herself for forgetting the mainland mages had that power. She would have taken it to Kirban, if she'd had the time to learn the trick before being sent off to marry. Had she been able to bridle the magic of others, they wouldn't be in this situation now.

"And what are we to do if we reach the rank of Master again?" Alira asked, looking between the two older women with a frown. "The college doesn't retain as many teachers as the temple did. I know no one here, and I'm sure the others wouldn't have us back on Elenhiise, not after—"

"The right to Elenhiise is not theirs to give!" Envesi snapped. "I was Kifel's wife. With no heir named and the temple's influence to back me, I should have had his throne."

"And yet here we are, locked away in a basement, doing chores for Masters and mages we've never met," Melora chuckled darkly and shook her head as she tugged the clothesline on its pulleys to run the clean wash to the edges of the room. "Wise of them to hold magic outside our reach.. If I could get hold of a single thread, I'd give them all a thrashing they won't soon forget."

Envesi lifted her head and gave the former Master of wind a shadowed glance. "If I have my way, you may be afforded the chance."

Melora paused. "I beg your pardon?"

"Pardoned." Envesi straightened band pushed her snow-white hair back from her face. She still looked every bit the part of Archmage, even in the coarse brown wool of a laundry maid. The other women lowered their eyes and she savored the way it felt. "I see no reason to halt the research I carried out in Kirban. I've only been set back by the fact they put one of my tools to the noose. He was useful for study, but only a minor loss. I began the research needed to understand free magic long before I brought him to be."

Alira sent Melora a questioning look. When the older woman's expression didn't change, her eyes shifted back to Envesi. "You mean Lomithrandel?"

Envesi heaved a sigh. The young woman had been full of questions when she'd learned the truth of the prince's birth, and all of them had been answered. She hadn't the patience to go over it again. "Melora, please?"

Melora shook her head. "Say it yourself or it won't be said at all. I'll not speak of the practices you pushed us into until I know there's no one listening."

Irritated, Envesi turned back to the wash basin. "When Lomithrandel was brought to be, we were able to do something that was, until then, unheard of. You know he was born to free magic." The words carried weight, and for good reason. For all the power mages possessed, they were limited by Affinity. Without a nearby energy source to tap, they were all but powerless. But free magic was different. It was limitless, unfettered and almost uncontrollable. Free magic was power that rivaled that of the Lifetree.

"And he was allowed to live after the magic warped him because it let you study how free magic worked," Alira sighed. "I know. But if Lomithrandel has been put to death, how do you mean to study his powers?"

"I remember the course the magic took when he was made," Envesi said, her eyes unfocused and her hands idle on the washboard. "I remember every twist and bend. I remember the moment the bindings of magic came undone, the way the power came to life in him." Then her jaw tightened and she exhaled. "And could I extricate that moment from the taint that twisted his body, I could unbind myself, as well."

Melora stared at her with wide eyes. "Such a thing isn't possible."

"Isn't it, though?" Envesi mused. "It was possible in Lomithrandel. To determine what went wrong, all I need is another like him. Another that's been twisted by corrupted flows..."

Alira's jaw went slack. "You can't mean to create another!"

"She can't create another," Melora said, scowling. "Not without a full council of mages, at least ten who are strong in their Gift."

"I do not mean to renew that project." The former Archmage folded her arms over her chest and turned to face the others. "I mean only to study another that has been twisted by the unbinding process."

Suddenly pale, Melora stepped back. "You cannot mean to unbind one of us."

The thought hadn't crossed Envesi's mind. She barked a laugh. "No, the two of you are too valuable. You, Melora, because you were there. And Alira because she knows too much to be safe." She smiled coldly as she gave the younger woman a sidewise glance. Alira grew ashen as she swallowed and shifted in place. Good, let her be afraid. Fear was useful.

"Who, then?" Melora demanded.

"I don't know." Envesi didn't like to admit it, but she hadn't gotten that far. Not when the Masters of the college held the flows beyond her reach. Not while she was under too much scrutiny to even consider the preparations she would need to take.

Who, indeed. Lomithrandel had been safe to keep around, if only because of his connection to Kifel. It made him weak, easy to control. His power had never been a threat. Another mage, already versed in the ways of their Gift, was out of the question. "A child, perhaps," she said at last. "One just beginning to exhibit the spark of a Gift. One who knows nothing, hasn't been trained. Not a mageling, and no one from the college."

"An orphan, perhaps?" Melora suggested. "We're in a large enough city. Surely there are dozens to choose from."

An orphaned child did seem like the best option, though how she was to raise one while climbing the ranks in the college, Envesi did not know. It had been easy with Lomithrandel; Kifel had done that part of the work for her. "Perhaps," she agreed as she reached for another piece of wash in the basin. "Perhaps more than one."

Chances were, after all, she would need a bit of practice.

LORE HAD CHANGED little in the time she'd been away. Not that Envesi expected it to be different. Mages came and mages went, and few returned to walk the hallways of the Grand College after graduation. Few ever had.

Her return was shameful, but it could be worse. Though the loss of her title as Archmage was frustrating, she'd stopped thinking of it as a crippling blow. A setback, but not devastating. Perhaps it even reopened doors that had been closed long ago, shut in her face when her family had announced their intention to see her married.

She had been a student under her uncle, then. Tanvar had been a powerful man, strong in his Gift and clever in how he used it. He had been part of the council of the Grand College, as well, and she had hoped to replace him someday. That had been impossible when she was trapped on Elenhiise. It wasn't impossible now. The thought made her smile and she stopped halfway down the open walkway between College buildings to lean against the balustrade and look across the sea.

The country of Lore was renowned for more than the mages it trained. While most of the population lived along the coastline, The Grand College and the palace both stood on the numerous islands just offshore. Unlike anywhere Envesi had seen in her travels, the islands of Lore rose from the ocean like towers. Great mansions of stone seemed to sprout from the tops of the oddly-shaped spires of jointed basalt, some sprawling over the edges and teetering precariously above the sea.

Building atop the columns would have been foolish for anyone but the mages. Their combined power protected the basalt from the crashing waves that would have otherwise toppled the islands centuries ago. Looking out across the islands with the sunset turning the southern sky to a rosy backdrop, even someone as practical as she could understand why they found it worth the effort. It was beautiful and it was defensible. The mages provided access to the islands and could cut off that access at any time.

Envesi lingered until the first stars began to appear in the dusky sky. Then she pushed herself from the balustrade and continued on her way. None of the passing mages paid any attention to a white-haired woman in the brown wool of a servant, even with her mage-blue eyes. A laundry maid was a laundry maid, and for the first time since her arrival, the former Archmage was glad of it. Magelings were not permitted to rove the city on their own. Being noticed would have been a hindrance.

This time, her destination stood at the far end of one of the Grand College's gardens. Bridges would have marred the beauty of the basalt islands. Instead, they were connected by a number of free-standing Gates set inside tall, black stone archways and held open by gleaming Gate-stones. The portals made no sound and gave off no sense of energy, despite the immense power required to make them.

The Gate she chose was only one of a number of archways that stood along the edge of the city. The portal's surface provided a clear image of what waited on the other side. A pleasantly cool wind flowed through it as if it were any other doorway. Envesi picked up her skirts and stepped into to the coastal city in a single stride. Few people used the Gates; only the wealthy had need to traverse the islands. The rest of Lore's people were content to stay on the shore, where the sheer number of inhabitants gave the city a low hum that never quieted.

Her icy blue eyes earned her a number of curious looks outside the college grounds, but when Envesi walked, people moved out of the way. No one questioned the intent of mages, and she liked that. It was one similarity between Elenhiise and the mainland she was grateful for, though similarities between the two regions were blessedly few. On Elenhiise, mages were avoided out of respect. In Lore, they were avoided out of fear. The number of mages on the mainland dwindled year by year as the old distrust she'd all but forgotten drove people away from the college. She could have changed that, she told herself. She still might.

Street by street, Envesi wound her way farther into the city, where dim oil lamps did little to illuminate the streets against the night. Her figure cast flickering, misshapen shadows down long alleys and avenues as she passed.

The wards the mage council had bound to her kept her from touching the flows, but they didn't keep her from sensing them. She felt everywhere, scouted out each tendril of energy or spark that indicated a person with an inkling of a Gift left untapped. Now and then she paused to watch urchins scurry about the alleys and streets. When she felt nothing, she moved on.

She had to credit Melora; an orphan would be the perfect choice for renewed efforts with her experiments. With any luck, it would only take one. Recreating something like Lomithrandel would be difficult without a full council of mages, but the three of them should suffice. They would be forced to work slower, but that was not a bad thing. A lack of speed caused caution, and caution meant fewer mistakes. Such caution would be necessary. No matter how slowly she'd tried to recreate the complicated flows of magic in the past, Envesi had never determined how they should have been laid in place of that twist, that one kink thrown into the essence of life by that infernal woman.

The thought of it always stirred Envesi's anger anew. Lumia

never should have worn white. Envesi still cursed herself for that mistake, the first and last time she'd allowed her council to sway her. The woman had been reckless, impassioned, driven by her own causes. That alone should have been grounds to reject her when she'd come to Kirban Temple. The former Archmage shuddered with anger and forced the thoughts from her mind.

It was of no consequence now. She walked the streets of Lore's harbor city, not Ilmenhith. A place bursting with people and prosperity, a far cry from the isolated island she'd left behind.

The graceful soaring towers and arches of the college made the rest of Lore seem particularly squat and dumpy, its low stone buildings with roofs of thatch or wooden shakes far from awe-inspiring. Boardwalks lined the unpaved streets, which churned to mud the moment it rained. It was dirty and often ill-smelling, but it would have to do. Try as she might to keep from it, Envesi couldn't help but compare the city to Ilmenhith. For a moment, she felt a pang of regret, and her step slowed.

But Elenhiise was behind her. She could only hope her manipulations of the weather had come to some fruition, caused enough trouble for the pitiful girl the mages had set upon the throne. That satisfaction, too, would simply have to do.

The edge of the city proper loomed ahead and Envesi released a quiet sigh. She'd walked from one end of the city to the next without sensing anything of value. But the exercise had put a warmth in her legs and lungs, both refreshing and empowering.

Or was it the walk that strengthened her? Envesi hesitated at the edge of the city proper. Something prickled at the edge of her senses, as if to beckon her onward. She straightened and stared down the road that meandered from the city off into the countryside. Had she come this far before? No; she'd had no need to visit the fields. The currents of power that rode on the air seemed closer here, as if to beg her attention. Surely she would have noticed. Envesi's eyes narrowed and she extended her own energy to grasp the flows. The wards the Grand College had burdened her with felt distant, just barely influencing the forces that skirted her reach. That the wards on her power were tied to the college itself, and not to her, had never crossed her mind. A few steps farther and she'd be free to do whatever she pleased.

Alira and Melora came to mind. They'd be interested to hear of such a discovery. A hint of a smile twisted her mouth and Envesi turned back the way she'd come, toward the Gate that would lead her back to the college and her colleagues. Perhaps their research wouldn't have to wait so long after all.

A GIFT OF WHAT WAS

"Tea, my lady?"

Firal started and looked up from the papers on her desk. She shouldn't have been surprised to see Medreal in the doorway, holding the tea tray she couldn't picture her without. It wasn't unusual for the woman to enter without knocking, but under normal circumstances, Firal paid enough attention to notice her approach. "Yes, please," she said, giving as warm a smile as she could muster and leaning back in her chair as her stewardess closed the distance between them.

Medreal's Gift was odd. The woman had never given any indication of being predisposed to magecraft, but having studied at the Kirban Temple for the entirety of her life, Firal knew what the Gift felt like in someone. Medreal's power was there, but different. She'd felt something similar before, though she couldn't quite picture where. It gave the stewardess a curious presence, one that was easy to identify even from afar.

Firal straightened when she saw the number of teacups on the tray. Three, and only two of them in the room. "Who is here to see me?"

Medreal glanced up, a ghost of a smile coloring her expression. "A rather important man, from the looks of him. He introduced himself as Davan and said you would wish to see him immediately."

"Davan!" She almost leaped from her chair. "Show him in at once!"

"Of course, my queen." Medreal bowed her head and left one full teacup on the desk before she hurried away to do as she was told.

Firal eased back into her seat and stared at her tea in disbelief. How long had it been since she'd called Davan to Ilmenhith? It had been just after her father's death, if she remembered correctly, the better part of a year before. She had resigned herself to the idea that none of the Underlings would answer her call. It was almost troubling for one of them to arrive at the palace so long after her summons had been sent.

Had she been in a position to do so, she would have traveled to Core long ago and spoken with the people she'd left behind in the heart of the Kirban Ruins. But she'd been ill, heavy with child, and she'd only just begun to feel like herself again. She hadn't expected recovery from the girl's birth to take so long.

Gathering her composure, the queen smoothed back her ebony hair, lifted her chin and folded her hands against the edge of her desk, looking as much the part of ruler as she could manage. When she'd married Vahn, she had assumed he would be the one to take the throne, but her father had been king, not his. Ilmenhith and half of Elenhiise were hers to rule, whether she liked it or not.

When Medreal opened the door again, she ushered in a man who looked much older than what Firal remembered. He murmured a thank-you and shifted a satchel on his shoulder as he turned to face her. He gave a deep and respectful bow, though his expression was less reverent and more worried. His hair had gone gray in not quite a year's time, his face more haggard than any of the Underlings had ever seemed before. He hadn't shaven, and his clothes spoke of long travel on foot. Still, he carried himself with an air of dignity. At least that hadn't changed.

"Davan," Firal began, her tone courteous and formal, her face placid despite the new worries his appearance spawned in her mind. "I'd given up on the idea of seeing you outside of Core."

"Begging your pardon, miss—ah—Majesty." Davan avoided meeting her eyes as he touched a knuckle to his forehead and bowed again. "I'd have been here much sooner, but I didn't expect it to take so long for all of us to travel."

Her warm amber eyes never left him. "All of you?"

"Of course, Your Majesty." His brow furrowed with concern. "The letter I received said we were to serve you, our queen, as people of your country. So we've come to do as asked."

Firal pursed her lips. Surely he didn't mean it. Not all of them!

"We've established a camp of sorts five miles from the city," Davan continued, seemingly unaware of the impact of his words. "We thought it best not to move any closer until things with your army's patrols were cleared up."

Patrols? So the approach of the ruin-folk hadn't gone unnoticed. Word simply hadn't made it to the queen. Her jaw tightened. "Davan, how many did you bring?"

He blinked, flustered. "Everyone, Your Majesty. All of Core has answered your call."

Firal blanched and lowered her hands to her lap. All of Core. Twelve thousand soldiers. Wives, children, workers, the elderly and infirm. She felt almost faint. Their numbers would increase the population of Ilmenhith by half again! How was she to house them? Feed them? The farms were still recovering from the weather anomalies caused by the previous Archmage. Ilmenhith already teetered on the edge of a famine.

The panicked thoughts shattered at the thump of Davan's satchel landing on her desk. "Minna asked that I bring this for you. She'd flay me if I forgot."

Firal swallowed hard. "Is Minna well?" Oh, Brant favor her if she was to feed all of these people.

Davan grinned. "Yes, Your Majesty. Tobias, as well. The two of them weren't eager to leave Core, but once they were on board, I thought Minna might leave me behind..."

The rest of his answer faded to a distant hum in her ears as she pulled the satchel near. Minna was dear to her, having acted like a mother hen when Firal first arrived in Core, but solving this new problem would require more help than what a mother hen could provide. She flipped open the satchel and dug inside. Her hand closed around what felt like a purse and she drew it out, brow furrowed. When she saw what it was, her heart fell to her stomach.

"I apologize, my queen. I did not mean to let your tea grow cold." Medreal reached between Firal and the satchel to top off the forgotten teacup. Then she turned to face their guest. "Will you take tea, Davan?"

Firal dropped the purse back into the satchel and reached for her tea instead, grateful for Medreal's subtle intervention. "Yes, Davan, please. Sit, share a cup of tea with me."

"I would enjoy it, Your Majesty, but I should not stay longer than our meeting requires." A pinched look came to his weary eyes. "Food is in short supply after our trip. I must see to my people before nightfall."

Of course food was in short supply. Firal nodded and forced a smile over the rim of her teacup. "I understand. I will see that supplies are sent to your camp as soon as possible. Tend to your men, and please send word when your officers are prepared to meet with me to discuss how we shall properly welcome you into the city."

"Yes, my lady." Davan gave an awkward sort of bow and started for the door.

"Oh," she called before he reached it, managing a much more genuine smile. "And please tell Minna I said hello."

He flashed her a warm but tired smile in response. "I shall," he said as Medreal opened the door for him. He bowed to her as well and slipped out into the hall.

Medreal pursed her lips as she closed the door. When she turned, she cast Firal a frown. "My lady, I do not mean to question, but you hardly spoke—"

"We spoke enough," Firal interrupted, returning her teacup and its saucer to her desk so she could rub her face with both hands. "All of Core! An entire army camped right outside my city, and this is the first I've heard of it. Why hasn't anyone told me, Medreal?"

Her stewardess looked uncomfortable. "I apologize, my queen." She shifted on her feet and licked her lips. It was the first time Firal could recall seeing her nervous. "I'd heard nothing of the matter, myself."

Firal stifled a sigh and slouched in her chair. It was no secret that Ilmenhith hadn't exactly welcomed her as queen. Were it not for the support and backing she'd received from the mages of Kirban prior to her coronation, she doubted the people would have accepted her at all. But the mages were as well-respected as her father had been. If the mages said she was their rightful queen, it was unlikely anyone would argue. Even so, the people meant to be subservient to her found new ways to disrespect her at every turn. She barely had control of the city. If not for the great amount of sway Vahn held over the military, due to his father's long history as a high-ranking officer, she might not have controlled it at all.

"I doubt our soldiers are concerned about having these visitors at our doorstep. Your husband would have heard something of it, otherwise." Medreal took the teapot again and filled a cup for herself.

"Or perhaps he has heard something of it, and merely decided I didn't need another thing to worry about." Firal couldn't help the bitterness in her tone. She reached for the satchel Davan had left and opened it again, just enough to see what else was inside. Her brow knit as she pulled out a small book and turned it over in her hand.

Medreal eyed the chairs before the desk, waiting for permission to sit. Firal granted it with a wave of her hand. The stewardess nodded her appreciation as she settled. "What is it, my queen?"

"A journal I kept when I was a mageling," Firal said with wonder. She brushed her fingertips over the worn leather cover before she thumbed through its pages. "I didn't imagine Minna would send this. I didn't think I'd ever see it again." She put it aside with a shake of her head and emptied the rest of the satchel's contents onto her desk. It held little; just a larger book on herbs and healing she'd written during her time with the Underlings, and three small purses. One jingled when she picked it up, the bumps and ridges inside familiar. It bulged with the unmarked gold coins she'd collected in Core, money useless to a queen. The sight of the other purses put a lump in her throat.

She didn't need to open them to know what they held. The smaller of the two contained a single lotus seed wrapped in layers of silk, the first gift she'd received from her husband. Her first husband, her real husband. Squeezing her eyes closed, she stood and shoved the purses away. Furry seed catkins spilled across her desk.

Medreal raised a brow. "Aspen," she mused as she sipped her tea. "I've heard such a tree can live a thousand years."

Firal shot her a glare. "A tree dies once you cut it down." She picked up her skirts and hurried toward the door.

"Yes," Medreal agreed, a smile in her voice. "But aspen grows back from the roots."

Firal hesitated before the doorway for a long moment before she bit her lip and slipped into the hallway without another word. She didn't have time to think about such things, not with ever-growing problems ahead of her. There were enough troubles on her plate without stirring up those that had plagued her mind and heart through the long months after her coronation.

Firal hastened her step to avoid being stopped and only slowed when she reached the doors to the private quarters she shared with Vahn. It had been strange to move into the royal apartment after Kifel's effects had been packed away. Medreal had offered to let her sort through them, but it didn't seem right to rifle through the personal belongings of a man she'd barely known. She'd have to look at his things eventually, but she was in no hurry.

Her quarters were far from the grandiose display Medreal insisted was proper for a queen. Firal liked it that way. She had been a guest in the palace once, when she attended the solstice ball with the other mages from Kirban Temple. When it was time to furnish her new quarters, she had requested the furniture from the room she'd stayed in; a small touch of familiarity to help her settle in. The four-posted bed looked woefully small in her new bedroom, but the rich forest greens of the bedding and curtains looked spectacular washed in the warm evening light from the arched windows that lined the far wall.

Firal breathed a sigh of relief as she closed the door behind her, smoothing her skirts and her hair before she made her way to the half-open door that led into nursery. She expected a nursemaid to be in the room. Instead, she was taken by surprise.

Vahn hummed softly to the bundle nestled in his arms, booted feet keeping the rocking chair swaying. His sword leaned against the cradle beside him, and the circlet that marked him as king-regent lay atop his folded purple cape on the floor. Firal leaned against the door frame and watched in silence with a lump in her throat. A time passed before he noticed her there. Surprise and then guilt spread across his face.

"I sent the nursemaid away," he said in a rush, putting both feet down to stop the chair and glancing to the child in his arms. "I hope that's all right. I just thought—"

"You're raising her, Vahn," Firal said with a smile tinged by sorrow. "If you wish to hold her, you don't have to justify it to me." She clasped her hands before her stomach and moved to stand beside him, where she could look down at the round face of the swaddled infant. The girl's pink lips puckered in a pout, her eyes closed and their long lashes brushing her rosy cheeks.

He relaxed into the rocking chair and brushed a dark curl from the baby's forehead with a fingertip. "It's good that she looks like you."

She chuckled beneath her breath. "My cheeks aren't quite that round, thank you."

Vahn offered a nervous smile in return. "Are you done with your duties for this evening?"

Firal nodded and held out her hands in request. He shifted the sleeping infant into her arms with some difficulty. She couldn't fault him for that; a month's time and he was still as nervous around the girl as the day she was born. "Medreal will be sending up an evening meal for us. She chastised me this morning for spending too much time on my feet."

He all but leaped from the chair, gesturing for her to sit. She gave him a reprimanding look, but eased down into the rocking chair and leaned back as she cradled her daughter against her chest. The girl favored her strongly, Vahn was right about that. But for all that Lumia looked like her mother, there was plenty of her father in her, as well. It pained her sometimes, seeing the girl's parentage reflected in her peculiar violet eyes. Firal brushed the thought from her mind. There were more important things to worry about now.

"I had an interesting meeting this evening," she said, trying to keep her voice level. "It seems that all of Core has uprooted from the ruins and set up camp a few miles from Ilmenhith's edge."

Vahn grimaced.

"So you did know, then?" Firal raised a brow.

"I didn't plan to keep it from you," he said, twisting a button on the cuff of his sleeve. "I just didn't want you to worry about anything else. You have enough to manage right now, and I thought... well, I thought I could take care of this before you heard."

"Take care of it how, Vahn? The Underlings are my people, perhaps even more so than the people of Ilmenhith." It surprised her how easy it was to keep calm. Had it been anyone else in the world, perhaps she wouldn't have managed it. But she owed Vahn a deep debt of gratitude. He'd never done anything but serve.

He shifted on his feet. "By arranging for provisions and lodging. I commissioned more fishing vessels when they arrived, since fish is about all that's plentiful now, and put out an order for more grain to be shipped from the mainland. Though it won't make much difference for a few months, at least." He paused then, looking away. "I hope I haven't overstepped my bounds, my lady."

Firal sighed. "Vahnil, how many times have I told you not to call me that? We're supposed to be married. And you are supposed to be king-regent, overseeing my affairs until I fully recover from childbirth."

"I know," he groaned, rubbing his brow. "I know. It's just..."

"Hard to keep pretending," Firal finished, turning her amber eyes toward the window. "I know."

An awkward silence fell over the room, punctuated only by the steady creak of the rocking chair.

"Please don't call me Vahnil," he said at last.

She smiled sarcastically. "Please don't call me your lady."

"So you aren't angry at me?"

That made her pause. "I'm displeased that you decided to keep such important information from me." She weighed the words before they left her tongue, a skill the Kirban mages were still trying to hammer into her. "But I appreciate the thought that went into your reasons. However, that does not change the fact that I am the ruler and you are my regent. It's fortunate that I learned of the Underling camp from Davan himself. Can you imagine what a fool I'd have looked if it had been anyone else?"

"I know. I'm sorry. I should have considered that first." His shoulders sagged. He took his sheathed sword and rested its tip beside the toe of his boot, a finger on the pommel balancing it upright. "I'm still learning too, you know."

Firal nodded in agreement, content to enjoy the quiet until their meal arrived and the scent of food drew her to the table.

She insisted on their portions being made smaller, but the amount of food the servants still brought to their quarters made her ache with guilt. Ilmenhith wasn't starving, not yet, but the price of produce had risen until only the wealthy could afford even sweet potatoes. Grain merchants emptied their stores and kept only enough to feed their own families, and livestock had grown so scarce that Firal feared the peasantry would take to slaughtering their work animals for meat before the rainy season returned. There were fish, of course; Elenhiise was an island. But while fish would feed hungry mouths, overfishing the waters nearest the island came with its own set of problems.

The months behind her blurred in lessons about the island's economy and lack of effective agriculture, taught by both Medreal and the temple mages. They still expected her to find a solution. She still hadn't. Her education as a mage had been focused on healing, not barter and exchange, not crops and farming. Elenhiise had always been a trading outpost between the northern and southern continents, a place for the trade of gems and spices and fabric and other things that lasted well during long months at sea. How was she to know how to bring food to the island?

There had to be something she was missing. She considered again how to seek help from the mainland. It was good that Vahn had ordered more provisions, but they needed something much more immediate. She could order the temple mages to open a Gate to the mainland, but with no idea who to contact, how was she to seek assistance? Was there even anyone in the temple who knew the mainland well enough to establish a Gate? If she'd been raised in the palace, surrounded by nobles, perhaps she'd have known who to seek. If Kifel had lived to see her crowned as heir, perhaps he could have set her on the proper path. But that path was nowhere to be seen, and her father was dead.

Not for the first time, Firal tamped down feelings of resentment and forced herself to breathe deeply and calm her mind. Her food had already grown cold.

The baby woke as Firal finished her meal, having tasted it little with how her thoughts were elsewhere. She returned to the nursery's rocking chair once more, cradling the girl to her breast and adjusting her swaddling. Half the palace was still scandalized by her decision to feed the girl herself, rather than calling for a wet nurse. She couldn't expect them to understand. It was the last shred of independence she had to cling to, the last scrap of self-sufficiency she could provide her broken family. Had Kifel never come to retrieve her and the girl been born in Core, things would have been very different.

"Firal," Vahn started from the doorway. She was surprised to see him still there, given the uncomfortable way he usually acted when she nursed the baby. "I've been meaning to ask for a while... I hope you understand."

She lifted a blanket and draped it over her shoulder and the baby in her arms. With her modesty restored, he seemed to relax. "Yes, Vahn?"

His brow furrowed and his tongue darted between his lips, as if to unstick the words. "Out of all the names you could have chosen for her, why Lumia?"

Firal's heart sank. She tried to smile and found she couldn't. Instead, she stared down at the cover that hid the infant from sight. "As a political gesture, I suppose. The people of Core answer to me. More than ever, we need symbols to unify our people. That was the name of their queen once. Now it will be again, someday. And because..." Her voice cracked.

She forced herself to go on. "Because a man should have his daughter's name etched on his heart." All the emotion she'd tried to tamp down through the day came bubbling up at the question. Tears blurred her vision and though she blinked hard, she couldn't keep them at bay. "Because he ought to at least know it, and what other names are there that he could never forget?"

Vahn grimaced. "I'm sorry, my lady, I didn't mean to—"

"The Masters knew him. I never would have thought walking away would mean his death. How could I have failed him so completely, Vahn?"

He moved to her chair and knelt beside her, wiped tears from her cheeks and cradled her face in his hands. "Master Anaide's actions are not your fault. You can't blame yourself for that."

"But I could have spoken! I could have said something—anything—instead of just walking away in anger. How could I have misjudged his intentions? Now I'll never see him again, and the last he'll remember of me is that I turned away and left him to those vultures!" The first sob almost choked her. Her hands trembled as she clung to the child, her only remaining anchor to the life she should have had.

Vahn moved closer and she buried her face in his shoulder, sobbing helplessly. He stroked her hair, steadfast and gentle, the only friend she felt she had left in the world.

"I couldn't be a proper mageling. I couldn't have survived without the mercy of the Underlings. I couldn't even save my husband in the moment he needed me most," she cried. "I've failed at everything!"

He hushed her, resting his cheek against her head. "You know that's not true."

"It is, and now I'm supposed to be queen? I've hardly been out of bed. I don't know how to rule, I never even had a chance to know my father before taking his crown. I didn't even want it! Now I'm nothing more than a puppet on the strings of the Master mages." She gulped back her tears and fought the rising wave of bitterness that swept over her. "Everything I've done has been at their behest. Even when dealing with Relythes and the Archmage I was little more than their mouthpiece, reciting what they drilled into me before the meeting took place."

"And in doing so, you protected the temple and the kingdom." Vahn rubbed her back and brushed hair from her face. "Every ruler starts somewhere, my lady, you must know that. You've taken the throne while quelling a war, carrying a child, and grieving the loss of both Ran and Kifel. Who could expect more from you?"

She sniffed and looked away. "Ran expected more."

Vahn opened his mouth as if to protest, but closed it again when her tears began anew. Instead, he wrapped his arms around her shoulders and held her while she cried, the baby sheltered between them.

Some time passed before Firal heard the footsteps of the maids crossing their apartment to join them in the nursery. She wiped her eyes and breathed deeply, doing her best to compose herself before they appeared at the door. Her drowsing infant remained oblivious to all that had transpired, something for which she was silently grateful. The last thing she needed was an inconsolable child. Vahn stood and brushed back Firal's hair one more time before he stepped back from her chair.

"Come now, my queen," Medreal said as she slipped through the doorway and reached for the baby in Firal's arms. "You have meetings with the Kirban mages early in the morning. We must get you into bed. Shall I have a maid tend the baby tonight?"

"I'll tend her myself, as always. Thank you, Medreal." Firal let the old stewardess usher her into the bedchamber. The other maids led her behind the standing screen in the corner to help her out of her dress and into a nightgown. She could dress herself, of course, but had long since learned it was easier to allow the maids to do it—if only because it stilled their tongues. She drew another deep breath and hoped her eyes were no longer red, lest their tongues wag about something else.

"Shall you need assistance, as well, master Vahnil?" Medreal asked.

Vahn shook his head. "I believe I can manage with my wife's assistance."

Medreal raised a brow and turned to look at Firal behind the screen. "Very well," she intoned, obviously amused. Firal gave her a darkening look.

Despite her insistence she could tend the baby on her own, the maids still diapered the infant and changed her clothes and swaddling before they surrendered her to Firal again. Then they turned down the linens on the bed, fluffed the pillows, and gathered up every scrap of wash on the way out. Medreal lingered at the door. "Shall I send breakfast in the morning, or would you prefer to eat with Master Anaide when she arrives?"

Firal's mouth tightened. Another lecture from Anaide was the last thing she wanted to submit herself to, but she couldn't afford to anger the ranking mages any more. Not after she'd named Nondar as Archmage. "Anaide and I will take breakfast in my office. Thank you, Medreal."

The old woman inclined her head and curtsied before she let herself out and latched the door behind her.

A long minute drew by in silence before Vahn released a sigh and scrubbed a hand through his short crop of blond hair. He sat on the edge of the bed to pull off his boots as Firal slipped beneath the blankets. "I don't envy you for having to deal with the mages," he muttered.

"I don't envy you for having to deal with peacekeeping between our men and all of Core."

He gave her a reproachful look, then turned away. She averted her eyes, studying the walls and ceiling as he stripped down to his undershirt and breeches. "I'll keep the peace in the city," he said, sounding determined. "It's my duty to my queen."

Firal snorted and cast him a sidewise glance. "Everything you do is your duty to your queen."

"Not everything." He pulled a pillow and extra blankets

from the bed and folded them into a pallet on the floor. He slid into it, drew the blanket halfway up his chest, and looked up at her with a mirthless smile. "Some is for my queen. And some is for a friend."

She returned his smile, unable to keep sadness from her eyes. "Good night, Vahn."

He nodded and sank into his pillow as she extinguished the lamp. "Good night, my lady."

4

ARENA

PREDAWN HOURS FELT THE SAME AS ANY OTHERS IN THE MUSTY dungeons, though they held fewer visits from guards. The jailers kept some semblance of normal hours and seemed to expect the prisoners to keep the same, for the guards at the front of the prison slept during the long night watch.

Sleep didn't come so easily for those inside the cells. Rune gave up on sleeping long before the armed guardsmen rattled the door of his cell to rouse him.

He had expected them to cart him off to the arena, but he'd also expected to go alone. The long line of inmates in the hallway between cells surprised him. Several looked as if they'd been beaten, though Rune hadn't heard any ruckus to indicate there'd been resistance. He sat up and stared at the armored guard who unlocked his cell door until the man shifted uncomfortably beneath his gaze. They remembered the fight he'd put up before, then; he wasn't sure if that worked in his favor or against it. He rose when beckoned and took his place in the line of inmates, holding out his wrists for the manacles he knew were coming.

The guard checked the manacles twice before he fastened one around Rune's wrist and fastened them to the heavier chain that held the prisoners in line. Rune held out his other wrist. His eyes never left the guard's face as the man closed the second cuff and tucked away the key.

With his cell nearest to the door, he was the last man added to the line. A handful of guards stood before the prisoners and another handful stood behind. One of the guards in the back carried an odd presence and Rune eyed him a moment before he realized the man was a mage, there to maintain whatever barrier it was that kept him from reaching the power that might have set him free. One of the armored men in the rear shouted an order and the whole line shifted forward without delay. The guards moved to flank the line as they marched the prisoners up the curved stairs and into the blazing morning light.

Rune blinked hard and turned his eyes to the ground until his vision adjusted. He'd not been in the city long enough to recognize anything that surrounded him, but he studied everything all the same, mindful not to let his expression change.

The buildings that loomed tall beside the streets seemed strange after the architecture on Elenhiise. Squared stone buildings stretched toward the sky, topped with tall, peaked roofs of dull clay shingles. Some bore balconies supported by sculpted columns, while others sported intricate carvings and reliefs along their roofs or the ground. Most of the buildings stood so close together that a grown man would have had to turn sideways to squeeze between them. Others had no space between them at all. If he escaped from the prison, he'd be forced to flee along the main roads.

The street they walked was curved, its end disappearing around the bend. Small trees separated the road into two avenues, grasses and shrubbery planted in stone-walled boxes around their bases. There would have been flowers too, he assumed, were the weather not so cool. Rune wasn't accustomed to changing seasons, but he figured it to be autumn now. There had been flowers in bloom when he'd first arrived on the mainland, six months before.

A jerk on the chain and an angry shout from the guards jolted him into motion again. He hadn't realized he'd stopped as he studied the plants he couldn't name. Perhaps if he'd known them, he wouldn't have ended up in such a mess to begin with. But he didn't know how to hunt in unfamiliar country and he didn't know how to forage when the flora was strange to him. Necessity had driven him into the city. Necessity, he reminded himself, would get him out.

People stood along the sides of the street, watching the procession of prisoners and guards. The farther they went, the more there were, some shaking their heads, others scowling, a few crying. Most of the prisoners tried to ignore them, marching onward until they reached the end of the curved street and the guards brought them to a pause.

The avenue widened and then ended abruptly at a wall of hedges, rather than the wall of stone one might expect to encircle a palace. Milky-white and gleaming under the sun, the Spiral Palace jutted into the sky like a twisted horn. Balconies protruded from its sides here and there. Three-striped banners of gold, green, and blue hung from their rails.

The prisoners weren't given long to stare before barked orders set them on the move again. Though they wound ever closer to the palace, it wasn't their destination, and Rune knew the arena the moment he laid eyes on it.

Close to the base of the Spiral Palace, teeming crowds milled around the arches and columns, eager to enter. The arena beyond looked something like an amphitheater, a great bowl carved into the earth with a deep pit in the center for combatants to be kept in. From what Rune could see, the tiered stands were already full. Just ahead, one of the other prisoners gave a long, dismayed moan. Uneasy as the sound made him, Rune remained stone-faced.

The guards gave the crowds a wide berth and led the procession to a small building set to the side, its gates watched by more men in armor. A heavy iron portcullis guarded the entrance, which proved to be the mouth of a tunnel that dipped beneath the stands.

The trip through the tunnel was shorter than Rune expected, and it ended with him and the dozen or so prisoners being pushed into a large iron cage. The door was shut and locked behind them with a loud, final clang. One of the men grabbed the guide chain and jerked the line of prisoners to the side of the cage so their manacles could be unfastened. Rune rubbed his wrists when they were freed. In the moment of stillness that followed, he studied this new cell.

Large as the cage was, there was scarcely room for the prisoners to move without bumping into one another. One wall was another portcullis, through which he could see the arena's pit. There was nothing in the dusty bowl, no shelters or obstacles —nothing but empty ground. His eyes narrowed and he moved closer to the portcullis to peer out. Another iron grill on the far side of the arena lifted as he watched. The crowd that ringed the arena erupted in a roar as an armed and armored knight strode into the pit. A handful of weapons lay in the cage behind the man, though not enough for all the prisoners to arm themselves. So it wasn't to be a battle, then. It was meant to be a slaughter.

Rune stepped back and blinked when the cell's iron bars blocked his path. The walls were closer than he remembered. And moving closer. He'd missed the clanking of gears with the noise of the crowd just outside.

A man on the other side of the bars turned a wheel that shrank the cage, forcing the captives toward the portcullis as it began to rise. Some of the prisoners pressed forward and eyed the weapons as their only chance for salvation. The rest moved to the back of the shrinking cell and resisted the push of the iron bars behind them. Rune set his jaw and stayed one step ahead of the cage wall.

Someone ducked under the half-raised grille and raced for the weapons on the other side of the pit. A surge of prisoners followed his lead, more than one stumbling in the dust.

Too many men, not enough weapons. Rune was better off with his magic. He gritted his teeth and reached for the flows of energy that swirled everywhere around him. They skirted his grasp and he spat a curse. He thought he would have power here!

Wheeling to face the guards that still stood on the other side of the shrinking cage, he laid eyes on the mage who held the flows just outside his grasp. Desperate, Rune threw himself against the bars and lashed out with one clawed hand. His claws grazed the fabric of the mage's shirt. The heavy gears clacked as the iron bars fell into place, flush with the arena wall.

Screams and shouts behind him signaled the first death. Rune spun just in time to see the armored knight pull his sword free from the corpse of the prisoner foolish enough to attack him. The knight beckoned the other prisoners, the sound of his gloating a tinny echo that was all but drowned out by the noise of the spectators. A handful of prisoners fell into a group and advanced on the knight. Rune cursed again, his eyes darting around the arena.

The pit was flat and broad, with no entries or exits beyond the two the combatants had entered through. Towering walls encircled the space, topped with pikes and ringed with iron fencing. There was no chance of climbing the walls, not with the bowmen waiting on the other side of the fence. He had to get a weapon. Claws would be useless against armor. He caught a glimpse of the dead man's knife, kicked about in the dust as the knight moved to face the prisoners.

Twisting and twirling, the knight deflected strikes from the men, their dull weapons glancing off his shining armor when he missed. It was a show, not a fight. The knight played with them, luring them to attack with feigned openings, fending them off with little effort before striking them down one by one. The other prisoners rushed in to seek blades lost by the fallen. The knight cleaved one of the men in two before he could rise with his newfound weapon, then paused, struggling to pull his blade free.

Rune darted forward to seize a weapon. He skidded in the dust, snatched something from the ground, and regained his footing before he looked at the weapon in his hand. His eyes widened when he found nothing more than the wooden handle of a broken axe.

The knight descended on him before he could curse again. He braced with both hands as his opponent's sword took a chunk from the scrap of wood in his grasp.

There had to be another weapon somewhere. Rune scanned the bloodstained ground and barely lifted his eyes in time to evade a second swing. He sprang back, slipped in the blood and grime, steadied himself with a hand against the earth. The other prisoners moved back, hugging the walls, none among the living brave enough to lend a hand.

Rune got to his feet, gripping the axe handle and waiting for the next move. He wasn't foolish enough to attack. Instead, he watched the way the knight paced to the side, forcing their movements to morph into a circle.

The knight lunged and Rune swung the handle to deflect the man's blade. Wood cracked with a shower of splinters as he knocked the armored man off balance. Something glinted in the dust and Rune lunged for it. A dagger. He shifted the splintered wood to his left hand and scooped the dagger into his right. The roar of his pulse in his ears made the jeering crowd seem distant.

As the knight regained his balance, he shouted something that sounded like profanity. He staggered forward, clearly flustered. Though the knight's blade was nowhere near him, Rune still moved back. The man swung wildly, angry words muted by his helmet.

Rune crossed his dagger and broken axe and brought them down hard on his opponent's sword. The blow drove the blade into the dirt. The man's hold on the hilt broke. The knight fell forward as he lost his weapon and Rune darted in to slam an elbow into the back of the man's helmet. The knight staggered and Rune followed with a swift kick to the chest. He regretted it the moment he struck the breastplate. A jolt of pain shot up his leg and he stumbled as the knight toppled backwards into the dust.

No time for weakness. Rune gritted his teeth and snatched the lost sword from the ground. His foot throbbed, protesting every step he took to put distance between him and his downed opponent.

The tone of the crowds above them changed, voices sounding concerned, surprised. There was no question who the crowds cheered for, but if their champion being disarmed caused that much distress, how unusual was it?

The knight spat words Rune couldn't understand as he climbed back to his feet. He cut off with a cough. Choking dust made it hard to breathe, every footfall stirring more of it into the air. The man clawed at his helmet and gasped for air when it came off. He wasn't quite what Rune expected—older, with salt-and-pepper hair and a pointed beard. His eyes were wild with anger, the set of his jaw saying more than his language could. He hadn't expected to encounter an opponent that knew how to fight. Still, he drew his off-hand blade and moved into a stance that invited attack, the prisoners cowering against the walls of the arena long forgotten.

Rune advanced on him, twirling the sword in hand. The knight had played with his opponents before striking them down. How well would he respond to being toyed with the same way? Flashy as it was, armor came at cost of mobility, and now that he had the better weapon, Rune had the upper hand. He darted in, his sword just skirting the man's armor, teasing a blow he could have landed.

The knight's shorter blade darted here and stabbed there, each strike short or swatted away. The noise of the spectators grew anxious, their fear reflected in the face of the knight he faced. Rune kept his own expression still, his mouth grim, his eyes cold and hard as the steel in hand. He circled the older man, taunted him with nicks carved into his gleaming armor.

Anxiety became fury, and with bared teeth and an angry bellow, the knight surged forward. He threw himself into a desperate lunge that drove his short sword toward his enemy's chest. Rune swept his sword upward and knocked the smaller weapon from the knight's hand. He twirled his blade as he caught the man's armor with his free hand and spun, hauling the man closer. The tip of his sword found a gap in armor and plunged into flesh.

Every voice above them fell silent.

Rune shoved the blade deeper. His eyes flicked up to skim the stunned faces of the bowmen perched above the pit. None of them held arrows ready. None of them looked able to draw, their bows beside their knees. He let the knight go and the man's body crumpled to the earth. Not even a whisper could be heard overhead as he turned and walked calmly back to the iron gate from whence he'd come. The other prisoners scattered, staring at him in a mixture of fear and disbelief, an expression mirrored by the guards on the other side of the bars. They heaved the cage wall back as Rune came near and dropped the portcullis behind him, separating him from the prisoners still in the arena.

He held out his hands for the manacles that awaited him, face solemn as the guards fastened his manacles to the lead chain. They pulled him from the cage and he walked with his head held high.

Behind him, the arena erupted in screams of panic and rage.

REDORAM BLINKED at the sound of voices and shuffled across his cell to peer out through the barred door. When he saw the guards, he grimaced, pulled back, and leaned against the wall.

Curiosity needled at him like a mosquito's nose, but he pretended not to pay attention. They never came back so quickly, not on arena days.

They sounded angry. Angry and concerned, and they spoke too fast for him to catch much of what was said. Something about combat, something about a knight. Then they came into sight and Redoram frowned. They dragged someone between them. Surely someone hadn't come back alive.

The men threw their captive into the cell across the hallway. The cluster of guards moved in after him. One threw the prisoner's lead chain over a hook in the ceiling and hauled their captive up onto his toes. Redoram saw the first swing of the club, grimaced again, and looked away. He'd seen many a prisoner beaten. He didn't want to see it again.

Closing his eyes didn't help him escape. He didn't have to look, didn't have to see them blacken eyes and bruise ribs, but he couldn't close his ears. The dull thump of clubs striking flesh and the sharp snapping of whips made his stomach churn. This time was different. It wasn't duty that drove the guards; they were angry. It went on far longer than it should have and stilled only when a shout from someone at the front of the prison beckoned the men back out.

Stroking his beard in feigned nonchalance, Redoram turned to look at the guards as if noticing them for the first time. They filed out of the cell and locked it behind them. Dark liquid stained more than two hands.

Only after they were gone did Redoram move forward again and peer across the hallway to see the poor sod who angered them so. When his eyes fell on the bloodied man that struggled to his hands and knees on the prison floor, Redoram's eyebrows lifted.

Beaten and dirty, but still breathing, still alive. The same creature, the same strange whatever-it-was that had left that very cell a scant few hours before.

Redoram glanced toward the front of the prison and listened

for the guards. Quiet. They were gone. "I didn't expect you would come back," he said. Despite their lack of company, he kept his voice low.

Only silence answered.

He frowned and went on. "No one's ever come back from the arena, you know."

The stranger across the hall looked at him, his peculiar eyes gleaming a baleful red in the dim prison. "I... can imagine... they wouldn't want to," he wheezed. He managed to sit up, though he gasped and grimaced as he leaned back against the cool stone wall.

"I take it you killed your opponent, then?" Redoram nodded without verification. The look on the other inmate's face made it clear he wouldn't get it. "Well then, I'm afraid you've embroiled yourself in quite a mess of politics."

The other prisoner's face twisted with displeasure.

Redoram paused and leaned against the bars of his cell's door, trying to get a better look at the stranger on the other side of the prison. Like the guards, he'd thought the prisoner some sort of beast. He chided himself for it now. The fellow was clearly some sort of man, and one with some measure of skill.

"You've had training with a blade?" When he got no reply, Redoram ducked his head in another attempt to get a decent look at his companion's face. It would be just his luck to have them put a man with a decent brain in the opposite cell, only to beat him to death the first time they had a chance. "Rune?" He made a face as the unusual name left his tongue.

"Some," Rune replied. Just that word seemed to take a great deal of effort. A long moment passed before he spoke again, but when he did, he seemed to have caught his breath. "I thought you said I'd have my magic in the arena?"

"I said I believed you would. And I did. The spectators usually like some fireworks." Redoram twisted the end of his beard around one finger. Would that the flows were free, so he might properly evaluate the man's Gift. He could feel the spark of it, but couldn't sense how it connected to the energies around them, not when they were both cut off from the source. "If they didn't loose the wards, they were likely afraid of you."

Again, he received no reply. Redoram sighed and tried to make himself comfortable against the bars. "I know you are weary, but you must listen while we are able to speak. You must understand what you'll be facing now. I didn't expect you to come back alive. The sort of people they send to the arena aren't the sort with the strength to kill a man. The prisoners here are nobody. People in the military are somebody. Somebodies have peculiar ways of avoiding prison, if you see what I'm saying."

"Then how did a somebody like a high-born mage end up in a cell?" Rune asked, never looking his way.

Redoram hesitated. "Garam Kaith is a good man, but like most good men, he listens when he is given orders."

"Kaith?"

"The Captain of the Guard. The man who came to visit yesterday, the one with dark skin. Were it up to him, I'm sure I wouldn't be here. Then again, I may not stay here forever, if we're clever enough." The old man smiled to himself. "Now, shall I teach you about the mess you're in?"

Rune turned his head just enough to look across the narrow walkway between their cells. Even as beaten and bloodied as he was, there was still a spark of spirit in his eyes. With luck, that spirit would be enough to pull them through. "I'm listening."

"Good." Redoram folded his legs beneath him and rested his knobby hands on his knees. "First, you must understand the men who enter the arena to kill prisoners are among the city's elite. The wealthiest and most powerful of knights, soldiers, and nobles venture into the arena to satisfy their want to kill. It poses little risk to them. The prisoners are usually little more than peasants who were arrested for being drunk and disorderly, or farmers who couldn't pay their taxes. Even if you'd had use of your Gift, the man you faced would have had a mage of his own on the sidelines, ready to shield him. The arena is open only once a week, and only for one round. It takes a great deal of money, power, or influence to be the one in armor on arena day. Sometimes all three."

"So I've made some high-ranking enemies." Rune snorted softly and glanced away. "Wouldn't be the first time."

Redoram raised a brow. "Some enemies, yes. There will be those who seek to avenge the fallen for sake of their allied houses. There will also be those who hope you'll continue to best your opponents, narrowing the field of competition among the Royal City's wealthy."

Wiping a trickle of dark blood from his upper lip, Rune sighed. "How many do I have to kill before they'll let me out?"

"Let you out?" The old mage chortled. "They don't let anyone out. I've been here for several years already."

"For expressing an opinion?" Rune asked. Skepticism burned in his tone.

"Indeed." An opinion that still seemed justified, in Redoram's mind. "But we'll go over that, in time. There's much I need to teach you, if you're to return to the arena. You must know who to kill and who to spare, in order to sway factions in your favor. In essence, the kingdom is split into three provinces. There's a province ruled by the Grand College of Mages in Lore, a province ruled by the ancient Aldaanan, and then Roberian, an agricultural province politically trampled between the two. Swaying one side or another is the only chance you'll have at being pulled out of here."

Rune's eyes narrowed. "And what do you stand to gain from helping me?"

The clank of armor at the forefront of the prison signaled the return of a guard. Redoram chuckled and held up a finger. "All in time, boy, all in time."

Some grumbling rose from the opposite cell, accompanied by

the low shuffle of its occupant trying to make himself comfortable. Redoram sat back against the wall, a wry smile twisting the corners of his mouth as the guard moved past. For the first time since his imprisonment, he thought he might live to see the sun again.

INCONVENIENCE

RUNE'S BRUISES WERE NOT HEALED BY THE TIME HE SET FOOT IN THE arena again. His body protested the battle but he didn't let it slow him, muddy his strategies or dampen his reflexes. With the mage still holding the flows just beyond his reach, strategy and reflex were two of the precious few things he had to swing combat in his favor.

The second trip into the arena ended the same as the first, with him striking down his opponent and being beaten for it when they returned him to his cell. Lessons with Redoram filled most nights, covering everything from political alliances in the Royal City to improving his grasp of the local tongue. The weeks fell into a rhythm of monotony. Only the weather seemed to change. Sometimes he was one of a dozen prisoners carted off to the arena, sometimes he was one of two. Sometimes his opponent was skilled, sometimes it was obvious they'd never experienced a real battle. Sometimes he was beaten with clubs after his victory, sometimes with chains.

And then a day arrived where many things changed.

Arena mornings rarely differed from one to the next, the prisoners fed their cold slop and left to sit while the guards awaited orders on which to send into battle. But this morning, his food was hot. Rune eyed it with a measure of suspicion before he cast a glance across the walkway to see if Redoram fared the same. He'd come to like the man, if only because he was a beneficial mentor. The old mage shrugged and gestured to the tray in his hands. His food steamed, as well.

The near-tasteless porridge was almost enjoyable while warm, and Rune savored the heat that seeped into his fingers when he held the bowl. Having spent his life in the tropics, he thought it odd how the comfortable summer days faded into cool mornings and downright chilly nights. It made sense that cooler weather might result in warmer meals, though if that were the case, why did Redoram seem as puzzled as he?

After he ate, the prison stayed quiet for longer than normal. And when the guards arrived with the guide chain to take inmates to the arena, they carried only one set of manacles. That wasn't unfathomable either, given how few prisoners remained. Crime came and went with the change of seasons, Redoram had told him. Harvests this time of year would keep men busy. When winter was deepest, the prison would fill again.

"Best of luck," the old mage whispered as the guards led Rune out of his cell and fastened him to the chain they held between them. Rune stared straight ahead and did not respond.

Commoners filled the city streets nearest the palace, as usual, but they whispered amongst themselves in excited tones as the guards led him toward the arena. He tried to pay it no mind, tried not to look at them. It was a relief when they reached the now-familiar tunnel that led to the pit that had come to rule his life. They locked him in the cage and removed his manacles. He turned to face the arena. Then he saw it.

A sword. Driven into the ground, only a step away from the gate at the front of his cage.

Rune threw a startled glance over his shoulder. The guards shook their heads and backed away. His heart beat quickened. What was different today? What were they doing? What had he done?

He wasn't afforded any chance to think. The gates on either side of the pit began to rattle and lift, the cage behind him shrinking to force him into the arena. Swallowing hard, Rune shifted forward. The portcullis lifted enough for him to pass and he ducked beneath it, tore the sword free of the earth, and moved to meet his opponent.

Steel rang as they met, blades first. The sound drew vibrant cheers from the stands overhead. With swords locked, Rune sized up his opponent. Short, fast, nimble on his feet and wearing armor over leather instead of chainmail. A subtle difference from the usual, but important. It betrayed him as a fighter who relied on agility, not strength.

Rune let his blade skirt off his enemy's as he slid to the side. He stepped right, planning to circle the knight and look for weak points in his gleaming gold-trimmed armor. He didn't get the chance.

Surging forward, the knight put him on the defensive, striking at him with precise and eager blows. Sparks flickered from their connecting blades and Rune was forced to check his footing more than once. A clever fighter, one who'd clearly studied his opponent beforehand. He seemed to know the patterns Rune used in battle, ready to counter every one of them.

An ill-timed thrust offered an opening. Rune darted in and aimed a strike for the knight's throat. But the man was fast and ducked just beneath the blade's edge, bringing the pommel of his sword up into Rune's stomach.

The blow knocked the air from his lungs and almost sent him to his knees. But a fall meant death, and Rune staggered back, gasping for breath as he readied his blade again. The people above them screamed, the noise a dull roar in the back of his mind.

Again the knight came at him, but he was ready this time. He parried and lashed out with a foot. He caught the man just above the waist, knocked him backwards and earned a cry from the knight that made the hair on the back of Rune's neck stand. He moved while his opponent was off balance, striking the knight's wrist, knocking the sword from his hand.

The knight stumbled and Rune rushed in with sword upraised. He fell upon his adversary, and as he bowled the smaller figure to the ground and tore the helmet from his head, the crowd above them went silent.

A boy. Wide-eyed with fright and barely old enough to have a sword of his own, no matter how skilled he seemed. The knight was a boy.

Rune held him fast, catching his breath, taking in the terrified look that filled the youth's blue eyes. His grip on the hilt of his raised sword tightened and his jaw clenched. Spitting a curse, he shoved the boy into the dust and cast his weapon to the ground.

Not a breath stirred above them, the arena silent for only the second time Rune could recall. He shook his head and backed away. A boy. They'd given him a sword to kill a boy.

Disgust wrenched his expression into a scowl as he turned to walk to the portcullis. He ducked beneath it as soon as it had lifted enough for him to retreat to the cage beyond. He'd killed knights. He'd killed soldiers. He'd killed his father.

But he wouldn't kill a child.

"WE HAVE A PROBLEM, CAPTAIN." The woman at the rail never looked away from the pit of the arena.

Garam pursed his lips and considered his response carefully. He'd known what this meeting was about before he'd answered the summons. Now was difficult to keep his tongue in check. He was in no position to speak to members of the council the way he wanted—especially not Lady Bryndis, considering how high she stood in the king's favor. He didn't doubt the councilors already knew how he felt about the situation, but he couldn't just bow his head and let it go. "You had a problem from the moment you decided it was a good idea to let him face an undefeated opponent. Would you prefer if a prisoner killed him?"

"No," Bryndis said slowly, tapping her fingers together as she watched the scene below. The balcony the councilors reserved to watch arena matches was far from optimal seating. The distance made it hard to see the nuances of what happened in the pit, but most councilors refused to mingle with anyone beneath them. "Our problem began when your prisoner didn't die in his first match."

It was hard to refute that. The Royal City had been abuzz ever since that day. It was rage, at first, the nobles scandalized to think a common criminal could best one of their own. But as the weeks carried on and the unusual prisoner won match after match, the tides turned. Garam almost dared say the crowd had developed a liking for the man, if only because the balance of power among the noble houses shifted with each death.

"And what do you expect me to do?" Garam asked. "To have him executed after he spared his opponent in a fair-won fight would incite outrage. People like him, whether you do or not."

"People are charmed by seeing a beaten dog rise, yes." She stroked her chin. "But he is not to rise within the arena again. This match was too close. You're in charge of peace in the city, are you not?"

The captain restrained the urge to grit his teeth. "Yes, ma'am."

"Then keep the peace." Bryndis rose from her chair and patted Garam's armored shoulder as she slid past. "How you do that, of course, is up to you."

Garam refused to watch the councilor leave. Instead, he stared down into the pit. He hated the way they tried to pull his strings and tie his hands with them at the same time, hated that he was in no position to contest it. The king was too busy to personally oversee things in the Royal City. Garam understood that. He just wished the council didn't oversee it in the king's place.

Stifling a sigh, he left the balcony and hurried down the steps. With the milling crowds so dense, it was difficult to locate one of his men. Even when he found one, he had to raise his voice to make himself heard over the din. "Where is he? The prisoner?"

"Still in the cage under the arena, sir," the man replied.

Garam nodded. "Good. Don't return him to his cell when you get him back to the prison. I want to question him first." What he meant to question him about, though, Garam wasn't sure. What was there to discuss? It wasn't as if the man could offer a solution to the problem he'd created. Or the problem created when the council decided to allow a mere child into the arena as a combatant.

"Yes, sir." The guard gave a quick bow before he disappeared among the crowds.

The moment the man was gone, Garam rubbed his forehead with a gloved hand and allowed himself an exasperated sigh. No matter how eager he was to get things over with, it was best if he took his time in heading for the prison. The guards would need a few moments to get the prisoner settled in the audience room set in the forefront of the prison, and he needed more than a few moments to decide what he was supposed to do.

He knew he was right, regardless of the disdain that had colored Bryndis's voice. Execution was out of the question. After the prisoner had defeated so many nobles, the noble houses would see it as an affront for him to be put down, the deaths of their men wasted on politics that went nowhere. Just thinking of their political games made his head hurt and Garam put them out of his mind.

He made his way into the prison and paused when he reached the bottom of the stairs. His eyes drifted over the shelves of armor and supplies. All of a sudden, he knew exactly what to do.

"He's ready for questioning, sir." One of the prison guards

appeared at his side with a tray of hot food. The smell of it made his mouth water.

"Good." Garam took the tray and gestured for the guard to bring a bottle from one of the shelves. "Let's get to it."

The audience room was small and held nothing other than a table and chairs. Their peculiar guest sat with his elbows propped against the table's edge. Garam crossed the room without hesitation, deposited the food on the table, and took the bottle of mead from the guard's hand. "Send someone for Lord Survas. Tell him his translation services are required."

"I do not need your Lord Survas," the prisoner said, turning eerily snakelike violet eyes toward the captain. "I do not like him."

Garam raised a brow. A wave of his hand sent the guard out of the room. The door clicked closed behind him. "You speak our language," he remarked as he pulled out a chair to sit across from the creature.

"I listen. I learn." His accent was as strange as his appearance, but the words were easy to understand. It was a step in the right direction, at least.

"Not a lot to listen to in the prison." Garam leaned against the table. "What was it you said your name was?"

"Rune," the prisoner replied, never moving, never blinking.

The captain stared at him for a long time. There were a lot of questions he wanted to ask, now that Survas wasn't in the mix. Things he wouldn't trust the nobleman to translate properly. But those questions weren't why they were there. Garam pushed the tray of food farther across the table and nodded toward it. "Good steak, decent mead. I'm sure you're hungry."

Rune shrugged. "I am not interested in... how is it said? Bribe?"

"Bribery," Garam corrected with a chuckle. "Your grasp of the language is impressive, considering you didn't seem to understand anything when you were arrested. How long have you been studying?" He reached for the bottle of mead, uncorked it, and took a sniff. Perhaps he'd lied. It didn't smell decent at all.

"I leave the ship, I listen. A man will understand after time." A vague answer, but the blank look on Rune's face made it clear he'd get no other.

Garam sighed and put down the bottle. "Do you know why you're here?"

"In prison?" Rune lifted a brow. "Because to eat, a man does what he must. In this room? Because I do not kill children." He spat the last word with contempt and venom, a hint of disgust creeping into his expression.

"And it's good for you that you don't. You've made quite a spectacle of yourself in the arena. There are more than a few nobles who would like to be rid of you now that you've been undefeated for months. They were trying to trap you. The boy you fought in the arena was Vicamros II, Crown Prince of the Royal City." Garam leaned back in his chair. "If you'd killed him, you would have been executed on the spot."

The words hung heavy in the air. The man across the table weighed them carefully. "And I am not to be executed?"

Garam shook his head. "Quite the opposite. Because you spared the prince's life, people are likely convinced you knew who he was. Now they're afraid of what ties you might have in the city. No one wants to face you in the arena again, but no one wants you killed without justification, either." He paused. "That makes you my responsibility."

Rune snorted a laugh and shook his head as he reached for the fork on the tray. He speared the steak with it and gestured toward the table. "A man is to eat without a knife?"

Now it was the captain's turn to raise an eyebrow. "What makes you think I'd trust you with one?"

The prisoner lifted a hand and wriggled scaly, clawed fingers before his face. "Because I do not need weapons to fight." He released the fork and lounged in his chair, folding his hands together against his stomach and looking amused. "You look at me strangely because I am part green and you are the color of earth. But we are both men. I know why I am here. Now, you tell me why you are here."

Garam stared back for a moment before he snorted a laugh. The last time they'd conversed, through translation, Lord Survas said something about the strange man speaking in an uncommon way. He was beginning to see why. "I'd like you to consider joining the Royal City guard."

Rune blinked and tilted his head. "Why?"

"Because you can fight." Garam shrugged. "It's fairly obvious you have military experience. If you can swing a sword and listen to orders, I have a place for you in the barracks. It gets you out of the prison and out of the way of the nobles. Everybody's happy."

"And if I say no?"

The question caught the captain off guard. "Then you sit in prison until you die, or you fight in the arena until you die. At least as one of my men, you'd have freedom."

That brought a scoff. "Not freedom. Taking orders is not freedom." Rune paused, then nodded. "But I consider your offer."

"That's it?" Garam's brow furrowed. "You don't have a lot of room for consideration, my friend."

"And you do not have room to assume I am your friend." Rune stood and offered a surprisingly respectful bow. "Return me to my cell."

The captain stared at him in disbelief. But the prisoner did nothing, just stood, waiting for him to act. Garam swallowed and rose from his chair. Survas was definitely right; the man was no common thief. The way he spoke and carried himself, even knowing his position as a prisoner, made it clear he thought himself Garam's equal.

Garam squared his shoulders and adjusted the gleaming gilded armor that marked him Captain of the Guard. He led the way to the door. The handful of guards waiting on the other side fell in to surround their prisoner as he was escorted back to his cell. "I expect an answer in the morning."

"And I expect a knife with my meal." Rune smirked and slipped into the cell. He settled cross-legged on the floor.

Garam's eyes narrowed but he said nothing more. He left the prison with only his fists clenched at his sides to betray his frustration.

He tried to put the whole situation out of his mind and think of something else as he made his way across the city to seek refuge in his quarters. He had enough to worry about without the nobles and their politics. With all the unrest in the city, it was easy to ignore the games they played. Nobles thought themselves more important than they were. They didn't see the way the Royal City bubbled with uneasiness, the way more and more commoners came in from the countryside as winter approached.

The peasantry feared it would be too difficult to reach the Royal City after the first snows. They hadn't said as much, not precisely, but the stories they carried were much the same. Before it's too late, they all said. Why they wanted to reach the shelter of the city walls was never said.

His thoughts scattered as he reached his door. The barracks were largely empty this early in the day, and he was grateful there were no messages in the box beneath the plaque that declared his name in bold letters.

Sighing and rubbing his forehead, Garam slipped inside and checked the lock behind him before he settled at his desk. While the nobles worked at forming rifts between themselves within the city, the provinces did much the same with each other. He still didn't understand how the king couldn't see the problem. The mages from the college were worse than the nobles, walking around with their heads tilted so far back in effort to peer down their noses that he wondered how they walked at all. The Aldaanan hadn't set foot in the Royal City in months, driven away by the spats he'd had to quell far too often. And the province of Roberian might as well not be a part of the Triad, given the lack of communication from the guard stations there.

There were times he wished the king had seen fit to give him a better title. Captain of the Royal City Guard seemed fine enough, but it barely brushed the surface of what was expected of him. Coordinating the guard posts across all three provinces was his duty, as was communication with and relations between the provinces' guard and the rest of the army. Then again, perhaps he'd been given the title he held simply because no one knew what else to call him. Either way, he was underpaid for the amount of work they piled on his desk and his shoulders.

Garam drummed his fingers against the edge of his desk and tried to ignore some of those piles of work now.

Things would have been easier if the provinces were united. Garam would never admit it, not out loud, but as unpopular as the suggestion had been among the council members, he still thought it best. But that suggestion had ended with Councilor Parthanus being stuffed in a cell to rot, and Garam would not risk sharing his opinion.

Ah, Redoram. The captain leaned back in his chair and rubbed his neatly trimmed beard. He should have remembered the man sooner. The councilor was clever, crafty, and educated by the Grand College. A good man, despite those questionable ties. Garam had forgotten Redoram was kept in the cell across the hallway from their new arena champion. No wonder the creature had picked up their language.

He grimaced. Man, not creature. He still had to stop and remind himself. Rune's words still lingered in his mind. Him part green and Garam the color of the earth, but both of them men.

And one of them a man who wouldn't eat without a knife.

Garam swore as he planted his elbows on his desk and buried his face in his hands. No commoner would speak the way that prisoner did. For that matter, a commoner would have eaten with his hands. Rune had picked up a fork and demanded a knife to go with it.

"Lifetree's mercy," he breathed. "What have I gotten myself into?"

He scrubbed his face with both hands, suddenly weary. He started to rise, but paused when he caught the title of a book on his desk out of the corner of his eye. Weeks ago, he'd asked for a number of volumes to be pulled from the library and delivered to him. His fingers slid down the spine as he lifted it, wondering which of the nobles had given themselves the pleasure of delivering the titles to his private quarters.

"A History of Kings," he read aloud as he settled back in his chair and opened the book. His thoughts turned to the kingsword still wrapped and hidden beneath his bed, and the very strange prisoner he'd taken it from.

"You're looking particularly not-beaten tonight."

Rune startled awake and blinked a few times before he realized it was Redoram's voice that woke him. He stretched and rubbed his luminescent eyes before he turned toward the old man's cell. The lamp in the hallway had gone out in the night. He could just make out the mage's features. Rune rolled off the suspended plank that served as his bed and moved to the door of his cell, the quiet padding of his footsteps accented by the click of his claws against the cold stone floor. "I'm as surprised as you are." He cast a glance toward the front of the prison and listened for any sign the guard might be awake. He heard nothing.

"Care to tell me what happened?"

Rune shrugged as he lowered himself to sit on the floor. He leaned against the bars and rubbed his eyes again. He hadn't meant to fall asleep; he'd grown used to their midnight conversations. Then again, he was tired from his fight and less bruised than usual. The plank was almost comfortable. "I spoke with Captain Kaith after the match. I guess he decided I didn't need a good beating tonight."

Redoram snorted. "Don't skirt the truth with me, boy. I can't help you if you do."

Rune hesitated for a time before he convinced the words to leave his tongue. "I fought a boy today. Not a knight. The captain said the boy's name was Vicamros II."

"Dear Lifetree!" the mage gasped, clutching at the bars. "Tell me you didn't!"

"I don't kill children," Rune said, scowling. "Scared him to death, but I let him go. Still, from the way he looked at me, I wouldn't be surprised if he wet his trousers in terror."

Redoram heaved a sigh of relief and rubbed his brow. "Thank heavens. I can't imagine the sort of chaos that would take the city if the heir was killed in the arena." He shook his head and his shoulders slumped. "And what did the captain have to say about that?"

Rune shrugged again. "He asked me to join the guard."

"Well now." The old mage tugged his beard, looking amused. "What did you tell him?"

"Nothing, yet. He's coming back in the morning to hear my answer." Not that he'd given the answer much thought. He didn't want to stay in prison, that was for certain. But he didn't want to serve beneath anyone, either. It seemed people were always trying to use him to their advantage. He was tired of it.

"You'd best think of your answer soon, then, given that it's not long until sunrise now." Redoram turned away as a grim smile wreathed itself on his face. "I'm glad you've found your way out and I'm glad I was able to assist. Lifetree knows I've been useless as a caged canary in here."

Rune bowed his head. "Thank you. Your help won't be forgotten."

The old man waved a hand and let silence fall.

It felt like hours before a guard appeared in the hall to re-light the lamp in the hall. It seemed like longer still before the clatter of armor heralded the arrival of Captain Kaith and a pair of his men.

Garam knocked a tray against the bars of Rune's cell. "Breakfast."

Rune pushed himself up from the plank again. He hadn't slept any more, but he felt rested enough. The food smelled good; he walked to the door of his cell to look at it. And the cutlery. "You brought me a knife," he laughed, flashing the captain a grin. "Good man."

"Do you have an answer for me?" Garam stepped back to let the guards unlock the door. Once it swung open, he pushed the tray into Rune's clawed hands.

"I will join you," Rune said. He speared a grape with the tip of the knife and popped it into his mouth. "On the condition my mentor comes with me."

Garam's expression tightened and he turned to glare into Redoram's cell. "I knew you were involved, you wretched old man!"

Redoram didn't stir from the back of his cell. "I never did pass up the opportunity to teach a man to survive in this city."

Garam rolled his eyes and turned away from the mage. "You're asking for something larger than you realize."

Rune tilted his knife in hand, studying its shape. "And my speech in your language is not best. Is there another who knows my mother tongue?"

"Lord Survas," the captain replied, flinching even as he said the name.

Redoram chuckled. "Good to see we all feel the same way about him."

Garam shot him a warning look. "Listen," he started. His eyes slid back to Rune. "I can't promise that will happen. This man has got a lot of enemies, and they had him put here for treason. If he wasn't a mage, he probably would have been executed, but we can't afford to offend the Grand College. I'll do what I can. But I make no promises."

Rune nodded and set the tray of food aside, putting the meal out of his mind. "You are a good man. So be it, then. I am yours to command." He bent at the shoulders in the slightest bow of respect, though his eyes never left the captain and his men. They stepped back and he moved forward, straightening his back and holding his head high as he strode out of the cell and into the hallway.

"How does it feel to be free?" Garam asked.

"I walk without chains, Captain." Rune shook his head with a wry smile. He hooked his clawed thumbs in the pockets of his tattered trousers and made his way to the front of the prison alongside the other guards. "That does not make me free."

But it was, at least, one step closer to it.

6

DISCORD AND DEBATE

Vahn sidestepped to avoid the wad of spittle a merchant sent into the street. He shot the man a glare that went unnoticed, then righted himself and adjusted his cape before continuing on his way.

He'd never seen the streets of Ilmenhith so crowded. Peasants and farmers had come in from the countryside to be away from the Underlings. Come to think of it, he hadn't seen a single Underling in the city. He didn't doubt when Davan said the merchants wouldn't deal with them, but if they'd run them out of the city altogether, that was another issue. Yet another thing to add to the list, he supposed.

Though he tried to stop thinking of his ever-growing collection of problems, his eyes drifted over the wilted and damaged produce for sale in a merchant's bins and concern crept to the surface again. How had Kifel ever managed to run the city on his own? Vahn couldn't fathom. Even splitting tasks between Firal and himself, they continued to fall behind.

The first of the new fishing ships had joined the fleets. Citizens had been offered the chance to petition for ownership of the vessels, a groundbreaking decision that turned the tides for a number of struggling families. Vahn had ventured into the city in hopes of finding people in better spirits, but with the Underlings camped right outside the city's limits, moods seemed more dismal than ever. There had to be a better solution, one that didn't involve waiting months for food to grow. The weather had righted itself after the former Archmage's exile, but Davan's travels across the island brought troubling reports of failing farms. The long and heavy rains had washed away good soil and left bare rock where there used to be fields.

Still, Vahn wasn't sure he wanted to rely on the Underlings for information. Regardless of what Firal said, regardless of the convoluted history those people had with Ran, he couldn't make himself trust them. It hadn't quite been a year since they'd marched against Ilmenhith—at the behest of a different leader, perhaps, but they'd done it. Davan claimed they were loyal to Firal now. Vahn didn't trust him, either.

Trust aside, though, he knew the Underlings had value to offer. Many of them were skilled with agriculture, having grown enough food within the limitations of the Kirban Ruins to survive for centuries. They had other skills, too; methods of mining and forging the smiths in Ilmenhith had never learned. He didn't doubt they could be useful, but until they *made* themselves useful, they were still a burden.

His very thoughts reached his ears as words and Vahn stopped short, startled to hear the sentiment from the mouth of a merchant. A handful of grumbles at Vahn's back made him cast an apologetic glance over his shoulder to his guards. He never went anywhere without an entourage anymore. Half a dozen men walked at his heels, all of them armed to the teeth. He couldn't be too careful. He wasn't Kifel.

A second merchant harrumphed and shook his head. "The queen says they're here to ally with us. I'll believe it when I see it."

The first barked a laugh and spat at the ground. "There's to the queen!"

Vahn bristled and his hand settled on the hilt of his sword before he caught himself. "You'd be wise to mind the way you speak." Though his fingers twitched, he didn't pull his weapon from its sheath. The men that fell in formation behind him stood ready to draw steel. Unnecessary show of force would only serve to damage what reputation he had.

Both merchants startled. They bowed and scraped and called apologies over the top of one another.

Forcing himself to relax, Vahn released his sword and gave the two of them a scowl. "Her Majesty wouldn't allow them near the city if she wasn't certain of their allegiance. She has met with their leader and they carry her colors with pride. Is that not enough?"

"Yes, King-regent," one replied in a hurry. He backed away as he bowed. "Of course, King-regent."

The title made his hackles rise, but Vahn nodded and turned away. "Be mindful of your tongues, lest they spill such treasonous speech in the street again."

His half-dozen men fell in step behind him as he moved on. The clank of their armor was familiar and soothing, and the noise helped draw his mind back into focus. He couldn't let such things distract him. He'd made his patrol; there was little else he could do in the city. Vahn turned his company back toward the palace and resisted the want to hold on to his sword. He'd seen enough troubles for the day and was desperate for a moment to clear his head, perhaps mull his thoughts over during a hot bath.

He'd only just stepped into the palace courtyard when he saw a familiar crest on a familiar cape disappear past the palace doors, and his stomach dropped to his knees.

The worst troubles, it seemed, were just ahead.

***

FIRAL ROLLED the single lotus seed between her fingers and held it up against the light. She and Vahn hadn't exchanged seeds after their wedding. They hadn't exchanged anything. Then again, she couldn't blame him. No doubt it would have been strange, swapping symbolism with a woman who carried another man's child in her womb.

Her hand drifted over her stomach absently. So much had changed in the course of a year; her body bore permanent marks to show at least part of her struggles. Perhaps it was best for things to be the way they were with Vahn. She couldn't imagine a man wanting her now, not with her sagging skin and the purple stripes that decorated her abdomen and hips. Medreal assured her they would turn silver as they aged. As if silver was any better.

Unsettled, Firal put the lone seed away in its pouch and moved to the window to gaze at the gardens below her office. She was still at a loss. She didn't know what she was meant to do, how she was supposed to fix her problems. The Underling camp had moved closer to the city under Vahn's direction. Banners proudly displaying the kingdom's colors—her colors— flew above the encampment. It was strange to look across the whole city and realize her best supporters were just beyond its edge. Stranger still to think of them as her people, and herself as their queen. She shuddered at the thought, rubbing her arms and turning away from the window just as the door to her office opened.

"My lady, a visitor to see you." Medreal nudged the door closed with a hip and carried a fresh tea tray to Firal's desk.

"See them in." Firal forced a smile. The words no more than left her tongue before the door opened again and a tall man in red-and-gilt finery let himself inside. Her eyebrows lifted, but she managed to keep her expression pleasant.

He was a fine-looking older gentleman, fair of hair and paler than most islanders. His squared jaw and blunted ear-tips marked his diluted bloodline, though from his state of dress he didn't seem to suffer socially for his lack of mage blood. "My lady." He swept back his cape to bend in a graceful bow with his fingers pressed over his heart. There was a familiarity about him, one she couldn't quite place.

"Do I know you?" she asked as she made her way to her desk. It certainly seemed she ought. He hadn't addressed her as a queen.

"I was at your wedding," he replied, a hint of humor in his voice. "Along with a hundred thousand others, I suppose. I apologize. I should have come to visit sooner, but it was—"

"Firal!" Vahn burst in the door, a look of wide-eyed panic on his face. "My father is—" He stopped short, words escaping when he saw the occupants of the room before him.

"—awkward for me," the older man finished, giving Vahn an amused look.

"Is he, now?" Firal struggled to keep from laughing, in spite of the miserable look on Vahn's face. She schooled her expression to a cheerful neutrality and looked back to their guest. "Forgive me. I'm afraid I've not been afforded the chance to know you."

"Of course." He brushed his cape over his shoulders and moved forward when Firal gestured for him to seat himself. "Ennil Tanrys, my lady. I suppose I'm the closest thing to a father you've got."

She pursed her lips, the only outward sign of the way his words made her bristle.

"Don't make that face at me. I knew Kifelethelas much better than you did." Ennil leaned forward to take the first teacup Medreal filled. She offered honey and cream, but he waved her away. "He was a close friend of mine, yet he never so much as mentioned you until the day he brought you back to the palace. But I don't doubt you're his. I know how the mages are. How his wife was. She'd cut off her nose to spite her face. Hid his blood child away from him and gave him something else to raise." He arched a brow as a mirthless smile twisted his mouth. "But here you are."

Firal struggled to keep her wits as every inch of her prickled with displeasure. This man made her skin crawl. How could he be Vahn's father? The two were nothing alike. "I'm the only choice the mages had."

"Oh, of course." Ennil leaned back in his chair and scratched the hint of stubble on his chin. "Now that our uncrowned prince is missing, hmm? Not that that's of any concern to you. I'm sure one of you even has an idea how he got out of that prison cell."

Vahn shifted on his feet and turned his face away. Firal watched him from the corner of her eye. They'd never spoken of the matter. What reason did he have to be uncomfortable? "It seems the royal family's secrets are not so secret as I thought." She couldn't help the ice that crept into her tone.

As if sensing she needed something to occupy her hands, Medreal pressed a warm cup into her grasp. Firal murmured a thank-you as she wrapped her fingers around it.

Ennil shrugged. "Lomithrandel's unusual condition was how the king and I came to be friends in the first place. My son always has had a particular skill for becoming entangled with the royal family." He gave Vahn a sidewise look. "I don't believe for a second that the boy killed his father on purpose. He was headstrong and foolish, but he loved his father dearly. Kifel's downfall was his own fault. He was too soft, too lenient with those he cared for. Let them walk all over him. Of course, that's how you were taken away from him to begin with, hmm?"

Firal gritted her teeth and clutched her cup so firmly, her knuckles turned white. "Why are you here, Lord Tanrys?"

"To offer my help." A fleeting hint of sorrow crossed his face and was replaced with a steely frown.

Help? What help could he possibly offer her? Her eyes darted to Vahn, his refusal to look at her stirring her ire. "I beg your pardon?"

Ennil set his cup on the edge of her desk. "To help you get a handle on the kingdom, put your head on straight. If you're what the mages think ought to rule us, you'd better be able to do it properly. Especially since House Tanrys is along for the ride. Vahnil is my only child. My only son. The livelihood of my family depends on him."

Vahn cringed and walked to the windows.

"Then perhaps you should have had more children," Firal replied frostily.

Ennil leaned forward and gave her a stare so hard it made the hair on the back of her neck rise. "And I would have, if the choice were mine. A sword took that decision from me when it took my cullions."

A flush rose into her cheeks and she looked away.

The man went on, unruffled. "Now all my expectations fall on him. I blame myself, really. I taught him to aim high. Perhaps I should have taught him to know his limits, instead. Don't mistake me, girl, it's not because of you that I've never come to visit before."

Firal's brow furrowed. "You have no reason to be angry at Vahn. He is king-regent and married to the queen. He's done House Tanrys an incredible favor."

"The only favor he's done House Tanrys is being responsible enough to marry you after you were with child."

After she was with child? Her eyes settled on Vahn's back as anger flared in her chest.

Ennil scowled and shook his head. "Now I'm here to fix this mess. I served your father as Captain of the Guard for many years before I took my retirement. I'll need a higher rank than that if I'm to sort out this disaster the mages handed to a pair of children."

"I am not a child," Firal snapped. "I'm a grown woman and fully capable of sorting this out on my own."

"Are you?" Ennil sneered as he pushed himself from his chair. "Well then. My apologies, my queen, but it doesn't look that way. When next you call your council together, I expect a summons to sit on it. Is that understood?"

Her eyes widened and her shoulders bunched. The heat of anger spread from her chest to her limbs.

"Understood," Vahn said from the window. "We will call for you. Thank you, Father."

Pleased, Ennil nodded and gave a bow almost deep enough to look sincere. "Very well. Have a fine day, my lady. May the Lifetree's leaves fall as blessings upon you."

Firal responded with the slightest incline of her head and stood to see him out. He didn't wait for her, brushing out of her office with his cape swirling behind him. He left the door wide open and Medreal grumbled as she went to close it. "I don't like that man." Her words were just loud enough for Firal to hear. "Never have, can't imagine I ever will."

The moment the door latched, Firal spun on her heel to hurl her teacup at Vahn's head. He barely dodged. The cup shattered against the wall. "*After* I was with child!" she cried, squeezing her hands to fists until they trembled at her sides. "You told him! How could you? After everything we've been through—"

"It's not what you think!" Vahn flinched as she snatched a second teacup from the tray.

"I'll thank you to stop breaking my porcelain," the stewardess said as she plucked the cup from Firal's hand. She took the tea tray from the desk and cradled it close. "You're more like your father than you realize, Majesty. And I don't mean that in a good way." She sniffed and marched out of the office before more of the tea set could be ruined.

Firal gritted her teeth and folded her arms across her chest. "So you want your family to think me a harlot? The entire purpose of you and I being together was to prevent that, and you went and—"

"Firal," Vahn interrupted, reprimanding. He moved forward, hands outstretched in gesture for her to settle. "They don't think ill of you. No one thinks ill of you. That's exactly why I told my father what I did."

"That I was pregnant out of wedlock?" she demanded.

"That it was my fault!"

She blinked, taken aback. It took a moment for her to shift the surprise on her face back into a scowl.

Vahn rubbed his forehead and squeezed his eyes shut. "You forget you're not the only one who had a relationship before this happened. One minute I was courting Kytenia, even thinking of asking to marry her, the next I'm being crowned as... as..." he faltered and waved a hand in irritation. "Whatever I'm supposed to be! Don't you think it was hard for me, too?"

Firal looked away. She hadn't forgotten his ties to her dearest friend, nor the way Kytenia had been the one to offer Vahn as a solution to her problems.

"I had to explain that to my family. They knew her, and they knew what she meant to me. So when my father asked why I was abandoning that to marry you instead, I..." He paused and wet his lips with his tongue. "I told him I'd taken advantage of you. That I'd sullied your honor and had to fix it. I told him Lumia was mine."

She bit her lower lip and watched him from the corner of her eye. "And he believed you?"

Vahn hesitated. "Yes, because I'd made a bit of a reputation for myself. Not true, mind you, of course not true. But a reputation, nonetheless." His expression softened as he moved closer and rested his hands on her shoulders. "If anyone thinks ill of the situation, it's because of me. Not because of you."

"If anyone thinks ill of the situation, they still think ill of me." She couldn't keep the edge from her voice. "No matter what people believe, someone's name is going to be dragged through the mud. You'll have to forgive me if I don't want to be remembered as the queen who was taken advantage of."

He sucked in a breath and held it for a long moment. She could tell he struggled to keep hold of his temper. It had never seemed difficult for him before; he was so much calmer in demeanor than she. It always took every bit of restraint for her to hold her anger in check. His silence made it boil harder within her now, and she clamped her mouth shut for fear she might shriek like a whistling teakettle.

"I'm doing the best I can," he said at last. "The only people who've heard that story are my mother and father, and they'll take it to their graves before they let it cast a shadow over the family name. Go ahead and think them untrustworthy if that's what you want, but you'd be well served to remember your own father trusted them with Ran's secrets. Those are much more dangerous than ours."

Firal snorted at that. More dangerous than their lie, perhaps. The truth was another story. She couldn't think of a worse secret to be keeping, not with how the city seemed wound tight and ready to lash against the Underling army camped right outside its border. Her child was the child of the man who'd led that army against Ilmenhith. The man who killed their king. She hadn't really come to terms with it, herself, but her personal problems were the least of what she had to be concerned about now. A queen had to be selfless, put her people before herself. There would be time in the future to deal with the rest. To bury the feelings she still had for Daemon. For Ran. *Rune,* she reminded herself. The name that combined his two lives into one. *The name I gave him when we started our life together.*

"Firal?" Vahn's voice jarred her back to herself. He stood with one hand raised as if he meant to touch her, but didn't know if he should. The concerned way he looked at her made her aware of the tears that traced lines down her cheeks.

She wiped them away with the side of her thumb. "What did your father mean?"

His brow furrowed. "About what?"

"When he spoke of Ran escaping." She'd been occupied at the time, dealing with the Archmage and Relythes, king of the island's other half. The relief of hearing Rune had escaped during their meeting had weakened her knees and brought tears to her eyes, emotions she'd been fortunate were mistaken for grief at her father's murderer escaping execution for his crime. But how he'd made it out, she still didn't know.

Vahn wavered.

Her chest tightened. "You know how he made it out of the dungeon, don't you?"

He bowed his head and swallowed before he managed a nod.

Tears pricked her eyes again. "Were you involved, Vahn?"

"You aren't the only one who cared about him." His voice was hoarse with emotion. "He was my best friend, Firal. I couldn't see him die."

"Is he alive? Do you know where he is?" Desperation colored her words. She struggled to keep from crying again.

"I don't know," he said, honest and apologetic, worry creasing his brow. "I hope so, but if he is, I don't think he's on Elenhiise any longer. The island is so small. Now that everyone knows about the city under the ruins, there's nowhere for him to hide."

Despite all her sensibilities, her heart sank. There was sense in what Vahn said, especially with the border between the two halves of the island closed to travelers. She forced herself to nod as she gathered her skirts and started toward the door.

Vahn moved after her. "Where are you going?"

"To see to my daughter. Do me a favor? If you venture into the city again, carry a message to the Underling camp and tell Davan I wish to meet with him." She drew a breath and collected herself, smoothing her hair and drying her eyes before she opened the door and stepped into the hallway. She didn't hear any affirmation from Vahn, but since he didn't follow her, she knew he wouldn't protest.

THE MEETING WAS ALREADY in progress when Envesi and the others arrived in the lecture hall. Melora and Alira walked before her. Envesi wished they would move faster. Most of the hall was already occupied, forcing the three of them to sit at the back, though the shape of the vast room and the amplification magic helped carry the sound of the councilors' voices to the farthest reaches of the hall.

"There's nothing to fear from Roberian. They're our primary source of food. Commerce is better than ever, especially since we've cut the Royal City and their taxes and tariffs from the middle. Aldaan is our only concern."

Envesi couldn't decide if the Master mage speaking sounded defensive or annoyed. His back was turned to the audience, but she couldn't have seen his face from that distance anyway.

The council met at a round table where a podium might have stood for a normal lecture. Had she known the lecture hall would be so crowded, she would have insisted they arrive early. But this was the first meeting of any importance that had been called together since they began their penance, and none of them anticipated the mages of the Grand College would be so interested in politics. Envesi squinted at the table, struggling to make out the faces of the councilors she'd tried to memorize. She thought the first fellow was Orneld, but she wasn't certain.

"We would be fools to move against Aldaan! The last time the Aldaanan pushed against us was when magic was bound, several thousand years ago. The last thing we want is to rile them again." Master Arrick was supposed to be seated beside Headmaster Tolmarni, but it looked as if he were trying to climb onto the table.

"Enough." The headmaster motioned for them to settle and the seventeen mages around him quieted, though few looked happy. "We're all aware of what the Aldaanan think of our magic. We don't need to go over that again. It's not a question of what they think, it's a question of how we work around them."

"What are they talking about?" Alira asked in a whisper. Envesi gave her a sidewise glance.

"I'm not certain," Melora said, frowning until her weathered face looked pinched. "This is the first I've heard any mages discuss matters of the region."

"There is no working around the Aldaanan." The Master who had been speaking when they first entered lifted his voice again. He was irritated; Envesi was sure of his identity now. She'd never met Orneld, but the college mages often muttered about his miserable disposition. "Either Lore and Roberian break away from the Triad, or the Grand College is done for. It's reached a point where our mages cannot even walk the streets of the Royal City! The whole place is warded against magic. Even our healers have been shut out. As long as they continue to bend to the desires of the Aldaanan and try to rob us of our power, we will continue to fail."

"And what makes you think Roberian would want to break away from the Triad alliance?" A woman spoke, this time. Envesi was surprised to see Minet sitting at the council table. The girl had been a novice in gray when Envesi left. "They're the weakest country out of the three of us. Only the laws of the Triad put us on equal footing. We'd be battling Aldaan and trying to consume Roberian at the same time."

"There's no need to push against Roberian," the headmaster interjected. "We stand against Aldaan, no one else. If the Aldaanan forfeit or are defeated, all that happens is Lore becomes bigger or their territory is taken by a different power."

"I still see no reason to go against them at all," another mage grumbled. His manner of speech so reminded Envesi of Nondar that it made her scowl. "The Grand College has enough power outside the Triad. If the Aldaanan continue to be a threat to our success, we're best served to move to wherever they are not. Our sway has lessened, but there are still places we are welcome and needed. Even in the reaches of the southern continent."

"And how long until the opposition follows us there, as

well?" Minet rose from her chair. "We cannot continue to flee from mages with the power to strip us of our Gifts. Without magic, we are nothing."

The headmaster nodded at that. "Minet is correct. We cannot run. We face the Aldaanan here and now. The Royal City has resisted every compromise we've offered, so now we are forced to oppose the Royal City, as well. And you know what that means."

Arrick fell back to his chair and clasped his hands together against the edge of the table. "War."

Envesi straightened. Melora shifted at her side.

"War?" Alira breathed. Her wide eyes made her look ever more like a child and less like the Master mage she used to be.

"So it is," Envesi murmured with a slight smile. "Mages at war."

"And mages at war means no one in the college to supervise what magelings are studying or experimenting on." Melora smiled in return.

Envesi leaned forward until her elbows rested on her knees. Her white hair spilled over her shoulders. "That certainly makes things interesting, doesn't it?" She rubbed her chin, turning the facets of the issue over in mind. If the college opposed the Aldaanan, they would have to face mages wielding the very thing she sought for herself. Free magic. Something precious, something wild, something so threatening that the Grand College now sought to stamp it out in their enemies.

The college Masters couldn't oppose such a power, not as they were. The bonds of affinity imposed on them in ages past made sure of that. But if Envesi could loosen those bindings, give even a few of them the ability to touch the power of everything around them, unfettered by affinity or element... She shivered at the idea.

"And who in the Grand College would turn against such a thing in wartime?" she mused aloud.

"What was that?" Melora eyed her with a frown.

Envesi didn't offer any explanation, too lost in her own thoughts. She pushed herself up and smoothed her skirts and hair. "Excuse me, my sisters." She slipped past the two of them and made her way to the stairs that led outside, then hurried off to find the headmaster's office.

It was a golden opportunity, after all, and she'd speak to him of the matter if it meant waiting by his door all night.

7

FAILING FUTURES

A SOFT BREEZE STIRRED THE PAPERS ON NONDAR'S DESK AND fluttered the leaves of the open book before him. He grunted as he paged back to his place, displeased to see the wet ink smudged on the opposite page. He leaned back in his chair, dropped his quill to the desktop, and rubbed his aching wrist with the gnarled fingers of his left hand.

His mood was sour despite the pleasant weather, the warm sunbeams and soft breezes carrying sweet scents from the garden doing nothing to improve his disposition. Pleasant weather didn't help him accomplish his work, nor did it help solve the problems piling up on his desk. He could have delegated some of it, but there were few mages in the temple he trusted to help with his work. Anaide and Edagan—his fellow Masters and the leaders of the two still-functioning houses of affinity—were the obvious choices. But he'd had enough of their pushing and prodding, wheedling and nagging. They resented the fact he'd been given the title of Archmage instead of one of them. Neither said it, but with the way they still tried to assert themselves over him, they didn't have to.

He couldn't fault the women for how they felt. As strong as he was in his Gift, they were several centuries older than he, with strength and experience to show it. And while they were older, Nondar showed his age in ways the two women did not—one of many shortcomings he had his half-mage heritage to thank for. His frailty did him no favors.

But he held no resentment for his Giftless blood and never had. His healing affinity tied him to life forces and gave him longevity to rival any Giftless Eldani. Their innate magic slowed their growth and let them live three centuries, perhaps four if they were fortunate, while his full-blooded peers saw their lives stretched to at least six. Almost to his fourth century of life, Nondar held nothing but pride for what he'd accomplished in his many years.

His eyes drifted toward the windows as he flexed his fingers. For as much as his joints pained him in the tropics, he dared not imagine how he might have fared if he hadn't come to the island. He'd seen the founding of Kirban Temple, saw the way the mages changed life on the island. Every major city had become home to a chapter house full of mages, and most minor cities had at least one mage of their own to look after their people. Or they had, before the disaster that had befallen the temple. Nondar grimaced at the thought as he pushed himself from his chair and made his way to the windows.

The view of the temple grounds still pained him, though it had improved. He had lived in the temple's central tower since he became Master of the House of healing, though his days as a mere teacher seemed distant now, buried beneath the ashes left in the wake of the fire. Much of the temple had been restored, and the garden below grew in lively greens, nourished by the ash. But a considerable number of repairs remained to be done, and workers proved scarce in the wake of controversy left by his predecessor.

Envesi had been an excellent Archmage, a shrewd woman with a sharp eye and sharper tongue. She had been skilled at keeping coin flowing from the cities, which had fed the magelings their suppers and fattened the purses of the Masters who trained them. If not for the woman's insufferable bullheadedness, perhaps their prosperity would not have ended. Any other woman would have been satisfied to be both Archmage and queen, but Envesi had rejected the latter title and struggled to break from her husband's rule. At the end, the king had refused to be pushed, and the temple had paid the price.

The damaged portions of the campus had begun to grow over with moss and creeping vines and looked less like the prestigious university he remembered and more like the crumbling rings of the ancient ruins just beyond the temple grounds. Every time he saw them, Nondar stifled a sigh.

Craftsmen tended toward patriotism. After Envesi's secession from Kifel's rule, few workers were willing to associate with mages, regardless of what Queen Firal did to repair ties between the temple and the kingdom. If there were more money in his coffers, he might have been able to overcome protests, but even the wealthiest cities had become reluctant to seek the services mages offered. Firal sent the temple a monthly pension to cover the expense of food for the mages, bless her, but the rising prices meant there was never coin left over. And the rising prices of food, of course, were something the mages were supposed to be able to take care of.

Nondar turned his head. A presence hovered outside his office door, and he wondered how long his wandering thoughts had kept him from observing it there. "Come in, girl," he called as his gaze drifted across the temple's walls and toward the ruins. He didn't like the place, even knowing it was now empty. But the Archmage was expected to work from the Archmage's tower, so he would learn to make do. "I didn't call you up here to use you as a doorstop."

Kytenia stepped inside and shut the door. He didn't have to look at her to know her cheeks grew rosy. As a healer, he had an innate sense of people. As her teacher, he knew her well enough to predict her embarrassment.

The girl cleared her throat. "I apologize, Archmage."

His thick white brows lifted, the only outward sign of his amusement. "For what, hesitance? You could have knocked, I suppose." He rested a knobby hand against his hip as he hobbled back to his desk. The short walk made him regret he hadn't used his cane to walk to the window in the first place.

"I suppose so, Archmage." She stopped before his desk with her hands clasped together and stared down at her toes. "What have you called me to assist with?"

"Patience, girl, I'll get to that." Nondar gritted his teeth as he sank into his chair. He dropped the last few inches with a sigh. "Would that we found a way to cure arthritis. I'd be a happier man, that's for certain." He rubbed his forehead and then smoothed his hair and his narrow white beard. Another cushion for his chair might help. He'd have to remember to ask for one later.

The mageling girl fidgeted with the hem of her robe.

Nondar laced his knobby fingers together. "I received a message from Ilmenhith this morning. Have any of the other Masters mentioned it?"

Kytenia shook her head, never looking up.

"Ah. Unusual, I expected them to be gossiping about it as soon as I was out of earshot. The queen has summoned me to the capital, but there's something I must tend to before answering." He chuckled, though he didn't feel a bit of mirth. "How are you faring, dear girl? As I understand it, you are one of the magelings working with... how are they saying it? Enhancing? Improving? Working with the earth."

She nodded in response, but said nothing.

He leaned against the edge of his desk with a sigh. "So you understand what the problem with the food supply is, then."

"That the previous Archmage scoured away the fertile soil with the torrential rains. We've managed some improvements, but earth-working isn't exactly my specialty, Archmage." She winced. "Archmage Nondar, you know my affinity is healing. Why have I been assigned to this duty?"

"Because, child, it's very important for you to understand the expectations people have for mages of the temple. If you are to wear the white of a Master, you will be expected to have a hand in all things." He smiled and gestured for her to make herself comfortable, waiting for her to settle in one of the chairs on the other side of his desk before he went on. "Your particular connection with our young queen makes you a vital key in this puzzle around us, which is why your group has been spread across so many tasks beyond your normal fields. You are her friends. Firal will trust your word more than that of the Masters. Maintaining a good relationship with the capital is important, especially considering that the queen relies on us to help with tasks like assisting the farmers. There's only so much we can do about that, however. The soil will recover with time, but repairing the temple's reputation is the forefront of my concerns."

Kytenia looked away. "I've barely spoken to Firal since her coronation. I don't know if we can still be considered friends."

He shrugged. "I am certain she will be pleased to include you in her new life. There will be errands that take you to Ilmenhith soon enough, but that isn't why I've called you."

The girl's expression didn't change. "How may I assist you, Archmage?"

Nondar glanced to the open ledger on his desk. He closed the book without another thought for the smudged ink. "You are right, I know healing is your strong suit. I'm afraid I'm beginning to reach a point where my age is a hindrance to my duties."

The mageling brushed at her robes. She'd graduated to green rank not long after his own promotion. It was nothing to sneeze at, but he wished she were already in blue.

Despite her fidgeting, she did not speak, so he went on. "I am in desperate need of an assistant now, one with good eyes and good handwriting. One who can ease the pains in this old body of mine, which means a student of the healing arts. As former Master of the House of healing, I have a great deal of knowledge

I can pass on to you directly, so it is not as if your efforts would be unrewarded." He paused, adjusting his spectacles. "There are also financial rewards to be offered, of course, since this would be on top of your existing duties."

Kytenia bit her lip and wrung her hands. "You mean, you want me to... You're offering me a position as Archmage's apprentice?"

He inclined his head in affirmation and smiled when a light sparked in her eyes. "I can think of no other I would trust with such a task. Given everything we've been through in the past year, I feel you are more than trustworthy."

"Thank you, Archmage." Kytenia restrained her smile, but the way her hands curled to fists in the skirt of her robes betrayed her enthusiasm.

"I take that to mean you accept, then?" Nondar chuckled when she nodded. "Very well. Your first assignment. I expect you to return to my office after your classes conclude this evening. Bring supper with you, if you would. I doubt my old legs will carry me down to the dinner hall a second time today."

"Of course, Archmage." The mageling jumped from her chair and dipped in a curtsy. She flashed him a single, brilliant grin on her way out of his office.

He watched her go with a smile, though his cheer faded after she closed the door. His eyes fell to the closed ledger and the abandoned quill beside it. What was done was done, but he didn't look forward to hearing complaints from Edagan and Anaide. They'd be snapping at his heels by morning. Dealing with sensitive matters, such as inquiries from the capital, had come to mean involving one of them. Their rank granted them authority to pen letters in his place when his hands ached too much to hold a quill. That he would replace them with a mageling, of all things, would rankle.

But he'd spoken the truth to the girl; there were no others he trusted with such a task. His choices were limited to the friends Firal had kept at the temple, and of the three remaining, Kytenia was the only one he knew well enough to rely on. She was a good girl, and strong enough in her Gift that he had no doubt she would wear blue shortly after year's end, if not before then.

Her strength, however, was not why he had chosen her. Kytenia already knew their young queen's most harmful secrets, and had shown herself willing to protect them. She had offered her own intended to protect Firal and her child, sacrificing the life she'd planned for herself. There were none more trustworthy than Kytenia. His only regret was that he had need to trust someone at all.

The old mage brushed the thought from his mind as he took his cane from where it hung on the edge of his desk. Its handle had left a permanent indentation in the wood. He eyed it with a sardonic smile as he got to his feet and waited to gain his balance. The first mark he'd made as Archmage was literal, and a sign of his physical failings, at that.

The warmth of activity eased the stiffness of his joints as he exited his office. The many stairs of the tower still presented a problem, though the station installed just outside his office door alleviated most others. A different mageling sat at the small station in the mornings and evenings, but there was always someone present and waiting to be sent on an errand. It was a girl in pale yellow robes today.

"On your feet, girl." Nondar waved a hand to hurry her along. "I must take a brief excursion. Fetch enough Masters to open a Gate."

The girl bobbed her head and ran off. Nondar leaned against the edge of the table where she had been studying. He didn't like waiting, but he had few options. The previous Archmage had kept a Gate-stone among her possessions, letting her come and go from the temple as she pleased. He'd seen her use it, but never where she kept it. His mages had turned the office upside-down looking for it at his request, but the thing never had turned up. A pity; such an artifact would have been quite useful. He doubted the likelihood of coming into possession of another.

The Masters arrived as he ruminated, and he nodded to each of them in silent greeting. Only once the last of the half-dozen mages was present did he speak. "Open the Gate to the queen's office in the palace of Ilmenhith. She has enough mages in the palace to have me returned, no need to wait for me. Be quick about it, now."

The Masters formed a half-circle around the door and he braced himself for what was to come. Using the doorway as a frame for the portal was unnecessary, but a common practice. Some mages had trouble keeping the energies focused without a frame to concentrate on. With so few Masters at his disposal, even one failing to support their share of energy could have disastrous results for the rest.

Nondar shuddered at the shift of the power currents in the air. White-hot, crackling light split the air and he shielded his eyes as the Gate opened. The portal hummed with power, making his skin tingle as if touched with electricity. Once the sound and sensation stabilized, he uncovered his eyes. The longer the mages held the Gate, the more energy it took, so he wasted no time in crossing to the familiar room on the other side.

The mages dropped the portal the moment he was through. The air currents behind him rippled as they settled.

Firal looked up in surprise, dropped her pen and all but leaped from her chair. A Gate without an anchor—either a Gate-stone or mages to catch the energy at the destination point—could only be seen from one side, lending him the illusion of having stepped from thin air. He thought he might have startled her, but the look on her face spoke more of relief.

"Good afternoon, child." Nondar opened his arms. Deep wrinkles swallowed his features as he smiled. The young queen almost threw herself into his embrace. He hugged her tightly, startled at how much smaller her frame seemed to be. He put a gnarled hand on her shoulder and pushed her back. "You've lost weight. Are you eating enough?"

She clung to his arms, as if afraid he might escape. "That's exactly why I've called you, Master. That is, Archmage," she corrected herself, chagrined. "I'm sorry. I gave you the title and I still can't remember to call you by it."

He patted her shoulder with a chuckle and gestured toward her desk. "It's quite all right, my dear. Imagine how I feel, having kissed skinned knees for a girl I now call my queen."

She looked embarrassed, but said nothing. He tried not to rely on his cane as he followed her to the chairs. She pulled one out for him, but he waved her off when she tried to help. Old as he was, he could seat himself, though he shifted awkwardly until he was comfortable.

"So," he started, leaning his cane against his chair. He paused when she sat next to him. She was the queen; he'd expected her to seat herself behind the big desk, not close to his side, like she had when they were mageling and Master. He tried not to let his discomfort show. "You've summoned me to discuss the fact you aren't feeding yourself properly?"

"No one is being fed properly, Nondar." Firal rubbed her forehead with her fingertips, as if to smooth away the lines of worry that etched themselves into her brow. "I can't feed my city. Vahn has commissioned more fishing ships and we mean to import grain from the mainland, but we need something more immediate. I thought that would be enough to see us through until the next harvest, when things ought to stabilize, but..."

"But?" he asked.

She worried her lower lip. "I don't want to think of them as a problem—they're my people, too—but the whole of the Underling city has uprooted from the ruins and staked themselves right outside Ilmenhith. They used all their resources to travel here, and now they look to me for support. How am I to feed them and the rest of Ilmenhith at the same time?"

Startled, Nondar sank back in his chair. He hadn't even heard a whisper of people leaving the ruins, never mind the whole city. "Brant's roots, girl! Did no one see them traveling?"

"They must have, but no one told me!" She threw up her

hands in defeat. "Even Vahn didn't mention it, and who knows how long he knew they were on the way. I can't support them, Nondar, there's no way. I thought maybe I could have mages open Gates to the mainland to establish immediate trade, but who would I trade with? I don't know the name of a single person in a seat of power there. All these lessons and lectures with Edagan and Anaide, and neither one of them will tell me what I need to know."

He patted her knee in a grandfatherly gesture of comfort. "Calm down, child. It's not the end of the world."

She looked at him with tears brimming on her dark eyelashes, a look that wrenched his heart, and he reached for her hand.

"Heavens. Why didn't you call for me sooner?"

"When it was just Ilmenhith, I thought I could manage on my own." Firal's lip trembled. "But now it's Core, too. I don't want to rely on the temple forever, but I don't know what to do."

Nondar's shoulders sagged as he exhaled. "Dear child, you may turn to me whenever you need. I thought I hammered that into your thick skull while you were still one of my students." He tapped his temple with a thick finger. "The temple is your best resource in instances like this. Had I known the situation in the capital was so severe, I'd have suggested it earlier. Yes, we can certainly open a Gate to the mainland."

Firal shuffled her feet and smoothed her skirts over her knees. "Where can we go, though? Who would be able to help us? Elenhiise has been self-sufficient for so long that maybe nobody thought it necessary that I have connections to the mainland, but I need them now."

"The temple has ties to an aggregation of mages on the mainland. Very old ties, but they do exist. It was to them that we sent my predecessor, if you'll recall. Going through the temple connects you to the Grand College of Lore, and if nothing else, they will know who to refer you to for whatever business you have on the mainland." He paused, rubbing his chin in thought.

"As a matter of fact, it would be wise to make sure the new generation of Masters is capable of Gating to the college, in case of emergencies. There are very few of us remaining who can." Truth be told, he suspected he was the last. He was the mage who led the opening of the Gate for Envesi's exile. Melora, the other Master he knew could reach the mainland, had gone with the former Archmage.

Firal drooped in her chair, the concern etched on her brow seeming to lessen. "So we can import food immediately?"

"Yes, of course." He patted her knee again and tried to smile without showing pity. The poor girl, overwhelming herself for nothing. Still, the notion he could have alleviated her burden earlier stirred guilt in his chest. The thought of opening immediate, direct trade with the mainland simply hadn't crossed his mind. "I would be more than happy to assist you with this. In fact, I can begin arrangements as soon as I return to the temple."

"Yes, yes. Please do. The sooner this is taken care of, the sooner I'll be able to rest." Firal wiped her eyes. "Thank you, Nondar. I don't know what I would do without you. You're right, I should have come to you sooner."

"Of course I'm right," he chortled as he leveraged himself from his chair and righted himself with his cane. "I am the Archmage, after all." He gave her a wink and a toothy grin. "Rest easy, child. And for Brant's sake, get something to eat."

"Yes, Archmage." Her amber eyes sparkled when she smiled and he felt the pleasant stir of the fatherly emotions the girl always had elicited from him. He stroked her dark hair before he made his way to the door. She hurried ahead to open it for him, then accompanied him the short distance to the parlor where the royal mages spent their day in practice and study. She clasped him in one last embrace at the parlor door. "Thank you again."

"Speak nothing of it, child." Nondar waved a hand as he waited for the mages to open a Gate. When it stabilized, he excused himself from her side to step through the portal and back into his own office. The poor girl, inheriting such a problem and then worrying herself sick over one of its smallest challenges. Nondar shook his head and turned his gaze to the ledger on his desktop. The temple's finances, now there was a problem to worry about.

He sighed with resignation and started toward his desk, staggering when his balance faltered. The cane in his hands was all that saved him. The floor looked so far away, all of a sudden. He held out a hand to steady himself for another step.

He never made it to his desk.

8

FREEDOM

IT WAS THE BEST THING HE'D SEEN IN MONTHS. RUNE EXHALED AND turned his eyes to the ceiling, mouthing a silent thank-you as he pushed the door closed behind him. Privacy was precious enough, but what stood against the wall of the small room had to be worth half his father's fortune at a moment like this.

He tossed aside the fresh clothing he carried and stripped out of the grungy, tattered garb he'd worn through his stint in prison and the months before. Dipping his clawed fingers into the steaming water proved it almost hotter than he could stand. Almost.

Tired muscles protested as he climbed into the tub and were soothed the moment he sank into the water's welcoming heat. The half-healed wounds from the prior week's beating stung at first; he ignored them until the sensation went away. He'd been told to make it fast. He didn't plan to. A proper bath was a luxury he'd not been afforded since leaving Elenhiise and he intended to enjoy it to the fullest.

The soaps on the shelf above the tub were simple and didn't smell like anything, but for a bath chamber inside the soldiers' barracks, he didn't expect anything otherwise. They suited his purposes fine, suds stripping the layers of filth from his skin and the grit from his hair. The water cooled before he finished and he considered reheating it before he realized magic still hovered just beyond his grasp. It seemed unlikely they'd still guard him after he'd agreed to join their ranks, but without Redoram nearby to ask for certainty, he'd just have to assume they still did.

Rune left the water feeling refreshed, and for the first time in ages, he felt human. Or, as close to human as he could ever feel. A wry smile crossed his face and he tore his eyes away from his clawed and scaled feet.

He toweled dry and dressed as best he could. The small buttons gave him some trouble, and he fumbled with them for some time before he got them through their holes. The uniform was simple; plain trousers and a collarless shirt in a matching dark gray, accented by broad bands of color at the tops of the sleeves. He recognized the colors from the flags that flew over the palace and the arena, each symbolizing one of the three provinces united by the Royal City. The uniform was to be worn under a soldier's armor, he assumed. They hadn't bothered to give him boots and his claws clicked on the wooden floor when he walked to the door.

"About time you were done." Garam waited on the other side with arms crossed and a sour look on his face. No matter his expression, Rune didn't figure he'd been waiting long. The man jerked his head toward the entrance. "Time for a haircut."

"What, you do not think mine suits a soldier?" Rune smirked and ran his fingers through his wet hair. It reached his shoulders now; with how matted it had been, he hadn't realized the length.

"Don't."

Rune's brow furrowed. "What?"

"You said 'do not.' If Councilor Parthanus isn't here to teach you how to speak, I suppose I'll have to do it myself. Say 'don't', saying 'do not' makes you sound archaic." Garam gestured for him to follow.

"My tongue is archaic. Your councilor says as much." It took effort not to sound irritated. Redoram told him he'd been fortunate to have months of immersion in the language before their lessons began, but even with total immersion and intense study, complete fluency was still some time off. He understood it better than he spoke it. Translating his own words in his head frustrated him. "I am doing my best."

Garam said nothing more. The captain led him out of the barracks and down several streets before they stopped at a small workshop that looked to serve no one but soldiers. Uniforms like the one Rune wore filled shelves along the walls. Racks of swords and spears and other weapons stood between them. The place was tended by an old man who muttered to himself as he folded uniforms and organized blades. In the midst of his work, the man pulled a stool from somewhere and pushed it to the middle of the room.

"Sit," Garam ordered, waiting by the door while the old man sharpened shears on a whetstone.

Rune did as he was told, tucking his chin into his chest and staring at his hands as the old man went to work. The shears clacked beside his ears and his damp, tangled hair fell away in clumps. Then the old man grasped his chin and turned his face this way and that. He mumbled something to himself as he released Rune's face and fetched a razor. There was little to shave, and it wasn't long before the man held out a mirror, inviting him to look. Rune glanced at it and then looked again, startled by the reflection.

"Look like a different man, don't you?" Garam chuckled.

Rune nodded and forced himself to look away. A man he didn't recognize, save the unchanging green of his hands and feet.

"You'll get used to it," the captain said.

The old man put the mirror aside and took up a measuring tape. He pulled Rune to his feet and made him stand with his feet apart and his arms up. Again, the man mumbled something Rune couldn't understand as he took measurements and wrote down the numbers.

Then Garam straightened and waved the old man away. "Any time you need a haircut or new equipment, this is where you'll come. He'll have your armor ready in a few days. Pick a weapon you're proficient with off the racks, then follow me. We'll get you shown to your quarters. Training begins in the morning."

"I need to speak to someone of a small matter before morning." Rune took a sword from the nearest rack without a second glance. "The energy flows here, they are strange. They move when I reach for them. Redoram said magic was held outside my reach in prison, but why can I not grasp it now?"

Garam stopped mid-stride. "You're a mage?"

Rune hesitated. "You did not know?"

"The only mage we knew of in the prison was Redoram." The captain muttered a curse, rubbing the back of his neck. Then he shook his head and resumed his path toward the barracks. "They should have known, why didn't they sense it in you? Ah, no matter. I can speak to them about it later. I'll bring someone to you after you're settled, have your abilities assessed and see what can be done."

Rune frowned as he fell in step behind the captain and turned the thought over in his head. They hadn't known of his power? Then what kept him from touching it now? And if not to keep the flows from his grasp, why had there been a mage present to escort him to and from the arena? He recalled the man's behavior, the guarded way he'd looked around while they walked. Always looking at something else. Looking *for* something else, he realized. The man had never been there to keep him from using magic; he'd been there to keep someone from using magic against him.

But what need was there to protect a mere prisoner? He considered it from every angle he could think of, turning up nothing but the idea that a noble could be offended if something happened to an opponent before their prized arena match. That had to be it, considering the odd games the nobles played.

Redoram had spent a considerable amount of time trying to teach him what to expect. A number of the nobles' practices here were questionable, but sending mages to assassinate prisoners in chains still seemed rather extreme.

"Here we are." Garam's voice jarred him from his thoughts and Rune cast a disinterested glance around the barracks as they stepped down into one of many near-identical rooms with a long row of beds inside it. "A bed to sleep in and a chest for your things. Not that I expect you own much."

Rune opened the wooden chest and laid the sword he'd chosen inside. "That would be it, yes." He caught a glimpse of Garam eyeing the sword and he closed the chest, struggling to keep his expression from darkening. All he had in hand, at least, but he was in no position to demand his father's sword. Not yet.

He wasn't thrilled about being without the blade and he wasn't pleased with being reduced to the status of a nameless guard, but it served a purpose for now. Food in his stomach and a safe place to sleep was hard to argue with. Assuming the captain kept his word and was able to pull Redoram from the prison, he'd have a chance to learn enough about the region to survive on his own.

"Good. Take a few minutes to rest and get your bearings, then head down the hall to the training arena. Watch some sparring matches to get a feel for what you'll be up against tomorrow. I'll fetch someone to address magic with you." The captain's face shifted almost imperceptibly at mention of magecraft, but it was enough to speak volumes.

"Thank you." Rune seated himself on the side of his bed and pulled up his feet. It was a stiff straw mattress with rough-spun blankets over the top, but it felt more like silk cushions after that plank in his cell.

The captain started back the way he'd come, but paused after a step or two. "I'll find something for your feet, too. Can't have you walking around the way you are."

Rune arched a brow at the choice of words, but he let it pass.

He rested only a few minutes before he got back to his feet and retrieved the sword he'd only just put away. Any longer in bed, and he'd fall asleep. He paused in the hallway and counted the doors to remember which room was his.

Despite the rooms looking alike, the rest of the barracks proved easy to navigate. The building was split by a long hallway, one end leading out into the city, the other open to what had to be the training grounds. The room with the bathtub was at that end of the hall, opposed by a staircase to the second floor, in which he had little interest. Rune slipped into a small armory beside the training arena and spared a glance for the shelves full of battered armor and damaged weaponry. A wrought iron fence was all that separated the armory from the arena. A pair of benches sat next to the dusty ring.

Several pairs of men sparred in the squared training grounds, but Rune was less interested in them than the tall buildings that surrounded the arena on all sides. Windows facing the arena might have allowed someone to watch, but all of them were shuttered to keep the noise and rising dust at bay. Looking around at the buildings above them, Rune almost missed the way one of the men elbowed his sparring partner and gestured toward him. The man's partner laughed, and another pair paused to look at him. Rune lifted a brow.

"So the captain was serious!" one of them said, wiping sweat from his brow. "Think you can fight real soldiers, instead of the gussied-up knights they had you pitted against?"

"A real soldier is made on the battlefield." Rune's brows lowered as he spoke, though his snake-slitted eyes drifted up to the shuttered windows again. "Not in a sheltered training ground."

Teasing mirth drained from the faces of the soldiers before him. The man who'd spoken first scowled and spat at the ground. "All right," he said, hefting his sword in hand and settling into a battle stance. "Let's see it."

Rune twirled his sword and stepped around the iron

fencing. He glanced down as he tested his footing on the hard-packed dirt. The sparring ceased and the remaining pairs of men turned to watch the fight. He considered stopping to retrieve armor from the shelves behind him, but dismissed the thought as soon as it came. He'd been without armor in the arena and lived to tell the tale. And that was against men who wanted him dead. He turned his thoughts to his opponent instead as he strode across the dirt. His blade darted with the first move.

The soldier parried and countered with grace and speed, catching him off guard. Rune gritted his teeth. He barely caught his opponent's sword and chided himself for getting cocky. He moved back, readjusted his stance and shifted his hands on the hilt of his unfamiliar weapon.

The other man floated just beyond the reach of his blade, darting in at every opening. Steel rang with musical notes over the jeers and laughter of the men watching them fight. Rune tried not to look at them, ignored their applause and chatter, and focused on his opponent instead. *Like a viper*, he thought. The only difference was the bite would be from steel instead of fangs. He pulled back, defending, observing.

Much like a snake, the soldier struck for the head, leaving his lower half open whenever he lunged high. Rune feinted one direction and ducked the other when the man fell for it. His sword snapped forward and its edge rasped against the soldier's cuisse.

The spectators howled, half of them with laughter, the rest in anger. Rune straightened with a smirk.

The soldier's eyes flashed with fury and the man lunged forward to grab Rune by the shirt, brandishing his sword.

"That's enough." The captain's bark startled everyone to silence. The men bowed their heads and turned away, most returning to their sparring matches. Rune's opponent scowled, but said nothing as he released him and strode back to his partner.

Garam raised a brow and folded his arms over his chest. "Making friends already, are we?"

Rune brushed at his shirt with his free hand. "I seem to be good at it." His smirk faded under the captain's stare, and a frown grew in its place. "Did you bring a mage?"

The captain nodded and jerked a thumb over his shoulder. Rune half expected the mage-guard that had walked with him from prison to arena and back again, or maybe a scholar from the king's circle. Who he saw instead wasn't what he'd expected at all.

The woman all but shoved Garam out of the way as she stepped out from behind him and planted her hands on her hips. Her skin was the same earth-brown as the captain's, but her ears bore a distinct point, exposed by the way her hair was drawn into a multitude of tiny braids and tied at the back of her head. Hair the unmistakable stark white of an experienced mage, he noted, her eyes clear blue to match. Rune glanced between the captain and the woman, but she spoke before he could make a sound.

"This? You brought me to see this?" Her brows knit and she slid forward, circling Rune with an appraising look. "Where are you finding these things, Garam? Did you scrape him off the underside of a rock?"

Garam sighed. "Just do what I brought you to do."

"Pah! I feel nothing in him at all." She fluttered a hand and turned as if to leave. Garam caught her by the shoulders and turned her around again.

"You haven't even tried yet, have you?" Garam pushed her forward. "Sera, this is Rune."

"Rune," she repeated flatly. She studied him a moment, then gave Garam a skeptical look. "That's his name?"

"The one he gave me." The captain stepped back and gestured for her to proceed.

Sera sighed, holding out her hands. "Fine. Come on, then, Rune, let me gauge your Gift."

Rune glanced between her and the captain and drew back. He'd linked energies with someone only once before. He tried not to think of her now. "I do n—ah—don't... think this is a good idea." He faltered over the word he'd been given earlier. Correct or not, it felt foreign on his tongue.

"Nobody asked what you thought." She grabbed hold of his scaled hands and seized his energies before he knew what she was doing.

He shuddered as the electric tingle of their merging energies ran through his body and gasped as magic surged into him, suddenly no longer out of reach. Sera shrieked. Power rolled through him, white-hot and intoxicating, growing until it roared within his ears. Gritting his teeth, he thrust her away and withdrew his power so fast it snapped back at him like a whip. He almost lost his balance.

Sera staggered backwards and fell into Garam's arms. "Lifetree's mercy!"

"What happened?" Garam demanded, his face twisting with confusion when she shoved him back.

"Are you trying to kill me?" Her voice cracked as she spun to glare at him and leveled an accusatory finger with his nose. "You didn't tell me he was a free mage!"

Garam's eyes widened. "I didn't know!"

"You didn't know what?" Sera snorted. "You ought to! Do his eyes glow in the dark, Garam? Did you even look?"

The captain fumbled for words.

"Of course you didn't." She sighed, rubbing her temples with her fingertips. "Ay, my head is killing me now."

"I am sorry," Rune started, glancing between the two of them uncertainly. "I would have said something, but—"

"No, no." Sera waved a hand and sighed before motioning for him to move out of the way. He did as directed. She dropped to sit on one of the benches and cradled her head in her hands. "I should have given you a chance to speak. You were right, it wasn't a good idea." She paused and gave him a wry smile.

"But you could have just told your captain you were a free mage."

He didn't reply. How she knew the nature of his power, he couldn't fathom.

"So you can't train him?" Garam asked.

She scrubbed her face with both hands and straightened. "I can teach him some. Enough to serve your purposes."

Feeling steadier on his feet, Rune reached for the flows and made an exasperated sound in his throat when they skirted his grasp. "I still cannot touch them! How did you seize them through me?"

Sera glared at him. "Patience, snake, I'll speak to you when I'm ready. Garam, what do you wish me to teach him? I'm hardly capable enough to deal with a free mage on my own, but—"

"Just the basics," the captain replied, cutting her short. "Just enough to make sure he's got himself under control. Not that it's a concern while he's in the city, but if patrols take him beyond the barriers, I want to be sure."

Barriers? Rune frowned. No wonder, then. If the entire city was layered with a barrier that kept energy away from mages, it explained why he was still powerless. But it didn't explain why Sera was able to reach through it, or why there was enough concern about magic that it warranted a mage escorting prisoners to and from the arena. Rune sighed and rubbed his eyes. More questions for every one answered.

Sera scratched the tip of one pointed ear and pursed her lips. "I can't promise he'll be a quick study. I've not worked with his sort of magic before."

"Just give it your best effort and I'm sure it'll be good enough. I'll let you get right to it. You know I have things to attend to." Garam patted her shoulder and offered her a fond smile before he left.

Rune looked away.

"Things to attend to," Sera grumbled, crossing her arms and

squinting up at Rune. "As if I don't. Sit down, snake! You're making me nervous, hovering over me like that."

He shot her a glare. "I am not a snake."

"Lizard, then? What am I supposed to call you? I've never seen a..." She waved a hand as if trying to summon a word as she studied his feet.

"You could try my name." He seated himself at the other end of the bench and leaned forward to rest his elbows on his knees.

Her eyebrows lifted until her forehead creased. Then she laughed, a bright and clear sound, altogether lacking the mockery he expected. "Maybe so," she said, tapping a finger against her chin as if the idea hadn't crossed her mind. "Very well, then, Rune. What sort of questions do you have for your new teacher?" Her nose crinkled as his name left her tongue, though her expression was more amusement than distaste.

There weren't many questions in his mind. Though Sera's hair and eyes were bleached, she did not wear the robes of a Master mage. He could feel the strength of her Gift well enough just by opening his senses to it. Having felt how quickly she was overwhelmed by coming in contact with his power, he had an idea of the extent of her control. His last teacher had not been stronger, but she'd been much more refined. He swallowed and pushed thoughts of Firal from his mind. "I cannot touch the energy here, it moves from my grasp. Yet you seem to have no difficulty touching power. Why?"

"Ah, yes." She pushed her booted toes at the ground. It was then he noticed what she wore—the same sort of shirt and trousers he'd been given. At first glance, it had looked like peasant's garb. It startled him to see the uniform on a woman, though evidently not enough for him to notice it right off.

"The barrier is relatively new," Sera said. "It covers the entire city and extends a little farther than the city walls. The shanties and markets outside the wall are protected as well. It was put in place to keep peace within the city, so the Aldaanan and the college mages would keep their magic to themselves. There was only the one incident, but one was enough for the barrier to be put up. There are a handful of mages in the guard who were given amulets to let us bypass the barrier, but you can keep the idea of you getting one out of your head. There are only a few, and each only works for the mage it was given to."

He remembered the college from conversation with Redoram, but the Aldaanan she spoke of were something they hadn't had time to discuss. "What happened between the mages and the people of Aldaan?"

"You don't know?" She looked surprised. "No, I suppose you wouldn't. The barrier was erected not long before you went into the prison. Garam said he didn't think you spoke our tongue when you were arrested, so I suppose I can't expect you to have heard." She twisted one of her many white braids around a finger. "The barrier has only existed for a few months, but the Aldaanan and the mages have been at odds for years. The Aldaanan wish to eradicate the college, while the college wishes to advance its power. It's just poor luck that both countries ended up as provinces beneath the same ruler."

"And this led to fighting in the city?"

"There was an incident where a college mage started something with a group of Aldaanan in the city. Or perhaps the Aldaanan started it, I don't know. Either way, it ended with the college mage trying to do something to them with his magic, and the Aldaanan severed him. Cut him off from magic entirely." She shuddered, rubbing her arms as if chilled.

Severed. The term hung heavy in his mind. It seemed like forever ago when he reflected on it, but the sensation of tearing Lumia's power from her was as fresh as if he'd just left her screaming on the floor. The tension of the power in the air, the palpable feeling of her ties to magic snapping when he pulled. It made the hair stand on the back of his neck and he shuddered, too.

"Exactly." Sera licked her lips before going on. "Since then, the college mages have demanded that the Aldaanan not be allowed to enter Lore or the Royal City. That can't be done, since the Royal City sits where all three provinces meet. It's part of all three territories, so no one can be denied entry. To keep matters peaceful, it was agreed that the Royal City would instead be made into a neutral ground, where no magic can be used. Except by the guard."

It was a reasonable explanation, though the issue itself seemed needlessly complicated. Rune lifted a hand to scratch his head, momentarily startled by the shortness of his hair. "Why did the king not unify the land when first he took it? Is it not more trouble to keep the provinces divided?"

"Your guess is as good as mine." Sera peered at him from the corner of her eye. "The way you speak is very backwards. How long have you been learning our tongue?"

"Not long enough, it would seem," he replied dryly, pushing himself up from the bench.

She quirked a brow. "Where are you going?"

"To rest indoors." And to think. The concept of severing someone from the flows was concerning. He didn't know how he'd done it, couldn't recall what made him think he could. It had been an accident before, instinct, another twist of power he didn't know how to control. Now it weighed heavily in his mind and made it hard to think of anything else. "I am to begin training tomorrow. Will that include magic?"

Sera nodded as she rose and brushed dust from her uniform. "Garam's orders. I will meet with you after your sparring matches. Hopefully you'll be cooperative once Garam's work has you worn out, and not fall asleep while I'm trying to teach."

Rune grunted in response and retreated into the barracks. Sera followed close at his heels. When they reached the doorway of the room he'd share with a dozen other men, she stopped at the stairs and let him enter alone. Her nose crinkled with disgust. "Ugh, those beds. I'm always glad I don't have to sleep here. Rest well, then, if you can. And don't let my brother work you too hard."

Rune glanced up and blinked when he found the doorway empty. Her brother? Well, he supposed it made sense, though the earthen tone of their skin was the only obvious resemblance between them. Then again, her pointed ears were an explanation for that, marking them as half-siblings. What it didn't explain was how Garam could have such an obvious dislike of mages when his own sister was one of them. Rune sat on the edge of his bed, running a hand through his dark hair and frowning at its shortness again.

He did look like a different man. It was fitting for the beginning of a rather different life, but he wasn't sure he liked it. He wasn't vain by any means; the reflection of the scales and claws he so hated served well to keep him away from mirrors. It simply wasn't a flattering cut, though it showed how far he'd come.

And how far *had* he come? Rune sank back into his bed, grateful for the stiff straw mattress and the stale smell of the down-filled pillow. Mostly down, he corrected himself as the quill of a feather jabbed his neck. He pulled it from the cloth and twirled the feather between his claws.

He hadn't thought much of where he was or where he was going, even in the long hours he'd spent in prison. He'd been so preoccupied with trying to figure out how to escape, he didn't know what to do now that he'd done it. Serve in the guard, learn about the city, but then what? Elenhiise suddenly seemed a distant memory, one he clung to in fear it might escape.

He missed the island. He missed the ruins, the complex and winding halls of the city beneath them. The soaring towers of the palace in Ilmenhith, the smell of the earth after the heavy tropical rains. The smell of Firal's hair.

Firal. His chest tightened with the thought of her and he laid a hand over his eyes. She'd smelled of herbs and lavender, her hair soft as silk when it brushed against his skin and caught in his scales. He could still see the way the sunlight spilled in from the hole at the top of their tent, the last morning they'd spent together. The way the light played over her milky skin and glinted off her hair, lit a sparkle in her fiery amber eyes. He could see the way she'd flushed and ducked her eyes, covering herself as if they hadn't been married a month before. More than a month, even. He curled a hand around the rings still tied around his neck, forcing himself to open his eyes and stare at the ceiling instead.

Going back was out of the question, with the mages and his father's men eager to see him at the gallows. And yet the thought of Firal—the memory of their last encounter, the pain in her expression and the tears in her eyes—was almost enough to make him try. There had to be a way, though he'd spent nearly every waking moment since he'd left the island trying to figure out just what it might be.

The sound of footsteps in the hall shattered his reverie and he lifted his head.

"In here, is it?" a familiar voice asked. Someone farther down the hall replied with something he couldn't hear. Then the man stepped into the doorway and Rune sat upright on his bed.

"You!" He crossed the room with long strides. "Captain Kaith said he did not know if—but you already—"

"Yes, yes," Redoram sighed, smoothing his grungy clothing with both hands. "And Captain Kaith is who sent me to fetch you. There are conditions to my parole, and one of them seems to be you."

Rune paused, uncertain.

"So I've come to collect you." The old man smoothed his beard and his bedraggled hair. "I didn't particularly want to cross the city looking like this, but my freedom is at the mercy of cooperation, so here I am. You have lessons with the captain and his dear sister in the morning, I've been told, but for tonight, the lessons are mine to teach."

"Lessons?" Rune asked. The mage started walking, and Rune followed him down the hallway and into the open air of the street. Light struck his face and he blinked hard against the glare of sunlight. With how tired he was, he'd almost forgotten it was still early in the day.

Redoram beckoned him with one hand. The man moved at a surprising pace, given his age. "I'll explain once we reach my home. Come! You aren't the only one who can appreciate a bath and trim, you know."

Rune hid a smile at that and fell in step beside the old man, not caring how odd the two of them might look. "I have many questions for you, my friend."

"I'm sure you do," Redoram said, his apparent gloom doing nothing to dampen Rune's newfound enthusiasm.

For the first time in ages, something seemed to be going his way.

9

RUNESTONES

Rune glanced up and folded his book closed when he saw Redoram in the parlor doorway. The old man looked better, wearing a robe of embroidered velvet in a deep blue with a biggin on his head to match. His hair fell in white waves about his shoulders, his beard trimmed and tidy. He looked more like a noble mage ought to, complete with jeweled rings on his fingers.

Redoram arched a thick brow at the book. "You can read?" He sounded more intrigued than surprised, though surprise was what showed in the crease of his brow and the frowning twist of his mouth. "You're a clever one, aren't you."

Rune put the book back where he'd gotten it from, squaring it atop the stack of tomes on the table beside his chair. "I used to think myself clever. I learned otherwise. It's the fools who think themselves smart, isn't it?"

The old mage chuckled and scratched his beard. His laughter came a bit too easily, making Rune uncertain it meant anything at all. "And that just shows you are clever, after all. Either way, you might want to keep that bit of information to yourself. I don't know how things are where you come from, but the ability to read is reserved for nobles here. You wouldn't want to give anyone the wrong idea about you. It's a good way to earn enemies." He sat on the plush couch across from Rune's chair and sank into the cushions with a sigh.

Redoram's house was luxurious, though there was no reason to expect anything else. The two-storied mansion stood near the Spiral Palace, maintained by a competent serving staff even while Redoram himself was imprisoned. From the sound of things, no one had expected him to be gone as long as he had been. Ornate furniture of dark wood and expensive upholstery decorated the pristine parlor, the only part of the house Rune had seen. He was more interested in the shelves that lined the parlor walls, each of them overflowing with books.

"My father said knowledge was best when shared." Rune leaned forward in his seat.

"Your father would have been a very unpopular man here." The old mage shook his head. "But that's enough talk in your tongue, isn't it? Idle conversation isn't why I was pulled from the prison."

Rune tilted his head. He'd shifted back to his native language without a thought and hadn't caught himself in the process. His brow furrowed and he switched to the local dialect, a tongue that seemed to have no proper name but was referred to as the trade tongue. It was nothing like the trade tongue used on Elenhiise, Rune mused with an inward grumble. That one, he spoke, and it meshed well with his mother tongue—which Redoram claimed was Old Aldaanan. Regardless of his skepticism over the name, it seemed to him that Old Aldaanan was a much more graceful language. "Why did they turn you free? The captain said he did not know if he could free you at all."

"That," Redoram said, pointing to Rune's face, "is precisely why the captain retrieved me from the prison. He informed me that since I started your language lessons, I'd best teach you to speak properly, because he lacks the patience for your stiff grammar and backwards speech."

"I am doing the best I can." Rune tried not to scowl, though his eyes flashed with anger.

"And that may be, but you must understand that Garam Kaith is not a very patient man. Learn that now, and you will be much better off." The mage adjusted his cap as a smug look worked its way onto his face. "Although I have to say it has worked to my advantage. I must thank you for getting me out of that dank cell, even if it's only because I'm now expected to be your teacher."

Rune looked down at the low table between the couch and chairs as Redoram pulled a checkered board out from underneath it and laid it on the tabletop. He glanced twice at the board. It stirred memories of evenings in his father's parlor. Memories he preferred not to recall. "What is that for?"

"Oh, I always had it out. For entertaining company, you understand. The staff hated trying to clean the board without disrupting pieces, so I'm not surprised they put it away while I was absent. It's been a few years, you see. When King Vicamros suggested eventually unifying the provinces into one country, I was the first to support the notion. My thoughts were not well-received."

"Why would that put a man in prison?"

Redoram shrugged. "Unification would be beneficial to most, but harmful to the agendas of quite a few nobles. You see, as they are now, the provinces are mostly self-managing. King Vicamros has final say in most things, but the majority of provincial political choices are made by their own nobles, the counts and countesses who oversee each region. Which means that, as things are now, Vicamros is little more to them than a figurehead. The nobles do as they please in their own provinces, and there are very few nobles who would wish to give up a position of power. You understand."

Rune nodded. The explanation made sense, though it made him question what he'd entangled himself in during his time in the arena. If the nobles were vengeful enough to imprison a man who disagreed with them, what would they do to a man who had killed almost every noble he'd faced? He tried not to think of it, turning his attention back to the checkered board on the table instead. "Tell me of this game. I thought it was a chessboard, but the marks are too few."

"Ah!" The mage grinned. He opened a drawer in the side of the table and pulled out a bulging velvet purse. "Would you care to play? Chess is a thinking man's game. Runestones is similar. If you're familiar with one, you'll likely enjoy the other."

"I played chess with my father." Rune leaned forward, watching as Redoram spilled colored stones across the board. Runestones, he'd said. The name did enough to catch his interest, but when he saw the marks etched into the surface of the stones, he slid from his chair and moved to sit beside the table. He picked up a stone between his claws and frowned at the engraving, its lines filled with gold. He turned his hand and stared at the matching scar Lumia had given him.

"You wouldn't usually use stones belonging to another. Unlike chess, you choose what pieces you wish to use on the board. Each moves differently. You assemble your own set by winning pieces from your opponents. You win a match, you keep a stone. Of course, if you don't have your own set, you've no choice but to borrow stones to play with." Redoram spread his pieces out, rune side up, on his end of the board. Then he pushed the rest of the stones across the table. "Choose fourteen stones and place them as you will. If you look at mine, that might give you an idea of how to start. This rune moves as a knight in chess, this one like a bishop—"

"What is this stone?" Rune turned the piece he held.

The old man squinted. "Mannei? It doesn't have an exact equivalent in chess, but it can move forward or backward and side to side. It can only be taken from a diagonal. It's a good enough piece, but can be difficult to use if you don't know what you're doing. There are more pieces that move diagonally than straight ahead."

The knowledge made him prickle with irritation. Rune put the piece on the board before him and stared at it with his brows knit. He knew Lumia thought of her soldiers as puppets in some sort of game, but seeing the mark she'd branded him with etched into a piece from an actual game made him seethe. "Which piece is the pawn?"

"None of them." Redoram turned a few stones over in his hand, pursing his lips as he inspected them. He selected a few and put the rest aside before he dug another handful out of his bag. "Each piece has its own strengths and weaknesses. Some move in the same fashion as others, some are like chess pieces, and others have their own rules. But there are no stones equivalent to a pawn, or a king."

Rune glanced down at the stones the mage selected. The marks on their surfaces meant nothing to him. "If there is no king, how is the game won?"

"Well, that's up to the players," the old man explained. "Before a game, you must agree on how many pieces must be taken to win. It can be as few as three or as many as all fourteen. Since this is your first game, I say we play to seven."

"And this will help my speech?" Rune frowned, skeptical.

"Not at all, but it will make you pay attention and concentrate while we are talking, which will work to your benefit. Hurry and pick your runes. Do you have any questions for me? About the game, or about the city?" Redoram finished setting his stones and pushed the rest across the table for Rune to see.

"Captain Kaith." Rune didn't look up again, focused on sorting through the unclaimed pieces on the tabletop. He didn't know what they did, nor did he recognize any other markings. Though he'd always known the runes Lumia used were foreign to Elenhiise, he'd never stopped to consider where she might have learned them. She had never spoken of her life before the Underlings. The thought she might have ventured beyond the island intrigued him, but he supposed it mattered little now. He chose his pieces based on which shapes were most interesting and nudged them around the board with his claws. "He does not like mages, but what of Sera? She is his half-sister?"

Redoram nodded. "Technically speaking, yes, though calling them half-siblings to their faces would be a great insult. The two of them come from a complicated culture, where families and even kingdoms are perpetuated by declaration instead of blood. When houses merge, the higher-ranking house takes precedence and all of its new members are considered part of that family from that moment forward. There is no jealousy over existing children when widows remarry. If you must refer to the two of them as siblings, say brother or sister, nothing else. Family is not always determined by parentage, after all."

Rune caught the inside of his lip with his teeth. The words resonated with him, stirred the old aches of longing he'd never managed to quash. Kifel had always been a father to him. He regretted how he'd never understood that until it was too late. Now that regret ate away at him on the inside. Had he understood, perhaps he could have fixed the sour turn their relationship had taken before the end. Rune set his jaw as he collected the stones he didn't want from the table and returned them to their bag. "So the captain allows exception for his sister?"

"It's less of making an exception and more that he chooses to turn to her in lieu of trusting anyone else. You're right, he cares little for mages. You and I would be wise to tread lightly around him. But with the tensions between the college and the people of Aldaan, it isn't safe for the guard to be without a mage who can warn him of potential problems. Sera is the best choice, so instead of returning to the college to finish her studies, she remains here. Or perhaps he keeps her here." Redoram moved a piece across the board and Rune leaned forward to see how he'd done it. He hovered a claw over his own pieces, uncertain. The old mage chuckled and pointed at Rune's stones. "That one moves like a knight, as I said. That one can move forward, either straight or at a diagonal, three spaces at a time. No less."

"This will be a long game if I must ask before every turn," Rune said, moving his piece and shifting to watch his new mentor's choice.

"Best get used to it, then," Redoram replied cheerfully, dropping his stone into place with a click. "We have many games and lessons yet ahead of us."

SWORDPLAY, patrol training, magic lessons, language lessons. The rhythm of activity stayed the same regardless of the day of the week, though Rune's meetings with Sera were least frequent. He preferred his lessons with Redoram. Each passing day improved his understanding of the language and the game of runes they played. He even kept a small bag of stones he'd won from his teacher in his trunk of belongings now, though he kept the rune that matched his scar in his pocket and studied it when he had free time. A game of runes would have been preferable, today.

He didn't enjoy his lessons with Sera in the least. She shared Garam's impatience, and her tongue grew sharp when they butted heads. The tone she took with him when they disagreed reminded him too much of the Masters back at Kirban Temple.

"Stop resisting when I try to gauge your energies! I know well enough not to try to seize them again." Sera glared at him when he rolled his eyes. Her hip cocked to the side and she crossed her arms. "Do you want me to teach you or not? I need to know what abilities you already have. Wild mages are hard to train."

"Wonderful." The sarcastic inflection of his tone made her frown. He ignored it and reclined on the bed in the room that was his new home. Lessons were a stage of life he couldn't seem to leave behind.

She puffed her cheeks and shifted her hands to her hips. "So?"

He glanced toward her. "What?"

She shot him a withering glare. "So, you're holding back and being vague and it isn't helping anything. Garam wants me to teach you control, and you've already been familiar with everything I've tried to show you. If you would just tell me your level of proficiency, everything would be easier. You're wasting both our time."

"You say wild mages are hard to train." Rune rolled onto his side, making himself comfortable. "Wild mages, or free mages?"

"Both. But the reasons for it aren't the same. Wild mages are those without any training, those who learn through trial and error. Free mages are those who can touch any source, unlimited by affinity." She fluttered a hand as she spoke, a gesture she seemed to employ when flustered.

"I know." His eyes narrowed and the corners of his mouth twitched with a suppressed smile when he saw the way she looked at them, noticing his vertically slitted pupils for the first time. "I am not a wild mage."

Her face slackened with surprise as her gaze locked with his. Then she snorted and tossed her head, breaking eye contact. "What are you, then?"

The double meaning of the question made him bristle and he struggled to appear unruffled. It was a question he'd tried to find an answer to on his own—and an answer he still didn't have.

"I think that's enough conversation for today," he said.

"I happen to agree." Garam's voice from the doorway startled them both. Sera turned to glare as the captain stepped into the barracks. Her irritation was short-lived. He waved an envelope and her eyes locked onto it in alarm. The wax seal on the back was broken.

"This was waiting on my desk upstairs," the captain said. "It looks like we have a small problem."

Sera snatched the envelope from his hand and pulled the

letter free. Her eyebrows worked up and down as she read. "A formal dinner tonight? Why would he send an invitation on such short notice? You are Captain of the Guard! We should have been at the top of the list."

"I think we were on the top of the list," Garam said, gesturing at the paper. "Keep reading. The handwriting is hasty. I think the whole thing was just thrown together, though I'm not sure why."

She frowned. "And a dinner being thrown together is a problem?"

"No," he shook his head and regarded Rune with a grim expression. "The problem is that I have specific orders to bring *him*."

Rune blinked and drew back. "Me?"

"You can't be serious! He was in prison until just a few weeks ago." Sera's mouth tightened as she read on. "Why? He is nobody!"

Garam wiped his face with a palm. "Since I'm supposed to bring him, they obviously feel he's my responsibility. Which means I'd better find something to put him in. Even the poorest turkey can be dressed nicely for the table."

Rune gritted his teeth and sat upright. They discussed him as if he weren't right in front of them. More reminders of the temple mages. He wasn't certain what a turkey was, but he didn't doubt it was an unpleasant comparison. "I can dress myself."

Both turned to look at him, faces stern.

"And perhaps you should find an apple to stuff his mouth while you're at it." Sera shoved the letter and its envelope back into Garam's hands and climbed the stairs to the hallway.

Garam turned after her. "Where are you going?"

"To get ready! If I'm to be embarrassed by being seen with the lizard, I'm at least going to look good." Her nose turned toward the ceiling as she disappeared from sight.

The captain sighed and motioned for Rune to follow. He climbed the stairs and turned opposite the direction Sera had gone. "Come on. I'm sure I have something that will fit you. I hope you bathed this morning. We've barely got time for both of us to get ready before we have to be there."

Rune said nothing and kept his jaw clenched as he followed Garam down the hall and up the staircase. It seemed he was destined to never have a moment's peace.

The captain's private quarters weren't as luxurious as he expected, though the simple functionality could have been as much a statement about Garam's personality as it was about his salary. Comfortable, but lacking frills, like most of the clothing hung in the wardrobe.

Rune didn't dare explore the man's quarters, but he craned his head to look on shelves and under the desk, searching in vain hope his father's sword would be out where he could see it. But it was nowhere in sight and he sighed in frustration as Garam held up coat after embroidered coat to his chest.

"I don't care what color it is," he said at last, snatching a coat from Garam's hands. "Just give me something to wear."

"I'm not looking at the color," the captain growled, "I'm checking the size." But he let it pass and put the other garments away.

It was a fine piece of clothing, a long, high-collared blue coat with elaborate white embroidery on the collar and sleeves. Though they were close in height, Garam was broader through the shoulders than he and it took some thinking to determine how to make the garment fit without a tailor's services. The simplest solution was to add padding in the form of more layers underneath. Rune peeled off his new uniform, folded it, and put it aside before he donned the first of the thin linen shirts. He caught Garam looking at the scars that decorated his back from the corner of his eye.

The captain cleared his throat. "Did my men do that?"

Rune looked away and reached for another shirt. "No."

It took a few tries before he layered on enough undershirts to make the coat fit right, though they added uncomfortable bulk across his chest. It would be a bit warm, but with a chill in the air and his fond memories of Elenhiise's sweltering heat, he didn't think he'd mind.

Black trousers and a belt that fit were easier to come by, though his hands and feet were still bare when Garam said they had to leave. Rune didn't care, but the way the captain looked at his claws with disdain made it clear he felt otherwise. He adjusted his posture and moved with a stalking grace, keeping his steps silent as they left the barracks.

Rune expected a carriage would have been sent to collect them, but the street outside the barracks was empty. He'd never seen a carriage here, now that he thought of it; not within the city limits. He'd seen nobles carried in sedan chairs, from time to time, but never a carriage or horse.

With the sun sinking beyond the horizon, they walked the familiar curved avenue, though the trip felt altogether different this time. Knowing their destination was the palace, rather than the arena, made the familiar route seem fresh.

People in the streets paid them little mind. To go unnoticed was an unfamiliar experience, but a pair of men dressed as nobles were less interesting than a procession of guards with prisoners, Rune supposed, even though the bold red-and-gold coat and trousers Garam had chosen for himself stood out against the drab colors of the city's crowds.

Rune's eyes drifted upward as they reached the point in the curve where the arena and palace came into view, something he'd seen often in daylight, but never once at night. The difference stilled the breath in his chest.

The twisted spire of the Spiral Palace glowed white against the sky, its curving edge glistening with so many lights it seemed rimmed with stars. The colored banners and streamers shimmered in what had to be mage-light, each snap of the flags in the wind flashing like a crack of lightning.

Nobles clustered at the foot of the tower, though most seemed less than eager to move inside. They milled about the entryway and found excuses not to enter. The crowd parted for Garam—and Rune by extension—and allowed the two of them to the forefront. The doors to the palace stood flush with the ground, the transition from rough cobblestone to polished marble almost as jarring as the movement from cool mage-light to the ruddy glow of candles and mirrored lamps inside.

Aside from the dim hallways that branched off to either side as soon as they set foot in the palace, the first floor seemed to contain nothing but a great ballroom. Spiral fluted columns with elaborately carved bases supported a vaulted ceiling. Rune squinted as his eyes explored. The ballroom was bright, countless mirrored chandeliers casting reflections of dancing candlelight onto the gleaming floor below. The low hum of voices filled the palace, accented by the music of a chamber orchestra Rune couldn't see through the crowds. He straightened his coat and started forward, halting when Garam caught him by the shoulder.

"I'm sure this seems overwhelming," the captain said in low tones, his voice almost lost beneath the noise of the people around them. "If you stay close to me, you shouldn't have to worry about—"

"Calm down." Rune brushed his hand away. "Swinging a sword isn't all I can do." He pulled away before Garam could protest and slipped into the throng, studying faces as he walked. With each step, he grew more relaxed, a cool facade of comfort settling over his face. He'd played this game enough times in the past, knew what behavior such affairs demanded. This language, he did speak.

Heads turned as he passed, nobles murmuring amongst themselves and averting their eyes when he looked their way. It wasn't until he paused to take a glass of wine from a tray carried by a servant that anyone spoke.

"Ah, the hero of the arena. You've come a long way in little time, haven't you?" The unfamiliar man claimed a glass of his own, looking Rune up and down with a sneer as he lifted the drink to his lips. He was positively unremarkable, as far as nobles went, draped in gold and jewels and fine silks and looking very much like the balding man behind him.

Rune lifted his glass just enough to catch the scent. "So I have. I'm touched by the city's hospitality. I would not have imagined nobles would be so eager to give me the honor of combat in their arena."

"Honor?" The man barked a laugh. Wine sloshed over the rim of his glass. "Not a month past, you wore nothing but rags. Where is the honor in that?"

"What a man wears to battle means little, as long as he wears it back out. As I understand, only the wealthiest, most influential of men in the Royal City set foot in the arena more than once. By my count, I've battled more than any man here." Rune smirked, sipping his wine as the nobleman's face fell. "So what does that make me, I wonder?"

"A man who would be wise to learn the limits of his station," Sera said as she slipped from the crowd to stand beside them.

The nobleman gave her a dark look. "Indeed. I thought your brother had a tighter rein on his men. Or is his grip slipping?"

"Garam cannot be held responsible for the loose tongue of a free man, Lord Fironan. As I recall, a loose tongue was the least of your nephew's faults when he served beneath my brother." She lifted her chin and looked the man straight in the eye until he shifted in discomfort and turned away.

Rune watched with interest as the man disappeared into the sea of people, though whatever amusement he felt disappeared as soon as Sera turned her look of disapproval on him. "What?"

Her eyes flashed and she jabbed a bejeweled finger into his chest. "This is your first foray into the world of nobles and royals. Remember that you don't speak for yourself. You speak for the guard, and through that, for my brother. Do not embarrass him."

He drew back and let his face fall to careful neutrality. Agitation itched between his shoulder blades and he bit his tongue to hold a retort at bay. She stared at him expectantly and he inclined his head. "Of course."

Sera crossed her arms and studied him for a time before she seemed to accept his word. Her posture relaxed and she turned her head with a jangle of gold beads and chains to look across the grand ballroom. Gems glittered in her hair, her white braids coiled at the back of her head and draped with precious metals. She looked every bit like a noble, he decided; her high-collared dress of green and gold brocade must have cost a fortune. A wide silk drape to match wrapped around her exposed shoulders. Rings of gold encircled her wrists, and green and gold jewels flashed at her throat. Garam's position came with rank, but he wasn't sure that explained hers. Once again, he wondered what he'd embroiled himself in.

Her head whipped about without warning and she glared. "What?"

Rune averted his eyes. "You don't look like a part of the guard."

"Neither do you." The glint in her eyes became something more playful as she looked him up and down. "You carry yourself well in a noble's clothing. One might be fooled into thinking you belong in it."

"What makes you think I don't?" He offered his hand. She pursed her lips and leered down at it. "For a dance," he clarified.

Sera's brows lifted and the corners of her mouth twitched upward. "And he dances, too! Did Councilor Parthanus teach you that during your language lessons?" She laid her fingers in his grasp and he pulled her toward the sound of the orchestra.

"I doubt he would have made a very good partner. We'd never be able to decide who should lead." He helped her place her hands and joined those on the floor in a familiar waltz. She stumbled over the steps and he tried not to laugh. "Though perhaps you should ask him for a lesson."

Her nose crinkled and she stomped at his foot, narrowly missing his clawed toes.

"Hey!" He gripped her shoulders and held her at arm's length. "I was only teasing. Do you want to learn or not?"

"I can dance. I just don't know this one. It's popular in Aldaan, but..." She hesitated. "You think you can teach me?"

Instead of replying, Rune nudged her feet into place with his toes and positioned her hands again before he swept her across the floor.

It was a strange experience to revisit. The memories of the last time he'd danced flooded back as they moved faster, the spinning crowds a blur and Sera's laughter a dim ring in his ears. He recognized the music, a ballad he'd heard before. One they'd played at the solstice, though not the one he'd danced to. He squeezed his eyes closed and pulled her closer. Her hand in his felt almost the same, the rasp of his scales against the silk of her dress just as he remembered, and when he opened his eyes, for just a moment, he saw a flash of amber eyes and ebony hair in Sera's place.

He let go, stepping back and breathing deep, blinking to right his vision and scatter the unwelcome visions. Sera stumbled, laughing so hard she pressed a hand to her stomach and still looked as if she might topple over.

"What are you two doing?"

Rune was relieved to hear Garam, though he took a step back as the man joined them. "Teaching your sister to dance."

The captain looked between the two of them before he took Sera's arm to keep her from falling. "He dances? No, never mind. Of course he does. I'm starting to think he belongs in the palace as much as we do."

"Of course he does." Sera wiped her eyes and gathered her composure. "Don't forget he was invited, too."

"I didn't forget." Garam's lips pressed to a thin line. "That's why I came looking for him. The king wishes to speak to him."

Rune stared at him, unsure he'd understood, though the captain's face showed he must have. What reason would the king have to speak to him? A member of the guard, a former prisoner? The arena flashed through his mind and he grimaced at the recollection of his last opponent.

"My thoughts exactly," Garam said with a grimace of his own. "Come on. It's best we don't keep him waiting."

Even had Garam not known where to go, it wouldn't have been hard to find the king. The nobles offered him a wide berth, which Rune could only assume was so none of them could be accused of eavesdropping on whatever conversations the king held. The man didn't seem to notice the empty space around him. He stood with a woman on his arm, the two of them talking and laughing with a pair of men who were as forgettable as the man Rune had spoken to before. Fironan, Sera called him? Finoran? He shook his head and adjusted his borrowed clothing as Garam led him forward.

The king looked just as Rune expected, based on his knowledge of kings and his encounter with the man's son. Fit and youthful in build, if not the rest of his appearance. His blond hair sported gray wings at his temples and fine lines decorated the skin around his eyes and mouth. The king was not quite as tall as Rune or Garam, but stood straight and proud, and the crown he wore resembled mountain peaks.

He turned to greet them with a pleasant expression, though his eyes were hard and impassive, guarding whatever impression he actually had. The woman at his side gave away little more, her dark eyes untouched by her smile as she studied them. She looked familiar, her gentle face and the silver wings in her auburn hair lending her a matronly look, but Rune couldn't place her.

"Ah, the champion of the arena! I can't say we've ever had one of those before." The king waved the other men away. They reminded Rune of rats, the way they hunched and scurried off at their dismissal, both of them leering over their shoulders.

"Sire," Garam said as he bowed in greeting. "Lady Bryndis."

Rune only inclined his head. "King Vicamros, ruler of the

three provinces and the Royal City. I could have recognized you without the crown, your son looks so much like you."

The king's expression remained unchanged, though Bryndis's smile faded.

Garam coughed.

"He does," Vicamros agreed. His eyes narrowed at the corners with the faintest of smiles. "He's a good lad, clever and strong. He's had a great deal of training with a sword, but things are different in a match where the outcome is death. It would seem I'm fortunate to still have the boy, given the way your match ended." The steel glint never left his blue eyes. "I find it unlikely you knew who he was. Tell me, what stayed your hand?"

Rune lowered his eyes and clasped his hands behind his back. "Had I known later matches would require me to fight children, I'd have thrown a fight much sooner."

"He is the prince. He knew the consequences of his actions long before he set foot in the arena," Bryndis said.

Garam shifted forward, but paused when Sera laid a hand on his arm.

"He is a boy," Rune said, surprising himself with the patience and evenness in his voice. "Too young to understand the consequences, too young to realize he isn't invincible. It wasn't so long ago that I was in the same position. I understand now how fortunate I was to live."

The king chuckled. "And fortunate to live yet, it seems. My son's pride is bruised and he'll endure some teasing for having lost and been spared, I'm sure, but it is better to be teased and alive than foolish and dead. I was not present for his match, and had I been there and aware it was to happen, it wouldn't have taken place at all."

"I'd heard rumors the councilors were displeased that Rune was pulled from the arena. It was suggested he be executed for shaming the crown prince, seeing how he was only an inmate."

Sera held tight to Garam as she spoke, though her pale eyes flicked in Rune's direction. "I take it you don't feel the same?"

Vicamros rubbed his brows with a thumb and sighed. "The councilors brought that shame down on him. I've already spoken to them about indulging his fancies. I don't share their opinion, no." He spread his hands in an earnest gesture as his gaze slid back to Rune. "I thank you for having mercy on the lad."

"Mercy would have been sparing him from his father's anger," Rune said, allowing himself a smile when he saw the curve of the king's lips. "I'm sure I have done the boy no services."

"No, none for the boy." Vicamros laughed, though his mirth faded quickly as he scanned the room. "Just for me. And not the last service there is to ask, it seems. If you're one of Captain Kaith's men now, you'll be doing me a great service in only a handful of days. I suppose there's no more sense in waiting to announce things."

Rune's smile died on his lips. Ominous words, made more ominous by the way the king cleared his throat and gestured for attention.

"His majesty speaks!" Garam shouted, bringing the room to silence. Nobles and servants alike turned to face their ruler. The music ended with a few strident notes. Sera pulled Garam back and Rune followed without being told, leaving a wide space around the king again. Even Bryndis stepped away, her face solemn.

"My friends," Vicamros started, his strong voice reverberating in the hall. "I am grateful to all who were able to attend on such short notice. It is my hope that this evening has served as a pleasant event for you to remember. I fear for some of you, it may be your last visit to the Spiral Palace."

Rune took another step back. He skimmed the faces of people around him as they shifted from merry to concerned. His mind went to Redoram, to the lessons on the country and its people, to his conversation with Sera just that afternoon about the conflict in the city. He saw Garam straighten as if to brace for bad news, saw Sera take his hand into hers. This was a speech they'd heard before, new only to him. A great service, the king said. Rune cursed.

"Early this afternoon, I received word from the province of Lore. The Grand College has announced its intention to rebel against the Triad. The college moves an army of mages toward Aldaan's border even now." Vicamros let his gaze drift over the countless people in the ballroom, though his eyes lingered nowhere. The crowd was a sea of solemn and fearful faces. "With the barriers in place to prevent use of magic, the Royal City itself cannot be harmed by their efforts. Our army will move to defend Aldaan against the mages and bring the college in Lore under control. The best men of the guard will be joining them. Between their numbers, I fear that accounts for a good many of you, and many more of your children."

An unpleasant murmur rolled through the room. "When are we to move?" someone asked from nearby.

The king seemed unruffled. "Our forces will begin to mobilize first thing in the morning. We cannot afford to wait any longer than that. Further orders will be given shortly, as I am about to meet with my council to determine which units are to be stationed where. Please, enjoy the feast and the festivities for tonight. Tomorrow, we are at war."

The words made Rune's stomach drop, and he cursed again.

TIES THAT BIND

EYRION TOLMARNI PRIDED HIMSELF ON THE DISCIPLINE INSTILLED IN his students.

They were not his pupils directly; he really had little to do with their education at all, but considering he had hand-selected every professor still practicing in the Grand College of Lore, it was hard to think of them as anything else. They were trained by teachers of his choosing, raised through the ranks of color by the council, and put in Master white by his own hand.

Knowing this woman had worn white without being raised to it by himself or his predecessor bothered him.

Eryrion never lost his composure, though he raised his chin an inch and squared his shoulders as he moved down the hallway to his private quarters. It was bad enough she'd come to his college dressed in the color reserved for Master mages, worse that she'd brought two others with her. But that he had recognized her—a fact he'd hidden from the rest of the council, pretending not to—was what bothered him most.

He didn't doubt there were factions of mages he didn't know about, groups scattered across the globe that had likely existed for just as long as the Grand College. He'd encountered one or two in his time, but they had their own methods for teaching and sorted their ranks according to their own practices, befitting their own societies. But this woman, with her hair and eyes bleached like his own, claimed the title of Archmage.

The very notion made Eyrion seethe. *He* was Archmage. Headmaster of the Grand College of Lore, leader of all mages beneath the rule of King Vicamros and beyond. And this woman, standing in the hallway in front of the door to his quarters, was a problem.

Envesi faced him when he approached and dipped in a curtsy he knew was insincere. She wore the rough-spun clothing of a laundry maid, but she carried herself no differently than she had when she'd arrived. "Headmaster Tolmarni."

"I have no laundry for you to collect this evening." He tried to ignore her, turning to his door as he drew a ring of keys from his robes. "I will send a mageling with it when I do."

"Forgive me, headmaster, but I am not here to collect laundry." There was an edge in her voice, like honed ice. "I have been hoping to speak with you, but it seems the past several days have kept us both busy. With the college mages preparing for the impending war, I thought we should speak of what you are moving against."

Eyrion couldn't keep from pursing his lips. "I am Archmage of Lore and leader of the Grand College. I know perfectly well what we move against without a laundry maid to tell me." He stepped into his quarters and was startled when she slipped in after him and positioned herself just inside the door. Annoyance twisted to anger, and he turned with admonishment ready on his tongue.

"Really, Eyrion," she said before he could deliver it. "Do you mean to send your people to war without first releasing their power?"

Though her presumptuousness made him bristle, her words gave him pause. He didn't even notice that she'd addressed him by name. Releasing their power? "What under Brant's shaking branches does that mean?"

The corners of her lips quirked upward, a look of amusement drawn on her face. "So there are no free mages in your employ? Curious. With how advanced the college claims to be these days, I'd have thought you would have unbound your Masters by now."

His eyes narrowed. He was not the only one who knew of her failed experiments, the convolutions and corruption of magic she'd spun on the remote island where she made herself Archmage. The council had not been pleased with his choice to allow her to remain in the college with her companions, but what other choices were there? Bylaws older than the college itself forbade the severance of power, and it was better to keep mages of questionable intent where they could be watched. Envesi's attempts to create a free mage had been the talk of the council for weeks—all the more reason for him to pretend they'd never met. But the concept of unbinding *existing* magic had never come up. A hint of curiosity pricked at the back of his mind.

She moved farther into his quarters and studied the fine furnishings with an unreadable expression. "The power of a single free mage could flatten an army, if they know how to wield it. How do you plan to keep your army safe?"

Eyrion did not reply right away. Instead, he studied her, his expression unchanging. It was no concern of hers, and yet he found himself drawn to answer, to see what other information might spill free if he humored her. "Even free mages can be barred from touching energy sources. My mages are trained well. If they are fast enough, they can place a barrier between any enemy and the flows."

"So you mean to take them by surprise?"

"Surprise may not be necessary." He closed the door and sealed them in privacy. His rooms were always warded against spying eyes and ears, but he found himself probing for the wards nonetheless. "Aldaan's numbers pale in comparison to ours. College-trained mages might even outnumber them one hundred to one." Whether or not that many college-trained mages would answer his call to arms, however, was yet to be seen. Mages had been trickling in for days, forming new companies to join those already on the move. Eyrion had sent mages not only toward Aldaan, but toward Roberian and the Royal City, as well. The latter were not meant as an attack force, but a defense against possible Aldaanan retaliation. Then there were major outposts to be guarded in Lore itself, and the college, which could not be left untended. Even with war brewing, life went on as usual within the college, classes and council meetings held like clockwork.

Then again, there was a laundry maid in his room, speaking to him of issues the council had raised as part of their protest at least a dozen times. A laundry maid who claimed she had been an Archmage, he reminded himself. A laundry maid who had once been his rival for position of headmaster. Perhaps things were not going on as usual.

"And even with a hundred mages to their one, if they fail to cut the Aldaanan mages off from the flows before they can take hold, they'll be smashed like ants beneath a free mage's foot." Envesi moved in a regal way, every bit a woman who was used to having power that came from rank, not magecraft. She did not seat herself, but she did stop before the low couches in the sitting room at the front of his suite, as if she expected a long conversation to come. "That's why I've come to speak to you, Eyrion."

The hair on the back of his neck stood, and he set his jaw. "The council knows of your practices. This isn't your secluded island, where you can expect to indulge in the same perversions of magic."

She sighed and spread her arms with a shrug that signaled defeat. "That creature was a mistake, one I've spent a great number of years regretting. I had hoped to rectify the problem and have the abomination unmade, but the plan fell through. Partially due to the patron of my temple. That is not, however, what I'm speaking of. I do not mean to create free mages for your armies. I mean to free the mages who follow you now. Unbinding their power, breaking fetters imposed on us by the ancient Aldaanan, so that we might rival their capability again."

Eyrion didn't recall crossing the room, but he found himself sinking into the cushions of a couch. He stared at her in disbelief. "Such a suggestion is madness. If there were a way to unbind affinities, surely one of the college mages would have discovered it by now."

"Oh, but one has." She seated herself across from him and clasped her hands in her lap. "My uncle began the research. I had hoped to assist him with it when I studied here, before my family offered me in marriage. I believe it is entirely possible to unravel the bindings and free our own magic and I believe I know the way, but there is a small problem to overcome, first."

A problem, a price. He should have expected as much. "What manner of problem?"

"The council heard of Lomithrandel's creation, but they were not told the whole truth of what he was. He was a monster, you see," Envesi said, as nonchalantly as if stating the weather. "Releasing the bindings of his power resulted in physical corruption, some sort of taint. It gave him a form that was part man and part beast."

Eyrion shuddered. "And unbinding my own magic would have the same result?"

She nodded. "Which is why we are speaking now. I am certain I can find a way to stave off the damage, but like anything else, it requires practice."

The pieces began to fit together in his head. There was an inflection in her words, a note he didn't like. But the notion of free magic—all the power of the world's energy at his fingertips—was tantalizing. He turned that thought over in his head, considered what it could mean. Eyrion Tolmarni, the first Archmage to practice free magic. He leaned back into the cushions and steepled his fingers together. "Go on."

Envesi smiled coldly and in spite of himself, the expression gave him a thrill.

KYTENIA LEAPED to her feet as the door opened, her heart in her throat. Master Edagan slipped out of the Archmage's private quarters and closed the door, her face stern as etched stone. She expected the Master to say something. When she didn't, Kytenia cleared her throat. "The Archmage, is he...?"

"A stroke," Edagan said with a stiff incline of her head. "He is fortunate you brought his meal when you did."

Kytenia exhaled and her shoulders sagged, the tremble finally gone from her hands. She'd thought him lost when she discovered him on the floor, unable to rise or speak. There was little magic could do to prevent the issues that came with old age and while a stroke was not entirely unexpected, the fact it had happened was still troubling.

"He's weaker now, his words a bit muddled. He will need time to rest, but I expect he will recover. I've done what I can, but it may be wise for you to remain by his side for the night," Edagan said. She was stronger in healing than Anaide, perhaps the strongest Master left in the temple after Nondar. If she thought Nondar needed supervision, Kytenia would not disobey.

"Yes, Master. Thank you." Kytenia bowed her head, touching fingers to her heart in a gesture of sincerity. What would have happened if she'd been late to return from dinner? The thought sent a shudder rolling up her spine.

Edagan sniffed and gave a slight nod as she brushed past and left Kytenia alone. She had always been a woman of few words —or, few words for magelings, Kytenia thought with a wry smile. From what she understood, the Masters all talked Firal's ear off.

Kytenia dashed that thought as soon as it arrived. Thinking

about Firal always led to thoughts of Vahnil, and even a year later, those thoughts made her heart wrench. Instead she smoothed her hair and her robes and bolstered her courage before she stepped into the Archmage's rooms.

The temple's central tower was not large enough to offer a luxurious suite, but the modesty of the furnishings inside surprised her. The simple wooden furniture was not all that different from what the magelings were given. A pair of padded benches stood in the near corner with a low table set before them. Full bookshelves were nestled in the corner opposite. A small bowl of fruit and a pair of pitchers stood on a table ringed by three chairs, and a canvas folding screen painted with lilies hid the last corner of the room. Kytenia closed the door behind her and crept forward to peer past the screen, to the bed where Nondar lay.

He rested with his eyes closed. Her heart hammered until she saw the slight rise and fall of his chest. With his pallid expression and his hands folded on his chest, the Archmage looked older and more frail than ever before. She stared at him until one of his bushy white brows lifted and one blue eye opened to look at her.

Kytenia gulped and tucked her chin to her chest. "I apologize, Archmage. I didn't mean to stare. I didn't want to disturb you if you were asleep."

"No," Nondar replied with some difficulty. He worked for a moment before he could say anything else. "Rather tired, but not asleep." He stirred—not much, but enough to move semi-upright against the pillows and open his other eye. He'd regained a great deal of mobility and muscle control in the hours Edagan had spent with him, but one side of his face still sagged, making his frown seem even more unpleasant than usual.

"Master Edagan said I should sit with you tonight." Kytenia put her hands behind her back, unable to keep from fidgeting. He hadn't known her when she found him in his office. She'd almost feared he wouldn't remember her at all.

Nondar snorted, curling his upper lip in disgust. Half of his upper lip, at least. "Edagan can kiss a goat. A night's rest and I'll be back to work, right as rain." His words slurred softly, and her brow furrowed as she listened to him. He didn't give her time to dwell on it. "Bring me a drink, girl. My mouth is dry."

Kytenia hurried to the table and looked into the silver pitchers. There was wine punch and water, as well as something that smelled like cider. She filled a cup halfway with water and took it to the Archmage's bedside.

His grasp was weak, but Nondar took it and lifted the cup to his lips for a long draught. "Ah, better. Fetch a pen and paper, will you?"

"I don't think you're in any condition to be writing, Archmage."

Again, he snorted. "Archmages don't write. Their apprentices do. Now hurry and fetch it, you've a... a... well, a message to write."

She bit her lip. "A dictation to take?" Her eyes searched the room again before she decided to check the shelves. They looked much like Nondar's office always had, stuffed full of books and scrolls and messily stacked papers.

"That's what I said," Nondar snapped.

Kytenia cringed as she hunted through the shelves to find a blank sheet. Then she fished a pen from a jar and found a mostly-full bottle of ink. Beneath another mess of paper, an ink-stained board lay half hidden. She wiggled it free and carried her supplies to the old mage's bedside. "Who am I writing to, Master?"

He stared at the paper in her hands for a long while. Eventually, his eyes lifted to her face as his brow knit. "You know, child, I've forgotten."

Kytenia lowered her pen. What relief she'd felt after speaking with Edagan faded, replaced with concern for more than just the old Master's health. She couldn't help but wonder what had been important enough to warrant a message sent from his bedside. That he'd forgotten so easily was worrisome. A side effect of a stroke, she knew, but the knowledge only made things worse. With his body so frail, how was he to control the energy flows well enough to wield magic? If his memory was failing, how was he to sit through meetings with the other Masters? How was he to lead the temple? He couldn't even speak clearly.

A knock at the door jarred the thoughts from her head and both she and Nondar turned toward it. There was just enough of a pause to be courteous before the door creaked open and someone stepped inside. Kytenia raised a brow when her sister rounded the privacy screen, her arms laden with pillows and blankets.

Shymin froze in place, clearly not having expected Nondar to be awake. She shuffled from foot to foot for a moment before she hefted the bedding in her arms. "Master Edagan told me to bring these up, Archmage. I apologize for interrupting. She said Kytenia would need them."

Nondar leaned back into the pillows, grumbling beneath his breath. "I am a grown man, I have no need of a mageling for a babysitter."

Shymin blinked, startled by his slurring speech. She shot a wary glance to Kytenia, who shook her head.

"I'm not your babysitter, I'm your apprentice." Kytenia put the writing supplies aside and stood to take the bedding from her sister's arms. "It's perfectly normal for an apprentice to stay close at hand, just in case their Master has need of something."

Shymin's eyebrows lifted with unspoken questions. Kytenia ignored them.

"And if I have need of something, I shall call for you then," Nondar protested, but Kytenia piled the blankets and pillows onto one of the couches anyway.

"Archmage, may I borrow Kytenia for a moment?" Shymin asked.

He waved one knobby hand. "Go ahead. Perhaps I'll recall what that message was about while it's quiet enough to think."

Shymin curtsied and gave Kytenia a shadowed look as she

started for the door. With a grimace, Kytenia followed her into the hall. The door of Nondar's quarters was no more than closed behind them before Shymin wheeled on her.

"Apprentice to the Archmage?" Shymin all but cried. "When did this happen? Why didn't you tell me?"

Kytenia made a hushing motion with both hands. "Just this afternoon. I wasn't keeping it from you. I meant to tell you tonight, but that was before he..." she trailed off. She didn't know if the other Masters would mention Nondar's condition to anyone else, now that she thought of it. There were plenty of reasons to keep it quiet, and she was sure they wouldn't appreciate her informing the whole Temple. "Before he fell," she finished. "He's supposed to have his cane with him all the time, but he leaves it hanging on his desk. He's to rest for a few days while the other Masters make sure he's fit to be up and about. You know how careful you have to be when healing the elderly. It's so easy to exhaust them."

Shymin eyed her suspiciously, but to her relief, she didn't press the matter. "So what do you suppose he means by making you his apprentice?"

"I don't think he means anything by it." Kytenia flushed in spite of herself. "I think I was just fortunate enough to be the mageling closest at hand when he decided he needed one."

"Aren't apprentices normally schooled for the purpose of—"

"I'm still a mageling, Shymin," Kytenia interrupted. "And in green, no less. I know his former position still hasn't been filled, but only Masters are qualified. Besides, he's the Archmage now, not Master of healing. Archmages can have whatever sort of assistant they need."

Shymin frowned, but nodded. "Well, all right. Though I still think it's strange. I suppose this means you'll be staying here for a few nights?"

Kytenia nodded back. "At least until Edagan is certain he doesn't have any more fractured bones. I'll still be attending classes, though, so I'll be down to our room first thing in the morning to change and get my notes."

"All right," Shymin sighed. She tugged at the collar of her robes. "It'll be strange not to have you nearby at night, but I'll get enough breakfast for both of us and we can talk about it then. Just try not to strangle the old goat before daybreak."

Kytenia laughed as her sister turned to leave. "I'll try. Oh, and Shymin? Please don't tell Rikka about all this. It'd be the talk of the temple before nightfall tomorrow, and I'd like to keep it secret until I know exactly what I'm in for."

Shymin's mouth took a sour twist, but she nodded before she disappeared down the hall.

***

"I STILL DON'T THINK this is a good idea."

Firal bit her tongue and struggled to keep from rolling her eyes as she adjusted her necklace one last time. It was a simple piece for a queen, but she preferred the pendant with its relief of Ilmenhith's seven-pointed star to the glittering jewels in which Kifel had draped her. She no longer thought of the necklace as a gift from her mother, but as a symbol of her father's legacy. It seemed a fitting choice for tonight. "You've said as much a dozen times already. It's not going to change anything, Vahn. We need to do this. In fact, we needed to do it a long time ago." She turned from the mirror and crossed to the bed where he sat, tugging on his boots. His cape lay across the foot of the bed. She picked it up.

Vahn grimaced, but stood to let her drape it over his shoulders. "I think we're overdressed, as well."

"I am the queen and you are my consort and king-regent. We can't possibly be overdressed. I'm sure your father will be wearing his finest as well." She adjusted the drape of the rich purple fabric and fastened the chain at the front. "You should be grateful this is just a quiet dinner in your father's home, rather than a palatial affair."

"That you think a dinner with my father is a quiet affair is the first indication you don't know what we're getting into," Vahn said.

Firal slapped his shoulder. "Go make sure the carriage is ready. I'll fetch Lumia and will be along right after you."

Vahn gave her one last disapproving look and turned to leave with a mutter beneath his breath. She paid it no mind, smoothing her hair with both hands as she made her way into the small nursery adjacent to their room. Medreal sat on the floor, fastening the tiny buttons up the back of the baby's dress. The stewardess acted as if she didn't see Firal coming, but a hint of a smile pulled the corners of her mouth.

"You don't have to pretend you didn't hear us." Firal knelt to take the girl once Medreal was done. "The door wasn't even closed."

"I apologize, my queen. It isn't my place," Medreal said, an almost wistful look in her dark eyes as she watched Firal settle Lumia against her shoulder. The baby burbled happily, and the stewardess hurried to fetch a cloth to drape over the shoulder of Firal's dress. "But Vahnil is more like his father than he realizes. They're both bullheaded when it comes to their relationship. No one party is at fault for this meeting being so long overdue."

"I know." Firal tucked the cloth in between the infant and her shoulder. "And this meeting couldn't come at a worse time. I've so many other things to worry about. It would have been nice if I'd received more than a day's notice."

Medreal frowned and clasped her hands in front of her apron. "May I speak as an adviser, my queen?"

"Of course, Medreal. You run the palace practically without supervision, you know your word is valuable to me."

The old woman inclined her head. "Meeting with Lord Tanrys is of utmost importance. I don't like the man or his ego, but he is a valuable resource to you. You want him on your side, my queen, believe me."

Firal quirked a brow and lowered her voice. "What more do you have to tell me?"

"That you're going to be late to dinner if you don't hurry along. Shoo, shoo!" Medreal waved her out of the nursery with both hands. "Shall I walk you to the door, or do you think you can find your way on your own?"

Snorting a laugh, Firal turned on her heel and swept out of the nursery. "There are some things I can still do on my own, thank you. We'll speak in the morning over tea."

"Of course, my queen." Medreal bowed and began to gather the baby's toys from the floor.

Firal stroked the baby's back as she made her way through the palace. The bustle castle business never changed. Young maids and servants ducked out of Firal's way with murmured apologies, while the older women among the staff always paused to peek at the baby and smile. Firal made her way down the grand, sweeping staircases in the throne room and paused to spare a glance for the dais.

By contrast, the throne room hadn't gone unchanged. Kifel's throne had become hers, but an equally ornate seat now stood beside it for Vahnil. She wasn't sure where the second throne had come from; Medreal had seen to its placement the day after the wedding. Firal couldn't help but wonder if it had been her mother's, stowed away after Envesi distanced herself from the king. She shook her head and hurried on her way. Vahn was unsettled enough as it was. She didn't want to agitate him further by making him wait.

A pair of guardsmen waited by the front doors. They bowed and she acknowledged them with a slight incline of her head as she slipped past, but to her surprise, the two of them fell in step behind her. She rarely ventured outside the palace, and though her few ventures were always accompanied by guards, she had assumed a trip to her father-in-law's house would be different.

Perhaps that had been foolish. Silent, she bounced Lumia against her shoulder and made her way toward the waiting carriage.

Vahn stood beside it with his hands clasped behind his back, a half-dozen horsemen from the city guard creating a semi-circle around the back side of the coach. Firal's brows lifted, but she said nothing aside from a murmured thank-you as Vahn helped her into the carriage and slipped in after her. She allowed herself a frown as she settled on one of the velvet cushions and shifted Lumia to her lap.

"What?" Vahn asked.

A footman closed the door and the carriage swayed as he, the driver, and the two guards who had followed her from the palace climbed to their places. Her whole body swayed as the carriage jerked into motion, and she turned her head to avoid Vahn's gaze. "Just thinking on how things have changed, I suppose. It's strange to recall that when I first saw this city, I walked its streets alone."

"Even Kifel didn't travel alone," he murmured.

Firal glanced past the curtain in the carriage's rear window. The horsemen followed close behind. "I just think eight men is excessive, that's all. And for the record, Kifel came to the temple alone several times."

He gave her a reprimanding look. "And was surrounded by mages in his employ. My father keeps an entourage, himself, now that we're married. Even he isn't guaranteed safety in the city. Eight men for the three of us is not many. Three for you, three for Lulu, two for myself."

She smirked. "Lulu?"

Vahn flushed. "Lumia. Sorry. It's just a pet name that seems to have stuck."

"No, it's all right." She smiled down at the infant in her lap, who kicked her legs and cooed when she saw her father. "Lulu. I like it."

He glanced in her direction, a hint of appreciation in his eyes, but he said no more. Both in front of and behind them, the sound of horseshoes rang against the stone streets, turning the noise of the city to little more than a hum around their carriage. Firal grew quiet, gazing through the fine glass windows.

While Vahn's family had resided within the palace walls during his youth, his family owned a stately home elsewhere. The Tanrys family had gone back to it after Ennil retired from his position as Captain of the Ilmenhith Guard. And while they were a family of wealth even before Ennil had scaled the ranks of the guard, the estate had only grown more resplendent after his decades serving as the king's protective hand over the city.

Most of the wealthy chose to keep manors just outside the city, where they could carve out larger pieces of land. The Tanrys estate, on the other hand, was nestled within the city itself. An acre of land would not have been impressive elsewhere, but in the midst of high, crowded buildings, it stood out as a remarkable oasis. Firal watched it loom ever larger as she gently freed a curl of her ebony hair from Lumia's grasp.

Gardens sprawled across the estate and spilled through the tall iron fences and scrollwork gates that kept the rest of the city at bay. Cool gray slate formed a walkway that led from the gates to the front of the manor house. A narrower path branched off toward the stables at the back of the estate. The house itself seemed similar enough to the rest of the city's buildings, tall and graceful and made of pale stone, though the unusual window boxes that spilled flowers down the front of the house did set it apart.

"I've never seen this part of the city," Firal murmured as the carriage halted. Outside, the driver and footman spoke to the guards on horseback in low voices. "I think I would recall this place if I'd seen it before."

"Father likes being different. He enjoys the recognition," Vahn said, though the words were devoid of the bitterness she'd expected. Instead, a hint of respect colored his tone. She eyed him curiously but he didn't say anything else as he shifted to open the carriage door.

His hand brushed it just as the footman opened the door from the other side. A hint of displeasure pinched the corners of Vahn's eyes and for a moment, Firal suspected he found their entourage as disheartening as she did.

Vahn slipped out of the carriage first and righted his cape before he turned to offer Firal his hand before the footman could interfere. She accepted the help, cradling Lumia against her chest with her other arm. Vahn helped her straighten her skirts while the footman smoothed the back of Vahn's cape. Before any of them were presentable, a man in livery appeared at the front door of the manor.

The half-dozen guards on horseback dismounted when they saw him. They positioned their horses in a half-ring behind their queen and king-regent as the gates of the estate swung open.

"Lord Ennil Tanrys gladly receives Your Majesties," the liveryman said, motioning them in with a wide flourish.

The guards exchanged a few quiet words with the carriage driver and then with Vahn. The two guards without horses remained beside the carriage as the rest of the gathering moved into the fenced estate. More liveried men came from behind the house, intercepting them to take the horses and allow the guards to fall in around their charges.

The men walked close at her heels and Firal didn't like it one bit. She tried to ignore them and inched closer to Vahn's side as they took the front stairs in tandem. Vahn caught her elbow and gave it a squeeze, offering both support and solidarity as they stepped into the house and the large receiving room where Ennil waited.

"My lady," Ennil said, dropping in a graceful bow that was more respectful than she'd expected, given their brief first meeting. "It is an honor to receive you within my humble home."

She tried not to laugh. The house was anything but humble, as magnificent inside as the gardens were outside. "Thank you, Lord Tanrys. I am grateful to be afforded your hospitality." Her eyes were drawn to a wide banner of scarlet and gold above the entryway, embroidered with the crest she recalled from the cape Ennil had worn when he visited the palace. She tried not to stare, unable to puzzle out what exactly the crest was. A bird of some sort, she thought.

Arched doorways led into sitting rooms and a formal parlor, each of them filled with elegance. Most of the furnishings were polished dark wood with red upholstery and gilt edging, though clashing accents in Ilmenhith's colors of silver and blue were sprinkled throughout. Firal didn't see any serving staff as Ennil led them past the parlor and into a grand dining room, but she didn't doubt their existence. Not a speck of dust marred the furniture.

The dining table was large enough to host twenty, though only four places were set. The dishes were delicate porcelain, accompanied by crystal goblets as fine as any the palace could afford. Trays of food were already present, though as they stepped in, a woman entered the room with another. "Ennil, would you—oh! You didn't tell me they were here already!"

A smile of surprising warmth split Ennil's features as he joined her and plucked the tray of vegetables from her hands. "Vivenne," he said, and placed a kiss on her cheek. "See to your granddaughter. I'll fetch the rest."

Vivenne's bright eyes sparkled as they turned to Firal and Lumia and, oddly, Firal felt a lump rise in her throat. Vahn bore more of a resemblance to his mother than his father, just as much spirit in her blue eyes as what could be found in her son's. Her pale blonde hair fell to her waist in tight ringlets, and though age had put gray at her temples and laugh lines at the corners of her eyes, her plump face was without wrinkles. A stained apron she seemed to have forgotten covered her green brocade dress. She hurried to join Firal and Vahn at the far side of the room. "Oh, let me see her!" she cried as she swept both Firal and the baby into a hug.

"She mothers everybody," Vahn muttered, earning himself a playful slap on the arm.

"Oh, hush you! I've every right to mother your wife. I am her mother now!" Vivenne held Firal at arm's length. "Oh, you're magnificent. I couldn't have asked for a more lovely daughter. And that baby! Why, her hair's just like yours. Here! Let me see her pretty face." She scooped Lumia up before Firal could do more than laugh.

"Mother, please. You act like you've never seen a baby before."

Vivenne gave him a reprimanding look as she cradled Lumia to her bosom. "I've not seen this one, and look at how big she's grown already! Oh, her head still bobbles, the precious dear! How old is she now, a month?"

"Two, almost." Firal's throat stuck. She swallowed hard. Vivenne looked every bit the part of a proud grandmother, and despite all she knew, she felt a pang of remorse for the relationship she and her own mother had never had.

"And here I am, just seeing her for the first time." Vivenne gave Vahn a shadowed look.

He cleared his throat. "You've prepared tonight's dinner yourself, Mother?"

"She thought it best that the staff be given the night off. Fewer prying eyes and ears." Ennil returned from the other room with a pair of wine bottles. He gestured toward the table with them as his eyes skimmed the armed men in the doorway. Firal raised a brow and he went on. "The royal family's business shouldn't be the gossip of Ilmenhith. And whether we like it or not, we're now a part of it. Sit, please."

Vahn pulled out a chair and motioned for Firal to seat herself. After she did, he drew back another chair for his mother. "And whether you like it or not, the royal family's business will always be the gossip of Ilmenhith. You can't avoid that forever, Father, no matter how you try to avoid us."

Ennil's mouth tightened.

"Oh, look at her eyes," Vivenne cooed, stroking Lumia's cheek. For all that she sounded distracted, her face was pinched with anxiety, and Firal felt a stroke of pity for the woman. Though Vivenne tried to diffuse it with the baby's presence, the tension between the two men didn't slacken in the least.

Ennil stared at his son for a long moment, and the silence grew so thick it made Firal's scalp prickle. Then at last he dropped his gaze to the baby in his wife's arms, dispelling the sense of dread. "They are an unusual color, aren't they?"

Firal straightened in her chair. "It runs in the family, it seems."

"Something to do with being the child of a mage, I suppose," Vivenne said, smiling up at her. "Just lovely. Such a dear. I had hoped to have more children than just Vahnil, though I suppose it's best that he ended up being our only, what with the handful he was."

"Is," Ennil grumbled.

Vahn gave his father a hard look as he filled plates for himself and Firal. "Carus," he called over his shoulder. One of the guardsmen stepped forward as Vahn lifted Firal's plate. "Test the queen's food."

"Don't be silly," Firal chided. She reached for her food and scowled when he lifted it beyond her fingers to pass it to the soldier behind her. "Vahn, we're at your family's home. Your mother made this herself!"

A look of amusement crossed Ennil's face as the soldier tasted everything on the plate. "Forgive me, Majesty, but your husband is wise." Firal turned to him, startled, and he gave a grim smile. "You should trust no one, my lady. Those who don't wish to kill you will wish to control you instead."

She tensed and cast a wary glance toward Vivenne and Lumia. The woman was pale, staring at her husband in disbelief. Slowly, Firal's eyes drifted back to Ennil. "And which party do you fall in?"

Ennil rested his elbows on the table, laced his fingers together and watched with a steel gleam in his blue eyes.

Vahn filled a pair of goblets with wine from the table and held one up for Carus to take. Firal didn't need to look to know the soldier would be as pale as Vivenne. She heard him sip and swallow hard, and then he passed both wine and food back to Vahn. "Safe, King-regent."

Vivenne exhaled heavily, her shoulders sagging with the weight of relief. Firal did not stir.

"Control, my queen," Ennil said at last. He filled his own goblet and took a long draught. "But only enough to keep the peace and set things straight in the capital. No more than your mages want of you, I'm sure."

Firal's eyes narrowed and she bit her tongue to keep it still. The mages scolded her often enough about speaking without thought, and though she knew they were right, the idea of heeding the advice of mages immediately after his jibe about their control made her seethe. He was right, though. There were times her council—the mages—squabbled over making decisions as if she weren't even there. Her jaw tightened, her anger stirred anew. "I have no intention of being a mouthpiece instead of a queen. The mages offer valuable counsel, but I will not let myself be a puppet on their strings or yours."

"Very well, not a puppet. A dancing bear, perhaps? Ready to maul us all, the moment she's off the leash." Ennil smirked, lifting his goblet as if in toast.

Vahn slammed his hands down on the table and thrust himself from his chair. "You will not speak to your queen like that!"

"And you will stop calling yourself king-regent!" Ennil snapped. "Your trepidation only makes this whole situation worse. You are ruling as your wife recovers, and your child is the heir to the throne. You could be king, boy! You bow to your wife as head of the kingdom and bow to no one else. Ilmenhith needs strength and decisiveness."

"And if I am king, you will not speak to me in that manner either," Vahn said through clenched teeth.

Ennil stared at him for a time, his gaze weighted, judging. Then he burst into laughter, put down his wine, and clapped slowly. "Very good! Much improved, and very quickly at that. Please, sit. If it pleases you. Now that your head is in the right place, there is much for us to discuss, Majesties."

Vahn blinked and shot Firal a confused glance. She raised a brow, inclining her head toward his chair. He sank back into it, eyeing his father distrustfully. She didn't blame him. Only an instant before, his father had been aggressive, power-hungry. The sudden, respectful shift in the man's tone threw her off.

Vivenne shook her head and stared at Lumia, the child now drowsing in her arms. "You know I don't like it when you play those games, Ennil."

"You have an unusual way of speaking to people. I see why you aren't popular in the palace." Firal drew herself up in such a queenly fashion that even the mages would have been pleased. "Allow me to make one thing clear, Lord Tanrys. You are not in my good favor, nor in that of my husband, and you are remarkably fortunate that you've not yet been arrested for your mouth tonight. That can change quite easily, of course, so I allow you one opportunity to explain yourself, before I have you dragged off to the dungeon for your disgraceful show of insolence and borderline treasonous suggestions to your son."

Ennil's brows lifted, the look on his face a mix of surprise and what she thought might be respect. "My apologies, Majesty. I don't wish to disrespect my queen, but I must know I have your full attention if I am to be of any assistance."

"And how would a retired noble be of assistance to me?" Firal asked, just a hint of impatience in her tone.

"I've already said. I will be part of your council, and we need to discuss matters now. You will need my presence desperately, if I am to extricate you from the mages as the balance of power shifts among them."

She kept her expression neutral, though a prickling sense of uneasiness crept up her spine. "Why would I need your help when I have the Archmage?"

"Because, my lady," Ennil said earnestly. "The Archmage is dying."

BASILISK

THE DOORKNOB TURNED, BUT THE DOOR DIDN'T MOVE WHEN HE pushed. Rune gritted his teeth and threw his shoulder against it. The latch strained but held fast. He glanced down the hallway behind him before he took a step back and kicked the door hard enough that the walls shook. He grimaced.

At any moment, the barracks would spring to life as soldiers scrambled to organize their belongings and prepare for departure. Any second, someone would realize he was gone. He flexed his toes and kicked again. Wood splintered around the latch. The door flipped open and banged into the wall behind it.

Rune darted into the dark office on the other side, his heart hammering in his chest. His eyes scoured the walls, the shelves, the space under the desk and table. It had to be there somewhere. The captain hadn't mentioned the sword again, not so much as a whisper. Books on weaponry still sat in piles on the desk, betraying the man's curiosity. It had to be there, if the captain was researching it.

He threw back the lid of the chest at the bed's foot and dug through it. Nothing. Growling, he dropped to his knees to look beneath the bed. The sword was the one piece of his life that was still at his fingertips, still within his control. He wasn't leaving without it. He jerked the wardrobe open and flung clothing aside. Nothing. He cursed, raking claws through his short hair as he turned to look around the room again. A shadow moved into the doorway and he froze.

"Looking for something?" Garam folded his arms over his chest, though his face stayed impassive.

A hint of red flickered in Rune's eyes. "You have something that belongs to me."

"Your uniform?" The captain didn't stir. "On the bed. Right where we left it. Going to need it when we ride out tomorrow."

Rune shook his head and scoffed. "I'm not riding anywhere. I left my homeland because of war. I'm not riding straight back into it."

"You'll ride wherever I tell you to ride," Garam replied, tone even, though his dark eyes glinted like steel. "You're a member of the guard now, which means you're under my command. You'll do as you're told, and you're not going anywhere."

"Try and stop me," Rune spat.

Garam lifted his chin, lowered his arms, and squared his shoulders. "All right, then. If that's how you want to play it, we'll play. Get past me and you're free to go."

Rune hesitated, studying the captain, but the man's face gave away nothing. "And if I can't?"

"Then you stay under my command and you don't go anywhere." Garam quirked a brow. "Because if I win and you try deserting, you'll regret that you ever survived your first round in the arena."

Silence fell between them and Rune's eyes searched the room one last time. He saw the captain's sheathed sword beside the bed, knew Garam saw him looking at it. There weren't many options to weigh.

He bolted for the weapon, jerked it from its sheath and spun to strike. Garam knocked the sword aside and caught Rune's sword arm, wrenching it behind his back.

Rune grimaced and lurched to the side to twist out of the

captain's grasp. But the man caught his ankle with a foot, swept Rune's legs out from under him, and sent him crashing down. His head hit the floor and his eyes flared crimson as stars burst in his field of vision.

Garam struck the sword from his hand and Rune answered with claws, tearing fabric and flesh. The slash yielded nothing from the captain. Instead, Garam split his lip with a backhand and pinned his sleeve to the floor with the sword. He twisted Rune's other arm and held him to the ground.

Spitting curses, Rune tried to jerk his arm free of the sword, but the many layers of fabric he'd worn to make his borrowed coat fit kept him anchored in place. Garam twisted his other arm a little farther. He gritted his teeth against the pain.

"Don't make me hurt you," the captain growled. "You're no use to me if I have to beat you the way you deserve."

Rune glowered at him and spat black blood.

"Give up yet?" Garam asked.

Again Rune tried to free his sleeve from the sword, but every movement made his opponent shift a little more. The pain in his twisted arm inched toward agony.

"I'll break your arm if I have to."

He tried to get to his knees, but found himself unable to move without his arm snapping like dry tinder in the captain's grasp. He cursed again and angled his shoulders to lessen the pressure. Unwilling to surrender yet, he pulled his sleeve against the sword until sweat beaded on his brow. Nothing. He collapsed against the floor, gasping for breath. The blade was so dull it couldn't have cut butter.

Garam eased his grip just slightly as he felt Rune's resistance wane. "You were good in the arena, I'll give you that. But I didn't get to be Captain of the Royal City Guard by luck or inheritance. Consider that, next time you get cocky."

"Let me go," Rune growled.

"Give up?"

Rune squeezed his eyes shut and cursed one last time.

"Yes or no."

"Yes." The single word escaped as an angry groan, the grumbling of wounded pride.

Garam let him go and jerked his sword from the floorboards.

Rune exhaled heavily. With his head bowed, he drew himself to his knees and gripped his aching shoulder. "You fight without weapons often?"

"When I need to. Less often, these days, but it's a good skill to have." The captain offered a hand. Rune eyed it distrustfully and Garam curled his fingers into a fist as he stepped back. "Get up and get your uniform on."

Rune struggled to his feet with a grimace. He'd been bested in fights before, but he couldn't recall it ever happening so quickly. He didn't know whether to be angry at the captain or himself.

"I gave you an order."

Rune gave him a dark look. "What makes you think I will obey?"

Garam crossed his arms. "Because you lost. Or have you really got so little honor that you'll still play the coward and run from your responsibilities?"

The captain's choice of words made fury flare in his chest, but Rune clenched his jaw shut so tightly it hurt. As much as he wanted to argue, he felt more of a coward than Garam knew. Not that the man would realize it, nor were his reasons any of the captain's business. Silent but still scowling, he stripped off his borrowed coat and peeled off the layers of shirts beneath. The sweat on his brow grew cool. The hair at his temples itched. He cast the clothing to the floor and retrieved his uniform from the bed, ignoring the ache in his back and strained arm. Another figure appeared in the doorway just as he finished dressing.

"There you are. I was wondering where the two of you—oh!" Sera clapped a hand to her mouth and rushed to her brother's side. She lifted his arm to inspect the bloody gashes in his sleeve. "What's happened here?"

"Nothing." Garam's tone made it clear there would be no discussion. "I'm fine. Good that you're here, though. You're going to take him to see Councilor Parthanus. Let him know what's going on and see what useful information he can give us. The councilor hasn't been sitting on any meetings just yet, but he has enough connections that he'll know what's happening."

"I don't need an escort," Rune snapped.

"If you think you're going anywhere alone, you're more stupid than I thought." Garam jerked his arm from Sera's grasp and turned to face her. "And you will stay with him until we move out tomorrow morning, understand?"

Sera glowered at him and planted her fists against her hips. "Why should I play babysitter?"

"Because you're one of few mages with power here, which means you can put him down without breaking a sweat. If it comes to it."

She raised one white brow and her eyes darted to Rune. "Oh, bitten by your new dog already?"

Rune gave her an ugly, mirthless smile.

The captain's seemingly perpetual frown deepened.

"Fine," she muttered. "Come on. I'm tired, and I'm sure Councilor Parthanus has fine beds in his guest room. Maybe even a nice place in the stable for you." Sera fluttered a hand in the air as she turned and strode out of the office with a sway in her hips.

Rune met Garam's eyes, just briefly, before he glanced away and sullenly trudged after her.

"WELL, that's what you get for thinking you stood a chance against Captain Kaith. Even the men you bested in the arena were afraid of him. They would have dropped their swords at his feet. King Vicamros chose him for a reason, you know."

Redoram pulled his bag of runestones from the table drawer and gave it a shake. "Time for a game?"

"The sword is mine by right. He has no business keeping it from me." Rune shook his head angrily, pacing between the couch and bookshelves like a caged animal. He felt like one, trapped within the Royal City, bound by agreements he shouldn't have had to make.

"Speak a language I can understand," Sera interrupted from her place across the table from the old man. "Else I'll have Garam throw both of you back in prison for conspiracy."

Redoram cleared his throat and slipped back into his own tongue. "Regardless, breaking into his office to take it back was foolish. I'm surprised you even tried. I heard them speaking about your sword when you were arrested, and if it really is a kingsword, Kaith is not unreasonable in assuming it came to you through illegitimate means."

Rune glared at him, irritated by both his words and the language he spoke them in. It was harder for him to speak the local dialect when he was angry, and stopping to translate in his head only made his mood worse. "I am not a thief," he snapped.

"And yet you were arrested for stealing," Redoram said, amused.

"Because my only other choice was to starve!"

"What is a kingsword, Councilor?" Sera asked, sliding gold bangles up and down her arm. She still wore her green and gold finery, though a member of Redoram's staff had scurried off to find something else for her to wear to bed.

Rune clenched his jaw. He shook his head and returned to pacing.

Redoram put his runestones back into their drawer. "An unusual weapon, named such because the only known kingswords were given to rulers across the globe. Gifts from a king of the ancient Aldaanan to his peers. There weren't many, fewer than fifteen."

"And he had one of them?" She jerked her head in Rune's direction.

"So it would seem," Redoram murmured. "To my understanding, there were only five accounted for before he arrived in the Royal City, most stashed away in treasuries or mounted above some wealthy king's throne. A pity, really. It seems a waste of a good weapon and an unusual artifact."

Sera leaned back and caught Rune by the sleeve, forcing him to stop. "Quit pacing, you're making me nervous. So what makes these swords so special? I'd think a king would rather have something gilded and crusted in gems to show his power."

"They are strong," Rune said. Both Redoram and Sera turned toward him as he spoke. "They cannot be broken."

Redoram nodded. "Precisely. The Aldaanan don't share their smithing secrets, but you know their fondness for spinning magic into everything they do. The kingswords were made to be the only weapon the kings would ever need. Never chipping, never cracking, never breaking. Practicality aside, they were meant to be a symbol of lasting unification in a more peaceful time."

Rune snorted and leaned against the back of the couch. "If they are meant to represent peace, it's no wonder so many are missing."

The old councilor gave a wistful sigh. "So it would seem."

A moment passed in silence before Rune spoke again. "Captain Kaith says we are to march into Aldaan tomorrow."

"Yes, I've heard."

The old man's dismissive tone made him frown. His claws dug into the cushioned back of the couch. "Is there nothing more you can tell us?"

Redoram shrugged. "That you will be working with the Aldaanan, and that some of them won't be happy to see some of you. While the Aldaanan get on well enough with most of the Royal City, they have little love for mages of the Grand College and even less for the so-called Eldani of the rest of the world."

Rune's brow furrowed. "So-called?"

"That's beside the point," Sera snapped, the gold beads in her white hair clicking as she shook her head. "Have you heard nothing about their numbers? The numbers of the college mages? Where we are to set up camp? Anything?"

"No, nothing. At least, not yet. Believe me, my lady, I am as anxious for information as you. There are some people I can speak to, but I likely won't have anything to tell you until the small hours of the morning. I am still getting reacquainted with council business, and it seems Lord Survas now holds my position as representative of the scholars, which makes it difficult to know where I stand." Redoram grimaced, but he clapped his hands together and rose stiffly from the couch. "That said, I would be happy to discuss whatever I learn with the two of you over breakfast. The city will be in such an uproar tomorrow that it would be much easier to have you close at hand, rather than trying to fight your way back here before your departure. One of my staff can show you to the guest rooms I have to offer."

"Just one room, Councilor Parthanus," Sera said.

Redoram's thick white brows lifted in surprise.

"Not like that, Redoram." Rune glowered at her back. "I'd sooner swallow a hornet than share a bed with her."

Sera scoffed. "As if I'd ever consider it! My brother's orders are that I'm not to let the lizard out of my sight. I trust you can arrange for separate beds."

"Of course, of course." Redoram sounded shaken. He rubbed his hands together and nodded, the gesture as meaningless as his laugh. "Upstairs, then. My staff will show you where you can wash and change."

"Thank you, Councilor." Sera gave a lofty sniff as she pushed herself up from the couch. With her head held high, she glided into the hallway to intercept a maid.

Rune rolled his eyes and started after her, though he paused when Redoram met him at the doorway.

"Do you have a moment?" the old man asked, casting a glance down the hallway to be sure Sera didn't hear.

"A moment, yes, but no time for a game. I didn't bring my runestones with me, anyway." Rune slipped back into his mother tongue.

Redoram didn't hesitate to follow his example. "Picking a fight with the captain was a foolish move, for more reasons than one. You've not made the best name for yourself here, and your actions haven't helped. If your sword really is that important to you, do yourself a favor and keep in mind that Captain Kaith has little respect for dishonesty."

Rune's shoulders bunched at the mage's words. There was something in Redoram's tone he didn't like, an echo of the way Garam had accused him of cowardice.

"You'll be at his mercy the whole time you're in Aldaan," Redoram continued. "Best to keep your head down and do as you're told. I know you're not eager to fight again after the arena, but you haven't got any options now."

"I never had any to begin with." Rune pulled away to follow Sera and the maid upstairs. "Good night, Councilor."

The old man sighed and turned back into the parlor as his guests departed.

Rune smoothed his sleeves as he made his way up the stairs. The dried blood from his split lip itched. He lifted a hand to rub his chin. As if in answer to his discomfort, a maid carried a fresh pitcher of water to the washstand in the room. A mirror hung above the basin, and the room held two beds. Sera inspected both of them with an approving eye. Then she shot Rune a venomous look and followed the maid back into the hall, muttering something about a separate washroom. Just as well, he figured. He didn't need more than a chance to wash off the blood, and he didn't much feel like sharing. Or waiting turns, for that matter.

He pushed the door closed and rubbed his tired eyes with the side of one scaly hand as he crossed to the washstand. The water in the pitcher was perfectly clear when he poured some into the basin. He'd forgotten what a commodity clean water was. What they'd given him in prison was cloudy and often tasted of dust.

The water was cold, too, and it made his upper arms rise with goose bumps when he splashed his face. It took some scrubbing to get the dried crust of black blood off his lip and chin. He studied the injury in the mirror when it was clean. It still hurt, but the swelling was already almost gone. Sighing, he leaned against the washstand and studied his reflection.

It was strange to see how he'd outwardly changed. Rune had never thought himself soft, but everything about the past year had served to harden him. Hard travels, hard times, a struggle just to survive. Time in prison and the arena had put more muscle on his frame, and proper meals had almost erased the gauntness of his face. Much had changed, and his circumstances had improved, but a year prior, no one ever would have called him a coward.

The accusation still rankled, a sting left long after the nettle was gone. Redoram hadn't helped, either, but what stung worse than his mentor's words was knowing he was right. He and Garam were both right. A coward, a thief, a liar. Rune locked eyes with his reflection. He was all these things, he realized, and the realization hurt. He saw them in himself, ugly traits the mirror threw back at him. He hated it, worse than he'd ever hated anything, even the inhuman form he'd been born with. And for the first time, he hated himself.

He felt it first. A prickling, crawling itch that crept over his skin, up his neck and across the side of his face. A shadow blossomed on his cheek, gray tendrils spiderwebbing from its center as his skin crackled and hardened, flakes falling away as it changed to stone. Rune threw himself back from the washstand with a panicked shout, flinging the basin into the mirror. Both shattered as he fell. His back hit the floor. Shards of the mirror rang as they crashed into the hardwood.

The door flew open. "I can't leave you alone for a minute!"

Sera all but snarled, though there was the faintest hint of concern in her eyes. "What happened?"

Rune glanced to the mirror shards on the floor, myriad reflections showing nothing out of the ordinary. He swallowed hard. "Nothing."

"Nothing?" Sera pointed at the broken glass and porcelain scattered across the floor. "You broke a mirror! Do you have any idea how much those cost?"

"Bad luck," a maid murmured behind her, earning herself a glare.

Rune touched two fingers to his face. Soft flesh gave way beneath his scaled fingers and he squeezed his eyes closed in relief. "I'll replace it."

Sera waved the maid away and crept inside to join him. She knelt at his side and picked up the biggest pieces of the mirror. "Haven't you gotten yourself into enough trouble for one night? No, don't answer that. I don't want to hear." She dropped the shards into the pitcher.

The maid returned with a broom and shooed Sera out of the way. She swept up the broken glass and took her leave while Rune crawled onto one of the beds. He cradled his head in his hands as Sera turned her back to him to change clothes.

"Well, with any luck, we'll have some sort of good news or information from Councilor Parthanus by morning." She paused and glanced over her shoulder. "Here's hoping that breaking a mirror isn't really bad luck, hmm?"

He didn't reply.

Sera shrugged and extinguished the lamps before she crawled into the second bed. Soft sounds of the house staff at work filled the darkness for some time. Eventually, she gave a heavy sigh. "Close your eyes."

Rune turned toward her in the dark. "What?"

"You're a free mage. Your eyes are glowing and the light is keeping me awake. Close your eyes."

He stared at the shadow of her beneath the blankets.

Deciding it wasn't worth an argument, he turned to lay on his side with his back to her. He closed his eyes but sleep didn't come easily, memories of a familiar face cast in stone haunting his mind.

IT WAS JUST before dawn when a maid appeared at the door and roused them from sleep with the declaration that Councilor Parthanus had returned. Sera excused herself to a separate washroom to primp and to change, trading her borrowed nightgown for the green dress she'd worn to the formal dinner the night before. Rune had only his uniform. He brushed a hand over the wrinkles as he trudged down the stairs and arrived in the parlor a few steps ahead of Sera. The wrinkles did not budge.

Redoram waited with a steaming drink in hand, looking both troubled and weary. "I hope the two of you appreciate everything I've been through. Dealing with the council is never pleasant, but dealing with the council in the middle of the night on the eve of a war declaration is worse than I could have imagined." He gestured to the breakfast tray on the low table in front of him. The runestone board had been put away.

Sera pushed past Rune and sat in the velvet-upholstered chair beside the old man. "I'm sure we both appreciate your struggle." She helped herself to a pastry and a hot cup of coffee. Rune made a face as she offered him a cup, and she raised a brow. "You don't like coffee?"

"I prefer tea." He settled on the empty couch across the table from them, resting his elbows on his knees.

She snorted. "Tea is a woman's drink."

Rune shrugged. "And a man's drink, if it's what's in his cup. Redoram, what did you learn?"

"The two of you are departing for Aldaan before noon, though I'm certain you already knew that. Fortunately, there were some tidbits that came from the meeting that you'll find more useful than that one." Redoram paused to sip his coffee, his shoulders slumping with fatigue. "I thought it odd they would send the Captain of the Guard off with the army. The Royal City needs little in the way of defense, especially against mages, but the guard and the army are separate entities. You understand."

Rune nodded in encouragement for him to continue.

"It's a political move," the old scholar said, "since none of the councilors are fit to go and King Vicamros will be busy here. They've chosen Captain Kaith as a representative of the Royal City. Those of you who are accompanying him will be sent to meet with the Aldaanan leaders and assist them directly."

"What makes you think we will be at Garam's side?" Sera asked.

"You're his sister, aren't you?" Rune studied the food on the tray without any appetite. He'd barely slept, the vision of what had happened at the mirror playing through his mind a thousand times and robbing him of rest. "That's reason enough for him to keep you close."

Her eyes narrowed and she studied him suspiciously for a long moment. Then she looked back to the old mage beside her and tossed her head. "Nevertheless, it's good to know where we will be. And good to know that Garam's position hasn't been forgotten. He is an important man. I had feared they were trying to make a statement by sending us with the first wave."

"They may be." Redoram peered at Rune over the rim of his cup. "The front lines would take care of several problems they seem to be concerned with."

"I know the council dislikes me. But I don't die so easily." Bitterness colored Rune's words. He felt a twinge in his side at the thought of being stabbed. Twice, now, his injuries had been grave enough he should have died. And twice he'd pulled through, with the aid of mages. He'd been closer to death then than any time he'd set foot in the arena, and if that was the best the Royal City had to throw at him, he wasn't concerned about the councilors and their knights.

But then, he reminded himself, this war wouldn't put him up against councilors. Mages were a different story.

Sera took another pastry from the tray, along with a handful of dark berries from a white dish. "Do you know much about who we will be dealing with in Aldaan?"

The question made Redoram frown. "Very little, I'm afraid. The Aldaanan tend to keep to themselves. They follow King Vicamros without question or fuss, but they interact with the other two provinces in the Triad very little. Aside from the occasional trade caravan that comes through the Royal City on its way into Roberian, we don't see them at all. I do know they have an elected leader amongst themselves, rather than an official ruler. Leadership changes every few hundred years, when the leader declares themselves wearied and wishes to rest. Sometimes they serve as leader again at a later time, other times not."

Rune glanced up. "They live so long?"

"They are free mages, they don't age like the rest of us." Sera gave him an odd look. "I would have thought you'd know something about that."

His brow furrowed. "There aren't many like me, where I am from."

"Is that so? Interesting," Redoram murmured. "I was under the impression free mages always flocked together and secluded themselves from the outside world. How many free mages are there, where you hail from?"

"Including myself?"

The old mage blinked. "So few?"

Rune took a pastry and turned it between his claws. "I suppose I shouldn't be included, as I'm not there anymore. So, not counting myself... one."

Both mages stared at him in surprise. Sera leaned forward, her face twisted with sympathy. "No wonder you know so little about your magic. I'm sorry. I would have thought you'd have a teacher, like in Aldaanan culture."

"A reasonable assumption, given that he speaks their tongue," Redoram said.

"My teachers were all limited by affinity. I didn't know my Gift was different until just before I left." He'd had time to consider that, too, while traveling. Rune still didn't understand why Medreal hadn't revealed her abilities sooner. He couldn't help but feel wronged by her secrecy. So much would have been different if he'd had a more capable teacher.

And yet, if he hadn't pursued lessons with Firal, perhaps nothing ever would have come to fruition between them. He found himself reaching for the leather strap around his neck, for the rings he always wore, and he forced his hand down. The thought of Firal spawned memories of Core, and those turned his thoughts to Tren's peculiar death—and the event that led to him breaking the mirror the night before. There were so many fragments of his old life that made little sense, but perhaps he had a chance to unravel them now.

"I do have a question," Rune said slowly. "It is not related to Aldaan."

"Speak it." The old man waved a hand.

"What do you know about basilisks?"

Sera snorted a laugh.

Redoram seemed surprised, but humored him. "Real basilisks, or the sort found in folk tales?"

"What's the difference?"

"One is an ordinary sort of lizard. The other is a legend from a culture on the other end of the world."

Rune hesitated. He'd never heard the name before he caught it whispered in Core, moments after Tren had died. Somehow he doubted the ruin-folk would be familiar with strange lizards. "What does the legend say?"

"That they're monstrous creatures, as tall as a horse, that turn their prey from living flesh to stone. Ridiculous, but there's a measure of truth in most legends. The lizards I've heard of are much smaller than a horse, perhaps the size of a house cat, but they have a venomous bite that can cause paralysis in its victims." The mage poured himself another cup of coffee. "Why do you ask?"

"No reason," Rune murmured, staring at his pastry. He forced himself to take a bite. "Just a... dream I had, I suppose."

Sera drained the last of her coffee before she spoke. "Well, that aside, is there anything else you can tell us? About the meeting, not venomous lizards."

"I'm afraid not. Much of my evening was spent catching up on affairs, and convincing the rest of the council that I still had a right to be there." Redoram stroked his beard, his mage-blue eyes glazed with thought. "I did learn that the Aldaanan are to send further instructions to Captain Kaith by wing, once the army is on the move. Once you depart, I will send word of new developments. If I hear any, that is. I believe they plan to have King Vicamros formally remove me from the council."

"Being imprisoned didn't remove you from it?" Rune asked skeptically.

Sera rolled her eyes and put aside her cup. "Politics here are complicated, lizard." She stood and smoothed her skirt. "Come along. The sun is up and Garam will be waiting. Thank you for your hospitality, Councilor."

Rune crammed the last of his pastry into his mouth and licked sugar from his claws. "And for breakfast. Though, next time, I'd ask that you have a pot of tea."

Redoram rose with a chuckle. "If there is a next time, friend," he murmured as he saw them to the door.

Sera slipped out first. Rune paused at the threshold, unsure what to say. Before he thought of anything, the old councilor clasped him on the shoulder and he returned the gesture in kind. Redoram kept his face neutral, though his eyes were grim.

Rune flashed him a disarming grin. "Remember, tea. Served with honey and cream." He pulled back, righted his uniform, and strode after Sera at an easy pace. He wasn't thrilled about marching to a war that wasn't his to fight, but he reminded himself of his time in the arena and tried to think of ways to work the situation to his advantage. There had to be some way it could help his standing.

Besides, he thought. *We're going up against mages. What could they do that I haven't suffered before?*

GREATER FORCES

SHOUTS FROM THE REAR OF THE PROCESSION BROUGHT THE ARMY TO a halt again. Rune fell out of formation to assist, alongside several others. Lightning crackled overhead, spooking the horses and making matters harder for the men who fought to keep them still.

The rain had begun not long after Rune and Sera set out from Redoram's house, the sort of downpour Rune hadn't expected to see outside of Elenhiise. In spite of Garam's effort to make an early start, it had been well past noon before they left the Royal City. The army hadn't even made it past the city limits before the wagon wheels churned the roads to mud and stuck fast. It had been slow going since. The army moved perhaps a dozen yards at a time, then paused to pull the wagons out of the mire. They couldn't move ahead without their supplies, not with several thousand men behind Captain Kaith's buckskin horse.

"And we're to travel all the way to Aldaan in this," a soldier muttered, hushing the horses as they tried to flail in the sucking mud. Odds were one of the animals would break a leg before the day was over.

Someone handed Rune a shovel, and he looked back the way they'd come. The barren trees surrounding the city were still visible, though the army had been on the move for hours. Had he been able to use his magic, he might have pulled the wagons free on his own, but the flows of energy that hummed in everything around him still escaped his grasp.

"For the safety of the city," Sera had said. "If you can see the city, magic is out of reach." It seemed overly cautious to him, but complaining wouldn't make any difference. Eventually they'd pass beyond whatever barrier held magic at bay and he'd have his power. Enough power to decimate the army he walked with, he thought bitterly. Enough to cause the sort of chaos and confusion he needed to escape. But he refused to leave his father's sword. He could wipe out a tenth of Garam's army on his own, but without the captain's help, he wouldn't find the blade again.

It took some time to free the wagons, but as they dug the wheels from the mud, they guided the wagons off the wide road and into the tall grasses alongside it. The horses would tire faster pulling the wagons on an unbroken trail, but it seemed their best chance for progress. The men moved back into formation, occupying the road the horses couldn't travel. Frigid mud squelched beneath Rune's feet as he took his place. The men weren't as hindered by the mud as the animals, though it stained their boots and uniforms black.

The march went on for several miles without interference, winding northwest until the last traces of civilization disappeared behind them and they reached the edge of the barrier that kept the Royal City free of magic.

It wasn't like the mage-barrier surrounding Kirban Temple. There was no prickle or tingle to feel as Rune passed through. Just the sensation of magic being beyond his grasp, then a sudden deluge, a frigid rush that made him suck in a breath and stop dead in his tracks. It was revitalizing and refreshing, and he found himself drawing power close just to savor the sensation of it being there. Men kept moving around him, men without a Gift, who didn't know what they were missing. He closed his eyes and held on a moment more, until shouts from ahead drew his attention.

Garam had halted. Sera stood beside his horse and the two of them leaned close to one another, to speak without having their voices carry. Rune had seen very little of Sera as they traveled, but she was a scout, not a fighter. He assumed her reappearance meant she'd found something important. She pointed up. He and Garam both looked to the sky. A bird circled overhead, spiraling downward. No, not a bird; too big, too oddly shaped. Rune's brow furrowed as he tried to make it out, but it was little more than a dark shape against gray-bellied storm clouds.

"Stop the wagons!" Garam shouted as he dismounted his buckskin gelding and passed the reins to a nearby man, who walked the horse back to the wagons. "Keep the horses back and keep them calm. We can't afford to have them injure themselves in the mud."

The airborne silhouette shifted to circle above Garam and Sera, obviously intending to land near them. Curious, Rune moved closer to the captain. The winged creature banked and he got a good look at it for the first time.

Its lean body was like that of a great cat, but instead of fur, its mane was tawny feathers. More feathers fringed its long tail and feathered tufts like an owl's stood in place of ears. Its head wasn't feline, but wasn't quite that of a bird, either, despite its sharp beak.

"What's the matter?" Sera grinned. He hadn't seen her approach, his eyes fixed on the strange animal. "Never seen a gryphon before?"

"I had no idea they even existed." Rune shaded his eyes with a scaly hand as the beast alighted not far from Garam. Almost more startling than the creature itself was the way it sat up on feline haunches, wiggled clawed fingers on its eagle-like forefeet, and plucked some sort of eye coverings from its face. It pushed them farther up on its head. Rune's jaw went slack. Sera slid a finger underneath his chin and pushed it shut.

"Can't have rain in her eyes, now, can she?" she teased.

Rune blinked. "How do you know it's female?"

"The plumage." Sera gestured toward her throat and chest. "Males have a bright patch in their mane."

"Captain Kaith, I presume?" the gryphon spoke, and everyone fell silent. The creature's voice was distinctively female and startlingly human, her words clear and crisp.

Startled, Garam eyed her from ear-tuft to tail. "Yes," he replied. "You'll have to forgive me. When I heard the Aldaanan were sending a message by wing, I expected a carrier pigeon."

The gryphon laughed, a strange trilling sound that made Rune's skin prickle. He fought an involuntary shiver.

"A pigeon, in this storm? Goodness no, Captain. I suppose I'll just have to do." The beast dropped to rest her clawed forefeet on the ground. Her head was level with Garam's when she stood on all fours. "I expected your army would have traveled farther by now, but it seems you've been more hindered by the weather than anticipated."

"We move as best we can," Garam said, irritated.

Rune frowned at the declaration. The mages in the Royal City weren't familiar enough with Aldaan to open a Gate for the army, but it still seemed like there should have been something they could do to make it easier.

As if reading his mind, Sera snorted and strode forward with her hands on her hips. "I've told you a dozen times that I could pull the wagons from the mud on my own. How much faster would progress be if you let me?"

"And have your magic spook the horses and half the men here?" The captain gave her a hard look.

The gryphon's ear-tufts raised. "A mage in your company?" She turned toward Sera, her golden eyes as piercing as they were keen. Then she paused and tilted her head as her gaze slid to Rune. "Two mages. Well now, that's not something I expected to see."

Startled, Rune took a step back. The gryphon trilled in

laughter again and padded toward him. He couldn't sense anything in the creature, no hint of a Gift at all. For a moment, he couldn't fathom how she'd identified his power. Then he set his jaw and reprimanded himself for the thought. He hadn't sensed Medreal either, and her Gift was the same as his own. It was foolish to assume he'd feel power in something as different as the gryphon before him.

"What makes you say that?" Garam asked. He looked as cautious as he sounded, his expression guarded.

The gryphon chuckled and clucked to herself. "Please, Captain. You are Garam Kaith! Your exploits are well known throughout the Triad's provinces, as is your dislike of anything magic in nature. No, don't look surprised, you aren't. News slanders a man as fast as it praises him, and I'm not offended. None of the Aldaanan are bothered by your opinions, so long as you're respectful to us. And you will be, won't you? Otherwise, you wouldn't be captain." Then she ruffled her feathers, shaking off raindrops and adjusting her wings against her back. "Now! I've come to give you direction, so let's start off in the right one, hmm?"

As the gryphon strutted ahead, Garam turned to bark orders for the men to move. The whole procession lurched forward. The captain hurried after the gryphon and spoke to the creature in tones so low Rune doubted he'd be able to hear if he walked right behind them.

"I'd best walk with them, get directions to scout ahead." Sera took a step, then paused and gave Rune a dark look. "And I felt what you were doing, you know. Don't go getting any ideas, now that your power is back at your fingertips. The Royal City isn't the only place where people can be kept from magic."

He raised a brow. It didn't sound like a threat, exactly, but he wasn't sure what else it was supposed to be. She didn't give him time to ask questions, turning and sprinting ahead to join her brother and the gryphon as the army moved into formation again. Rune took his place and fell in step alongside countless strangers, marching on toward the rise of mountains on the distant horizon. As conversation between the men resumed, he lifted his head in effort to see the gryphon again. Looking at the creature made him feel strange, but not in a negative way. For the first time he could recall, he didn't feel so unnatural.

RAIN CEASED after the first night, though the mud lingered for days. The army wound toward the northwest at a steady pace after the storm passed, halting only occasionally to pull wagons free. More than once, Rune heard Sera complain about not being allowed to use her magic to help, but Garam did not waver in his decision. Rune thought better of saying anything, regardless of whether or not Sera was right. Agitating either one of them wouldn't help.

They moved from the neutral territory that surrounded the Royal City to the lands of Aldaan without fanfare or notice. There were no markers, and the land looked no different than that near the city, though the farther they went, the hillier it became. Only snippets of conversation Rune overheard between Garam and the gryphon betrayed their location.

Almost a week passed with nothing of interest to report. No news, no trouble, just an endless march through an unremarkable landscape. Then an afternoon came where storms rumbled on the horizon and Garam brought the army to a halt early to make camp where they were.

Most of the men seemed relieved. Whatever merriment had filled the campsite the first few nights was gone now. Breaks had grown rare, and the weary army seemed to suffer in their absence. Rune didn't know how they expected to survive a war with an army that was, as he understood, mostly untried. The seasoned warriors among the ranks were all older, though Captain Kaith himself seemed unfazed by what lay ahead. Garam was difficult to read, but he was Captain of the Guard. It was unlikely this was his first battle. Rune studied the faces of the men in the camp and paused when he found the gryphon doing the same.

She turned her head under the weight of his eyes, her feathered mane ruffling as she stared back. Her expressions were oddly human, and there was no mistaking the curiosity in her birdlike face. She rose and flicked her wings as she padded toward him at a lazy pace. He shifted but stayed in front of the tent he had to himself—a luxury and an insult, since the fact he didn't have to share stemmed from the way the other soldiers avoided him.

The gryphon slowed as she neared him, and she leaned in to study him with sharp golden eyes. She tilted her head this way and that, observing his figure and his peculiar reptilian feet, though her gaze always went back to his eyes. "You're an odd one, aren't you?" she murmured at last, sitting beside him and fluffing her feathers. "A free mage, if I'm not mistaken. You feel like the Aldaanan, but you certainly don't look like them."

"And you don't feel like a mage at all." Rune narrowed his eyes at her, pretending to inspect her with the same scrutiny.

She cackled. "Gryphons don't use magic, we are magic. There's quite a difference." But she smiled, another expression he was surprised to see. "What's your name?"

"Rune."

"Liar."

He raised a brow.

She made a clicking sound with her beak and nodded toward his hands. "Men are named at birth. Scars like that come later. What is your name?"

He hesitated for a time, then shrugged and looked away. "It was Ran. Now it's Rune."

"I see." The gryphon's eyes wandered elsewhere. She seemed to have determined he didn't like being stared at. "My name is Ria. Now it's Ria, anyway. Brantmen aren't very good at speaking the language of gryphons. It was easier to change."

"Brantmen?" he repeated, unsure he'd heard her right. The term was wholly unfamiliar.

"Humans," Ria said. "And Eldani. The Aldaanan. Two-legged fleshy things, like yourself."

"None of whom can speak your language?" Rune gave her a sidewise glance. "What was your name before?"

She ruffled her feathers and let out an odd warble that reminded him of a creaking door. Then she adjusted her wings and snorted. "So, as you can imagine, it was just easier to change it."

He stifled a laugh.

"Ah, that's better. A bit of personality in you after all, hmm?" Ria trilled a laugh of her own. "Well, now that the ice is broken, indulge me. Your birth name is Aldaanan, but you're certainly not. Were you descended from Eldani, before you were changed?"

Humor died and a serious look drew itself on his face. Changed? "What do you mean?"

Her ear-tufts rose in surprise. "I can feel the taint in you clear as anything, friend. No one is born with that sort of shadow hanging over them. You're something off, something out of place in the world. Those sort of things happen, when magic goes awry."

"I've always been this way," he replied, though his brow furrowed. He knew he'd been made, rather than born, but he'd always assumed his power had been tainted since he drew his first breath.

"Is that so?" Ria mused, tapping her beak with one claw. "Hmm, perhaps. But perhaps Filadiel can tell us more. He's a bit of an expert in magic, and free magic besides. Most of the Aldaanan are. I'm sure he could look at you and see what's the matter right off. Oh!" She clamped her forepaws around her beak and made a miserable sound. "I'm sorry, that was rude. Therad is always scolding me for nattering on. Sometimes my beak gets away from me."

"Who is Filadiel?" he asked, ignoring the rest of her chatter.

"The leader of the Aldaanan. We'll have an opportunity to meet him once we get to where we're going. If you'd like, that is?" The gryphon looked hopeful. "He can probably tell you about the taint in the magic that courses through you. I won't say he can purge it, but if you wish to isolate or contain it, his teachings may be of some help."

Rune frowned. Of course he wanted to contain it. But if containment was possible, why hadn't the Kirban mages suggested as much?

She withered beneath his stare. "Well, just a suggestion, of course. I'd like for you to meet him. He's always writing his discoveries down for the elders to read. Gryphons like learning about as well as they like flying, which is quite a bit. In any case, we'll reach the Aldaanan valley in a week or so. You can think about it until then. I'll give you some peace." She stood and stretched like a cat before she started off the way she'd come.

"Ria," he called after her. She paused and peered at him over her shoulder. He licked his lips before going on. "You've seen tainted magic before?"

"Oh yes." She bobbed her head in mimicry of a nod, a gesture that looked even more odd than her human-like expressions. "I've seen them reversed, too. Filadiel is good at that sort of thing. Which is why I think you ought to meet him." She smiled at him again and gave her tail feathers a flick before she moved on.

He watched after her, a thoughtful frown pulling at the corners of his mouth. Then his eyes fell and he studied his hands. *Could* something like that be reversed? Kirban's mages had never mentioned the possibility. From everything he'd ever heard, he'd been a monster from the moment his life began. He hadn't thought it an intentional design, though it offered limited advantages to a fighter. Intimidation, claws, both things he'd trade for normalcy in a heartbeat. The idea of it being tied to something that could be undone seemed too good to be true.

And it came at a strange time too, with him ready to escape as soon as he could recover his sword. Convenient that there might be something that could aid him waiting at the army's destination.

Rune sighed in exasperation and retreated into his tent as the first raindrops fell. No, he couldn't suspect anyone of trying to coerce him to their destination. Even Garam had been both surprised and displeased to see the gryphon, and if the captain held as little love for magic as Ria claimed, there was no reason for him to orchestrate anything involving it. Rune tried to shake the thoughts, staring at the tent's ceiling in the dark. But the more he tried to empty his mind, the more nagging the idea became.

What if the corruption of his power could be undone? He laid back with an arm tucked behind his head and reached for the rings hidden beneath his shirt. He rolled them between his green-scaled fingers until the larger of the two caught on a claw. He slid it down his finger, rubbing it with his thumb. His hand no longer felt strange without it, but when he wore it, it still felt right. As if he'd never taken it off. He studied the ring as it reflected the light of his glowing eyes.

If what made him a monster could be undone, he wouldn't have to hide. The realization made his breath catch in his throat. He could bleach his hair, return to Elenhiise as Ran. He could return to Firal without worry of execution, explain all the mistakes he'd made, set things right. He swallowed hard, removing his ring, holding it tight with Firal's in the palm of his hand. If Ria was right, perhaps he'd have the chance to give her ring back after this war was over. He tucked the rings back under his shirt as his mind settled. To the heart of Aldaan it was, then.

There was no harm in trying.

THOUGH ALDAAN APPEARED similar to the rest of the Triad, the difference soon became apparent. Bitter winds swept over the army, turning their breath to mist and the mud underfoot to ice. It made travel easier, the wagons back on the roads, but the cold cut to the bone. The rest of the army seemed unbothered, but Rune couldn't keep his teeth from chattering. His bare feet ached until numbness took his toes. In spite of the cold, he found it easier to walk now that he wanted to reach their destination.

Most of the other men gave him a wide berth, but Rune didn't walk alone. Sera strode beside him, her chin up and her eyes bright. He wasn't sure why she'd chosen to travel at his side. Since she'd fallen in step with him, she hadn't said a word. Rune found he didn't mind the quiet. He almost preferred it to crude jokes and constant complaints he heard from the soldiers around him. The two of them were near the front of the marching army, close enough to see the captain and the gryphon as the pair led the way. The road they followed snaked up into the mountains that loomed just ahead.

"The mountains have no name, you know," Sera said, breaking the silence for the first time that morning. "Not an official one. Depending on where you are, it might be called the Aldaanan range or the Ribs, but both are just nicknames."

Rune gave her a sidewise look. "Ribs?"

She returned his glance, puzzled. "Because of how they branch off the mountains that split the continent. Haven't you seen a map?"

"Not a very recent one," he admitted. The maps Redoram had shown him had been of the Triad, but the mountains had not been labeled. The only time he'd seen a map of the known world, it had been in an ancient book in Kirban Temple.

"I would have thought Garam would show you," she murmured. "His men are sent all over the Triad. Basic geography is important for the job."

"In our defense," Rune said, "I haven't been one of his men for long."

She said nothing else, marching alongside him in silence with a distant look in her mage-blue eyes.

Rune watched her from the corner of his eye for a time before he spoke again. "Why do you walk with me? Instead of at the front, with the captain?"

Her eyes narrowed and her lips pursed. Then she shrugged. "We're alone, you and I. Hundreds of men around us, but only we are mages. We experience things differently, always aware of the ebb and flow of energies around us. You're the only one here who understands, even if your Gift isn't the same as mine."

Rune frowned as he thought that over. It made sense, but it was strange to think of an army so large without any other mages in it—especially when mages were what they moved to stand against. And stand beside, too, he reminded himself. The Aldaanan were mages as well. He shook his head. Sera's reasoning made sense, but the army's lack of magic did not. "How is it that Captain Kaith hates magic so much when his own sister is a mage?"

"It isn't that he hates magic, he just... distrusts it." Sera peered at her brother's back, that thoughtful look returning to her eyes. "Most who live in the Royal City feel the same way. They've been sheltered from magic for years. Garam hasn't seen the incredible things we've seen, likely never will. He'll never understand the benefits. He and everyone else in the city figure they can get by without it, so why should anyone want or need to use it?"

"But he trusts you. Why? You couldn't have grown up together." He rubbed his hands together and breathed into them to restore feeling to his fingers. "You are Eldani, are you not? You would have been grown before he was ever born."

She tossed her head with a small laugh. The golden beads in her white braids clicked noisily. He didn't know why she hadn't removed them. "That's the problem with you northerners. You always try to fit families into one category. Yes, I am half Eldani. Garam and I share a mother. She was a powerful mage in her own right. I was mostly grown before Garam came along, but being older doesn't mean I'm any less of a sister to him. I helped raise him. Upbringing of the children is the responsibility of everyone in the house, regardless of their parentage."

Northerners? He lifted a brow, but said nothing of the label. Where he was from was no concern of hers. Let her think he was from the northern continent, if it suited her. "Where I am from, widows do not often remarry. They might for political reasons, but rarely any other. The living family sees to the widow's needs. Is it different in your homeland?"

"Sometimes. Noble houses often merge to forge lasting alliances. If two houses choose to ally, that alliance persists even after the death of the original union's members. The bond persists in children who bear the blood of both houses. So in some respects, rather than being weakened by loss, the death of a spouse can be what drives a house to new heights." A faint, sad smile crossed her face. "In my mother's instance, her first husband—my father—was slain while escorting a trade caravan through the wilds, which freed her to marry Garam's father years later. So the alliance grew to encompass my mother's house, Garam's father's house, and my father's house, too."

Rune twitched at mention of her father's death. His own father's slaying sprang to mind too quickly for comfort. He pushed the thought away. "I'm sorry to hear of your loss."

Sera waved a hand. "I was too young to remember. She did not remarry for many years. My uncles served as father figures to me, and Garam's father was a good man. He was kind to everyone in the family. There is nothing to be sorry for. I never thought anything was missing." She paused, then laughed and nudged his arm. "Now it's your turn."

He furrowed his brow. "My turn?"

"To tell me something about yourself. Your homeland. Your family. Are there more like you where you are from?"

None of those were subjects he wanted to discuss. Rune stiffened and stared straight ahead. "We spoke of that with

Redoram. I was one of only two free mages. As far as I know, that is."

"I don't mean mages like you." She glanced to his feet, just in time to see him stumble. He spat a curse as the offending rock left a claw cracked and bloodied.

"It's too blighted cold," he grumbled, crouching to clutch his toes.

Sera dropped beside him and reached for his foot to heal it. Her fingers brushed his scales and she jerked back with a yelp. "You're freezing! Why didn't you ask for shoes, if you're this cold?"

"Do I look like I can wear shoes?" he asked through clenched teeth. He didn't mean to sound angry, but he thought unclenching them might let them chatter right out of his head.

She rolled her eyes and slapped his hands out of the way. He felt her push against his energy as she touched him, an entirely different sensation than the methods Firal had used. Instead of linking with him and guiding his own body's strength to heal him, a trickle of Sera's own energy poured forward to mend the injury. "There are craftsmen with us who can make something for you to wear. If they can make goggles for gryphons, I'm sure they can make shoes for a lizard."

Growling, Rune pulled away.

"You're welcome!" she snapped, pushing herself up and tossing her head. "How did you ever stay warm before?"

"Home isn't so far north as you think." He rubbed his feet to restore feeling to his toes.

Sera's brows lifted. "I'd have thought you Aldaanan. At root, if nothing else. The Aldaanan are the only free mages left."

Rune tilted his head to look up at her. "Apparently not."

The sparkle in her eyes showed her curiosity was piqued. "So where are you from, if not Aldaan?"

"The tropics. Where there is no need for shoes or—" He stopped short as something white drifted between them. His eyes tracked its descent. Then he looked skyward, his irritation melting into wonder.

Sera blinked, looked up, and laughed when she realized what he was staring at. Thick white snowflakes fell from the gray sky. They disappeared in her hair and melted against her dark skin. "So I see. Very well, then. I'll talk to Garam. He should have seen that you had proper equipment before the army moved. Try to keep up without hurting yourself."

He didn't reply, watching the steady fall of snow as the rest of the army slowly filtered past. Eventually, he rejoined their movement.

Time crawled no faster than the army climbing the mountainside. The long, cold hours were made to feel even longer by how little progress they made. The mountain paths wound in long, serpentine lines around ridges and peaks, keeping them away from the dangers of steeper slopes at cost of speed. Days dragged by and fresh layers of snow greeted them each morning, slowing them further.

A cobbler traveling with the supply wagons provided Rune with simple leather foot coverings after the first snowfall. He was grateful to have them, and less grateful for Sera's meddling. The mage walked with him most days now and chattered about her home, a city perched on a ridge between desert and jungle in the southern half of the world. He could tell she expected him to share stories of his own, but he said nothing of Elenhiise, instead using questions to lure more information from her.

He wasn't surprised to learn she'd studied at the Grand College. From what he gathered, there was nowhere else in the north where one could study magecraft. Far from reassuring, really. If the mainland proved to be anything like Elenhiise, mages were plentiful, and the Grand College was what they prepared to battle now.

Snow grew deeper on the paths as days wore on. Nights turned colder and spirits fell, until Garam announced they would break into the Aldaanan valley some time the next morning. Then the campfires seemed merrier and the simple stew tasted a little heartier. The stars twinkled bright overhead, except where clouds blotted the horizon. They threatened to swallow the sky before the army settled for the night, and Rune found himself surprised when the gryphon joined him in pitching his tent.

"I was told yours was the most likely to be empty," Ria explained as she helped drive stakes into the ground. "There'll be an ice storm tonight, I'd bet my tail feathers on it. Captain Kaith suggested I ask to share quarters with you instead of sleeping under the stars like I normally do."

"I'm sure Captain Kaith gives me no room to refuse," Rune muttered, checking twice to make sure she'd done everything right.

"I won't be any trouble," the gryphon reassured him as he settled next to his small fire. She sat beside him. "I can't fly if my feathers are damaged in an ice storm. There are no private aeries anywhere near here, so I can't roost anywhere else, and the other tents will be much too full for me to fit. Once you and your leaders meet with Filadiel, I imagine we'll be parting ways."

He grew quiet, studying his hands. The green scales looked dull in the dying light. He tried to imagine his arms without them and found he couldn't. He knew what it would look like; he'd seen it for years in the illusion his amulet spun for him—the amulet left abandoned in the caverns under Elenhiise. But having actual skin instead of an illusion of skin was different. He couldn't imagine what it would feel like. Coarse scales and clawed fingers were all he'd ever known. "Do you really think Filadiel can help me?" he asked.

"If anyone knows how to help, it would be him. I'm curious to see what he can do. Wisdom to tuck away for the future, hmm?" She trilled a laugh. "Gryphons live for knowledge. Since we can't wield magic of our own, it's a topic we know very little about. But getting to see something as incredible as corrupted magic being cleansed? Oh, what a delight that would be! Something to fill the books with once I return home."

It was no wonder Garam had sent her to bunk with him. It made sense to keep the oddities of the army together. The gryphon's presence was strangely comforting, made him feel less out of place. He stared at the ground, his eyes unfocused. "I didn't plan on heading to Aldaan, you know. I never wanted to be part of the army. Didn't plan on staying part of it."

Her ear tufts lifted. "What made you change your mind?"

A wry smile pulled at the corners of his mouth. "Hope."

She remained quiet for a time, though she eventually lowered her head to scrutinize him with one golden eye. He felt her studying every nuance of his features, from the cracked claw on one toe to the shadow of hunger that hadn't yet left his face.

"You've seen hardship," she murmured.

"Who hasn't?"

"But you aren't used to it. I can tell. I can see it in the way you carry your head." Her voice softened, her tone motherly. "You're right, struggles come for everyone. But how we emerge from hardship has a way of changing us. Sometimes the things we perceive as misfortune are actually greater forces pushing us in the direction we're meant to go."

Rune's eyes narrowed as he considered that, the events of the past year rolling over in his head. A fall from being royalty to being a mere prisoner intended for slaughter. A path marked by one long string of misfortunes, mistakes, and misunderstanding. If there were greater forces at work, he couldn't see them. Nor could he see how his place on the path to Aldaan was anything other than coincidence. Remarkable mages could have been found anywhere.

The only thing about the situation that struck him as unusual was the fact the mages he sought were Aldaanan. Too many things were Aldaanan. His given name, his language, his magic, his chance for normalcy. That, too, could have been coincidence; old countries spread their influence far and wide. But he couldn't help but feel there was something else, something missing. *Something pushing me there,* he thought.

Perhaps there were greater things at work after all.

"Ah, there's the ice." Ria interrupted his thoughts, getting up and turning to slip into the tent just as a frigid wind kicked up and the biting ice began to fall.

Rune followed her inside and settled on his pallet. He gathered his blankets close and shuddered as he lay down. The gryphon settled close by and tucked him beneath her wing to share the warmth of her feathers. The night passed peacefully, though the winds howled outside the tents.

When morning came, he looked down into the valley of Aldaan for the first time, the forest transformed to crystal by ice.

ALDAAN

Mountain slopes fell away before them, spilling into a deep valley. Forests filled the nook in between the mountain ranges, a mix of bony branches and evergreen, both encased in glittering ice from the night's storm. Patches of snow marked clearings between the trees, most of the gaps made by lakes or waterways. More mountains stood in the distance, blue shadows against the gray, snow-heavy sky.

Mountain ranges bordered the valley on three sides, leaving the western side open farther than the eye could see. If there were cities to be found inside the valley, they were nowhere to be seen. Only one structure rose from the trees—a lone, pale stone spire that towered over the forests to the northeast.

Rune slipped to the head of the army at the first chance he got, eager to be out of the mountains and into the valley, if only for the shelter the trees could offer from the shrieking winds. But the procession slowed as they reached the edge of the forest, and Garam and the gryphon paused to exchange words. Then Ria turned and paced toward Rune while Garam shifted to speak to Sera instead.

"We'll be parting ways for a little while," the gryphon said, fanning her wings as she came to a halt before him. "I'll miss our conversations until you arrive. The road through the forest is clean and well-maintained, it won't hinder you at all. I am to fly ahead and let the Aldaanan know the army will be joining them at the aerie."

He assumed she meant the tower. His eyes flicked toward it and a frown twisted his mouth. "So far into the valley?"

Ria nodded. "Aldaeon, the aerie, is what you would consider a major city. It's the only one in Aldaan, in fact. The others are small villages, minor outposts, nothing worth an enemy's notice. When the mages come, they will come to Aldaeon."

"How long will it take to travel that distance?" He tried not to sound anxious, but he was as eager to escape the cold as he was to meet the leader of the Aldaanan.

Trilling with laughter, she rose on her haunches to clasp his shoulder in one taloned forepaw. "Rest easy, friend. It won't be long." She pulled back before he could speak, drawing her goggles down over her eyes. The gryphon crouched and thrust herself from the earth with a mighty stroke of her wings. Snow scattered in the winds of her takeoff, settling only after she caught an updraft and soared above the treetops. "May fair winds bless your travel!" she shouted, circling the army once before she turned to the northeast.

Rune shaded his eyes and watched her shadow ripple over the treetops until a call from ahead set the men into motion. The jostle of movement around him kept Rune from staring after her for long. When his eyes fell to the path ahead, he froze in place. Both Sera and Garam watched him. The captain leaned close to share a word with his sister and she nodded with a frown. Then Garam started forward, and Sera trudged back.

"It seems you and the gryphon became fast friends," she called as she neared. The way she walked with one hand on her hip seemed dangerously casual.

Rune shrugged as he took his place in the ranks. "Two oddities in a normal army, what do you expect?"

She fell in stride beside him. Her lips pressed to a thin line.

"Ria told Garam you're to meet with the leader of the Aldaanan when we arrive. Is that so?"

Amused, he glanced at her. "Do you think your guide would tell falsehoods?"

"Answer the question," she snapped. The venom in her tone startled him.

"Yes," he said slowly. What did it matter to Garam? "They are free mages, are they not? She believes it would benefit me to meet with him."

Ice crept into her mage-blue eyes. "And how would it benefit you? The whole truth, lizard. Your speech slips back into archaic patterns when you're trying to be sneaky."

He blinked. "It does not."

"It just did! Now why are you meeting with the Aldaanan? Garam told me to get the whole story out of you, and I'll have it if I have to beat you for it."

The idea almost made him laugh, but he bit his tongue to keep silent. As spirited as the woman was, he doubted Sera could beat anything out of him if she tried. He considered challenging her, just to see if she would, but the scuffle would slow them down. By his guess, the aerie was at least a full day's walk in ideal weather. He didn't want to waste any time. Instead, he shrugged again. "If they really are free mages, it means they are the only ones who can teach me to use my magic properly. Ria suggested I speak with their leader because if he can't help me, he will know who can." It was the truth, if not the whole of it. The exact nature of the help he hoped to gain from Filadiel was none of her concern.

Sera's eyes widened. "She believes they'll teach you?" Now excitement colored her words, brightened her face. "Imagine the knowledge they could share! Arts lost to the Grand College for centuries!"

"Arts they probably wouldn't want to share," he said.

She snorted. "As if I could do any of it. You're a free mage. Our Gifts are as different as swimming and flying. But oh, just to hear of it..." She slapped his shoulder. "That settles it. If they do teach you, you have to let me know what you learn. Show me, that is. Even if I can't learn to do it myself, I'd like to see. Understand?"

Rune lifted a brow. "I don't have to show you anything."

"But you will have to show Garam. Or did you forget that he's your commanding officer? He'll want to know everything you do, especially if it involves magic."

"Because he hates it?"

"Because he needs it."

He stopped, unsure he'd understood. He rolled the words over in his head a second time. "He needs... what?"

"Magic." Sera halted a few paces ahead and turned to look back at him. Her expression softened, a mix of pleading and concern. "Don't you understand?"

Rune stared at her.

Sighing, she inched closer. When she spoke again, she lowered her voice. "We're to fight mages. That means you are more important to this army than a dozen swordsmen. As much as he distrusts our Gifts, Garam knows he needs them. Me and you. People who can protect the army while they fight, keep them safe from magecraft. If the mages in Aldaan can help you learn, help you grow stronger, Garam will encourage it. But he won't lose you to them, either. Remember, we're the only mages in this army. And of the two of us, you are more valuable."

Admitting he was of more use to the army hurt her; Rune could see it in her eyes. He tried to think of something to say to offer comfort, but turned up nothing. He shook his head. "The Aldaanan will be more useful than any of us. They have centuries of practice doing things I may only begin to learn now. This is their fight. Their home, a battle to be fought on their doorstep. And very close to yours. I have no stake in this war, Sera. I'm here because of circumstance. Nothing more."

"And circumstance will require you to fight for your life," she replied sharply, turning on her heel and moving ahead.

Rune winced, but hurried back to his position in the ranks, sparing her a sideways glance that went ignored.

He had no desire to fight, but he'd done nothing else since he'd arrived on the mainland. Perhaps it was to be expected by now. Or perhaps, he thought as he glanced toward the tower through the skeletal branches of bare trees, this time would be different.

THE ROADWAY WIDENED as they neared the tower. As desolate as it had seemed from the mountains, it was hard to believe the tower before them was the same spire. Manicured gardens sprawled between the trees, a variety of evergreen plants making them bright and merry even under inches of snow.

Low buildings of white stone might have stood out any other time of year, but now only the bright curtains and candles in windows kept them from blending into the wintery background. People bustled in the winding avenues around the foot of the tower, carting firewood and toting wares, though many stopped to stare as the army reached the city's edge. Rune studied them just as intently. He'd expected the Aldaanan mages, and perhaps some Eldani, but all he saw—and sensed—were Giftless human men and women. Gryphons walked in the crowds as well, though their numbers were few. Each of the creatures seemed more unusual than the last, ranging in color from the same tawny brown as Ria to an inky blue-black male with a crested head and a spill of brilliant scarlet plumage in his mane.

The procession stopped at the edge of the city and the few commanding officers collected near the front to take orders. Rune watched the windows of the tower above them as curious faces peered out at the army. He only half heard Garam's directions for camp to be made and men to be sent through the city to purchase needed supplies. The sound of his name made him start and he turned, tearing his eyes away from a dark-feathered gryphon who stared at them from one of the uppermost windows. On the ground, Garam met and held his gaze with a glare.

"I said, you'll be with Sera and me for the night." The captain didn't look pleased at having to repeat himself. His expression grew hard before he turned back to the officers. "If there are any questions, send someone into the aerie to find me. I imagine we'll be there a while, if not all night."

The officers saluted and bowed away, one at a time, to attend their tasks. Garam adjusted his gloves and righted his uniform as he started toward the tower. Sera trailed close behind him, frowning darkly. Rune fell in step behind them, gazing up at the aerie once more.

Great doors of polished brass stood open, welcoming the flow of people that moved in and out of the tower. The narrow tunnel of the entrance stretched on at least a dozen paces before they reached the tower's central room. Despite the press of people, Rune stopped in his tracks and stared up at the tower's interior in disbelief.

To the left, a wide ramp rose from the floor to begin a clockwise spiral around the inside of the spire. Doorways opened regularly along the path, no marks beside them to show where they went. The spiraling pathway bore no railing, the center of the tower open to the darkening sky overhead, and cool-colored mage-lights kept everything bright.

"It's beautiful," Sera gasped. She pressed her fingertips to her mouth as she strode to the middle of the tower's open central shaft, staring up at the dusky sky. With as warm as it was inside, the snowfall should have left puddles underfoot. Instead, the polished gray granite underfoot was bone dry.

Rune took a slow step forward, eyes wide with disbelief. "I've seen this before."

"You've been to Aldaan before?" Garam asked as he turned toward the ramp.

"No," Rune murmured. "But I've seen someplace just like this. Only..."

Sera took his arm and dragged him along as her brother started up the spiral walkway. "There's another tower in Roberian, though I hear it's very different. There are several similar towers scattered through the north, and one in the south, in our homeland."

"Are there any underground?"

She laughed. "If it were underground, it wouldn't be a tower. No, there's nothing like that. Not that I've ever heard of."

Unconcerned by the lack of railing, Rune walked near the ramp's edge, peering upward. The spacing of the ramp was exactly the same, the distance between the doorways in the wall the same. A perfect copy of the central spiral in Core, but reaching upward instead of down. "Who built these towers?"

"Who can say?" Sera tugged him away from the edge. "Perhaps the Aldaanan can tell you more, if there's time in between everything else they'll have to teach you."

Garam cast a dark look over his shoulder, silencing both of them. Neither spoke again as he led them upward through the tower.

Fewer people walked the path near the top, though the mage-lights were just as plentiful. The sky grew purple overhead and stars sprinkled the deep color by the time they reached their destination. At last, Garam turned toward the only closed door that bordered the spiral path. It swung open on silent hinges when the captain touched it. All three of them blinked against the brighter light on the other side.

"Ah, Captain Kaith." A friendly voice beckoned them in. "Wonderful that you've arrived! And your friends, as well."

"My apologies for our late arrival, Filadiel." The captain slipped in first. Rune and Sera pushed through the doorway behind him at the same time.

A man at the edge of the room rose from his chair to greet

them, and when Rune saw him, he felt an odd stirring of surprise and curiosity.

Rich russet robes, and bright jewels set the man apart from the other people sitting in the room and made it clear he was their leader, but Rune had expected something else. Filadiel stood a head shorter than Rune, his long, stick-straight hair a mousy brown that almost blended in with his clothing. His expression was warm and his face narrow and angular, making him look as if he'd never outgrown awkward adolescence. But the most unusual facet of his appearance was his ears. Unlike any Eldani Rune had ever seen, Filadiel's long, slender ears stood flat against the sides of his skull. They rose at least two inches above the top of his head, their pointed tips twisted backwards.

Undeterred by Rune's staring, Filadiel smiled when they locked eyes. "And look at you! My, my, I almost thought Ria was fooling with me when she said there was a free mage in your midst." He took a step forward, and the entire room seemed to resonate. A shockwave of power flowed from the small man, his dull green eyes flashing with an inner light.

The other Aldaanan lifted their heads, each answering with an energy wave of their own as they turned glowing eyes toward the newcomers. Without knowing what he was doing, Rune let his own power roll forth, responding in kind.

Filadiel laughed, clapping with childlike delight. "And so you are!" He strode closer, cheer fading to leave his face a somber mask. "I see she didn't exaggerate the state of your corruption, either."

"You are familiar with tainted magic?" Rune asked.

Nodding grimly, Filadiel crossed his arms and tucked his hands into his sleeves. "I am. Though nothing so severe as this, I must admit. Physical corruption to go with polluted magic is new to me, but I am sure we can both learn a great deal from a simple examination, but we will speak of such matters later. I am sure the three of you are weary from your travels. Shall I have a meal and wine brought for you?"

"It would be much appreciated," Garam said.

"Of course. Please, sit, all of you." Filadiel gestured to a number of plain, empty chairs scattered between the people already seated. He inclined his head, and another man of short stature rose from his seat at the edge of the room to slip out the door in response to the silent command. Rune watched him go. There was an invisible hierarchy, it seemed; he'd have to pay attention to ensure he didn't violate it.

Mysterious ranks aside, it didn't take more than a look to realize the people in the room were some sort of council. There were perhaps two dozen Aldaanan in the room, all of them with tall, twisted ears and a sense of magic about them that was so strong, it hummed in Rune's senses. Most of the council members were dressed finely, some adorned with jewels to rival what Filadiel wore. All of the women wore thin earrings in the very tips of their ears, the loops connected with fine gold chains above their heads. Some wore more chains than others, but from the look of their robes, it had more to do with personal preference than rank or wealth.

Some of the Aldaanan regarded him with curiosity, though most gazed at the floor, as if lost in deep introspection. Introspection was likely all the room was good for, unremarkable as it was. Glass-paned windows along the curved outer wall held snow at bay, and thick velvet curtains offered a sense of comfort to the otherwise featureless room. There was no hearth or fire, but the chamber was still warm. With so many mages in a room, Rune supposed there was no need for other methods of heating. He sat near the window and watched as Garam and Sera tried to make themselves comfortable nearby, relieved to find he wasn't the only one who couldn't settle. The chairs were narrow and short, leaving no comfort to be had.

"I apologize for our late arrival, Filadiel. The weather slowed us enough to concern me." Garam leaned forward, resting hands against his knees, managing to look at ease despite his awkward perch. "Have you seen any indication of the college mages' approach?"

"Yes, and I'm afraid they are part of the reason for the weather." Filadiel shifted on his feet and rubbed his forehead as if he could smooth away the growing lines of worry he found there. "We don't like meddling with nature, but we thought it the best way to slow their progress. The college mages move in small groups, which makes them less of a threat, but it also makes it harder for the gryphons to spot them. They stand out better against the snow, and they haven't the manpower to trample a path with any sort of ease."

Sera's eyes grew wide. "You altered the weather?"

"Not something we like to do, as I said." Filadiel wrung his hands. "We'll all sleep better, knowing your army is here. Though there may not be much sleep for us tonight. I'm sorry to say I won't be able to rest easy until we've developed some sort of plan of action. The college mages don't come in numbers great enough to attack us yet, but there are bands of them that must be serving as scouts no more than a day behind you."

"A day!" Garam exclaimed, rocking back in his chair. "Surely we would have known if anyone was following that close."

"I don't think so." Sera frowned and rubbed her lips in thought. "No one could miss our army marching through the mountains. The mages would have taken an alternate route."

"Precisely." Filadiel moved to the door and pushed it open before the people on the other side could knock. The man who had left the chamber moments ago carried a low table to the middle of the room. Several women followed with dishes, trays of food, and pitchers of wine to set upon it. "You went to the left of a mountain, they switched their path to the right. It wouldn't be hard for a small group to evade notice. Please, share a drink with me."

Sera moved first, sliding out of her chair and settling on the floor beside the table as Filadiel sat across from her. He filled goblets with wine, passed one to her, and set the others at the empty places. Rune and Garam joined them at the same time. Bowls of fruits and trays of meats with thick sauces sat in the table's center and a small, dark-crusted loaf of bread sat beside each plate.

"What are these?" Sera lifted a dark blue, plum-sized fruit from one of the bowls.

Rune all but snatched it from her fingers. "Maluiri! I didn't know they grew here."

Filadiel raised a brow.

"Mal-what?" Sera took another from the bowl.

"Maluiri fruit," Filadiel said. "Though they're typically called Brant's berries, these days. Maluiri trees are known for growing big, gnarled trunks and flat-bottomed canopies. Not very common here, though a few groves can be found in Lore." His eyes glinted with suppressed light as he turned toward Rune. "Are they common where you are from?"

Rune took his knife from the table and cut the fruit into thin slices. The sweet-tart aroma made his mouth water. "Common enough, but we aren't allowed to eat most of the fruit."

"Why not?" Garam asked.

"Most of the trees grow in a place considered sacred." Rune picked up a slice of the dark-fleshed fruit and held it out for Sera to take. "My father had one in the garden, but it was old and didn't flower often."

Sera held the fruit to her nose and inhaled deeply before taking a bite. She squealed and clapped a hand over her mouth. "Oh, it's sour! That was a dirty trick, you rotten—"

Filadiel interrupted her with a laugh. "Yes, quite sour. That's why we serve them with a bowl of sugar." He passed the bowl across the table and gave Rune a curious look. "There are few places where they're known as maluiri, Aldaan being one of them. Is Aldaanan spoken where you are from?"

Rune opened his mouth to speak, but paused when he realized the question had been posed in Aldaanan and he'd almost replied in the same. Sera watched him with interest. Garam's face was dark. "It is my mother tongue," he said after a moment, mindful to use the common language Redoram had spent months drilling into him. Garam seemed to relax, realizing he wasn't going to be left out of the conversation. "I speak it better than I speak this tongue. Forgive me if I insist on practicing. Captain Kaith dislikes my archaic manner of speaking."

"Is it not archaic?" Sera teased.

Laughing again, Filadiel nodded. "Of course, of course. You are free to practice, by all means. Simple curiosity on my part. It makes things much easier, though, knowing you speak Aldaanan."

Garam's eyes narrowed. "How so?"

"If I am to investigate the corruption of his magic, I will need the help of several who don't speak your tongue, Captain Kaith."

Rune dipped a piece of fruit in the bowl of sugar as Sera passed it to him. "I don't mean to press," he started slowly, flinching when all three sets of eyes at the table turned toward him. Neither Sera nor Garam looked pleased he had spoken. He paused and glanced over his shoulder. None of the other Aldaanan were watching, each staring at the floor as they had when the three of them arrived. He put down his fruit and cleared his throat. "I realize you have many important things to discuss with Captain Kaith, but if there is anything I can do to improve my ability with magecraft before the battles, I'd like to start. When can that begin?"

"Tonight, if you really wanted," Filadiel said nonchalantly, swirling wine in his cup and then taking a sip. "There are just a few things to be done beforehand, simple cultural procedures to prove your intentions before we begin lessons."

"Cultural procedures?" Sera's brow furrowed with concern.

Filadiel waved a hand. "Nothing unusual, I assure you. Just a matter of tradition. There are many here much older than I am, sticklers for traditions and things. You can finish the initiation rites by sunrise and begin practicing with the elders tomorrow morning."

Rune glanced to Garam, wordlessly seeking permission. It was still a blow to his pride, deferring to someone else, but the chance the Aldaanan could correct the taint in him was worth the deference.

Garam lifted his wine for a long sip. "The sooner he's got a solid hold on what he's doing, the better. As long as it doesn't interfere with his orders or responsibilities to the army. I have few mages among my men, I need all of them I can get for this."

"Excellent, excellent. We'll start on that after dinner, then." Filadiel grinned. "Now, on to the less pleasant business. The maps will be up shortly, but since you just came through the mountains, Captain, where do you think we need to have sentries stationed?"

Rune half-listened as Garam began to explain the strategies he'd come up with. The food on the table was tantalizing and most of Garam's plans didn't involve him, anyway. He filled his plate and managed to get his fork into his mouth before Sera leaned close enough to speak in a harsh whisper.

"Why would you agree to their terms without knowing what their initiation is?" She didn't bother trying to hide her anger. Her blue eyes flashed fire.

"Because," he murmured back between bites of food, "they're mages, not barbarians. A bunch of mages can't have traditions any worse than the sort I've seen before."

"What are you talking about?" she snarled in a whisper.

He lifted his left hand, just enough to draw her attention to the prominent rune-shaped scar on its back. Then he turned his hand over and stared thoughtfully at the less noticeable scarring in his palm.

Her eyebrows lifted.

"Believe me," he said. "There are worse things."

14

HARD LESSONS

"DYING!" FIRAL RAKED HER FINGERS THROUGH HER UNRULY HAIR, torn between screaming and crying. She did neither, turning so fast her skirts whirled and tangled about her legs. "And no one told me? A man retired from the city guard knew, but no one saw fit to tell their queen?"

Vahn bounced the baby against his shoulder, trying to soothe the girl's cries. "Firal, please, calm down."

"Why should I?" She wheeled to glare at him with tears brimming on her dark lashes. "How can you be so calm about this? Nondar is the only thing keeping the other Masters from running roughshod over me!"

"You're upsetting the baby."

Firal blinked hard and pulled Lumia from his arms. "And this is upsetting me." She sat on the foot of the bed and hugged the baby close. She didn't feel like reining in her emotions, but making the infant squall wasn't going to help anything. Pressing kisses to Lumia's dark curls, she rocked side to side and made soft hushing sounds. The baby nestled close and quieted.

Vahn sighed and rubbed his eyes. He looked more weary than the late hour could account for. She felt a tinge of guilt. Perhaps their visit with his father had been more taxing on him than she'd realized. He didn't complain, but he folded his arms over his chest and stared at the midnight sky on the other side of the windows. His shoulders remained stiff, his expression closed-off and defensive. "If you hadn't sent the mages back to the temple, you would have known Nondar's health was fragile."

The way he said it wasn't accusatory, but it still irritated her. She patted Lumia's back and scowled. "I sent the mages back to the temple to protect myself. At least this way they can't gang up on me. I'll only ever have to deal with a few of them at a time. What if I'd left them in Ilmenhith? I'd have every mage in white breathing down my neck every day. How am I supposed to rule like that?"

"It gives you a little distance, yes, but it doesn't keep them from pushing you around. Nothing will. If another Master steps into the role of Archmage, it's not going to give them any more influence over—"

"You don't understand," Firal interrupted, her voice cracking. "It isn't just that he's Archmage. Nondar is the closest thing to a father I ever had, Vahn."

His brows rose as his expression melted first into understanding, then concern. "I'm sorry," he said after a moment. "I always assumed he was just a teacher."

She sniffed and wiped her eyes. "The best teacher. He was grumpy, but always kind to me. Even after I was expelled from the temple. I haven't been a mageling for close to two years now. Nondar is the only tie I still have to what my life used to be." Her throat tightened as she spoke, threatening to choke off her words. It felt like she spent too much time crying these days, but she couldn't help herself. She swallowed against the constriction and forced herself to spill the thoughts that haunted her mind with ever-increasing frequency. "I don't think I can do this. Not without his help. I'm not as strong as I need to be."

It was obvious from the way Vahn shifted that her words troubled him, though he managed to limit their effect to a slight shrug of his shoulders and a shadow of worry in his blue eyes. "You don't have to do it alone, but you have to do it. There's no one else, Firal. Even your rule is disputed in the streets. Were it not for the mages backing you, the country would be in turmoil. If you can't lead us, who will?"

She shuddered and hugged Lumia close. The girl wriggled drowsily. "Is that supposed to help?"

"It's supposed to make you think." He paced forward and stood at the foot of the bed as if unsure whether or not he should sit. "I know ruling is hard, but you'll always have help. Even the mages want what's best for the kingdom. They're just... opinionated about what that is."

"And your father?"

"He'll help," Vahn said with a nod. "He already promised to be here for your meeting with Master Anaide in the morning. He's a hard man, but that might work in your favor. Archmage Nondar is a hard man, too, and that seems to be the buffer you need between you and those old harpies."

Firal scoffed quietly and wiped her eyes again. She couldn't disagree with the description, especially considering Edagan's sharp beak of a nose.

"Now come on." His voice softened as he offered a hand. "Lulu is tired, and you are, too. Let's get you both to bed."

She dried her fingers on her skirt before she took his hand and let him pull her to her feet. "I'd rather keep her close, tonight."

Vahn smiled. "I understand. I'll drag her cradle out from the nursery."

She paced by the window, rocking the baby in her arms while he moved the cradle to the bedside. It was the first moment of peace she'd felt since leaving the Tanrys estate, though looking at Lumia's dark curls and rosy cheeks put an ache in her heart. She tucked the baby into her cradle and stood beside it while Vahn stripped out of his finery.

"Do you need help with your buttons?" he asked quietly.

"Please." Firal pulled her hair over her shoulder and turned so he could unfasten the dozens of tiny buttons that ran the length of her back. She held the bodice to her chest as the dress came loose, waiting until he was done before she slid it off. The silk chemise she wore underneath clung to her skin but left her cold. She hugged her arms to herself. Polite as ever, Vahn looked away as she climbed into bed and drew the blankets to her shoulders. He lingered at the bedside a moment before he remembered himself and reached to take the extra pillows and blankets for his pallet.

She worried her lower lip. "Vahn?"

He paused and looked up.

"I feel... ah..." Fidgeting with the edge of the blanket, she licked her lips and swallowed hard. "I just... I don't want... to be alone, tonight."

Vahn stared at her in surprise, then his face softened. "Of course, my lady."

Firal offered a sorrowful smile as he put out the lamps and slid into bed beside her. She nestled against his shoulder and pulled the blankets to her chin as her tears finally escaped.

THERE WAS HARDLY a pause between the knock at the door and the sound of it opening. Firal jerked awake, then squeezed her eyes shut and turned her face toward her pillow. Vahn shifted beside her, letting out a quiet groan to express the displeasure she didn't dare voice herself. After a late night, morning came too soon. Firal wrenched her eyes open and promptly squinted against the sunshine. She'd forgotten to close the curtains.

"Good morning," Medreal called from the doorway. She carried a breakfast tray in her hands and pushed the door shut with her foot. "I've brought a pot of coffee with breakfast. I thought you might—" She stopped short, her eyebrows climbing as Vahn pushed himself upright in bed.

Firal stared at her stewardess groggily a moment before she realized what the woman was looking at. She shoved the blankets aside and righted her chemise, her cheeks turning crimson. "Leave it, thank you. I'll feed myself this morning. Prepare my office for a meeting, would you?"

Vahn scrubbed a hand through his mess of blond hair and squinted at Firal's back before he looked down at the bed, amusement drawn on his face.

"Of course, my queen." Medreal deposited the breakfast tray on the table and spun to face the door. "Shall I take Lumia with me?"

Firal paused to peer into the still-quiet cradle. "She's still asleep, I'll let her rest. It was a late night for everyone."

"I see," Medreal intoned, never looking back. "Very well. I'll be in your office if I am needed, my queen." She paused at the door, hesitating before adding, "My lord."

Firal cringed as the door clicked shut. She bit her lip as she pushed herself from the edge of the bed. She hadn't expected to sleep the whole night. Normally, Lumia woke her before she could. "Good morning," she said over her shoulder, unsure what else to say. Her cheeks still burned with embarrassment. "Did you sleep well?"

"Quite well, actually. The bed's a lot more comfortable than the floor." His tone was half joking, though it held a note of chagrin. "I apologize. I meant to get up after you fell asleep, but I guess I was more tired than I realized."

"Don't worry yourself. You needed the rest. I'll speak to Medreal later and clear up any improper thoughts she might have." She took a pale green dress from the wardrobe and knelt to find matching slippers. There was nothing wrong with resting in the same bed. She'd shared a bed with Rune several times before they married and shared in other things. The thought of those *other things* kept her cheeks rosy as she stood, but when she turned and saw Vahn looking at her, she thought she might blush all the way to her toes.

He looked away as soon as she met his eyes, but the serious, contemplative look she'd caught on his face had been enough. She didn't have to explain what thoughts Medreal might have, but she hadn't expected to see him thinking them, as well. Perhaps she'd chosen her words poorly. Perhaps she'd put the thoughts there, herself. Her ears burned and she hurried behind the folding screen to change. Once she was out of sight, she scrunched up her face and buried it in her hands.

Aside from Medreal and the Master mages on her council, only her dearest friends knew of her first marriage, the reason Vahn still slept on the floor. It was a struggle to maintain the illusion of a content marriage, the image of a happy young family with their first child. Things would have been simpler if she *had* taken Vahn to her bed. In fact, the mages encouraged it. Even if they had chosen to recognize her first marriage as valid, her husband was a traitor and she was a queen. They would have freed her of her previous vows and seen her marriage to Vahnil as legitimate. But the legality of her union didn't concern her. Legality bound her to Vahn, but her first vows still bound her heart to someone else. Not for the first time, she felt the pulling of guilt. Guilt for remarrying, and guilt for robbing Vahn of his chance to be happy.

She tried not to think of it any more, pulling the laces in the front of her bodice just a little tighter. Then she put on her slippers and stepped out from behind the screen, finger-combing her ebony hair.

Vahn had dressed, and he flashed her a nervous smile as he tied his boots. "I wish I could help with your meeting this morning, but Medreal left a note on the tray with breakfast. I'm to meet with Davan, it seems."

"Hopefully he has an idea of how we can feed his people." Firal crossed to the table and poured herself a cup of coffee before she sat. She was not fond of the flavor, but she'd grown accustomed to having it before morning meetings. The bitterness seemed to help her focus. "I never should have asked them to leave the ruins. If I'd told them to stay in Core, they would have planted their crops as usual and I wouldn't have to worry about having more mouths to feed. Things in the underground had improved so much. They even had livestock besides chickens and boar. Instead, they used all their provisions just to get here."

"It isn't your fault, Firal. You had no way of knowing what you were taking over. Even if Kifel were still alive, we'd be in the same mess." Vahn buckled his sword belt at his waist and leaned over to steal an apple from the tray. "Besides, that's why you're meeting with Master Anaide this morning, isn't it? To make sure your plans to trade with the mainland are still moving forward?"

She groaned. "That's another problem. Your father mentioned it last night, just in passing, and I've not been able to get it off my mind since. Even if we are able to move forward without Nondar, what are we supposed to trade?"

He rolled the apple between his hands. "What do you mean?"

"We were a wealthy island because of how many merchant ships used this as a waypoint between the northern and southern halves of the world. They counted on us for a chance to replenish their stores. Elenhiise was always known as an island of bounty. Now the fruit groves are all but barren because of having too much rain and then not enough. Every bit of coin we had has gone to feeding us, and you'd be a fool to think anyone is charging us a fair price."

Vahn's face fell. "But that means—"

"We're poor, Vahnil." The words left her mouth dry. "We haven't the money to feed the island for another season."

His expression grew grim and he nodded slowly as he put the apple back on the tray. The movement was so laden with guilt that she almost laughed. "We'll figure something out," he said.

"I hope so," she murmured.

He nudged the apple with a fingertip to send it rolling across the tray. "You eat, then. You have a big meeting right after breakfast. You'll need your energy."

She took the apple, though she didn't eat it. Instead, she shifted it between her hands and then returned it to the table. "And you?"

"Me?" He laughed. "I don't have to deal with my father." He slid back to the cradle to press a kiss to the sleeping baby's brow. Then he flashed Firal a teasing grin and slung his cape around his shoulders on his way out of the room.

Firal snorted a laugh and shook her head. She finished her coffee and nibbled a pastry, then went to rouse Lumia. When the baby was fed, clean, and dressed, Firal cradled the girl close and took a deep breath before she strode into the hall. She drew herself up to look every bit the part of queen as she made her way to her office.

A pair of chairs sat ready before her desk, a tea tray on the desk's corner with three cups upside down on their saucers. Medreal barely glanced up when Firal entered, though she offered a bob of respect before she lowered her eyes to the papers she was sorting.

"Thank you for seeing to the office, Medreal." Firal nudged the door closed, kissing the top of Lumia's head on her way to her chair.

"Only my job, my queen." The stewardess pulled back the large chair behind the desk and dropped a stack of papers in front of Firal the moment she sat. She slid another stack into a ledger.

The top paper was a report on food stores in the palace. Firal flinched and made herself look away. She studied her advisor's face instead. The old woman remained intent on her work.

Firal pursed her lips. "It isn't what you think, Medreal."

Medreal glanced up, clearly surprised, though she kept her face neutral and busied herself with the tea tray. She filled one cup. "It's not my place to think anything, my queen."

"But you're a smart woman. You do think, don't you."

The stewardess paused, drumming her fingertips on the teapot. Eventually, she set it down. "Yes, my queen."

Firal leaned back in her chair, shifting Lumia in her lap. "And what do you think?"

Medreal shifted on her feet, her fingers twitching as if she longed to pick up the teapot again. With her hands empty, her emotions had nowhere to hide. She sighed and settled for adding honey to the cup before she placed it in front of Firal. "That it isn't my business. It's been a year, but only you know if it's time for you to move on, my queen."

It wasn't much of an answer, but Firal hadn't expected anything else. There were times she thought the silver-haired woman was too polite to say an ill word about anyone—most certainly not about the queen she served—but that tact was not why she kept the stewardess around. "May I ask your advice?"

"Of course, Majesty."

"What would you do, in my position?" Firal lifted the teacup and twisted in her chair so she didn't hold it above the baby. She blew on it and took a sip. It was not as sweet as she'd grown used to, but that was one of many sacrifices she'd learned to make in the face of hunger.

Medreal frowned thoughtfully, wiping her hands on her apron. She stayed quiet for a long time, though her lips twitched with words unspoken. Eventually, she shook her head. "I don't know that I can advise you on that, my lady. Vahnil is a good man, but only you know your heart. I cannot tell you which way it pulls."

As noncommittal as ever. Firal smiled sadly and put her teacup aside. She cradled Lumia close against her stomach, listening to the girl's happy burbles for a while. The sound stirred delight and heartache in her at the same time. Those feelings constantly warred within her. The baby looked so much like her that no one thought anything unusual, but she saw things others didn't—things beyond the unusual color of the girl's eyes. A twist to the baby's mouth when she cooed, the way her face crumpled when she became frustrated. Little glimpses of her father that always put a lump in Firal's throat. She swallowed against it now, breathing deeply to keep her feelings in check. Her voice quavered when she spoke again. "Do you think I was hasty to marry him?"

"Which 'him' do you mean? That might change the answer considerably." The old woman didn't bat an eye. Her unapologetically sarcastic response brought a rueful smile to Firal's lips.

"Ran."

A shadow of sadness darkened Medreal's eyes and for a moment, Firal regretted the question. Medreal had raised him; she'd been the mother he'd never had. But the shadow was fleeting and the stewardess tried to smile. Instead, her face filled with regret—though for what, Firal didn't know. "I think you were like the rest of us. Swept up in all his fire, then lost in the wake of his storm."

Firal's eyes fell to the floor. Medreal was always polite, but the truth still hurt. More than once, Firal had looked back at the chain of events that catapulted her into the palace and wondered at the way it all swirled together. Like a hurricane, drawing in and destroying everything in its path. She'd never seen it coming, too close to the calm center. Too close to him, the eye of the storm.

"But you were young," Medreal continued, her words gentle. "Just coming into womanhood, just finding yourself. You didn't know any better, and he was so easy to love. He was full of passion, ambition. Full of determination to shape the world into what he wanted. It's only natural to be drawn to that sort of strength at such a tender time."

"You speak of him as if he's died," Firal said, blinking against the prick of tears.

"I speak of him as if he's gone." Sorrow traced lines in the old woman's face and she turned away. "Sometimes the difference isn't all that great."

Silence fell between them. It was interrupted by a knock at the door.

Medreal lowered her voice as she crossed the room to answer it. "Our paths are never straightforward. They wind like a serpent's trail in the sand. Your marriage to Vahnil is a necessity, my queen. Best for both the kingdom and the safety of your family. You shouldn't punish yourself for that decision, and you shouldn't rob yourselves of whatever joy your life together might offer. But that's only my opinion, my queen. Only you know what you must do to be happy."

Firal's chest tightened, but she had no time to reflect on her advisor's words or the grief that constricted her heart. Another knock sounded, more insistent. She straightened in her chair as the stewardess opened the door. Ennil stepped past Medreal with little more than a nod of acknowledgment.

"Majesty," he greeted. He dipped into a formal bow, his eyes falling to the baby in her lap. "And the little princess. Good morning."

Firal forced a smile. "Good morning. Lulu won't be staying for our meeting, I'm afraid. She'll be going with Medreal as soon as Master Anaide arrives."

"Only Master Anaide this morning?" Ennil seated himself without direction, adjusted his fine gold-trimmed coat, and scooted his chair closer to the desk. He watched Medreal fill a teacup for him and waved a hand in dismissal when she offered honey and cream to go with it.

"Master Anaide is bad enough," Firal grumbled. "I don't think I could stomach more than one Master at a time."

Ennil chuckled as he transferred the teacup and saucer to his lap. "I've dealt with them before. Mages were on your father's council, as well. I can't imagine they're any worse now than they were then. This would be easier if we'd had more time to discuss your plans, but we'll make do."

His mood was altogether more pleasant than when she'd met with him before, and she found herself relaxing as he spoke. But this was different. Vahn had been present for their previous meetings, and though her husband remained tight-lipped about his relationship with his father, it wasn't hard to tell they mixed as well as oil and water. "Thank you, Lord Tanrys."

"Ennil will do when we're in private, my dear. We are family, after all."

She arched a brow, but a knock kept her from replying.

The Master mage ignored the stewardess who opened the door and paused just inside the office, as if startled to find someone else with the queen. Anaide stood taller, straighter, and clasped her hands together before her stomach. "Did you forget we were to have a meeting this morning, my lady?"

"Of course not," Ennil said before Firal could speak. "The commissioned fishing ships are complete and need inspection, and King Vahnil is off to meet with the Underling faction on the edge of the city, so the rest of the council is unfortunately too busy to join us. It seems it will be just the three of us this morning."

Anaide's face twisted with displeasure. "I don't recall there being any open seats for councilors."

He gave her a smile that seemed too broad to be genuine. "I don't recall the queen needing a mage's permission to add members to her council."

The Master mage glared at him.

"Lord Tanrys served my father unerringly for years. He has been most gracious to give up retirement to take a place on my council." Firal stood to pass Lumia into Medreal's waiting arms, kissing the girl's brow before the stewardess left. Then she motioned to the second chair in front of her desk and gave Anaide an expectant look. "As you were not a part of my father's council, Anaide, you may not realize how exceptional Lord Tanrys is at managing city affairs. With the need to integrate the Underlings into the city, his assistance will be a necessity."

Ennil smirked, leaned back in his chair and lifted a booted

foot to rest his ankle on his knee. "And we are meeting about the state of affairs in Ilmenhith, aren't we?"

Anaide looked between the two of them, her too-blue eyes narrowing as she sank into her seat. "Yes, we are."

"Good." Firal settled behind her desk again, propping her elbows against its edge and lacing her fingers together. "Help yourselves to tea, both of you. Medreal won't be attending us today." Tea was one thing of which the palace still had plenty, at least. It was easy to come by in a city that was desperate to trade luxuries for food.

"I suppose the first thing in order is to determine when and where the Gate to the mainland will be opened." Ennil rubbed his chin thoughtfully, balancing his teacup on his thigh with his other hand. "People are desperate. We can't trust them to behave rationally when the supplies begin to come through. We'll need to plan for it to happen in a secure location. Perhaps even on palace grounds."

Anaide's brows knit together. She retained her composure too well to appear confused, but the subtle shift in her expression and the fact she said nothing gave her away.

Firal lifted her chin. It delighted her to see the woman caught by surprise, though she supposed she ought to feel guilty over such petty pleasures. The mage had upset her often enough in their lessons, though, and seemed to delight in that. Perhaps it was only fair. "What's the matter, Master Anaide? Nondar did pass directions on to the rest of the Masters, didn't he? I'd think he'd have plenty of time to devote to planning while he's trapped in bed. How is he recovering?"

"R-recovering, my lady?" Anaide stammered. It was the first time for that, as well. Firal struggled to contain her smile.

"I understand he's taken a fall, hasn't he?" Ennil lifted his tea as if to take a sip and let his cup hover before his lips. "Very dangerous for a man his age."

"Oh, yes." The Master mage leaped at the slight falsehood to recover, almost to Firal's dismay. "He is as well as can be expected, but the road to recovery for the elderly is often long and troublesome. Edagan and I will be acting as Archmage in the interim, as he mends."

Firal smiled sweetly over the rim of her cup and noted the look of discomfort on the mage's face. No one intended to serve her, and Anaide still hadn't poured tea for herself. Firal couldn't help but wonder how long her pride would hold out. She put her teacup back on its saucer with a noisy clink. "Then you'll know all about the avenues of trade we intend to open."

Anaide's mouth tightened, but this time, it wasn't with uncertainty. Her eyes flashed with disapproval. "And just what, exactly, do you intend to trade?" Her air of haughtiness returned as quickly as it had disappeared. "You don't even have the means to entice Relythes to reopen trade routes over that wall he's erected along the border. What makes you think you can convince anyone else to trade with a destitute nation?"

A *wall* along the border? Firal barely kept her mouth from falling open. She'd heard of no such thing, not even from Nondar. The idea that the Archmage she'd chosen was still hiding things from her made her blood boil.

"Trade and economy are none of your concern." Ennil's tone was as biting as it was commanding. "Your job is only to see that we have mages on hand to open a Gate to the mainland and sustain it while goods are transported through. Can you do that or not?"

Whatever vulnerability their conversation had first exposed, there was nothing but steel resolve and cold scorn in the Master mage's eyes now. Anaide barked a laugh and waved her hand in dismissal. "Direct trade with the mainland cannot be done."

"And why not?" Firal asked, annoyed.

The white-haired woman sneered. "You're a mage, aren't you? Have you never tried to open a Gate, girl?"

Firal glared back. "Opening a Gate on my own would be suicide."

"And opening a Gate somewhere we haven't been is impossible."

"Don't be ridiculous." Ennil glanced between the two of them. "Gates to the mainland have been opened before. Am I really to believe it can't be done now?"

"Believe it," Anaide huffed and crossed her arms. "In all of Kirban Temple, there were only two mages familiar enough with the Grand College to open a Gate to it. One was our previous Archmage, and the other was the one who led the opening of the Gate for her banishment."

Firal's shoulders sagged and she squeezed her eyes closed. "Nondar."

The Master mage smirked. "Precisely."

Ennil's eyes narrowed. He drained the last of his tea and set his cup aside. "So trade waits for his recovery?"

"Trade may not happen at all," Anaide said, her words mirroring Firal's fears. "Even if Nondar does recover from the incident, there's no reason to think any mainland nations would want anything to do with us. Elenhiise is minuscule, a dot on the map. When we had wealth, supplies, we mattered. Not now." She shook her head, her expression stormy. "This matter should have been discussed with all the Masters responsible for leading the temple."

"The queen doesn't owe you a discussion of anything," Ennil snapped. "She's given an order and it will be followed."

"The queen sits on her throne because the mages put her there," Anaide replied, ice and venom in her tone.

Ennil gave her such a withering stare that Firal was amazed the woman didn't wilt in her chair. "The queen sits on her throne because it belonged to her father. That the mages brought her heritage to public attention is the only thing to your credit."

A small smile played on the mage's lips. "The temple's word is all there is to say she belongs there. What makes you think removal wouldn't be as easy?"

A chill rolled down Firal's spine. The threat was clear, but it was the implication behind it that put ice in her stomach. Who *had* told Kifel that she was his daughter? That the information had come from the mages was all she knew. In the frenzy of war and her desperation to stop it, she'd never given it a second thought. What if the temple's word *was* all the claim she had to the throne? "Enough," she barked. Both Ennil and Anaide turned toward her, surprised.

"This will be discussed no further," Firal said. "Anaide, you will return to the temple and poll your mages. There is always a possibility we have another mage from off-island who can lead the opening of a Gate."

"But Majesty—"

Firal raised a hand. "End of discussion." Nerves dried her mouth, but she refused to let the mage see her squirm. "There are other things that demand my attention and I will not waste another minute with this. Both of you are dismissed."

Anaide's lips puckered as if to restrain a frown. She rose from her chair with a jerk, bowed stiffly, and spun on her heel. Firal watched until the white-robed woman made it through the door.

The moment she was gone, Firal seized her teacup and swallowed the last of the tepid drink.

Slowly, Ennil stood. "Firmly said, Majesty. I applaud that you held your ground." He gave a formal half-bow, the look in his eyes a combination of respect and concern. "Are you well?"

Firal glanced away. "As well as I can be. Thank you for your support, Lord Tanrys. There are things I must review now, but if there is any change in this situation, you will be notified at once."

"Of course, Your Majesty." He touched a hand to his heart and bowed again. He adjusted the cuffs of his sleeves on his way out.

The door clicked closed behind him and Firal sagged against her desk, burying her face in her hands. She trembled now that she was alone, shaken to the core by Anaide's threat to remove her from power. It wasn't just fear that shook her. It would have been easier if it was. Instead, the fear of being deposed as queen mingled with guilt. She *wanted* to be deposed.

She'd never wanted to be queen. She'd never wanted more than the opportunity to be a mage and a teacher. But when the Masters brought her news of Kifel's death, she'd gotten her first glimpse of their intent to see her crowned. They'd thought her tears were grief over the loss of her father. Instead, she'd cried for loss of her freedom. She'd closed herself in her chambers to try to think of a way to escape, and she had come up with nothing.

Then she'd seen her father's killer.

Her chest still ached when she thought of him, the pain a wretched mixture of sorrow and heartbreak. She'd not forgiven herself for her mistake, for thinking Rune had gone to war for another woman's sake, that he'd used her as a pawn in some sort of game for power. But he had eyed the throne long before Firal had come into the picture. What else was she to think? Yet she hadn't recognized the emotions on his face when they'd presented him before the throne for sentencing. Surprise, concern, confusion. Relief and hope. They all seemed so clear in memory.

Salty tears made trails down her face as Medreal's words echoed in her head. *You were young. You didn't know any better.*

She knew better now.

Firal thrust herself up from her desk, scrubbing tears away with the sleeve of her dress. She'd trusted Anaide to pass fair judgment in her stead. That had been her first mistake, the first falter in her rule. A chink in her armor, through which they slid their knives and pushed just far enough to poke and prod her in the direction they wanted her to go.

No more. Stubborn determination welled up within her and she clenched her hands to fists as she slid out of her office. A dancing bear, Ennil had called her at their first dinner. The comparison had rankled then, but she began to understand the accusation. The mages thought she would dance, or else be easy to remove and replace. It wouldn't happen. She wouldn't be controlled any longer.

Firal hurried down the hall to the parlor where her court mages waited. It was a trip she'd taken countless times since her daughter's birth, desperate to fix her mistakes. The mages had given her the same answer at each visit and she had let herself be cowed every time.

No more, she repeated in her head. She would not be denied again.

Eight mages in blue-trimmed white jumped to attention when the door flew open. Fewer than she'd hoped for, but enough for what she needed. "Prepare to open a Gate," Firal ordered, watching with a stony expression as the mages hurried to form a half-circle around the archway in the center of the room. She felt the surge of energy as the mages tied their magic together.

The woman closest to the arch turned toward her. Temar had served the royal family since before Kifel had been born. When the temple severed its ties with Ilmenhith, Temar had been the first to declare her loyalty to the crown alone. Firal had liked her since their first encounter, during the solstice ball. She had always been warm, pleasant. Yet she had denied Firal her independence at every visit. It seemed she anticipated another argument. Her mage-blue eyes bore a careful guard. "Where shall we send you, Majesty?"

Firal stepped forward. "Tie with me."

All eight mages looked startled.

"I will lead the opening of the Gate. None of you have the familiarity needed to open it. Tie power with me and I'll lead."

A flicker of doubt crossed Temar's face. "Your Majesty, we've been over this before."

"That was not a request," Firal snapped.

The mage made a soft, soothing motion with both hands. "Peace, Majesty. I mean no offense. The Archmage has not yet declared it safe for you to wield magic again."

Firal gritted her teeth. Her power had been forbidden since the moment the Archmage detected the child in her womb; the fragile, budding life within her could not withstand the force of magic. Tradition demanded mothers abstain from touching power for a year. Nine months for a child to grow, three more for the mother's recovery. "And if the Archmage should die before he declares me free to practice magecraft again?"

A small gasp rolled through the mages in the room.

"We are not trying to hinder you, Majesty," Temar pleaded. "We're trying to protect you."

"I don't need your protection, and I will not be denied any longer." Firal scowled. "I will lead. That is an order."

Temar's mouth tightened, but she said nothing. A moment later, tendrils of energy pushed toward Firal. She snared them, wove them together with her own strength.

She had studied the opening of a Gate, though she had never done it, herself. From her understanding, she wouldn't need to. The other, more experienced mages could guide the power. All she had to do was tell it where to go. No different from directing healing, she assumed, and she had plenty of practice with that.

Yet nervous queasiness stirred in her stomach. Somehow, she hadn't believed she'd get this far. She'd never mentioned her intentions, afraid the mages would try to stop her. Uncertainty made her grasp of the power waver, but regret for the number of times she'd surrendered burned too deeply for her to give up.

"Are you certain you wish to lead, my queen?" Temar asked.

Firal glared, steeling her resolve. Instead of replying, she squeezed her eyes shut, turning all of Nondar's teachings over in her mind. Then she cleared her mind of thoughts and focused on creating a clear visual. She pictured every detail, feeding them into threads of energy, and spun those threads into a web within the archway.

The air crackled. Light zigzagged between the sides of the arch, brilliant even with her eyes closed. She traced each detail over in her mind and brought it into precise focus a second time.

The texture of his skin, the line of his jaw. The color of his eyes, reflected every day in his daughter's gaze.

The Gate sizzled, white-hot with energy. She opened her eyes and her heart leaped as she caught a glimpse of her vision reflected in the ripples of the forming portal.

A deafening shriek filled the room, rising in pitch until the tendrils of energy shattered and the Gate collapsed on itself with a deafening boom. Power snapped back against her, knocking her to the floor. Firal scrambled upright, shaking so hard she could barely sit. She wasn't the only one who had toppled. All eight court mages lay on the floor. "What happened?" she cried.

"Not enough mages to contain a broken destination," one woman groaned, struggling to her knees and rubbing the back of her head.

"A broken destination?" Firal glanced between the mages as they got up, uncertain what the woman meant.

"Trying to open a Gate to something that has changed," another mage explained. "Something must have happened to wherever you were trying to go."

Firal's heart sank.

"There just weren't enough of us present to hold the misdirected energy in check." Temar got to her feet and offered her hand. "I apologize, my queen. We should have been prepared for that possibility."

"No," Firal said bitterly, waving the mage away and standing on her own. "It's not your fault. I wasn't prepared for that possibility, either."

The mages bowed and shuffled back to their chairs to sit and groan over the bruises they'd have, come morning. Firal stared at the empty archway with a new ache in her heart. Silently, she sent out another wave of energy. A gentle beckon, pleading and filled with sadness. Broken destination or not, the Calling was a method of contact that didn't need a clear mental image to send. It was tied to someone's essence, someone's energy, taught to mages for times where simple contact was needed.

She stood waiting for what felt like an eternity, hoping to receive a Calling back.

Just when she thought nothing would come, the door to the parlor flew open.

"Firal!"

She spun on her heel, startled to see Vahn in the doorway. He rushed forward and clasped her hands in his. "I know what we're going to do!"

She hadn't Called *him*, but the look of elation on his face drove everything else out of mind.

15

HARD CHOICES

"A MINE?" FIRAL REPEATED, SURPRISED. SHE SIPPED HER TEA, watching Vahn pace in front of the couch. He hadn't given his cup a second glance after she set it on the low table.

"With enough gems in it to buy the island itself. The gold from the river alone will be more than enough to refill the treasury." He paused to grin at her, a sparkle in his blue eyes. "I couldn't believe it. Davan tried to explain it, but he said something about the ocean and seams of the world that didn't make a bit of sense to me. Either way, he's bringing a map as soon as he can get his hands on it, and we can plan from there."

She smiled back, though her ears burned with embarrassment. She knew there were mines beneath Core and gold to be panned from the river. Why hadn't she thought of them before? The ruins were on her lands and the ruin-folk answered to her now. There was no reason she couldn't claim those resources for herself. Especially for the purpose of feeding hungry mouths. "I just can't believe you thought to mention it to him."

Vahn paused his pacing and finally reached for his teacup. "I didn't. It came up in a roundabout sort of way, while we were discussing the cost of food. All I said was that even the palace can't afford to feed everyone forever, and Davan said he'd have spent time in the mines before coming if he'd known how bad it would be."

Nodding thoughtfully, she tapped her nails against the side of her cup. It was both a relief and a new problem, pushing everything else to the back of her mind. "There's the issue of getting people to do it, though. Mining is hard work. It'll be difficult to find people willing to take the job. Then there's the trouble of getting it back to Ilmenhith. Not to mention keeping the workers from pocketing the gold and gems for themselves."

"Yes, we discussed that a little. But it's a start." His chipper attitude didn't waver and for a moment, she felt guilty for the discouragement that weighed on her shoulders.

"Yes," she agreed. "It's a start."

She had just enough time to finish her tea before Davan arrived with rolled maps tucked beneath his arm. He looked a little more worn each time Firal saw him, which stirred a new wave of guilt. She'd meant to visit the Underling camp to spend time with Minna. She still hadn't gotten to it.

"Your Majesty. Your Lordship." Davan bowed so deep he almost dropped the maps. He shuffled them in his arms. "I apologize for the delay. It's just that it's hard to find things when all your belongings are still in the back of a wagon." He didn't sound unhappy or inconvenienced, merely tired. Even after she'd spent months living among them, the Underlings still managed to surprise her with their tenacity.

"I completely understand." Firal cleared her desk to make room for his maps. An informal meeting would have been more comfortable, but the small couch and table beside the windows didn't offer the space they needed. The men joined her and Davan rolled a map out across her desk as soon as she had it clean.

The map was marked with symbols she didn't recognize and

written in a language she didn't understand, but the features themselves were easy to interpret. Having the map spread out in front of her made her heart race in delight, stirring memories of the many nights she'd spent trying to draw just such a thing. "This is the entirety of the ruins!" She traced the curving, twisting lines of the labyrinth's paths with a fingertip.

"Aye," Davan laughed, laying the other scrolls to the side. "You didn't think we'd live there for centuries without mapping it, did you?"

"But this is incredible! Every hallway, every entrance to the underground—" She stopped short as he unfurled another map on top of it, one depicting the lay of the subterranean passages. Her mouth fell open.

"Lord Vahnil mentioned it would be difficult getting ores in and out of the mines without mages Gating them back and forth." Davan searched the desk a moment before he cleared his throat. "Does milady have something I might use to mark the map?"

"Oh, yes, of course." Firal leaned back and fished in a desk drawer. Davan's maps were drawn on skins. She imagined they were the only copies that existed, which made them priceless. She produced her softest chalk in hopes it could be cleaned from the map's surface easily when they were done. He took it from her fingers without looking away from the maps, rubbing his chin all the while.

"There are better ways in and out of Core than the hallways, though they need someone who knows how to work them. Her Majesty, our, ah... former queen..." He paused as if uncertain how Firal would take to the woman being mentioned, shifting nervously before going on. "She kept books on how to work them, but they'll have to be retrieved from her quarters and studied by someone who knows how to read better than the lot of us."

Vahn's brow furrowed. "How to work what?"

Davan traced a hallway with a fingertip and marked a point along it. "The lifts, my lord."

Firal stared at the mark, unable to picture its location. "Lifts?"

"Aye, several. The fastest way in and out of the ruins." He made another mark, this one at the mouth of the river, near the giant waterwheel. "There's one not far from the mines, which means getting men through the ruins is the only challenge."

"And not much of a challenge, if we can mark the path," Vahn murmured, lifting the corner of the map to look at the layout of the ruins again.

"I'm more interested in these lifts," Firal said. "What are they, Davan? Why didn't your people use them when they lived in the underground? I never heard mention of them."

"Not much reason to use them, Majesty. No reason to visit the surface so often. How to work them fell out of common knowledge. But as I said, our former queen had books on them." Davan shrugged as he marked a place near the throne room, and another beside the spiral path that led to the gardens. "They're easy to miss, just a door in an alcove. Some may need repair before they'll work again, but a lift can carry a dozen men. There are big wheels and workings for them all over the place, but these are all the lifts I know of."

Her eyes lit with understanding. "They're powered by the waterwheel!"

Davan grinned. "Aye, Your Majesty. But that's as much as I know."

"So we just need someone to retrieve the books that explain how to use the lifts?" Vahn glanced between them for verification. "Then we can decide which lift is easiest to use with the mines, maybe even lay a roadway through the ruins. That would sure make it easier to move ore to Ilmenhith. The next problem is finding people who will want to work there."

Davan handed the chalk back to Firal and cleared his throat. "Begging your pardon, your lordship, but I think that may be the easy part. Not all of Core was happy to leave. If Her Majesty grants them special permission to return to the underground, on the condition they work Her Majesty's mines…"

"Problem solved." Firal put away the chalk with a smirk. "I suppose there's just one thing left."

"Which is?" Vahn asked.

"Getting the books." She raised a hand before either man could speak. "Which I will do myself."

Davan looked uncomfortable. "I can send any number of men to—"

"No one needs to be sent," she interrupted, gazing at the map. She committed each lift's location to memory, but her eyes lingered on the one beside the spiral path. She'd never ventured any lower than the path to her own cavern-house. The lift's alcove had to be somewhere below that. "It could take weeks for them to return. I have a dozen mages at my disposal. I can retrieve the books by myself. No arguments." She glared at Vahn as he opened his mouth, though her eyes softened when he closed it again. "I'm the best one to send. I'm familiar enough with the underground to find the books on my own without getting lost. As soon as I have them, I can Call the mages and have them bring me right back. The hard part will be convincing them to let me lead another Gate."

Vahn frowned. "Another Gate?"

Firal hesitated. She didn't speak without thinking very often any more. Davan looked at her curiously, but said nothing. She lifted her chin. "I'll discuss that with you later. Right now, this is more important. Davan, how soon can you have a group of miners ready? And what are the odds of having some of them be men already experienced in working these mines?"

"Very soon, my lady," Davan said. "As for miners, I have some suggestions."

She nodded, but even as she listened to his list of names and explanations of their former positions in the underground, she found her thoughts wandering to her failed Gate. Her desperate Call was still unanswered.

ALIRA SPUN, watching her pale gray robes swirl around her ankles. As Master of the House of fire, she'd looked down on magelings. She never would have expected to be pleased to see herself in gray again. Much had changed in the months since she'd reached the Grand College. She was beginning to think it was change for the better.

She'd always been a prodigious mage, strong in her Gift from an early age. One of the youngest mages in all Elenhiise to be named Master, and the youngest to be named Master of a House of element. Now she realized her skill—and the recognition of it that once meant so much—had never done her any favors. The shame of her exile from the island and her punishment in the college had been worsened by her pride. But the pride she felt now was different. It felt like progress, like something earned and deserved. It was strange that gray robes and the title of mageling were the first things she'd ever truly had to work for, but the strangeness didn't diminish her pride.

"Stop twirling," Melora snapped. "You're acting like a child."

Alira grew still, but didn't move from her place before the mirror. Melora and Envesi wore the same gray robes, though neither seemed pleased. They sulked at a table and looked bitter —Melora more so than the former Archmage beside her. Alira studied them both in the mirror, frowning. "You ought to be happy. Our title might be mageling, but the title isn't the important part." She didn't have to name it. Melora had almost wept with relief when the barriers were lifted and they were able to reach the energy flows again. Long months had passed without any of them working magic. Alira had missed the pleasant tingle of power more than she could say.

"You think it's important because you assumed they could

block you from your power wherever you go," Envesi murmured.

Alira pursed her lips and turned toward her. She expected the woman to go on and felt a twinge of annoyance when she didn't. Still, when she spoke, she was mindful to keep respect in her tone. "What do you know?"

The former Archmage shrugged. "Even if we hadn't been made magelings, we could have easily passed beyond the Grand College's reach. The barrier extends no farther than the edge of the city. One step into the field on the other side and you'd be free to wield your Gift again."

"Free to be treated as wild mages, you mean," Melora said. "Better to be a mageling on the bottom of the ladder than a wild mage. At least the uniform commands a bit of respect."

"It's true." Alira lifted her chin, allowing herself a taste of defiance. Envesi no longer had real authority over her, but years serving the woman had ingrained deference. "Being recognized as part of the college is a benefit."

Envesi snorted. "Within Lore and the rest of the Triad, perhaps. But outside these three regions?" She shook her head, a look of disgust on her face. "I trained in the Grand College once, long before I was Archmage of Kirban. Respect for mages was failing even then. Now it's worse than ever."

"Mages are a vital part of civilization," Melora argued.

"Not according to Eyrion." Envesi's use of the headmaster's first name caught both of them by surprise.

Alira hesitated a long moment before she shrugged and inspected her robes again. "What difference does it make? We're within the Triad, within the Grand College, and now we're magelings. Free to use our power whenever."

Envesi stood and pushed in her chair at the table. "Which will make our work simpler, to be sure. There is, however, a small problem on our hands."

"Of course there is," Melora said. She plucked a loose thread from her robes with a sneer. "You never should have involved the headmaster. He complicates things."

"Had I not involved him, we'd still be washing laundry," Envesi snapped. "But he expects results, and expects them soon. We still haven't even tried to perform an unbinding, and he expects unbound mages at his fingertips within a fortnight."

"What?" Alira cried. "So soon?"

The former Archmage looked grim. "Already he moves mages into Aldaan. What do you suppose will happen when one of Eyrion's armies goes up against a city of free mages?"

"Surely you don't mean for us to start experimenting within the college," Melora protested. "There are over a thousand mages here to sense what we're doing."

"Even if they sense it, they won't recognize what we're doing because they've never seen it done. Mages who ask questions are nothing to worry about, since we're working under direct order from the headmaster." Envesi relaxed her shoulders, as if to illustrate how unconcerned she was. "In fact, the college is the best place for us to work. The mages expect students to test their skills here. Wielding power outside the city might draw unwanted attention, especially with the unified countries moving into civil war."

It made sense, but Alira still frowned. Whether or not they operated with Headmaster Tolmarni's blessing, she didn't think that would exempt them from punishment if they were discovered by the council. She didn't know what that punishment might be, but it had to be worse than having their rank stripped. All things considered, she thought the punishment they'd already endured had been rather light. The mages of Elenhiise had presented them to the college in the only light they could without casting shadows of blame back on themselves. Lomithrandel and the atrocities of his magic had never been mentioned. Instead, the Elenhiise mages had only accused them of wielding magic to commit treason.

But wasn't that what the college was doing now? Using their

mages to strike against their own king? Perhaps that was why they seemed so unruffled by Envesi's efforts against Kifel. Alira didn't think they would have shown the same kind of leniency if Lomithrandel's existence had come up.

"Headmaster's orders or not, what you want us to do is still forbidden," Alira said at last. She wished she sounded more sure of herself, but speaking against Envesi at all was difficult.

Melora's brows lifted in amusement.

"Excuse me?" Envesi asked.

Alira braced herself. "You want us to practice forbidden magic with street urchins in case something goes wrong, because failure results in alteration of the subject's physical form. That's no better than what you did with Lomithrandel. I don't think the Grand College differentiates between forbidden arts."

The darkening of Envesi's expression told her she'd overstepped her bounds. The former Archmage drew herself up, shadows welling in the corners of the small room they shared. "You think you may speak out of turn because we both wear gray?" The woman rose until she seemed to tower over the room. The color of her robes shifted lighter; together with her white waves of hair and frigid blue eyes, she resembled a beacon of light in the darkness. Alira shrank back, suddenly afraid.

"Do not forget the reason you wear a mage's robes again!" Envesi thundered, fury brimming in her rigid form. "You stand at a precipice with a difficult decision to make, girl. We can do this without you, but you know too much to simply walk away. Do you dare turn against us now?"

Alira's mouth went dry. A weighty decision to make, with only one option presented. Fear churned in her stomach and weakened her knees. There was only one part in which the woman was wrong.

She'd reached the precipice long ago, the moment she'd sided against Kifel.

"No, Archmage," Alira managed, the title slipping from her tongue without a thought. "I stand with you."

Smug satisfaction wreathed itself on Envesi's face, and she sank back into her chair. "Good, because we begin our efforts tonight."

The words made Alira's stomach heave and she struggled not to retch. *I stand with you for now,* she told herself. *Because I have no other choice.*

16

TRUST AND FEELINGS

EXASPERATED, SERA STORMED ACROSS THE SNOWY FIELD. THE novelty had worn off long ago. After years of enduring the frosty winters of the northern continent, she couldn't make herself enjoy the season any longer. Winter was nothing but slick ice and chapped lips, not a hint of wonder to it.

The early morning sun cast a rosy golden glow over the camp. The illusion of warmth was the only pleasant part of leaving the tent she shared with her brother. She would have preferred to have her own tent, but Garam insisted she stay close. At first she'd thought it a ridiculous act of chivalry, meant to protect her from the ranks of men. She was the only woman in the army he'd led to Aldaan, and he'd muttered concerns about the way men's judgment could be clouded after months of discouragement and loneliness. She'd thought that reasoning ridiculous. Garam's men would behave themselves; if they couldn't, they wouldn't have been Garam's men. Even so, she almost would have preferred chivalry to the real reason he wanted her close at hand.

At some point during the night before, she came to understand he wanted her close not for her protection, but for his own. With a mage sharing his tent, he thought no one would dare wield magic against him. Lore's mages were nowhere near their encampment, and she hadn't thought the Aldaanan a threat, but he made her sit up half the night to keep watch while he slept. It wasn't until morning, when Garam roused her with orders after only a few hours of sleep, that she realized who he was afraid of.

Sera planted her hands on her hips as she reached her destination and glowered down at her new charge.

Rune met her eye and then looked away, hunkered down in the snow like a sulking child. He held a snowball to his mouth. "I don't wanna hear it."

She crouched in front of him and shoved the snowball away from his face, grasped his jaw, and forced him to face her. His tongue was swollen, a silver stud through its middle. She thrust the snowball back into his mouth. "You're more stupid than I thought."

He spat it back out. "It'th a tradithion, they wouldn't teach me wifout it." He grimaced at his slurred words, licked his lips and touched a claw to the stud. "Filadiel thaid ith thuppothed to—"

"Brant's branches, shut up! I can't stand to listen to that on top of your accent." She scowled and pressed fresh snow into a new ball for him as she stood. "You can tell me the whole story when the swelling goes down and you can speak properly again. For now, just answer some questions. Yes or no. They're going to teach you?"

Rune glared, but nodded.

"And this thing in your mouth is a requirement for their teachings?"

He hesitated, then nodded again.

The hesitance made her pause and she resisted the urge to demand an explanation. Instead, she handed him the fresh snowball and watched as he stuck out his tongue and pressed the snow to the fresh piercing. She had always known the Aldaanan were strange, but this exceeded everything she knew about their practices. "Are the lessons going to interfere with your responsibilities to the army?"

He shook his head.

"And will they affect your loyalties?"

He didn't respond, staring at her in silence. She could see him thinking it over, though his expression never wavered.

"Answer the question," Sera ordered.

Lowering the snow from his mouth, Rune spoke slowly, forming words as clearly as he could. "You make it sound like Garam had my loyalty to begin with. I am here because of the Aldaanan mages. No other reason."

She crossed her arms. "Not even to win back that kingsword?"

Eerie light flashed in his eyes.

Unsettled, she dropped her arms and sat in the snow beside him. "Listen, I'm only here because Garam asked me to speak to you. He thinks the Aldaanan are up to something by taking you in and teaching you their ways."

The way he stared made her uncomfortable, his face as unchanging as carved stone. "What do you think?" he asked.

"I don't know," she replied honestly. "Sometimes my brother is needlessly concerned about mages. And other times, he's right. I don't know what they want or why they're helping you, but I don't feel at ease about it, either. The Aldaanan are reclusive, rarely visiting the Royal City and never letting people into their cities. That we're here at all is unprecedented."

Rune seemed to consider that, his expression finally softening.

She shifted in the crunching snow, wishing he would speak, waiting a long moment to see if he would. When he didn't, she leaned close. "I didn't want to ask this, but Garam told me to." She cast a wary glance around them. The rest of the camp milled in the snow as if they weren't there. "I realize having mentors who can teach you to use your Gift properly is important to you. But if you find out that they mean us ill, be it through conversation, lessons, overhearing or anything else, will you let him know?"

His peculiar snakelike eyes narrowed. "No. But I'll tell you."

Sera blinked. "Me?"

"The only other mage in the army. Better to stand together, right?" He pushed himself up and started toward his tent.

She rose just as fast. "Where are you going?"

"Bed. The ritual took all night." He didn't wait to be dismissed, ducking into his tent with a snowball still in hand.

Worrying her lower lip, Sera turned away. A tightness gripped her chest, yet a weight lifted from her shoulders. It was a pleasant surprise to discover he trusted her, but unpleasant to find she was right to suspect he harbored a dislike for her brother. She couldn't fault him, but she couldn't fault Garam either. It was obvious that the men weren't interested in sharing their knowledge or concerns with each other. Were they both mages, she would have made them sit and talk the matter through.

But they weren't mages; they were men of weapons and war. *Except mages march against us now. What better are they?* The thought was bitter. She'd studied at the Grand College, treasured her days there. In her time, they had taught pacifism. She wondered at how different their teachings must have become for her one-time colleagues to pursue violence.

She'd left the college when Garam was a child, abandoned her education to return home and help their mother after Garam's father finally succumbed to illness. His death wasn't a surprise. He'd struggled with fragile health from the moment they left their homeland. An illness born of humidity, the healers said. Sera thought it an illness born of heartache. They'd fled home to escape war, sacrificing everything they'd ever known to keep their family safe. She had already been a member of the Grand College for some time by then; she'd already said her goodbyes. Garam had been too small to remember. Leaving hadn't impacted them. It had crushed their parents.

Would things be different if she hadn't left the college? If her family had never been driven from their home? She could have easily ended up on the other side of this battle. The thought chilled her, and Sera tried to think of it no more.

"You," she called, stopping to catch the attention of a soldier nearby. "Is Captain Kaith still in his tent?"

The soldier nodded and Sera hurried across the camp. Garam wouldn't be happy to hear of their conversation, but the sooner she told him, the better.

She pushed past the tent's flaps with a quiet grumble, though she was grateful to be back in the warmth. As much as she wanted to explore the city while things were calm, she was loath to venture into the snow. "Garam, I spoke to—" She stopped short as her eyes adjusted. The gryphon, Ria, stood at her brother's side.

The gryphon sat on her haunches, her upright posture reminding Sera of the dust-colored rodents she'd once seen in the plains. The creature gave a cheery whistle and adjusted the strange goggles atop her head. "Ah, lovely timing! I just came to see if the pair of you wanted anything for breakfast. Captain Kaith was preparing a list for me."

"Thought that meeting would take longer," Garam murmured, never looking up from his lap desk.

Sera raised a brow. "That's a long list for breakfast."

"Adding a few things I'll need to work efficiently. More ink, for one. Someone dropped my box and broke most of the bottles." He frowned as he dipped his pen in the inkwell and tapped it carefully against the side, mindful of every drop. "What did he say?"

She crossed her arms and snorted a laugh. "Not much. They pierced his tongue."

The gryphon's ear-tufts rose. "Oh! They've taken him in for training?" Sera and Garam both glared at her and she snorted. "Well there are only two mages in your army, and only one of them is male. It's not much of a mystery who we're speaking of. Still, I'm surprised they'd take him in so quickly."

Sera frowned. She wanted to be agitated that Ria had spoken uninvited, but the gryphon lived with the Aldaanan. As untrusting as Garam was of the beast, even he had to admit she could serve as a useful point of contact. "Do you know what it's for?" she asked as she settled on the floor. Unlike the other tents, theirs had a thick woolen rug instead of bare earth. One of the comforts of being in a position of leadership, she supposed.

"Didn't he tell you? Oh, I guess he couldn't, if it just happened. He'll probably have trouble speaking for a day or so, but he'll get used to it. All the free mages pierce their tongues. It's an old tradition, held over from when they served as the first clerics," Ria chirruped happily, dropping to all fours and ruffling her feathers before laying down. "They say the tunnels Brant's roots left behind were lined with silver, a remnant of the Lifetree's purity. The clerics wore it through their tongues to remind them to speak only pure words. Free mages wear it now to remind them to use their magic only for pure reasons. Just old symbolism, really, but important to quite a few of the Aldaanan elders."

Sera cast Garam a troubled glance. A mask of concern darkened his face and furrowed his brow. She forced herself to look away. "When you say pure reasons, winged one, what do you mean?"

"Well, I don't know the specifics of it," Ria admitted. "It's not my place, since gryphons aren't mages. There are all sorts of books on the matter up in the aerie, though, if you're interested in that sort of thing. I suppose you would be, being a mage and all."

Garam pushed back his tray and put his pen aside. "I just want to know if this is going to be a problem. He's part of our army, first and foremost. We need every mage we can get in the battles we all know are coming."

The gryphon clicked her beak. "I couldn't say. I'm not a mage.

Are you done with your list? I'll just take that and be on about my errands." She rose to all fours and plucked the paper from Garam's tray with a taloned forepaw. Her claws were nimble, for their size. She rolled the paper neatly and tucked it under the strap on her goggles. As if the gryphon wasn't already odd enough, she looked ridiculous with the paper sticking out beside her tufted ear. "I'll see the two of you another time, my friends. I'll send someone along with the things you need before midday." Ria turned to leave and Sera held the tent flap open for her. She folded it closed again after the gryphon had gone.

The moment they were alone, Garam's face crumpled into a scowl. "So I'm down to one mage, now."

"That isn't true." Sera moved into the middle of the floor and made herself comfortable. "I asked Rune to let us know if he learns anything. He knows the Aldaanan may be planning against us. He said he will tell us if he hears anything concerning —or, he'll tell me, rather."

He raised a brow. "Only you?"

She batted her eyes in response.

Garam scoffed. "You're getting too comfortable with that man for my liking."

"And just what is wrong with that, Garam Kaith?" The accusation in his tone made her face crumple into a scowl. "He's a powerful mage and a skilled fighter, and—"

"He's not human!" Garam snapped.

Sera's eyes darkened. "Neither am I."

He grimaced, clearly regretting his words. "Sera, I don't mean it like—"

"And how do you mean it?" she demanded, thrusting herself from the floor. "You dislike him for something he cannot help! Do you dislike me for my Eldani blood, too?

He started up out of his chair, reaching for her. "Sera—"

She stepped back. Anger warmed her like tongues of flame against her skin and it was all she could do to keep from slapping him. "He's on our side. That should be enough reason for you to like him. And he is a mage much stronger than I. That is enough reason for us to be friends. There's a great deal I can learn from him, Garam, and I'm not going to let you stand in the way." She whipped the tent flap open before he could speak and bolted back into the snow.

———

IT WAS COMFORTING to retire knowing the army wouldn't move again for some time. While Rune was eager to begin lessons with his new teachers, the night had been long, filled with tests of power and finishing with the piercing of his tongue. Healing the wound was forbidden, Filadiel said. Sleep offered sweet respite after the night's events.

Yet his dreams were far from peaceful, filled with images of strife and bloodshed. He saw faces that seemed familiar in glimpses too fleeting for him to recognize them, and other faces he knew so well he wouldn't have needed more than a glance to know them. He heard his name spoken like a caress, felt a surge of anguish and need. He saw her reaching for him through a crowd that faded like ghosts when she pushed through. Fire and urgency scorched in his veins, and his skin burned as if pricked by a thousand needles. The urgency grew. He tried to reach her, grasping for her extended hand, only to have her vanish the moment their fingers touched.

Rune jerked awake, gasping for breath in the icy air. Cold sweat slicked his body beneath the blankets, his skin still aflame with a stinging sensation the likes of which he'd never experienced. Light peeked in through a gap between the flaps of his tent. Desperate, he tried to cling to the image of Firal's face, to the image of her reaching for him. He trembled as he wiped sweat from his brow. His mouth was dry, but he still swallowed hard.

"Are you awake or not?" a voice called from the other side of the tent. Fingers drummed against the outside of the canvas before they swept back the flap. The daylight that poured in was all but blinding. "It's past midday, you need to eat something before—" Sera slid inside and stopped short when she saw him. "Are you all right? You look ill."

He was not all right. He was shaken, uncomfortable and confused. But he nodded, unable to form words.

She frowned at him, but swung a basket of food into view. Better than travel fare or rations, it was filled with fresh fruits and breads, along with smoked meat and a bit of cheese. She crouched and leaned forward to put it on the ground beside him, then rested her elbows on her knees and peered at him with a look he almost thought was concern. "Are you sure you're all right?"

Rune reached for the basket and tried not to look at her again. "Just a dream."

He lifted a piece of seed-topped bread out of the way to get a look at a jar of something underneath. He pulled it free and tilted it to watch dark liquid slosh inside. Wine, he figured, putting the bread back and opening the jar first. It smelled of berries with a hint of honey. He tested it and, finding the taste pleasant, took a long drought.

Sera waited to speak until he'd put down his drink and picked up a piece of bread. "May I ask you something?"

"Won't promise to answer," he replied, not looking up. A maluiri fruit rested in the bottom of the basket. He picked it up, amused.

She sat on the ground and crossed her ankles. "Garam told me why you were arrested. Why you ended up in the arena. But how did you come to be in the Royal City to begin with? You had no grasp of our language until Councilor Parthanus began teaching you, and you obviously know nothing of the area. You speak Old Aldaanan, but you're clearly not from here."

It wasn't as invasive a question as he'd expected. Rune shrugged as he chewed his mouthful of food. Redoram had warned him that his behavior gave him away, made his status as a noble in his prior life too obvious. But he couldn't shake the manners his nursemaid spent the better part of a century driving into him. "I don't know how to hunt here. The animals are unfamiliar. Foraging was poor along the coast. Didn't want to risk staying in one place too long, stole what I needed and followed the main roads north. A man does what he must to survive." He tried not to indicate he noticed the way she watched him eat. Too close, too intent. Studying his every move.

Cradling her chin in her hands, Sera leaned forward. "The coast? So you made landfall from somewhere else?"

Rune blinked. Out of everything he'd said, he hadn't thought she'd latch onto that. "The harbor was in Roberian, I believe. The land there was interesting. I'd like to go back."

She grinned. "I've heard Roberian's harbor is the biggest in the Triad, but I haven't seen it. When I left my homeland, I took a Gate straight to Lore. Are mages rare in your homeland?"

"Aren't they rare here?" He lifted the jar of wine to his lips again. "There are next to none in the Royal City."

Her face fell and she gave a slight shrug. "Mages are not held with the same regard they once were. It's a dying art, I'm afraid."

Considering the rank and honor that came with magecraft on Elenhiise, he couldn't imagine mages on the mainland being scarce. "But there's the Grand College."

"Which serves the entire world," Sera said with a wave of her hand. "Sure, they have a few thousand mages. Out of how many people? How many countries? If I am to be honest, my family was disheartened to learn I wanted to be a mage. They thought I would do better to marry young and forge new alliances for our house. My mother was a mage, but she only learned to utilize her Gift because her parents wanted to strike up an alliance with an Eldani bloodline. It was all politics, nothing to do with passion."

Rune smiled ruefully. He knew those kind of games all too well. "What made you want to learn?"

"Because I wanted to make a difference." She flexed her toes and stared down at them. "Mages are distrusted in my homeland after their role in the war, but I thought I could restore people's faith in mages if I honed my skills to perfection. I thought I could show them that mages were still needed, even with the way the world had changed."

A pang of sympathy stirred in his chest. Her words reminded him of his own ambitions, and he struggled to quash the disappointment that rose every time those memories stirred. They were only a year gone. He couldn't bury them deep enough.

"I don't understand," he murmured, studying her face. She looked genuinely regretful, lending that much more weight to what she said. "Mages can heal, they can cure illness, they can manipulate weather. Why wouldn't they be needed?"

"Because people can live without them."

It was simple honesty, but it still jarred him to silence. He'd never stopped to consider it before, but now the realization struck him with painful clarity. For all that Kirban Temple meddled in politics and shuffled mages around like pawns on a chessboard, they weren't necessary. A convenience, certainly, but not a necessity. Elenhiise functioned largely without Gates or healing, the only two arts he could think of as vital. Core itself had functioned for centuries without a healer. Firal had been a boon, but if he hadn't taken her to live among the Underlings, what difference would it have made?

"But it's strange to think of a world where mages are not common," Rune said at last, pulling the basket of food closer to look through it again. From the unusual selection of fruits, he thought it a gift from Filadiel or one of the other Aldaanan. "If anyone ever told the Masters back home that their services weren't needed, there would be an uproar all across the country."

"So mages carry more authority where you are from?" Sera asked.

"Some." Rune offered her an apple and she took it with a

smile. Now it was his turn to regard her thoughtfully, to study her until she shifted uncomfortably. He took a bite of fruit. "Why the sudden interest in me?"

Her shoulders lifted and her expression hardened as her guard rose. "Have you noticed anything unusual about Garam's army?"

"Half the men are only half as sharp as their swords. The other half seem offended their swords are steel instead of silver, like the spoon in their mouths when they were born."

She burst into laughter.

"What?" he asked, agitated.

"Just your way of speaking." She wiped her eyes with the side of her hand. "And that's not what I meant, though I can't say it's not an accurate description."

He bit into one of the small loaves of bread and gestured for her to go on.

"It's just that you and I are the only mages. We're also the only soldiers under Garam's command who aren't human." She turned the apple in her hands, not eating. "I don't think he planned it that way, but I don't think he's unhappy about it, either. He's always been uncomfortable around the Eldani. I'm surprised he's not more suspicious of the Aldaanan than he is."

Rune narrowed his eyes. "So he doesn't like magic, he doesn't like the Eldani, he doesn't like me... anything else I should know about your brother?"

"He doesn't trust magic, or the Eldani, or you. There's a difference between not liking and not trusting. You can love someone dearly without trusting them." She laid a hand on his arm. "But I trust you. And I think he's being ridiculous if he thinks the Aldaanan might use you against us."

His eyes darkened and he pulled away. "If you knew me better, you wouldn't trust me."

She startled him with a smile, so warm and genuine it made her seem like a flower opening to the sun. "Knowing you better is why I'm here."

He put down his food. He couldn't fault her for seeking someone to relate to, but if she thought he was it, she was mistaken. "You asked how I came to be in the Royal City." He pushed the basket aside and finally threw back his blankets. He tugged on the open-toed leather footwear that had been made to protect him from the cold, then reached for his sword and belt. "I fought a war my actions helped begin. I lost friends and family in the battle and afterward. I committed treason. I came north by ship to flee execution." His words shocked her and he was satisfied to see it. He rose and strapped his sword to his hip as he brushed past her. The tent's canvas flaps did nothing to hold the winter at bay, but he still felt the urge to flinch against the cold when he pushed back the flap and paused. "So if you trust me, know your trust is misplaced."

He slipped out into the snow and breathed deeply of the frigid air. It was already past midday, and his new mentors would be waiting.

***

"OH YES, that does sound unsettling, but it's not an uncommon occurrence. You really oughtn't worry about it much." Filadiel filled a second cup, not quite to the brim. He took both teacups, leaving the teapot and tray on the table beside the window. "Dreams can sometimes influence our power, and power can influence our dreams. After all, dreams are an expression of emotion, sometimes drawing on feelings that aren't even known to us. I'm sure you've noticed how much impact emotion has on your abilities. I've seen your eyes." He placed a teacup in front of Rune and cradled the other in both hands as he sank to his knees beside the low table in the middle of the room.

Rune wasn't surprised their first lesson would be held in private, but he had been surprised to find Filadiel himself waiting for him in the empty council chamber. There had to be a thousand other things for the short-statured leader of the

Aldaanan to tend, things far more important than dealing with a novice mage. Taking his teacup, Rune savored the warmth as it seeped into his fingers. "What about my eyes?"

Filadiel shrugged. "Well you can't control their light, that much is obvious."

It hadn't been so long ago that Rune thought the otherworldly glow of his snake-slitted eyes was just another abnormality that came with being what he was. He thought of Medreal and the way her luminescent eyes looked in the dark prison cell below his father's castle. She had told him he would learn to control the glow, but she hadn't mentioned how, and he hadn't been in a position to ask. He sipped his tea, grimaced at the bitterness, and turned his thoughts to another question instead. "Why do they glow?"

"Why, because of your power, of course." Filadiel chuckled, as if answering a silly question posed by a child. Then he tasted his tea and flinched. "Oh, that is awful, isn't it? Well, that's what I get for trying to make it by myself. Have you ever paid attention to how many flows of energy course through you at any given time?"

Rune shook his head and took another sip of tea. Bitter or not, at least it was warm. "There are too many to keep track."

Filadiel grinned. "Precisely! You see, free mages don't call for magic. Magic calls to us. It seeks us, thousands of threads of energy flowing through us at any given time. It's power that wants to be touched, wants to be used. The reflection of that is the glow of one's eyes. Until they learn to hold the energy at bay, that is."

"Why would you want to hold the energy at bay?" The explanation was a stark contrast to the lessons in magecraft Firal had given him, and Rune's brow furrowed as he tried to understand. She had to reach for power, often expending much of her own strength in trying to grasp it.

"Several reasons, I suppose. The largest being privacy. Powerful emotions can affect what energies are attracted to you and how you express them. If left unchecked, these feelings betray themselves by altering the color one's eyes glow."

"Like turning them red?" Rune asked.

Filadiel choked on his tea.

Rune shifted uncomfortably. "What? What does red mean?"

Clearing his throat, Filadiel put down his cup. "In your culture or mine?"

"Yours."

"Oh. That would make sense, I suppose I couldn't answer questions about your own culture. Ah, well, I suppose I ought to explain that the colors can also be affected by your perceptions. A greenish glow, for example, is an expression of happiness among my people, while I believe human cultures associate the color green with other, less pleasant emotions. And then of course, red is, for my people... well, lust. In any case, since you've not been brought up in Aldaanan culture, we may want to curtail that light in your eyes for propriety's sake, hmm?" Filadiel smiled, though he was obviously flustered.

"I see," Rune murmured. He stared at his tea for a time before he spoke again. "Have you ever trained any mages from outside Aldaanan culture?"

Filadiel's tall ears twitched. "No. We never have. There's never been a free mage outside of our people, though we knew it was possible one could be born after the magic of the Eldani was bound. Unlikely, but possible."

Everything Filadiel said only raised more questions. Rune frowned. He didn't think his inquiries bothered the man; if they did, he certainly didn't show it. But asking so many made him feel like a clueless child. It was worse than taking lessons from the mages in Kirban Temple, where they expected students to arrive knowing nothing. This was personal, focused on the unfathomable power he'd struggled to contain and control for his entire life. It felt like he should know more about it. Instead, he knew almost nothing.

"Why is the magic of other mages bound by affinity?" he asked at last.

The question seemed to surprise Filadiel, who blinked a moment and then tilted his head, boggled. "To keep them from using their power, of course. Why else would we have bound it?"

Rune shook his head. He knew he'd heard right, he just didn't understand. "*You* bound it?"

Filadiel's face grew grim. "Yes, and there are some among us who wish we'd bound it off completely, instead of just limiting other mages to their affinities. They worry that access to any magic at all gives them room for more corruption, more atrocities. Sometimes I fear they may be right. But what's done is done, and all we can do is wait for bound magic to fade from existence. It grows weaker all the time, the distance between new mages and the blood of our people growing greater with each passing year. Being born with free magic makes you quite the anomaly, my friend." The mage offered a smile that was rife with pity. "And we can see the effect it's had."

Self-conscious, Rune put down his half-empty teacup and rested his hands on his thighs beneath the low table. "There's so much I want to know," he sighed. "I don't even know where to start. Everything we discuss reveals something else I don't understand. Your culture, your origins, how free magic is different from everything I've learned—"

"You've been taught to use magic from a bound perspective?" Filadiel interrupted.

Rune hesitated.

"Show me," the Aldaanan councilor insisted. "Show me something you've learned."

For a moment, Rune wasn't sure what to do. There were a dozen things he could try. His brow furrowed as he ran through them in his head. Something simple was probably best. He scanned the table for something to use before he remembered the runestone in his pocket. He pulled it out and turned it over in his palm, studying the etched front that matched the scar in his hand. Now that he looked at the stone, he realized he didn't know why he'd taken to carrying it. He was just drawn to it, fascinated by the symbol he'd never seen anywhere but the back of his hand. It had been the first stone he'd noticed in Redoram's set of stones, the first stone he'd taken to start his own collection. It had felt like seizing his life, taking full control for the first time.

Rune held the game piece out where Filadiel could see. The stone began to glow as he poured energy into it to make a mage-light. He realized a moment later that creating a light had been his first lesson with Firal, as well.

"Oh dear," Filadiel muttered, rubbing his forehead. Lines of worry formed beneath his fingertips and he sighed. "Terrible. Terrible! That's all wrong. I didn't expect that at all."

The mage-light faded. Confused, Rune curled his clawed fingers around the stone. "What did I do wrong? I did just what I was shown, and—"

Filadiel raised his hands defensively. "Oh no, no, not you. It isn't your fault, I apologize if I made you think that. Yes, what you did would be perfect if your magic were bound, but it isn't. Bound magic is a dreadful thing. It forces people to work differently, expend more of their own energy. When a free mage works magic, they shouldn't use any of their strength at all."

"Then how am I supposed to do anything?" Rune asked, his brow furrowed with frustration.

"Simple." Filadiel smiled, taking a spoon from the table and laying it flat on his upraised palm. "Remember, the flows of energy want to work for you. If you want them to do something, all you have to do is ask."

The spoon began to levitate. Threads of energy moved around them like currents in the ocean, rushing power that raced to answer Filadiel's silent call. Rune's snake-slitted eyes widened as he watched, and as the spoon took on the warm glow of a mage-light, he felt it, and he understood.

SUCCESSION

"ERRANDS AGAIN?"

Kytenia rolled her eyes at Rikka's playful ribbing. She couldn't do much else with her arms full of books. "Better than to be lounging about in the library."

Rikka grinned, pushed herself up from the reading table, and moved to join her. "Should I carry some for you?"

"No, these are an urgent request out of Ilmenhith and the Masters are unhappy enough that I know what they are. I'd appreciate it if you would open the door, though." Kytenia stopped beside it and tried to be patient. The tomes were almost more than she could lift. She didn't know why Firal wanted a dozen books on machinery and mechanisms, but the request had come through Nondar's office, so it wasn't her place to ask questions. Anaide had grumbled so much when she shared the request that Kytenia knew there was something going on.

Rikka pulled the door wide and ushered Kytenia through with a bow. "After you, your apprentice-ness."

"Being an apprentice doesn't give you a fancy title. In fact, I'm fairly sure 'apprentice' is the opposite of a fancy title. Who wants to be an apprentice?" Kytenia hefted the books against her chest to balance them as she made her way through the temple courtyard. "Do you know if there are any Masters in the Gate rooms right now?"

Rikka shrugged, padding alongside her friend. "There always are. Are you sure you don't need help?"

Kytenia grunted. "Positive."

Rikka trailed along beside her anyway.

The Gate rooms had been added at Firal's behest after Kirban's mages returned to the temple. Similar to the parlor in the palace kept aside for safe Gates, Kirban's Gating rooms hosted nothing but empty arches used for framing portals. The old office building that contained them had never been fully repaired, but a handful of chairs sat scattered through the rooms so people could wait their turn in comfort. With the temple once again serving as the primary base of operations for mages, there were almost always people coming and going. It was an inconvenience for some, having to Gate halfway across the island to tend their duties in other cities, but the bustle meant there were almost always Masters present to manage the Gates. Nondar had mages who could open Gates at his beck and call. As a mageling, Kytenia had to hope she could catch the Masters when they weren't busy.

The room she chose was half filled with Master mages. A pair of Gates already stood open. One white-robed woman turned to look at them with one eyebrow raised.

"To Ilmenhith," Kytenia said, peering at the Master over her books. "I am to deliver these to the queen on behalf of Archmage Nondar."

The Master sighed. "Very well, we'll send you in a moment." Then she turned her eyes back to the open Gates.

"Are you meeting with Firal?" Rikka asked, mindful to keep her voice low. Their friend's ascent to the throne had changed a great deal, including how they were expected to speak of her. Referring to the queen in a casual manner was likely to get them both in trouble.

"I don't know," Kytenia admitted. "She's so busy these days.

I've only seen her once since the baby was born." Which was not as bad as it could be, she reminded herself. Had Firal stayed in the ruins, she likely never would have seen her again.

Rikka nodded, though her face fell. The changes had been difficult for everyone, but Kytenia often thought Rikka had it worst. After Firal left, Kytenia still had Shymin, even if her new apprenticeship made her relationship with her sister strained. But her duties left no time for anyone else, which meant that for Rikka, the loss of Firal and the death of Marreli—Rikka's childhood best friend—left her all but alone.

"I'll tell her you said hello if I see her," Kytenia offered.

"Tell her she owes us a visit, too." Rikka smiled, though she still looked sad. Kytenia freed a hand to pat her friend's arm. Then the air surged with power at the opening of a new Gate.

"The queen's Gate parlor," one of the Masters called as it stabilized. Kytenia shifted the books in her arms and strode through the open portal at a brisk pace.

More than a dozen court Masters looked at her in surprise as she appeared in the palace's parlor. The Gate dropped closed behind her and Kytenia blinked. It wasn't unusual for a handful of Masters to be present, just in case someone needed a Gate, but so many meant something must have happened.

"May I help you, girl?" A white-robed court mage stepped forward from the other side of the room.

"The queen requested these books from the temple library," Kytenia explained. Not for the first time, she wondered if she would benefit from some sort of marker on her mageling's uniform to identify her as the Archmage's apprentice. Her life would be easier without mages questioning her at every turn.

The court Master nodded. "Her Majesty is out at the moment but should return soon. Come along, we'll leave those in her office." She led the way into the hall without stopping to see if Kytenia followed.

Kytenia knew the woman led the mages stationed in the palace, but she didn't know her name. She should have, she realized, having spent so much time in Ilmenhith. And time in the palace, to boot. She made a mental note to review the lists of Masters in leadership positions when she returned to the temple. If she was to work as Archmage's apprentice, it was likely something she'd need to have memorized anyway.

She already knew the way to Firal's office, but it would have been rude to refuse the escort. The trip down the hall was short and a moment later, the Master mage pushed the office door open wide and held it with one arm. Kytenia bowed her head and slipped inside.

The office was empty, though the curtains were open and the room was bright and tidy. Firal couldn't have left long ago. An empty teacup still sat on her desk. Kytenia sighed, carried the books to the desk and divided them into two neat stacks. If only she'd been a bit earlier.

"Were you given any other orders?" the court mage asked.

"No, Master, that's all." Kytenia wiped her hands against the front of her green robes. Many books in the temple were still dirty with ash. The dust left her hands dry. She glanced at the books again before she returned to the doorway and stepped into the hall.

"Kytenia?"

The familiar voice made her heart leap into her throat. When she turned and saw Vahn behind her, the warmest of smiles wreathed itself upon her face. He looked magnificent, wearing blue silks and the rich purple cape of royal consort, with a silver circlet on his brow. She opened her arms and stepped toward him.

He stepped back.

Her face fell. She dropped her arms to her sides, her enthusiasm cooling. "My lord," she murmured.

"Good morning, Lord Vahnil," the mage said.

"Good morning, Temar." His face was the most neutral Kytenia had ever seen it.

"The mageling brought the books Her Majesty requested."

Temar gestured toward the office door beside her. "I was about to return her to the temple. Did you have need of her services?"

Vahn stared at Kytenia for a time before nodding. "Yes, actually. I'll send her to you shortly. Thank you, Temar."

The court mage bowed her head and turned to make her way back to the Gate parlor on her own.

Kytenia shifted on her feet. "What did you need, my lord?" She kept her tone frosty, her hazel eyes just as cool.

"Nothing." He offered a nervous smile. "I thought we could talk a moment. Unless you need to go."

"Not at all." She looked to the office door. "There, or here?"

Wincing, he looked at the floor. "You're a beautiful woman, Kytenia, I can't be with you in private. People would talk."

Her brows lifted. "You are a king now. What does it matter if they talk?"

"I'm king-consort," he replied heatedly, rubbing the back of his neck the way he always did when he was uncomfortable. "And acting as king-regent. There's a great deal riding on my reputation right now. I can't do anything to risk it."

Kytenia's lips pressed to a thin line. "I see."

"Don't be angry at me, Kyt. I'm here because you told me to be."

She knew she couldn't be angry, not if she wanted to be fair. But it still hurt that he wouldn't so much as touch her, not even to offer the casual embrace of friends. Her heart broke all over again."It doesn't appear to be a burden. You seem very comfortable in your new life."

Vahn shrugged. "This isn't where I planned to end up, but I'm making the best of what I have. I'm sure you do the same."

"I suppose so," she said.

He cleared his throat, and moved his weight to his other foot. His hands twitched at his sides as if he wanted to do something. Touch her, perhaps. Or rub his neck again. "I guess I'd best let you get back to the temple, then."

"And you should return to your work," Kytenia said. "The Archmage is waiting for me."

"Of course." He turned to the office door. "It was good to see you."

Kytenia smiled and dipped in a curtsy, unable to say the same. She restrained herself to a walk on her way back to the Gating parlor.

If only she'd been able to trade places with Firal. Her new position beneath Nondar opened a great number of opportunities, though most meant staying in the temple. She imagined she would end up as a teacher after graduation, able to pass on whatever she learned from working with the Archmage. But it wasn't the life she wanted. Teaching had been Firal's dream.

Vahn had been hers.

"You shouldn't be walking on your own, Archmage."

Nondar knew the girl meant well, but the way she spoke to him as if he were a doddering old man grated on his nerves. He glowered, then felt a wash of guilt the moment Kytenia shrank back. He had appointed her as his assistant. It wasn't fair to be angry at her for trying to assist. He forced his expression to soften. "I am still capable of walking from one end of the tower to another. We aren't going far. Besides, walking is why you fetched this for me." He thumped his cane against the floor and managed a chuckle.

It was a struggle to walk, but he wasn't about to let a mageling see that. This was the first time he'd escaped his room in days, and there was more to do than just sit in the garden for fresh air. Of course, a visit to the temple garden wouldn't be unwelcome after business was taken care of. The new plantings were coming along, and the fire-scarred trees were covered in leaves. The worst of the damage had been pruned out and the new growth promised a full recovery.

Would that the temple itself could recover so well. Nondar's eyes darkened and he hobbled on down the hallway with Kytenia close at his heels. She rarely left his side, neglecting her studies to tend him—the poor, frail Archmage—through all hours of the night and day. He would have to remember to push her studies, encourage the girl to keep up the practice of her magecraft. She was a skilled healer. Were things different, she might have made a good head for the House of healing after she graduated to Master white. Too many positions still sat empty, too many Masters carrying outside obligations that kept them from being considered. But it could be worse. They could have been trapped in Ilmenhith, unable to tend the chapter houses scattered across half of the island.

Kytenia hurried ahead to open the door to his office. Edagan and Anaide already waited inside, sitting at the council table and conversing in low tones. They grew quiet when he appeared in the doorway. Edagan's face remained placid, but Anaide couldn't quite contain her sneer. Nondar's jaw tightened, but he said nothing. He was Archmage and deserved respect, but didn't have the energy to reprimand her, knowing the fight it would begin. He often thought the two women resembled vultures, both circling above his failing body and waiting to strip the title of Archmage from his bones.

"Did you know Ennil Tanrys has given himself a seat on the queen's council?" Anaide demanded.

Nondar's thick white brows lifted, though he was careful to mask his surprise with amusement. He hadn't known, but Ennil was a shrewd man—if single-minded. If he sat on Firal's council, it meant Nondar no longer had to shelter the girl from these harpies on his own. "A man cannot give himself authority. He must receive it from the queen. If he sits on her council, it's because Firal wishes him there."

"You aren't concerned?" Edagan sounded startled, but a hint

of curiosity colored her tone. She was willing to hear him out. Anaide was not.

The Archmage did not reply right away, watching Kytenia cross to the table to pull out his chair. Even if Ennil's involvement was acceptable to discuss in front of magelings, he wouldn't want to speak of it in front of her. Kytenia should have been heiress to House Tanrys, instead of a green-ranked mageling in a dying school of magic. As Nondar sank into his chair, he offered the girl a smile. "That is all for now, my dear. Go tend your studies. I will send someone to fetch you when you are needed again."

"Yes, Archmage," Kytenia murmured with a bow. Nondar knew she worked hard to keep her composure, but she couldn't hide the sadness in her eyes. He knew what loneliness was like and he pitied her, but there was little to be done for it now.

Turning his ice-blue eyes to the two women at the table, Nondar folded his hands together and waited until he heard the door close behind him. Then he sighed and his expression hardened. "The two of you speak as if the Tanrys name isn't trustworthy. Do you fear him?"

Anaide scowled. "He will try to turn her against us. He knows how close we are to controlling the throne. There's no doubt he'd want to wrest the girl from our grasp. He'll want his own family in charge, and we're all that stands in his way."

Nondar leaned back in his seat. How he'd become entangled with so many mages who prioritized political power over magical prowess, he'd never know. "His family is close enough to power. He'll wish only to strengthen Firal's hold over Elenhiise. Or did you forget that his grandchild is next in line for the throne?"

"And how long will he believe the girl is his grandchild?" Edagan asked. "She looks enough like her mother that no one questions it now, but looks change, and something of her father is sure to surface. She has his eyes already."

The Archmage waved a gnarled hand. "Eldani children are

slow to grow, especially those with strong mages for parents. Firal herself is barely into adulthood. At twenty pents, she's the youngest ruler we've ever had. Ennil Tanrys is Giftless and aging. He will be gone before there is ever a doubt."

Both women fell silent, neither able to combat his point. Satisfied, he went on. "Now, let's move on to why I've called you. I wish to raise magelings through the ranks, and protocol requires I speak to you first." That had been one of his first changes to temple rules after he became Archmage, unanimously supported by the other Masters. It was a mild inconvenience, but he preferred inconvenience to the role of Archmage being like that of a monarch, who shouted orders and expected them to be followed.

"Which magelings?" Edagan asked.

"I have a guess," Anaide murmured.

Nondar gave her a sharp look. "My apprentice, yes. Kytenia is a dedicated student and a skilled healer, but there are some things I cannot teach her—formally, at least—until she is given the rank allowing such lessons."

Anaide's eyes narrowed. "Why such a need to rush?"

The old Archmage barked a laugh and rapped his cane against the edge of the table. "The look in your eyes answers the question. I am the former head of the House of healing. There are skills in healing I have mastered that some don't realize exist. If I am to pass on this knowledge, time is of the essence, and there are few healers still in the temple who are talented enough to learn."

Edagan looked thoughtful, drumming her fingers against the tabletop. "And the other magelings? Her sister?"

"No. Not yet, at least." Nondar hesitated. How hard would they resist? "But there are two others. Ellaith, a girl brought in from the chapter house in Wethertree. And Rikka, a girl you both are familiar with. All three are green magelings."

Edagan nodded. "I remember speaking to Ellaith after exams,

following our return to Kirban. A reasonable girl. Good head on her shoulders."

"I would say Rikka is an odd choice, given her wind affinity, but I do know she has redoubled her efforts in learning healing after the battle outside of Ilmenhith." A somber expression crept over Anaide's face, but she shrugged. "So you wish to raise all three to blue? I've no complaints."

The Archmage's eyebrows twitched, the only outward display of his surprise. He had expected a fight, but their gentle acceptance of his need for haste was more unsettling. "Excellent. I will have their new robes issued immediately."

"There is another matter we'd like to discuss, while we are here." Anaide laced her fingers together and rested her hands atop the table. "Something somewhat related."

Nondar knew where she was heading, but said nothing. He gestured for her to go on.

"You know the temple is faltering. Mages struggle to find consistent work and the hunger spreading across the island will soon find us here. With that in mind, and considering your health, Edagan and I feel it may be best for a certain matter to be settled."

His eyes narrowed. "Are you so eager to chase me into my grave?"

"Naming your successor is vital," Edagan insisted. "Especially in a time like this. We need to show the rest of the island that the temple has planned for the future. That the mages will be a part of it. With the state things are in, some of the noble houses of Ilmenhith believe the temple dies with you."

It took effort not to show his anger, but Nondar allowed himself a quiet scoff. "They have a number of surprises in store for them." He pushed himself from his chair, wishing he didn't have to strain to stand up straight. He took his cane as he lurched toward the door. "I have plans for the temple. There's no need for the two of you to worry. You will have my successor's

name in writing and marked with the queen's seal soon enough.
I only need the time to pen it."

Neither woman spoke and he smiled bitterly to himself as he
walked, wondering if either one realized he could no longer hold
a pen.

He opened the door. Just outside it, Kytenia squeaked and
leaped to her feet. Surprised, Nondar moved into the hall and
shut the door behind him. "Heavens, child, didn't I tell you to
see to your studies?"

"You did, Archmage." She brushed wrinkles out of her robes
and tried to smile. "But I thought you might need me sooner
rather than later, and—"

"Well, it's good you stayed," Nondar interrupted with a sniff.
"I need you to fetch two magelings for me. Find Ellaith and
Rikka and bring them to my private quarters."

Kytenia started to leave, but Nondar caught her sleeve and
she froze in place. "One more thing," he said. "Bring fine paper
and one of those nice pens from my old classroom, the ones with
the brass nibs."

"Yes, Archmage." She bobbed her head in deference before
she sprinted down the hall.

Sighing, Nondar made his way back to his quarters. He
rarely walked the halls alone anymore, and when he did, he
found himself saddened by how difficult it was to move. He
didn't remember growing old; it had crept up on him while he
was distracted, while he thought he had more time. He would
have liked to return to the mainland one last time, perhaps visit
friends. He'd not been there in ages. *Not since the founding of the
temple and Lomithrandel's creation.* The thought made him
shudder.

If he could change one decision, it would have been that. Had
he never been involved in that abomination of a project, he could
have gone to his grave with a clear conscience. But there was no
way to change it now, and with the poor wretch escaped, rather
than executed, at least he could sleep easy. Idly, Nondar

wondered where the boy had gone. He'd vanished without a trace, not a hair or scale to be seen on Elenhiise again. The mainland was Nondar's only guess.

Frowning, the Archmage rested a hand against the wall to aid his balance. The mainland came to his thoughts often now. There was a reason it kept coming to mind, something that made it hover on the edge of his awareness. But the thought always escaped when he tried to grasp it, slipping through his fingers like the smoke trail of a snuffed candle. He tried not to think of it again. There were more pressing matters at hand.

He left the door open as he slipped into his quarters and settled at the small table usually reserved for meals.

It did not take long for Kytenia to arrive at his doorstep, flanked by the other two magelings he'd summoned. All three looked bewildered. The Archmage didn't summon magelings often, except for errands, and there was no reason to call three of them at once for that. He gave a wry smile as he waved them into his quarters.

"No need to close the doors, girls, I'll be brief. Did you bring the paper, Kytenia? Ah, good. Bring it here." He folded his hands together and studied their faces with a hint of amusement. They thought they were in trouble, he realized; Kytenia and Rikka kept exchanging glances that made him wonder if they'd done something they oughtn't. Then again, he reminded himself, the two of them were better behaved than Firal had ever been. If anything, they had stayed up after lights were to be put out.

"Do you know why I've called you here?" He knew they didn't, but after seeing the way Rikka and Kytenia looked at each other, he couldn't help but ruffle their feathers. Their expressions became alarmed, while Ellaith looked confused.

"No, Archmage," Rikka said finally, ducking her eyes and tucking a strand of her fiery hair behind her ear.

"The three of you have been called because you all have something in common. I've just left a meeting with Masters Anaide and Edagan. After a review of the state of your studies and behavior, we've reached an agreement." Nondar paused just long enough to let them shift in discomfort, then smirked. "From this moment forward, the three of you are Kirban Temple's newest blue magelings."

Rikka's jaw went slack. Ellaith clapped a hand to her chest and exhaled in relief. Kytenia only stared at him with wide eyes.

"The three of you will begin study under me immediately," Nondar continued. "Under normal circumstances, I would extend this offer only to magelings with a healing affinity. However, Rikka, I understand that you strive to take a profession in healing despite your affinity being air. This puts you at a disadvantage, but I am confident you will still benefit from our lessons."

Rikka flushed to the tips of her ears. "Thank you, Archmage!" she cried, bouncing on the tips of her toes.

He motioned for her to settle. "Our lessons will begin first thing in the morning, with all three of you meeting me here. Kytenia, write an official order for me?"

"Of course, Archmage." Kytenia gulped as she dropped into a chair at the table and spread out the paper, pens, and ink she'd gathered.

Nondar cleared his throat. "On this, the twenty-third day of the eleventh month, first year of the rule of Queen Firal of the Penedhionn bloodline, let it be known that Rikka of the green robes, Ellaith of the green robes, and Kytenia of the green robes have been found worthy. By decree of the Archmage and his council, they are elevated to status of Blue Mage, effective immediately." He paused and leaned forward to watch as she finished writing. He held out his hand and Kytenia gave him the pen. He struggled to hold it steady, bracing his arm with his other hand to scrawl his name at the bottom of the page.

The magelings beamed as he finished and blew on the ink to dry it.

"Now," he said, passing the pen back to Kytenia. "Rikka and Ellaith, the two of you may go to the storerooms and request your robes. Take this notice with you and leave it with the woman working the storerooms today. I'll have Kytenia bring it back. Kytenia, I have another dictation to make, if you would stay."

"Of course, Archmage." Kytenia flashed a grin to the other girls as they curtsied and murmured thanks.

"Close the door behind you!" Nondar called after them. It slammed closed and he grimaced. He couldn't blame the girls for being excited, but he wished they would remember their manners.

Kytenia dipped the pen into the inkwell and held it ready above a fresh sheet of paper. "What shall I write for you, Archmage?"

"Something urgent, I'm afraid." A grim look settled on his face.

He'd spent so much time in reflection, yet he still worried about his choice. He knew the importance of declaring his successor, but even after weighing the merits of Anaide and Edagan and reaching his decision, he worried what would happen after the formal proclamation. Would the mages turn on each other if they didn't like his choice? They hadn't turned on him, but they'd also known how fragile his health had grown. Closing his eyes, Nondar drew a breath and gripped his cane until his knuckles turned white.

"On this, the twenty-third day of the eleventh month, first year of the rule of Queen Firal of the Penedhionn bloodline," he started, willing himself to relax and speak slowly. The declaration had to be made, whether or not he was ready. "Let it be known that the Archmage, Nondar of the Parthanus bloodline, officially declares selection of his successor. Upon his death," he cringed at the weight of the word, "the title and rank of Archmage, leadership of Kirban Temple, and the permanent position of Adviser to the Queen, shall fall..."

Kytenia glanced up as he paused.

The Archmage smiled. "...to Kytenia Silaron."

RHYLLYN

Alira couldn't make herself watch. It was bad enough she was here, that she was involved, without having to watch the others prepare for the experiment. She heard them opening the crate but couldn't bring herself to look. She stared at the table before her instead.

The table was no better. Crudely fitted with straps and ropes, it looked like something out of a torture chamber. Perhaps it was, she thought, clutching the skirt of her robes to keep her hands from shaking.

Behind her, the child wept. Alira flinched at the crack of flesh on flesh when one of the others struck him.

She should have run. She should have abandoned the Grand College when it became clear Envesi wouldn't let her escape this. Melora might have been all right with the former Archmage's schemes, but Alira was not—not when an innocent child was involved.

It was too late to flee now. The others would strike her down before she made it out the door. If there weren't two of them, she might have a chance.

If there weren't two of them, she might have tried.

"Children are such wretched creatures," Envesi grumbled as

she dragged the boy from the crate with Melora's help. Alira couldn't help but glance their way. She didn't know how the boy had come to be in the crate, or the crate in the shack beyond the city's limits. She did not want to know.

He wasn't a large boy, or very old; Alira guessed he couldn't have been more than six. She thought him human at first glance, but the spark of a budding Gift glowed in her senses when they brought him near. He was of Eldani descent, then. It was just so diluted that his ears bore no hint of a point.

The child's knees buckled and the two mages let his legs drag against the floor as they pulled him across the room. He had no fight left in him. Ugly welts marred the exposed flesh of his arms and legs. Together, the two women wrestled him onto the table.

"Alira, the straps," Melora snapped, jolting her out of her thoughts.

Alira swallowed hard and, with trembling fingers, buckled the child's legs in place.

Envesi stuffed a rag into his mouth and dusted her hands together. "That ought to keep the wretch quiet. We may be beyond where the college mages can feel us working, but there's bound to be someone near enough to hear if he shouts."

That they perform their experiments outside the city had been one of Headmaster Tolmarni's requirements. Though the Archmage of Lore granted them permission to practice unbinding, it was clear he did not want their efforts associated with the college. Should they be caught, it would be elsewhere, outside his immediate control.

The headmaster had allowed them a considerable amount of freedom when it came to research, but not practice. Envesi had insisted on examining a number of mages in the Grand College, volunteers who hadn't yet earned the right to gray robes, but they had only studied—they hadn't tried to unbind any of them. Envesi said the means for experimentation would be provided, but Alira hadn't expected this.

The former Archmage checked the straps as Alira moved to the head of the table. "Shall we begin?"

"Yes, Envesi," Melora said, standing at the table's foot.

Alira stared down at the boy's face. Wet trails glistened on his cheeks, pale stripes in the dust that coated his skin. His bright blue eyes shone with fear. Her heart wrenched and she wiped away his tears.

"Alira?" Envesi prompted.

"Yes, Envesi," Alira replied hastily, tearing her eyes from the child again.

"Good." The former Archmage sniffed, pushing up the sleeves of her dull gray robes. She tied her energies with Melora first and Alira resisted the urge to shrink from their combined strength. Then Envesi caught her in the net of power, too.

Alira gasped as the woman reeled her in. She'd thought her involvement would require her to participate directly. Instead, Envesi siphoned power through with such speed and force that it made her head spin. A shadowy haze crept in on the edges of her vision.

"Stay on your feet," Envesi ordered. "Don't lose the link."

The darkness grew speckled. Stars flashed before her eyes and Alira squeezed them closed, bracing herself against the table.

Envesi guided their combined energies on her own. The torrent of power filled the room with humming static and made Alira's hair stand on end. At the edge of her senses, their twined powers touched the spark of the boy's Gift. It burst and twinkled, ignited by the brush of power. Magic simmered within him, not linked with theirs, but snared by it.

Dizziness made the room rock beneath her, but Alira struggled to stay upright as the former Archmage pushed instead of pulling, and the twined threads of their power caught on the boundary of the child's affinity. Envesi pushed until their power strained, then drew it all back so tight that every thread of energy became defined. The burn of magic grew brighter and brighter in Alira's senses, until she could hardly stand it.

Then everything erupted into chaos, the torrent of power swirling too fast for Alira to follow. Whatever force Envesi commanded, the complicated twirls and turns were so far beyond her skill level that she couldn't comprehend the whirlpool of raw energy that threatened to sweep them all away.

"It's twisting again!" Melora screeched. The older woman was right. Alira shuddered as everything seemed to go sideways, her field of vision warping, skewing.

Raw energy lashed back against them, snapping the delicate threads that wove their magic together, flooding her with power so vile it made her stomach heave. Alira sagged against the edge of the table and clapped a hand to her mouth. Melora fell to the floor and retched.

"No, no, no!" Envesi screamed. She pulled fistfuls of her white hair and gnashed her teeth, her eyes flashing with fury. "This was different! She wasn't even here!"

The wave of nausea passed and Alira gulped, struggling to catch her breath as she forced her eyes to open.

The boy still lay beneath her, his eyes closed, tears still streaking his dirty face. He trembled and jerked with silent sobs, unable to move beneath the straps that held him down. Melora was still on the floor. Only Envesi remained steady on her feet, though her face was twisted with anger.

"Another failure." The former Archmage released a heavy sigh. She struggled to compose herself. Her hands swept over her face as if to wipe away her emotions before she smoothed her hair. "I must report this to the headmaster. We simply cannot do this without more hands to control the flows. I will have Eyrion assign more mages to this project."

"You mean for us to try again?" Melora asked, voice thick with disbelief.

"Within a few days, yes." Envesi pulled down her sleeves and turned to the door. "I will find the headmaster and explain the situation. Take some time to compose yourselves, then dispose of the evidence before joining me."

Alira blinked. "Dispose of—"

The former Archmage stepped outside and slammed the door.

"She means the boy." Melora's lip curled with a sneer. "Make it fast and put him out of his misery."

Alira looked down. When she saw the boy looking at her, her stomach gave a flop. His eyes were no longer human. They glowed a soft blue in the dim light of the shack, their centers slitted like a snake's. Yet they were more human than anything she'd ever seen. Fear and pleading warred within them.

She looked at Melora. The older woman grasped the side of the table and dragged herself to her feet. She still panted, obviously weakened by the tainted magic that had struck them both. Muddy green scales caught Alira's eye. The child's arm. Alira swallowed against the knot in her stomach and met the boy's eyes again.

"I can't." She'd been foolish to go along with it this far. She wouldn't have innocent blood on her hands.

"Then move over," Melora growled. "I'll unmake him for you."

Alira stepped forward and put a protective arm across the boy's body.

The older mage's eyes darkened. "It's bad enough that one exists. We can't allow the second to live."

"I realize the difficulty Lomithrandel's existence caused for you," Alira said. "But in this, I'm afraid Envesi has made a terrible mistake."

Melora's brows lifted. "What?"

"She involved me." Alira slammed her palms together and a pulse of energy exploded outward. It struck the other woman hard. Melora pitched backward and hit the floor hard, a cry of pain escaping her throat.

Grasping the flows around her and fighting back fear, Alira

looped waves of air around the older mage to trap her in place. Then she spun to the table, jerked the straps free, and dragged the boy to his feet. He staggered and clung to her legs.

"Traitor!" Melora shrieked, writhing against the air currents. Alira felt her prying at the flows, trying to wrest them from her grasp. Closely matched in strength as they were, the older mage still had the upper hand in skill. Alira darted forward to seize the woman by her robes and hair. Melora screeched as Alira hauled her to her feet and threw her against the table.

Melora twisted with a cry of rage. Alira backhanded the old woman and strapped down her arms while she was stunned. Then she wheeled, caught the boy by the arm, and bolted for the door.

"Alira!" Melora shrilled, flailing against her bonds. "I'll have your head for this! Envesi will—"

Alira slammed the door on the woman's words and almost tripped over the child. She clamped a hand on his shoulder and spun him toward the north. "Run!"

Frightened, the boy scrambled upright. He made it two steps before he stumbled, unable to move on his changed feet. Alira paced backwards, squeezed her eyes closed, and seized power. It seemed woefully inadequate after the torrent Envesi had pulled through her, but it was all she could do. She poured her focus into a single pinpoint. The shack erupted in flames with a deafening boom, and the force threw the boy to the ground.

Alira swept him into her arms and ran. The boy clung to her neck and wept into her shoulder. Behind her, the magic-fueled flames grew into an inferno. She ran north from the coast until her legs could carry her no longer, but she did not dare stop. Envesi could not have gone far. Alira pulled energy from anything she could to replenish herself, not caring if she damaged or unmade anything in the process. All that mattered was running. Her chest ached and her arms burned from the weight of the child she carried. Her throat grew so dry that coughs racked her body.

The fields of Lore gave way to forests and she plunged into the trees, racing through the underbrush until she no longer had the strength to draw energy to restore her aching muscles. At last, she stumbled, slowed, and finally sank to the ground with the boy on her lap.

"I must rest," she gasped against his hair. "I must. I'm sorry."

The child said nothing, his arms still wrapped around her neck, his face still buried in her shoulder. He trembled, though with tears or fright, she couldn't tell which. Gulping air, she stroked his head and wrapped her arms around his frail body. No strength remained within her, but she swayed anyway, rocking until they both grew calm.

After a time, Alira sat back, cradled the boy's face in her hands, and looked him in the eye. He was pale beneath the smudges of tears and dirt, but his expression was solemn. "Are you all right?"

He nodded.

"Are you hurt?" She couldn't imagine the transformation had been comfortable, but she didn't want him to suffer lingering pain.

He shook his head.

Frowning, she smoothed back his hair. Grit and dust coated her fingers. "Can you speak?"

He lowered his eyes and nodded again. "Yes, ma'am."

Her shoulders sagged with relief. The regional dialect was crude, but she'd grown used to it since her arrival in Lore. The Grand College was home to many foreigners and she had been forced to adapt. Her thoughts turned to the college and her place there, where she'd scraped together a simple life and a handful of belongings. All forfeit now. She couldn't return. Strangely, she felt no regret.

Alira offered the boy a smile. "Well. Let me have a look at you, hmm? Make sure you're all right." She doubted he felt comfortable with her after what he'd just witnessed, but he didn't fuss when she straightened his mussed clothing.

He was a street urchin, she decided. His clothes were little better than rags. But now that she took a better look at him, he was a cute boy. His eyes were a bright blue, made more vivid by the eerie light his now-unbound magic gave them. His tangled hair was a light chestnut, though darkened by dirt and dust. All of him was smudged with dust, in fact, though his hands and bare feet showed no dirt against his new scales. Those were a dull olive green, their color as unremarkable as the child had been that morning.

He stared at his hands as she examined them, his expression growing pained. "Am I gonna die?" he asked in a hushed voice, fear shining in his eyes. Alira was surprised he didn't cry, but they were tired. She figured he'd cried himself out while they ran.

She waved a hand in dismissal, trying to put him to ease. "Pish, no. Why, you're the strongest and healthiest you've probably ever been."

He didn't look convinced.

Alira restrained a sigh. "What's your name, boy?"

"Rhyllyn."

She opened her mouth to ask for a surname, but closed it just as fast. Whether he'd forgotten to share it or whether he had one at all didn't matter. If he had a family, it wasn't likely they'd welcome him back as a monster. "My name is Alira. Can you walk? We can't linger here. We must keep moving in case the others decide to follow us."

Rhyllyn nodded and slid off her lap. He wobbled on his feet and spread his arms to keep from falling. He watched his legs as he adjusted his footing and regained his balance. Alira stood and took his small, clawed hand in hers. His luminescent eyes trained on their fingers and the stark difference between them. "What's happened to me?" he asked in a whisper.

"I don't know, exactly," Alira said. Teaching had never been her specialty. Even had it been, she hardly knew how to explain the concept of affinities and unbinding to a mere child. "Come.

Once we're someplace we can rest, I'll see what I can learn about what's been done."

They walked side by side. Leaves crunched underfoot and birdsong filled the air overhead. The birds were a good omen. If more people entered the woods, they likely would go quiet. With the happy trills and warbles overhead, they could pace themselves for now. Alira's legs still ached, but their unhurried walk brought comfortable warmth back into them.

"Where are we going?" Rhyllyn asked. His voice was small, but steady.

Alira blinked. She hadn't considered where they might flee to. Her only concern had been escaping with the boy in tow. She couldn't go back to the college and returning to the coastal city at all would be foolish, especially with him by her side. She didn't know where she could take him. She didn't know where he would be safe. "North," she said eventually, smiling as if she had it all planned out.

He stumbled and used her hand to right himself. "What's north?"

"Well, there are mountains, and..." And what? North was where the college had sent mages for war. North was the center of conflict, a place bound to be full of soldiers and battle. An idea sprang into her head and she smiled down at him again. "And soldiers, of course. The soldiers fighting the mages. There's no one better to keep us safe from them."

He eyed her doubtfully. "You're a mage."

"Yes," Alira agreed, and her smile faded. "A strong one. Though not as strong as I thought, I suppose." Had she been stronger, she might have understood what Envesi had done to the flows, might have had an idea how to undo the magic-inflicted twist in the boy's body. Then again, her weakness wasn't just in her Gift. If she were stronger in other ways, she might have had the will to stand against Envesi sooner.

Not for the first time, she hated herself for the choices she'd made. When the temple divided, she thought she'd been wise in siding with the Archmage—that she'd acted in effort to keep the mages together. She'd thought the dissent of the other Masters was a sign of treachery. It wasn't until she'd learned of Envesi's experiments that she realized she'd taken the wrong side. By then, it was too late.

Despite having been stripped of her title and rank, she didn't regret her time in the Grand College. She'd gained a new appreciation for her Gift after having been deprived of it for so long, and she'd learned new methods of utilizing her fire affinity.

But the greatest changes had been in her demeanor. On Elenhiise, she acknowledged she'd often behaved in an arrogant and haughty manner. Gaining a high title at a young age hadn't done her any favors, but most of her attitude came from the idea she had something to prove to the other Masters. When the college put the three of them on equal footing, they all balked at punishment. Frustration had been enough to make her cry, but seeing the way Envesi and Melora faltered at the same challenges, Alira had realized she didn't have to prove anything. Her newfound humility had gotten her farther with the college instructors than anything else.

"How far is it?" Rhyllyn asked, snapping her from her thoughts.

Alira hesitated to answer. Geography had been one of their fields of study as magelings in the college, but there was a difference between looking at distances on an unfamiliar map and trying to traverse them by foot. Worse still, they were traveling without supplies. Her pockets were empty and she knew the boy had nothing. Not a single coin between them to pay for food or lodging. She regretted the circumstances, but looking at the boy who walked with his tiny hand in hers, she couldn't regret the decision.

She gave his fingers a gentle, comforting squeeze. "It's quite a way to travel, but we'll be all right. Mages travel the whole world, you know. Traveling from here to the mountains isn't half as far as I've traveled before."

The boy's eyes widened. "Really?"

"Oh, yes." Relieved he didn't question how they'd manage the trip, she spun grand tales of Elenhiise, the ruins, and the temple as they walked. If nothing else, she could recite old history lessons or folk tales from memory while her mind spun cartwheels. The soldiers in the north would likely kill them on sight, but the Aldaanan—other mages—might be open to negotiation. Keeping the child calm and happy was important, but not so important as buying time to think of a plan.

NEW LESSONS

EVERY TIME RUNE MET HIS TEACHERS IN THE FIELD JUST SOUTH OF Aldaeon, the gryphon was there. He didn't know how she knew; most of his lessons occurred in the tower. Perhaps one of the Aldaanan told her, though he couldn't fathom why. She never approached the room in the tower where they held his lessons, and never set foot on the field itself when practice was in session, but she was there.

Her golden eyes glittered and her ear-tufts stood straight, like the ears of a cat at attention. Rune caught her gaze and held it as he took his position at the meeting place in the center of the field. The snow was still trampled, a dirty gray-brown ring in the middle of the empty space. He was early, and his teacher was not yet present.

The gryphon noticed. Her feathered mane ruffled and she stood straighter. She tried to hide the way she glanced about, but the way her hindquarters lowered and wriggled gave away her eagerness. If he hadn't known better, he would have thought she looked about to burst. Rune cocked his head at her. She took it as an invitation and padded forward across the snow.

"You always watch," he called as she approached. "Yet you never join us."

Ria trilled in her peculiar gryphon's laugh. She laughed as a human might sometimes, too, but it was a raspy, foreign sound. Her trills were pure delight. "Ah, if only I could. But how would I? We are not all so Gifted as you."

He considered that for a moment, his brow furrowed. "Aren't you?" Strange as the gryphons were, he'd never stopped long enough to think about them. They were stories come to life, but Ria was so personable that it dashed all sense of wonder. Or, almost all of it. A small tingling of wonder still rolled through him as she stopped two paces away and sat on her haunches, studying him the way one might admire a piece of art.

"Certainly not. Gryphons bear no magic." Her ear-tufts drooped a shade. Rune fought the urge to touch them, to see if they were merely feathers or if delicate flesh hid beneath. He shook the notion free of his head. No matter how comfortable he was around the gryphon, he had to maintain some sense of propriety.

"Are you certain?" The words escaped before he could stop them.

Ria perked, then let out a little trill once more. "Oh, I forgot, you aren't familiar with us. You feel it, don't you? A little spark of something special?" Her beak parted in some semblance of a grin. "You aren't wrong. And yet, you are. Gryphons cannot wield magic. We *are* magic, you see."

He did not. A thousand questions leaped to mind and he opened his mouth to let them spill forth, but the gryphon stiffened and looked past him before he could.

"Your teacher's here," she said, a hint of disappointment in her voice. Her head drooped and her feathers flattened. "I'd best get out of the way. Good luck. I'll be watching."

Rune turned back toward the city. An Aldaanan woman trudged toward him through the snow. Her short stature and gray-brown dress, coupled with her darker hair, gave him the impression of one of the dark-headed snowbirds he'd seen outside the army's camp.

"Pardon me for being late," the woman panted, her breath forming small clouds of white. "I was at the top of the tower when someone informed me I was supposed to be here."

"I haven't waited long." Rune offered a half smile. He tried not to seem too eager. He needed their help—and the precise training only they could give—but eagerness implied vulnerability.

The woman smiled politely in return. "Shall we begin?" Her magic flickered at the edge of his senses, small and fleeting.

There were a number of mysteries that still surrounded their congruous power. The difference in strength between the two of them was one. The small Aldaanan woman before him was not the first Rune had sensed was weaker than him, yet the idea that anyone could be weaker when the world's power still answered in full force made no sense. He would have to remember to ask Filadiel about it another time. The leader of the Aldaanan had established himself as the key informant when it came to such things. Rune assumed it was because some things were meant to remain secret, and as acting leader, only Filadiel had the authority to decide what could and could not be revealed.

Rune relaxed his shoulders and opened himself to power, answering her question.

Her smile faltered, though she was quick to catch and restore it. "I am told you struggle in healing. We shall practice today."

A surge of uncomfortable emotions filled his chest. Rune closed his eyes and turned away to hide their shift of color. Too late, it seemed, because the Aldaanan woman tilted her head, the chains suspended between her tall ears jingling.

"You are not ready." It was not a question.

"No," he agreed. Firal still haunted his thoughts both day and night, drove every decision he made. How could he venture into her domain without her there?

"Very well," the woman said, smoothing her skirt with both hands. "Another time. Filadiel has other concerns. He says you are still too forceful in everything you do. Perhaps we should meditate together? I know a number of techniques that may be useful in convincing you to relinquish that hold you try to keep on everything."

This time, instead of discomfort, Rune bit back frustration. It proved easier to bridle. "Fine." He took a half step back and lowered himself to the ground. The ice and snow was far from pleasant to sit on, and he sucked in a sharp breath when the frigid wet immediately seeped through the fabric of his pants.

A sparkle lit the Aldaanan woman's eyes. "The ice builds character."

"So does war," he replied through clenched teeth.

Her eyes glittered, a shadow in their depths. "We'll see."

The sensation of power answering her call flooded his senses. It had been disorienting, the first time he'd felt someone else open themselves to magic. It ached, pulled, like they tugged at the fabric of his being. Like their magic siphoned his own power. In some ways, he supposed it did. They were both tied to the same energy sources, and there was only so much to go around. Bound mages called so little, he'd barely felt their pull. He'd never realized that others might have to compete.

"Open," his teacher prompted.

Rune closed his eyes and exhaled. He understood what he was meant to do, but it did not come easily. Magic flowed everywhere around him, permeated everything, yet he found himself reaching for it instead of acknowledging it was already there.

"Open," the Aldaanan woman repeated.

He rested his clawed hands on his knees and tried to ignore the cold that seeped through his wet uniform to attack the backs of his thighs. It clawed at his flesh and burned like embers. He gritted his teeth and seized power to dry the ground beneath him.

"Stop."

He froze, still latched onto the heady flows of magic.

The woman raised a brow. "You cannot gain control over

yourself or your power if you seek to remove every impediment to concentration. You think you will always be able to chase away the cold? Still the rain? Ignore it."

"I can't."

"Then you can't meditate." She shrugged as if it didn't matter. "If you truly joined with the magic you seek to wield, instead of forcing it to bend to your will, then it would solve those discomforts for you." Her eyes fell closed once more.

Frustrated, he sat back and stared at the mage. Unlike with his previous teachers, there was a lot he could learn from the Aldaanan by watching alone. Their power moved like his, flowed against his, fed off the same source. The woman before him appeared tranquil, comfortable, but when he opened the strange floodgates that held magic at bay to let himself sense what she was doing, her peace became harder to understand.

Threads and rivers of magic coursed both around and through her, as if she wasn't there at all—or as if she were part of the scenery, instead of a living being. The endless tide rolled straight through her, no point of entry or merging. And the ice— the wet and snow and ugly slush beneath her—did not touch her skin at all.

Rune's frustration grew.

"Mind your feelings," the woman prompted gently. "The way you feel calls power to you. Mind what forces you are open to."

His hands tried to curl into fists. The claws on his fingertips jabbed his knees before he caught himself. "I thought I was supposed to be open to everything?"

"Yes, but your agitation will limit you. What the spirit calls is what will answer. To be answered by everything, you must be calm."

The ice still bit his skin. Rune set his jaw and squeezed his eyes closed. He couldn't will the discomfort away, but he tried to ignore the way it chewed its way to his bones. His teeth tried to chatter. At first, he resisted. Then, gradually, he tried to surrender. His teeth rattled so hard his whole body shook. The magic simmered just beyond himself. He could touch it. Taste it. Dip in a claw. Perhaps then the nameless mage in front of him would be satisfied enough to move on to the next lesson. He braced and opened himself to power.

Magic fell over him like a wave, rushed in as if to drown him. It crashed against him and scattered like mist.

"You are not a rock among the waves," his teacher said. "Every stone becomes sand in the end. Do not force it to break you!"

Exasperated, he threw up his hands. "What else am I supposed to do?"

"Let go. Completely. You can't control free magic any more than you can keep thunderheads on a leash."

"I've done it before," he argued.

"You've fought errant strands into submission. It's not the same thing."

His eyes flickered red. "What else can I do but fight?"

"You fight, but the world is not your enemy," the woman said without so much as stirring. "You are part of it, born of it, birthed by its essence. You fight magic, but not because you want control."

"I fight it because I must," he growled.

She shrugged. "You fight it because it is you."

For a moment, even his shivering stilled.

"This is the natural order of things," the woman added, softer. She met his eyes, her gaze gentle and sympathetic. "No matter what you feel about what has happened to you, this is the way things should be. The way you should have been. One with us. One with the power that made you."

"But it wasn't supposed to make me." His voice cracked, despite his best efforts. "I'm not like you. I'm damaged, twisted—"

"We're all broken," she interrupted. "You simply wear your scars more openly than most. But you feel it, don't you? The way the power wants you? You've learned wrong, fought its embrace your whole life. What if, just once, you let go?"

Rune hesitated. Magic did want him. It always had. It was always there, pressing against him, filtering through him though he tried to control it, its wild surges and shifts reflected in the curious glow of his eyes. "Why would it want me?" Somehow, he'd never thought to ask.

The Aldaanan mage raised a brow. "Why would it not?"

He had no answer.

She chuckled and raised her hands with a shrug. "Brant, His power—they do not make mistakes. Your battle is your own, but this is as you should be. You feel it, too, don't you? Otherwise, you wouldn't be here." Her eyes drifted closed and once again, she melted into the tide of magic.

Rune exhaled hard and stared at the mud-stained slush before him. Magic tingled against his skin, crawled across him like some shapeless creature driven by curiosity. He trained his thoughts on it. No matter what the Aldaanan said, he still held his doubts. He didn't want control, he needed it. Unfettered magic had made him what he was. Opening himself to it as freely as his teachers suggested seemed dangerous, even foolhardy.

The currents of power against his skin slowed, as if in response to his thoughts. It didn't feel dangerous. That was why it troubled him. It was warm, welcoming, like a laughing brook on a summer day. Only he knew the current was swift, wild, and its waters deeper than what he could navigate. Yet his teacher would not be satisfied until he tried. Stifling his growing frustration, he exhaled again.

He could argue all day and it would go nowhere. Silent, grudging, he tried once more. His breath deepened and his shoulders sank. This time, he opened to embrace the magic that surrounded him slowly.

At first, nothing happened. Power hovered nearby, as if waiting, hesitant. To feel it was different from grasping it, he reminded himself, and nothing would come of mere feeling. He started to reach for it—as he had so many times before—and caught himself at the last second. No; he couldn't force it. Couldn't will it. It had to come to him.

Please, come to me, he pleaded silently. How was he supposed to communicate with something that wasn't alive? A troubled feeling stirred in his chest, weighty and dark, and he chased it away before it could settle.

Something else stirred. Fleeting, foreign, and yet it felt as if it should have been there all along.

Rune's breath caught in his throat and he willed himself to be still.

"Breathe," his teacher prompted. "Think of your breath, nothing else."

The suggestion summoned a thousand wild thoughts to mind. He fought them back until they scattered like white serpent's-tongue flowers on the wind.

No, he inwardly snapped. *Like nothing. Nothing.*

Stillness returned after a handful of breaths. And then something else stole in with his breath. It spread within his chest, suffuse warmth that crept into his limbs and tingled within his flesh. His awareness of the world around him faded, and with it, the discomfort of the ice beneath him disappeared. Comforting heat blossomed in his lungs, swelled until his ribs ached with their fullness. Power unlike anything he'd ever known coursed through him, stealing a gasp from his lips and replacing his air with *more.*

Searing pain shot through his limbs. Rune's eyes shot open and his gaze darted to his arms. Fat blotches of black spread and seeped at the elbows of his shirt. Itching, burning heat exploded just beneath his skin and panic gripped his heart. He tried to tear the fabric, but his fingers were too numb. He wrenched his sleeve up his arm instead.

Thick beads of ichor bubbled between the scales at the rough transition between beast and human flesh. It sizzled against his skin, blistered the tiny plates of emerald-green. A startled cry escaped him and in an instant, the magic retreated.

The weight of all his senses hit him like a hammer blow and he all but fell to the frigid ground, gripping his bloodied arm.

The Aldaanan woman opened her eyes, a hint of a smile playing at her lips.

It was all he could do not to snarl. "What was that?"

"Progress," she said, simply. When she stood, her dress was dry.

Rune glared at her back as she left without another word. His breath came fast, ragged, the winter air biting in his chest. Slowly, the pain in his limbs subsided, and he lifted his hand. Black, sticky ichor clung to the palm of his hand, and a small, blistered patch of scales peeled away from his arm.

In a heartbeat, his panic evaporated and a small spark of wonder ignited within him, lit by the hope he hadn't dared kindle.

New, perfect skin waited underneath.

CLEANSING

"IT'S THE MOST INCREDIBLE THING. LIKE WHEN YOU HAVE AN EMPTY cup and you hold it down in a basin. The water rushes in to fill it from every direction, just because it's there." Rune shoved another spoonful of food into his mouth and made a face. He still couldn't get used to the bitterness of molasses, but the army had nothing else to sweeten their morning porridge.

Sera laughed, her blue eyes sparkling with amusement. "Your descriptions of things are ridiculous, you know that?"

Mealtimes had become invaluable for explaining the extent of his lessons, and Sera often took breakfast at the cook fire closest to his tent. Once he joined the Aldaanan for the day's exercises, they did not release him until he was too weary to speak. His meetings with Sera were almost as exhausting, with the amount of effort she put into wringing information from him. Sometimes she offered tidbits of news in return, information about the army and Garam's plans. Today she offered nothing, but she was garbed in white to blend into the snow. She would be on scout duty, it seemed.

"I cannot think of a better way to describe it. Can't," he corrected himself with a wince. "Sorry. I try to have the Aldaanan teach me in this tongue instead of theirs, so I can practice, but speaking your tongue is still difficult sometimes. And sometimes their concepts don't translate well."

"I appreciate that you try." She leaned forward and patted his knee with a sympathetic chuckle. "You've gotten much better. But tell me more about this magic! It sounds incredible. Being that full of power all the time, exerting that little strength to twist the flows..." She gave a wistful sigh.

Rune shook his head. "It isn't like being full of power. It's just like I said. You are the cup and the water is the power. It fills you, but it also moves through you, moves all around you. It fills you when its presence is needed, but the way you float within it is what makes it amazing."

"And it feels like that all the time?"

"No, only when I need it." He shrugged and spooned the last of his porridge into his mouth. "It's difficult to explain."

Sera clicked her tongue and stared at the bowl in her hands. "I'm going to hate telling all of this to Garam. He'll be terrified to think all the Aldaanan have that much power at their fingertips."

"Would you like me to tell him instead?" He didn't relish the idea, but he was trying to stay on the captain's good side. Thus far, he hadn't invoked the man's ire. There were many reasons he kept his experiences with the Aldaanan to himself as much as possible. What the Aldaanan could do for him was all that pushed him to cooperate with the army in the first place. The fingertip-sized patches on his arms where human skin had replaced scales represented hope in Rune's eyes, and would mean inevitable loss in Garam's. There was no hiding his marked improvement in mood, though, and Rune knew the captain had noticed.

She made a face. "No. He still thinks I'm sneaking all this information out of you, instead of you sitting and spilling your guts like a child who doesn't know how to keep his mouth shut."

Rune snorted and put his bowl aside. "I can keep my mouth shut just fine." He dusted snow from his knees as he pushed himself up.

"Can you?" she teased.

"Yes. After all, you still don't know my birth name."

"Hey!" she shouted, scrambling after him as he turned away. "You can't tease me like that! I thought you told Garam your real name was Rune?"

"I did," he agreed. "And it is. It just isn't the name I was given when I was born." He flashed her a grin and wove between the tents on his way toward the pale tower at the edge of the city. He'd taken too long to eat; he was sure to be late.

A snowball struck the back of his head and he stumbled. Growling, he glared over his shoulder and dropped to the ground to make one of his own. Sera's eyes went wide as he turned to throw it, but it wasn't until a hand caught his wrist that he realized her expression wasn't for him. He turned his head and his face fell when he saw Garam.

"Both of you. My tent. Now." The captain released him, the hard look on his face dashing any mirth the two of the might have felt. Sobered, Rune fell in step behind him.

He and Sera weren't the only ones summoned, as they discovered when they stepped inside Garam's tent. A messenger and a handful of lieutenants already waited around the table in the tent's center. Ria sat in the corner. Her ear-tufts lifted when she saw Rune. He offered a nod of greeting in response, momentarily unsure why he'd been called. When he noticed the figurines atop the map that lay on the table, he understood.

A large number of robed figurines stood in clusters across the map's mountain ranges. Mages, no doubt. Garam's army was represented by figurines in armor, serving as a sharp reminder that Rune and Sera were the only mages in his command.

"The gryphons have spotted campsites while flying over the mountain ranges," Garam said, pacing around the table to stand behind it. He leaned forward and rested his hands against the map. "After locating the groups of mages, they began tracking them. They followed these groups over the course of several days. Their movement leads us—the gryphons and me—to believe they mean to band together and strike us."

"So we move against them before they have a chance to rally together," one of the lieutenants said. "Scatter their forces again."

"They'd flatten the army if you tried," Rune muttered. The officers glowered at him. He answered by raising a brow. "Have any of you fought mages before?"

Sera scoffed. "Of course not. Mages have never gone to war. Not since the battles that saw dragons eradicated from the Triad."

He gave her a hard look. "Mages are going to war now. They know what they're doing, or else they wouldn't be here. The mountains make Aldaan difficult to invade. If they're gathering in visible camps, it's because they hope to lure us out."

One of the lieutenants began to protest, but Garam raised a hand to silence him. "Go on," the captain said.

Rune gestured to the map. "You have a formidable army, but only two mages. The Aldaanan are strong, but they number too few to protect us if they're split up between fighting squadrons, and the mages from Lore must know it. They mean to draw your forces into the mountain. Then they will withdraw, and when your men pursue them, the college mages will sweep in from either side and crush them. Mages are scholars. They have a greater understanding of tactics than you know."

Garam's eyes narrowed, boring into him like dark coals. "Have you fought mages before?"

"I've fought before, that's enough." Rune folded his arms over his chest and shifted uneasily. "Getting close to the mages will be difficult and dangerous. They use barriers that can protect them from arrows and thrown spears. Getting close enough to strike them with a sword means putting yourself well within range of their power. The weakest mage can toss a grown man like a rag doll, armor and all."

Sera nodded in agreement, drawing a chorus of frustrated sounds from the lieutenants.

"Then how are we supposed to fight them?" one asked, exasperated.

Rune cast him a sidewise glance. "Why would you fight them? With our camp at the foot of the aerie, we have all the Aldaanan and the gryphons ready at our backs. We have food and the gryphons can bring in more of anything we need without being hindered by the enemy. It is winter and the mages are just now moving into the mountain ranges. Better to wait them out, make them desperate. They will run short on supplies before long, and their numbers are likely too few in each group to open Gates to retrieve more."

"I don't think King Vicamros sent me to wait them out," Garam said through gritted teeth.

"I don't think King Vicamros sent you at all," Sera murmured. The captain shot her a scowl and she glared back. "Just admit it, Garam. The council sent us here to get us out of the way. The Triad is three large provinces. Kingdoms in their own right. Your army is a paltry number of men compared to what they could scrape from the countryside if they decide they need more. How can you think they expect you to win a war against mages when they've only sent you with two of your own?"

Garam's face darkened with anger. "We have the Aldaanan—"

"Who can't even agree on whether or not they want to fight," Rune interrupted. "Becoming involved with bound mages again is the last thing they want."

"I don't care what they want!" the captain roared. The room fell silent, even the lieutenants appearing taken aback. "I am here because King Vicamros put me here. Because King Vicamros expects me to solve this problem. It is my rank, my life, my sister's life on the line. I... Will... Not... Fail." He jabbed a finger against the table to punctuate each word.

"Then listen to the only man present who has any idea what you are up against." Rune's eyes flashed in the dim light of the tent. "Wait them out, or you are sending good men to their graves." He sent the lieutenants a meaningful look and then turned to leave.

"You are not dismissed," Garam snapped.

Rune turned one baleful glowing eye toward the captain. Undeterred, he threw back the flap that covered the tent's entrance. "Try and stop me."

No one moved. Satisfied, he slipped outside and breathed deeply of the biting, frigid air.

It felt good to be defiant, to let his frustration and anger free. It felt like reclaiming a piece of himself. He didn't like who he'd been forced to become; a shell of a man who'd been pushed into compliance with threats of prison and worse. He'd been a leader before. Not as experienced as some, but more experienced than the lieutenants clustered around Garam's table. He had seen war. A war against mages, no less, but that was something he didn't intend to share. He didn't know how far word might have traveled from Elenhiise, but with the Master mages intent on his death, he didn't mean to find out.

The frosty air burned in his chest, giving him something else to focus on. He willed himself to be calm and tried to think of the lessons he'd had with the Aldaanan.

He'd tried desperately, but hadn't again reached the state of calm meditation he'd entered that caused that small number of his scales to fall away. Control over his Gift would come with control over himself, they told him each time he failed. The reassurance hadn't eased his frustration. Rune wiped his face with both hands and struggled to rein in his emotions. Eyes were a portal through which one could see the soul, Filadiel said. It made sense the turbulence inside him would be visible there, but walking into his lesson with his eyes aglow would only earn him a reprimand.

Thus far, his lessons had taken place in the south field or in the council chamber at the top of the tower. Today, he'd been instructed to seek a teacher inside the tower. The south field was empty. His composure returned as he climbed the tower's ramp.

It was unusual for more than one of the Aldaanan to teach at a time, which added to Rune's confusion when he opened the door at the top of the tower. The room went silent. Every seat in the council chamber was filled, and more Aldaanan sat on the floor. All eyes turned in his direction. Many of the free mages present were people he'd never seen before. He drew back. He was late for his lesson, but he hadn't expected council to be in session already—not when his lessons were hours long.

"Come in," Filadiel called from the far end of the room. "Shut the door. Sit. If you are to be one of us, you should be included in this discussion. Perhaps you can offer insight from another perspective."

A handful of the Aldaanan frowned, but no one protested. Rune slipped inside and closed the door. There didn't seem to be any order or arrangement to seating. He moved a single step to the side and sat on the floor. Nobody spoke. After he was settled, everyone looked back to Filadiel.

"As I was saying," Filadiel began, his voice holding none of the flightiness Rune had grown used to hearing, "I am well aware they need more mages for this. We can defend Aldaeon for a time, but only if we are here. I do not think Captain Kaith has any idea the number of enemies lurking in the mountains. He has asked for fourteen free mages to shield fourteen groups, but fourteen is a small number for such a large mountain range. If we divide our numbers, Aldaeon is weakened. Who's to say that's not exactly what the mongrel-mages want?"

A woman with the same mousy coloration as Filadiel gave a snort. "Were it not for the army King Vicamros deposited in our lands, there'd be no need to defend Aldaeon at all. We could have made for the northern mountains, left the city empty. It's not our land they're after, if you recall. It's us."

"You forget the other people who live here," another woman protested. She was dark-eyed and gray-haired, and Rune thought he remembered her from his first visit to the council chamber. "We have protected the humans in Aldaeon for generations. And even if not for them, what are we without our land?" She shook her head, as if to answer her own question. She wore more chains in her tall ears than the others, and the jewels that hung from them bounced with the motion. The others in the room grew solemn and she went on. "We are Aldaanan. We have lived in this valley since the gryphons built their first nest. True, there are some who have scattered, small pockets of free mages to be found all across the known world, but they are nomads at best. Aldaan is our home."

"Which is why this is not easy." Filadiel rubbed the worried wrinkles from his brow and turned his gaze to Rune. "Has Captain Kaith called his officers for briefing?"

Rune hesitated. Their eyes on him grew heavy. The last thing he wanted was to walk a political tightrope between the Aldaanan and Garam's armies, but he was pulled taut between the two groups. He should have known it wouldn't be easy to escape. "He called for his officers and mages. It's why I was delayed."

"Delayed?" Filadiel blinked. "Oh, yes. Your lessons. I'm afraid there will be none today, my friend. As you can see, there's much we need to discuss. Tell me, did the captain disclose the desire to move against the mages of Lore?"

"One of the lieutenants said they wanted to move against the mages," Rune said. "I told him it was a bad choice. That with the mountains around us and not enough mages in Captain Kaith's army, the best thing we could do was wait them out."

The woman with the many chains in her ears frowned. "You're very young to be making suggestions of strategy."

Rune met her eyes and twitched, startled to see a flicker of glowing color in her gaze. Now that he studied her, there was something hauntingly familiar in her face, though he couldn't put a finger on what. He licked his lips when he realized she expected a reply. "I was in a position of leadership once. Briefly."

She gave a wry smile. "Your entire life has been brief, boy." The color in her eyes flashed and she turned back to Filadiel. Her expression melted into cool neutrality. "But he is right. Scattering our forces to the mountains is the last thing we should do. If we are to involve ourselves in this fight, we must defend Aldaeon."

"I know, I know." Filadiel sighed, running a hand over his face. "But this isn't an easy decision."

"Which is why the council was called together in the first place," someone said. Rune tried to see who had spoken, but everyone sat with grim faces, most looking at Filadiel or at the floor.

Filadiel caught Rune's glance and held it as he leaned forward in his chair. "What would you do? If war would force you to sacrifice lives to violence, or force you to leave your home to save loved ones from strife, what would you choose?"

The question made Rune's skin crawl and he squeezed his eyes closed. He'd not spoken a word of what he'd been through; it was only cruel irony that he'd landed in the middle of a situation so like that he'd only just survived.

The woman with the many chains made a sound of annoyance. "It isn't his place to speak in matters he doesn't know about. He may become one of us, but he isn't one yet."

"And you are not current speaking leader of the Alda'anan, Indral." Filadiel gave her a hard look, and she sank back in her seat.

Rune's ears perked at the odd inflection of their title, but it was not the time for questions. He stared at the floor in front of him, unable to make himself meet the eyes of all those who studied him. "Do you wish me to speak as a man in the military?"

"I wish you to speak as a man," Filadiel said.

For a moment, Rune wasn't sure how to answer. If he had the choice to make over for himself, what would he have done? Had he not become involved in Tren's war, everything could have been different. He could have returned to the border village and retrieved Firal, taken her to safety in Core. He could have waited a day to recover, opened a Gate to Ilmenhith, and spoken to his father before battle erupted. But he'd done the best he could, not knowing how things would unfold. He'd had no reason to think Firal wouldn't make it to safety on her own. And no way to know if she had.

Thinking of his mistakes, his lapse in judgment and his violent reaction, made bitter bile rise in the back of his throat. "I would rather protect my loved ones," he said at last, lifting his snake-slitted violet eyes to meet Filadiel's gaze. "Even if it came at a price. I realize it's selfish, but I would gather them close and take them to safety while I knew there was still time."

"You would abandon your home?" Indral asked.

"I already have." Rune glowered at her. "The only difference is that I failed to bring the ones who mattered most along with me. Home can be anywhere, but it's nowhere without them."

Filadiel's face melted into a soft, sympathetic smile. "I see," he murmured. "Thank you for your contribution. Please, head to the lower floors and rest for a while. We may have time to fit a lesson in after this meeting is adjourned."

Bowing his head at the gentle dismissal, Rune pushed himself from the floor and slipped back into the hall. The door no more than closed behind him before the council chamber erupted in furor.

WHEN HE REACHED the bottom floor of the tower, Rune found it empty except for a lone tawny-feathered gryphon sitting at the foot of the ramp.

Ria looked up, her eyes brightening when she saw him. "Ah, I thought you'd be in their meeting all day."

"I thought you'd be listening to the captain and his officers all day." He tried to force mirth into his tone, but failed. Beyond the vacant ground floor, gray clouds cloaked the skies and tiny snowflakes danced on the wind. His spirits felt no brighter than the weather. "Where is everyone?"

The gryphon clicked her beak and fiddled with her goggles. "The soldiers are all still in their camp. The other people who call Aldaeon home are in a meeting of their own, gryphons included."

He raised a brow. "Except for you."

Sheepish, she ducked her head. "I wasn't supposed to leave, but I'd had enough of the bickering. They are bound and determined to spill blood as soon as possible. I don't want anyone from Aldaeon hurt, but I don't want anyone from the college hurt, either."

Rune gave her a weak smile. "I understand. I feel the same." He stared at the snow, unsure what to do. He had expected there to be more people in the tower, perhaps someone who could fix him a better meal than the army's near-flavorless porridge cooked too long over a campfire. He certainly wasn't going back to the camp, knowing Captain Kaith would be furious he'd left without permission.

"Were the Aldaanan fighting too?" Ria sounded concerned, an almost human look of sadness on her face.

He spread his hands in a gesture of defeat. "They aren't in agreement, but it's probably a lot less heated than the discussion happening back at the camp. The Aldaanan are unhappy, but they don't get as riled as the captain's men."

The gryphon's ear-tufts drooped. "I feel dreadful about all this. I want to help, but I want the aerie to up and wing off to new nesting grounds, too. We could make do in colder weather and the mages are unlikely to follow us far. I hear there used to be a tower in Quaris. We might try going there."

Rune tilted his head and his brow furrowed. "Where did you say?"

She looked at him oddly, her feathers ruffling. "Quaris, a region north of here. Haven't you seen a map?"

He frowned. Sera had asked the same thing while discussing

geography, and he was beginning to regret he hadn't taken the time to study Redoram's maps in depth. "Not a recent one," he said at last. It was the same answer he'd given Sera.

"Well," the gryphon sighed, adjusting her wings. "I can fix that. It's not like we're doing anything else. Come with me, will you?" She pushed past him and started up the ramp with an awkward, overly-cautious gait. The ramp was steeper than what the gryphons could traverse with ease.

She led him up several floors and stopped at a closed door marked with unfamiliar writing. She struggled with the doorknob for a time. Rune pushed her out of the way and the gryphon made a sound of exasperation as he opened the door himself.

The smell of books greeted them and Rune blinked in surprise when he saw the room. Deep and curving, the library was so wide it had to wrap around half the tower. Bookcases stood in rows between windows paned with stained glass. Tables rested at the end of each row, most so piled with books and scrolls that their surfaces couldn't be seen.

"You do read, don't you?" Ria asked. She clucked pleasantly to herself as she made her way into the library.

"Some," he said, tilting his head to study the spines of books on the low shelf beside the door.

"Well, I suppose some is the best I can hope for in a soldier." She jerked her feathered head toward the left. "The map racks are this way, come along. Most of the time, only the scholars are allowed to touch them. Fortunately for you, messenger gryphons are a special exception."

Rune followed her between the shelves, marveling at the collection. It was even greater than the temple's library, and not a single title he saw looked familiar. He reached for one and the moment his claw touched it, a shock shot up his arm.

"Careful," Ria said as he shook numbness from his finger. Her eyes sparkled with mischief. "You *aren't* a special exception."

He grunted softly in agreement.

The gryphon stopped at the far end of the curved room, where rolled maps were piled in carefully labeled cubbyholes. She hummed as she searched the labels. Her feathered tail twitched when she found what she was after. She carried the map to a table and motioned for him to pull out a chair. "Here we are. Sit down, have a look."

He seated himself as she unfurled the map across the table. It was wide and detailed, depicting four land masses, crisscrossed with guidelines and littered with notes. Ria removed weights from a drawer and placed them on the corners to hold the map flat. Then she sat on her haunches and edged close to the table. "Here's where we are," she said, tapping a place on the northern continent with a talon before drawing a line to the north. "And here is the kingdom of Quaris. Is that name familiar to you?"

Rune leaned forward and studied the line that represented the border between Aldaan and Lore. "There was a city named Quaris back home. I can't imagine they're related, but I never went there. It was on the opposite end of the island—" He stopped short and bit his tongue. A moment too late, it seemed, as Ria's eyes brightened.

"Oh, you're from an island! Hmm, where at? Let me see." She shoved him back with both forepaws and hunched over the map. "I'm sure you don't mean that marshy mess to the east. Most of the world recognizes the chain islands as a single unit, hmm? There aren't many islands outside of Lore, though..."

Despite himself, he found his eyes drawn to Elenhiise, little more than a speck in the middle of the sea. It was strange to see how insignificant it was compared to the rest of the world. The politics, the arrogance of the mages and nobles, the war that forced him to flee—how foolish it all seemed, considering the island's size.

Ria's claw laid against the image of Elenhiise, jarring him out of thought. "Here? Really?" She looked at him in surprise. "But that island is nothing. Too small to even take notice of."

He looked away and said nothing.

The gryphon opened her beak to speak, then closed it when her eyes focused on something behind him. Rune turned his head and frowned when he saw Filadiel hurrying toward them.

"I shouldn't be surprised to see you here," the short-statured elf huffed, glowering at Ria. "You bird-headed troublemaker, you left the library door open again! You know how terrible it is for the books to be exposed to all that humidity."

Ria harrumphed. "It's cold outside, there isn't any humidity."

"Is the meeting over already?" Rune asked.

Filadiel nodded, his face grave. "It is. I'm glad to see you didn't go far. I was just on my way to send someone to the camp to find you. Walk with me, would you? I'll explain our decision on the way to the aerie's peak." He turned on his heel and started back for the door at a brisk pace.

Rune cast a glance to Ria, then hurried after him. The gryphon huffed and crammed her maps into a box before she followed.

"It's not an ideal arrangement," Filadiel said, waiting for the gryphon to step out of the library before he closed the door. Then he led the pair of them toward the tower's top. "But I feel it's the best we can do in these circumstances. Our forces will divide. The majority of us will depart, heading northward to escape the reach of the mages of Lore. They will then arrange for the evacuation of the other inhabitants of Aldaeon. We hope that this decision will cause Lore's mages to abandon the invasion and fall back, since we are the targets and will no longer be here. It leaves Captain Kaith's army weakened, without the Aldaanan to back it, but it's the best we can do for the safety of our people and those who follow us."

It was a reasonable strategy, and if the city was empty, it meant the army could focus on their opponents instead of the lives they needed to protect. But Rune shook his head, staring at the sky as they wound their way toward it. "What does that have to do with me, though?"

"Ah, yes, that's why we're going to the aerie's peak." Filadiel rubbed his hands together as if in anticipation. "We promised to help you, and we will. But this must be done before we depart. Many mages will be needed, and the rest of the council has already gathered at the peak to take part."

Rune's heart leaped into his throat. He'd come to Aldaan in hope, but hadn't dared hope they would cleanse him so soon.

Behind him, Ria squawked. "Oh, you must let me watch! Please, Filadiel? I must see this! I have to see how it happens so I can write it down as new knowledge for the library!" She pranced in place, her claws scrabbling against the cold stone.

Filadiel made a sound of displeasure. "You may watch, but you must stay back. There will be a great deal of power at work, and you know the dangers of being exposed to it."

"Certainly, certainly!" The gryphon trilled in delight. She whistled merrily as they climbed.

The aerie's peak was precisely what it sounded like. At the top of the wide walkway, they passed through a narrow opening in a sheet of crystal that served as the tower's roof. Nearly a foot thick and perfectly transparent, it sheltered the inside of the tower from the falling snow. Its surface was slick, and while Filadiel stepped onto it without batting an eye, Rune lingered by the solid stone walkway of the ramp. A wide stone path ringed the sheet of crystal, dozens of robed Aldaanan along its edge.

"Come along, now!" Filadiel called, beckoning him toward the center of the aerie's peak.

Ria nudged his back and Rune stepped from the path. Transparent as it was, the crystal felt no different than the stone he'd just left. He made his way forward, willing himself not to look down. Icy wind gusted around them, tossing the mages' hair and robes, though they all stood as still as statues.

Filadiel closed his eyes and one by one, the Aldaanan mages sent rolling waves of energy in greeting. Rune answered unconsciously, shifting on his feet. He shook, though not just from cold.

"We are ready to begin," Filadiel said, extending a hand.

Rune laid his clawed fingers in the shorter man's grasp. Waves of energy flowed from the other mages again, but this time, they twisted and merged, forming a mesh of power that spun itself around them. It spiraled about their feet and Rune couldn't help but look down. His stomach dropped to his knees when he saw straight to the bottom floor of the tower, hundreds of feet below.

Then the mesh of energy drew up around them and draped around their shoulders like a mantle. Rune felt Filadiel reach for it. The leader of the Aldaanan pulled each thread of the web closer, tied them one by one into his own energies. And then, through their touching hands, Rune felt the energy surge.

"I had hoped to teach you this lesson differently," Filadiel said, holding him fast. "I don't expect you'll yet understand."

Suddenly wary, Rune drew back. "What are you talking about?"

"Your taint is rooted deeper than flesh," the elf said, his face twisting with repulsion as he spoke. "Though it is no fault of your own. Power given form is always twisted. But you are not to blame. Please understand, we do this to help." Light flooded Filadiel's eyes, whirling myriad colors before darkening to the deepest shadow of sadness.

Wind howled around them. Thunderheads piled in the skies, lightning crawling across their underbellies. The surge of power struck him again and pain lanced to his core. Rune gasped, falling to his knees. "Wait!" He tried to lift a hand. The web of power closed around him and drew tighter. It threatened to choke him. Shockwaves of pain forced him down.

"We are the guardians of magic," Filadiel shouted to make himself heard, his voice high and reedy over the wind. "And so we understand that magic must be brought to an end. You will learn, my friend, but I am sorry for how."

Each of the Aldaanan lifted a hand and drew a line of power from the web, tempered it into a spear of energy.

Panic clawed at Rune's heart and turned his stomach. Desperate, he reached for the hem of Filadiel's robe.

The mage moved beyond his grasp and drew back a spear of his own.

Rune looked up and immediately wished he hadn't. The mages threw their hands forward. Their spears of power plunged into him, burning everything away until there was nothing but darkness and the haunting vision of Filadiel's face, transformed to a mask of sorrow.

BOUND

Snow scoured the top of the tower, driven by howling wind. Pelting ice stung his cheeks and crept into his bones. His limbs were so stiff he feared they were frozen. But his numb fingers did move, and Rune pushed himself to his hands and knees. Pain throbbed in his head. Gray clouds masked the sky, yet everything was bright enough to be blinding. He couldn't tell how long he'd been atop the tower, but it didn't matter. He was alone.

He tried to stand and felt his legs give way. He landed hard. Grimacing, he rested his head against the crystal floor of the aerie's peak. When his eyes opened again, he stared down into the tower. It was empty, not a soul to be seen. The mage-lights had been extinguished, leaving the tower's interior bathed in shadow. But whether or not it was empty, it was bound to be warmer, and he tried again to move.

Dragging himself toward the spiral ramp into the tower took everything he had, but staying in one place meant freezing. His teeth chattered as movement restored circulation to his limbs, numbness gradually replaced with pins and needles and aching cold. He slid onto the stone ramp and exhaled in relief to be out of the wind.

The ache in his head made it hard to think. He remembered shouting, he remembered pain, but everything was a blur of agony and confusion. Belatedly, he realized his hands were unchanged. He gritted his teeth and trained his eyes on a doorway ahead. He had to start a fire, warm himself and figure out what happened. Unsteady, he got to his feet. He leaned against the wall for support and willpower alone kept him up and moving.

The door to the council chamber was open, every chair empty. There was no fireplace, but at least the chairs would burn. He staggered in and reached for the energy flows that would let him make a flame.

Pain exploded in his head and everything went sideways. He collapsed with a shout and gripped his head in his clawed hands. The sensation was slow to ebb and left him panting with exertion. Confused, he tried again. Once more, pain answered and magic escaped his grasp. Panic gripped him, colder than the biting wind outside. His last clear memories flashed through his head.

Magic must be brought to an end, Filadiel said.

No. They couldn't have. They were supposed to free him! Rune tried again, gathering every ounce of strength he had left. He pushed past the pain that left him trembling, desperately trying to snag a tendril of power. He brushed it. It did not answer, and instead slid free of his grasp. His stomach turned and he let his head fall to the floor.

"You're alive!" a voice cried from the door.

He didn't have the energy to turn and look, but the relief in her tone made him relax. Ria. The gryphon had come for him. His lightless eyes slid closed.

Ria's feathered tail whispered against the floor as she moved close, lowered one of her wings, and picked him up. She was surprisingly gentle, mindful of the talons on her birdlike forefeet as she slung him over her shoulder and halfway onto her back. It wasn't until then that he realized how large she was. She moved him as easily as if he were a child. With what little strength he had, he gripped the thick feathers of her mane.

"Now hold on." She made sure he was secure before she started down the tower. Her gait was awkward and her footing unsteady, and her forepaws slid out from underneath her more than once. But she moved faster than he could have hoped to manage on his own, and when she reached the ground, she broke into a steady trot and released a bright warble. "I've got him!"

Rune heard voices and the rattle of armor as people ran toward them, but all he could do was hold on to the gryphon's mane.

"Get him into that tent!" someone shouted, the voice unfamiliar and distant. "You, call the healer!"

The gryphon moved inside, the shadow of the tent soothing and comfortable after the bitter wind. "There, everything will be all right now." Ria sounded confident and calming as she lowered him to the tent's floor. She wrapped him in blankets and nestled close, her feathers soft against his face. She smelled of fresh air and sunshine, and the scent stirred memories of Elenhiise. Releasing a quiet sigh, he curled up in the blankets. The thought of tall trees and white trumpet flowers drifted through his hazed mind as he succumbed to exhaustion again.

"I KNEW nothing good would come of this. I told you." The captain's voice boomed in his head.

Rune flinched and turned away.

"Shh, Garam. Not now." Sera spoke softly. Her voice was close by and pinched with worry.

Rune shuddered and shifted closer to something soft and warm beside him. Feathers tickled his cheek. He twitched and forced his eyes open.

Everything around him was dark. He could only just make

out the outline of Sera above him. He tried to focus on her face, but his eyes were too bleary to make out her features. Groaning, he lifted a hand to his head.

"Oh, he's awake!" Ria whispered excitedly, though her tone was tinged with worry. She stirred, twisting her head toward him.

"Take it easy," Sera murmured, brushing fingertips against his brow. Her fingers were cool. Comforting, despite the chill in the air.

"What happened?" Rune croaked. The sound of his own voice made him grimace. He swallowed hard, his mouth dry and his throat raw. "I was at the top of the tower, and then—"

"The Aldaanan tried to kill you," Garam said.

Sera shushed him angrily.

"Don't you shush me!" the captain growled. "They've deliberately crippled our army! He would have died if the gryphon hadn't—"

"Enough!" Sera snapped, waving a hand. "Go worry about your army somewhere else. That's the last thing he needs to hear. He's weak as a day-old kitten and your shouting isn't going to help him recover."

A heavy silence fell and a tense moment dragged past before Garam grumbled beneath his breath, swept back a tent flap, and slipped outside. A blinding flash of daylight flooded the tent and Rune hissed, turning toward Ria's feathery chest and praying for the pain in his head to subside. The gryphon shifted to lay a wing atop him. The warmth helped; he hadn't realized he was shivering until the cold began to fade.

Sera sighed. "I'm sorry. He means well. He is concerned for you, he just doesn't know how to show it. Can you speak?"

Rune licked his lips and tried. His breath escaped in a hoarse rasp before he managed a word. "Drink?"

Sera slipped away, then returned to press something close to his mouth. He struggled to lift his head as cool liquid splashed against his lips. He gulped it down and choked when the sweet-yet-bitter liquid left a burning trail across his tongue and a heat in his throat.

"What is that?" He choked again and wiped his mouth.

"Brandy. It'll help warm you up."

He squeezed his eyes shut and pushed the bottle away when she offered it again.

Ria made a soft purring sound and bowed her head. "I'm glad you're awake. I'm so sorry, I wanted to get you sooner, but Filadiel forbade it and I had to wait for the mages to leave, and—"

"That's enough," Sera said. A cutting sweep of her hand brought the gryphon up short. "He needs to rest. Both of us need to be at full strength."

"No," Rune managed, forcing his eyes open again. His head still throbbed, but his vision was clearer. He could just make out the worried expressions they both wore. "Tell me what happened. Filadiel said something about power given form, then..." He trailed off, recalling the way the flows had slipped beyond his grasp. Was it because of what they had done, or was it because of the pain in his head?

"I couldn't see much," Ria admitted sadly. "There was too much power being used. I couldn't risk being close enough to understand what was happening. But the mages were upset, and whatever they did caused you a great deal of pain."

"There was a fight after whatever happened up there," Sera added. "The Aldaanan came into the camp and told Garam they were leaving. He wouldn't let me speak to them. He wouldn't even let me out of the tent. We knew something had happened to you, but it wasn't until after the Aldaanan left that Ria brought you down from the tower. I thought you might need healing, but there was nothing for me to heal. But you kept speaking in your sleep, repeating something I heard the Aldaanan say. Power given form, like you said."

Rune grimaced. "What else did I say?"

Sera made a soothing motion with her hands and lowered

her voice. "Please, listen. I realize you are a secretive person. But if there's something about your magic that makes the Aldaanan so angry that they abandon their city without a second thought, I need you to tell me what it is. You and I are the only mages left to fight the college."

He fell silent and stared at the tent's ceiling through the dark. The Aldaanan hadn't seemed angry to him. If anything, Filadiel had been distraught. But Sera hadn't seen what happened atop the tower. He wasn't to blame for the mages leaving, but who knew what had happened in their argument with Garam? Still, explaining the nature of his power was the last thing he wanted to do. He rubbed his eyes. The pressure granted small relief from the pain in his head. "I need to rest," he murmured at last.

"I'm not going anywhere until you explain things." Sera folded her arms over her chest, making it clear she didn't mean to budge from the ground beside him.

Frustrated, he sighed and rested one scaly hand over his eyes. "Fine. Ria, leave us."

The gryphon seemed surprised, but Sera nodded. Reluctantly Ria pulled herself up, stepped over him, and let herself outside. As hungry for knowledge as the creature was, there were some things he didn't want her to hear. He was in no mood for her questions.

The tent grew quiet, Sera's uneasiness filling the air.

"Well?" she asked at last.

"You can tell Garam the Aldaanan didn't leave because they were angry. I'm sure he thinks I have something to do with it, but I don't." His headache throbbed behind his eyes. He covered his face with a hand, silently resenting the scales that were still there. "They told me they were leaving, and that they meant to empty the city. But if everyone else is still here, I don't know how long it will be before they come for them."

She regarded him thoughtfully for a time before she dropped her arms and leaned closer."Tell me what happened at the top of the tower."

"They said they were going to help me," he replied. Putting it into words, it sounded naive. "I thought they meant they were going to cleanse the taint in me."

"The taint in your power?" She sounded confused.

"The taint in me," he repeated. He reconsidered the drink she'd brought. He'd never had much of a head for alcohol, but another swig or two might help his headache. "Filadiel said power given form always takes a twisted form. My form. I thought it was just my Gift, tainted when it was unbound, but—"

"Wait, unbound?" Sera interruped. "You weren't born a free mage?"

"No. At least, I don't think so." Then again, he wasn't sure he'd truly been born at all. Birthed by magic, perhaps, by the energy of the world around them, but he had no birth parents. Despite himself, he thought of Kifel and his throat constricted. "Let me have that drink again. And let me rest."

She handed him the brandy with a begrudging frown and leaned forward to rest a hand against his brow. "At least you're not fevered any more. Very well. Rest. I'll be back in a few hours to check on you."

Rune said nothing, but took another swallow of the burning liquid as she left him alone in the dark.

WHEN RUNE AWOKE, the pain in his head had subsided. He lay unmoving in the shadows inside the tent for a long time, still weakened but no longer exhausted. He couldn't tell what time it was without rising, but with warmth finally restored to his limbs, he wasn't eager to move from the heap of blankets. Dim, warm-hued light penetrated the canvas, but it could have been from a campfire or the setting sun.

It was his tent; he recognized his sparse belongings now that he had time to look. He didn't remember Ria carrying him that far. Then again, he didn't remember much. Not clearly, at least. It was just as well—he wasn't sure he wanted to remember.

After a time, he sat upright, stretching slowly to test his limits. He didn't feel stiff, and he hadn't lost any fingers or toes to frostbite. That was probably to Sera's doing; he did recall someone calling for a healer. If the Aldaanan were gone, Sera was the only healer left. The thought put a bitter taste in his mouth.

Once more, he reached for the energy around him, seeking his magic and finding himself empty-handed. His head didn't hurt this time, but a strange pressure filled his skull and an uncomfortable tightness pulled in his chest. The sensation reminded him of what happened if he held his breath too long, and he didn't like it at all. Swallowing, he looked down at his hands.

He didn't understand. No matter how he played events through his head, he couldn't figure out why the Aldaanan had turned on him. They—and Ria, for that matter—made it sound like they'd seen tainted magic before, and they'd seemed so confident they could fix it. What was this supposed to teach him? Why did they want to bring magic to an end? It wasn't as if he could help the actions of the mages who came before him. The Aldaanan had been eager to teach and he'd been a willing student. He curled his claws into his palms and clenched his fists in his lap as he tried to tamp down his rising anger.

Red light flashed on his glossy scales. Startled, he moved his hands and watched as the color of the light changed. His eyes. Rune scrambled out of the blankets and jerked his sword free of its scabbard. The otherworldly glow of his eyes reflected in the polished steel. The light was dimmer, faint enough that the light vanished when he looked at its reflection directly, but it was still there. So they hadn't bound him. Or at least, not completely. Frowning in confusion, he sat back on the blankets and stared at his sword. If his eyes still glowed, there had to be a way to use his power.

He tried to recall his lessons from the temple. There had to be something, some bit of knowledge about contacting power sources he might have been told before. But nothing came to mind. He grimaced and cradled his head in his hands as he tried to think. He'd never realized how little he'd learned.

A horn sounded in the camp, shattering his concentration. Rune grimaced as it blared again. He grabbed his armor as the sound of soldiers rousing to answer the call filled the camp outside.

For him, the warning couldn't have come at a worse time.

The glare of the setting sun threatened to make his headache return the moment he stepped from his tent. The camp boiled in a frenzy. Half-dressed men ran to retrieve armor and weapons. Others filed into ranks. Rune spat a curse and pushed through the growing crowd, making his way toward the captain's tent.

Garam intercepted him halfway. "You're up? You're moving." He swung an arm toward the mountains to the south. "The college mages have breached the mountain pass. Sera's moving against the eastern band, but there's a company gathering on the southern edge of the camp and they need a mage."

Rune's stomach dropped like a stone. "I can't."

"I gave you an order, now move!" the captain barked, shoving past him to shout at other soldiers.

Gritting his teeth, Rune moved after him. "And I said I can't!"

Garam stopped and turned to glare at him, but the moment their gazes met, the captain's anger disappeared. "Your eyes," he breathed. He didn't have to say anything else.

Sober, Rune nodded once.

His magic was gone.

GLOSSARY

Affinity – One's natural inclination in magic. There are five major affinities: Earth, water, fire, wind, and life. These provide the primary source of power a mage can draw from and manipulate. While there are smaller subcategories affinities may fall into, granting specific talents in narrow fields, they are generally related to one of the five and, as result, only the five major affinities are recognized.

Aldaan – One of three provinces in the Triad.

Aldaanan – A faction of free mages.

Alira – (*uh-LEER-ah*) – Master of the House of Fire.

Alwhen – (*OWL-when*) – The capital of the eastern half of Elenhiise island, a region known as the Giftless Lands.

Anaide – (*uh-NAYD*) – Master of the House of Water.

Archmage – The leader of Kirban Temple, generally recognized as the leader of all mages.

Core – An underground city beneath the ruins, home of the Underlings.

Daemon – (*DAY-mun*) – An Underling soldier. His tainted magic has twisted his body into a monstrous form.

Davan - An officer among the Underlings.

Edagan – (*ED-ah-gan*) – Master of the House of Earth.

Eldani – (*ell-DAN-ee*) – The only inhabitants of Ithilear who are known to be Gifted. Eldani are long-lived, due to their magic, and differ from humans only in their pointed ears. Diluted bloodlines are recognized by the reduced point of an Eldani's ear, which directly corresponds with their prowess as a mage.

Elenhiise – (*ELL-en-heese*) – A small island in the middle of the Lantaaran sea, generally used as a waypoint in trade between the region's northern and southern continents. The island is ruled by two factions, the Gifted Eldani and Giftless men.

Ennil – (*in-ill*) – Full name Ennil Tanrys. Former Captain of the Guard of Ilmenhith. Vahn's father.

Envesi – (*in-VESS-see*) – The Archmage of Kirban Temple.

Eyrion Tolmarni – (*EAR-ee-on toll-MAR-nee)* – Headmaster of the Grand College of Lore.

Filadiel – (*fil-LAD-ee-ell*) – Leader of the Aldaanan mages.

Firal – (*fur-ALL*) – A green-rank mageling at Kirban temple.

Flows – The natural ebb and flow of magic, which mages are able to seize and manipulate.

Garam – Full name Garam Kaith. Captain of the Royal City Guard. Sera's brother.

Gift – The ability to use magic.

House – A subsection of mages, ruled by a particular affinity. Mages within the House of Healing, Fire, etc. may take classes together, but their education is overseen by the Master of their House.

Ileara – (*ill-ee-ARE-ah*) – The second moon. The smaller of the two, Ileara is known as The Mother and is stationary in the sky. As it is only visible in the far western regions of the known world, such as the Westkings and the Chains of Raeldan, some residents of Elenhiise and the other eastern regions do not believe Ileara exists.

Ilmenhith – (*ill-men-HITH*) – The capital of the western half of Elenhiise island, which is under Eldani control.

Ithi – (*ith-EE*) – The first moon. The larger of the two, Ithi is known as The Soldier and circles Ithilear once per day. The thirteen months of the year are framed around Ithi's phases; its cycle is 28 days.

Ithilear – (*ith-ILL-ee-arr*) – The world. The name is derived from the two moons, Ithi and Ileara. In folklore, the moons are lovers. Ithi ventures forth to patrol and protect their child, Ithilear, while Ileara remains in one place to provide a stable home.

Kifel – (*kiff-EL*) – Full name Kifelethelas Penedhionn. The Eldani king and ruler of the western half of Elenhiise island.

Kirban Temple – (*KER-ban*) – Founded by Archmage Envesi, Kirban Temple is the only school of magecraft on Elenhiise

Island. A prestigious college sponsored by the Eldani crown and located near the southern edge of the ruins.

Kytenia – (*kit-teen-yah*) – A yellow-rank mageling at Kirban Temple and Firal's best friend.

Lore - One of three provinces in the Triad.

Lumia – (*loo-MEE-ah*) – Queen of the Underlings.

Mageling – A mage in training. Magelings are divided into five ranks before they graduate to Master and wear robes in corresponding colors. The five ranks are gray, lavender, yellow, green, and blue.

Marreli – (*mah-RELL-ee*) – A gray-rank mageling at Kirban Temple. One of Firal's friends.

Master – A mage recognized as skilled enough to wield magic without supervision. Masters outside the temple act as healers and scholars, and are in charge of scouting Gifted children to send for training. Masters who remain within the temple are generally teachers. Master mages are the only mages allowed to wear white. Court Masters and Masters of an affinity mark their eyes with black ink to distinguish their rank.

Medreal – (*mee-dree-al*) – King Kifel's stewardess.

Melora – (*mel-LOR-ah*) – Master of the House of Wind.

Minna - An Underling woman who befriends Firal.

Nondar – (*non-DAR*) – Master of the House of Healing, also known as the House of Life. Nondar is one of few recognized half-Eldani Masters and is unparalleled as a medic.

Ran – Full name Lomithrandel. A blue-rank mageling at Kirban temple and the only part-time student allowed. He considers Firal a friend, while she considers him a nuisance.

Redoram – (*RED-or-AM*) – Full name Redoram Parthanus. Former councilor in the Triad's Royal City.

Relythes – (*rell-uh-THEEZ*) – The Giftless King, ruler of Alwhen and the eastern half of Elenhiise island.

Rhyllyn – (*rill-in*) – A street urchin from Lore.

Ria – A gryphon messenger and amateur cartographer.

Rikka – (*RIK-kuh*) – A yellow-rank mageling at Kirban Temple. One of Firal's friends.

Roberian – One of three provinces in the Triad.

Royal City – The capital of the Triad.

Ruins – A sprawling labyrinth in the center of the island. The ruins fall entirely on Eldani lands.

Rune - A new name given to Daemon.

Sera – Full name Sera Kaith. A mage in the Royal City and a scout for the guard. Garam's sister.

Shymin – (*SHY-min*) – A green-rank mageling at Kirban Temple. One of Firal's friends and Kytenia's elder sister.

Tren – Full name Tren Achos. Lumia's general.

Triad – An empire in the north, composed of three provinces—

Aldaan, Lore, and Roberian—and ruled by King Vicamros.

Underlings – Giftless people driven into the ruins by war, rumored to be monsters and believed to be legend.

Vahn – Full name Vahnil Tanrys. A low-ranking soldier in Ilmenhith's military.

Vicamros – (*vi-CAM-rows*) – King of the Triad.

Vivenne – (*viv-INN*) – Full name Vivenne Tanrys. Vahn's mother. Ennil's wife.